Praise for Michael Connelly

'His methods of killing and eluding detection are infernally ingenious, adding an intellectual charge to the visceral kick of the hunt' *New York Times*

'Connelly is a crime-writing genius. His Harry Bosch stories are genuine modern classics . . . Unmissable'
Independent on Sunday

'Connelly has great skills. One is the creation of characters who live and breathe, so that we care about them far more than we do for the cardboard figures stamped out by most thriller writers. His second skill is mastery of pace. His books are page-turners, and the author is in sublime control of the speed at which we turn those pages'
Mail on Sunday

'While the themes of Connelly's LA crime novels are familiar (power, envy, corruption), his plotting is anything but' *Esquire*

'A superb legal thriller that manages three final twists . . . The first line of *The Brass Verdict* is "everybody lies", so there are plenty of surprises. And, of course, as a writer of fiction, Connelly proves to be a brilliant liar'
Evening Standard

'A clever plot, full of twists, to make a first-rate legal thriller' *Sunday Telegraph*

MICHAEL CONNELLY

Void Moon

An Orion paperback

First published in Great Britain in 2000
by Orion
This paperback edition published in 2000
by Orion Books
an imprint of The Orion Publishing Group Ltd,
Orion House, 5 Upper St Martin's Lane,
London WC2H 9EA

An Hachette UK company

Published by arrangement with
Little, Brown and Company Inc., New York, NY, USA

Reissued 2009

A CIP catalogue record for this book is available
from the British Library.

Printed and bound in Great Britain by
Clays Ltd, St Ives plc

The Orion Publishing Group's policy is to use papers
that are natural, renewable and recyclable products and
made from wood grown in sustainable forests. The logging
and manufacturing processes are expected to conform to
the environmental regulations of the country of origin.

www.orionbooks.co.uk

To Linda,
for the first fifteen

All around them the cacophony of greed carried on in its most glorious and extreme excess. But it couldn't make a dent in their world.

She broke the connection between their eyes just long enough to look down and find her glass and then raise it from the table. It was empty except for ice and a cherry but that didn't matter. He raised his glass in return, maybe one swallow of beer and foam left in it.

'To the end,' she said.

He smiled and nodded. He loved her and she knew it.

'To the end,' he began and then paused. 'To the place where the desert is ocean.'

She smiled back as they touched glasses. She raised hers to her lips and the cherry rolled into her mouth. She looked at him suggestively as he wiped the beer foam out of his mustache. She loved him. It was them against the whole fucking world and she liked their chances just fine.

Then her smile was gone as she thought about how she had played the whole thing wrong. How she should have known what his reaction would be, how he wouldn't let her go up. She should have waited until after it was over to tell him.

'Max,' she said, very serious now. 'Let me do it. I mean it. One last time.'

'No way. It's me. I go up.'

There was a whoop from the casino floor and it was loud enough to break the barrier surrounding them. She looked out and saw some ten-gallon Texan dancing at the end of one of the craps tables, just below the pulpit that reached out over the casino floor. The Texan had his dial-a-date at his side, a woman with big hair who had been working the casinos since all the way back when Cassie was dealing at the Trop for the first time.

Cassie looked back at Max.

'I can't wait until we're out of this place for good. Let me at least flip you for it.'

Max slowly shook his head.

'Not in the cards. This one's mine.'

Max stood up then and she looked up at him. He was handsome and dark. She liked the little scar under his chin, the way no whiskers ever grew there.

'Guess it's time,' Max said.

He looked out across the casino, his eyes scanning but never stopping and holding on anything until they traveled up the arm of the pulpit. Cassie's eyes followed his. There was a man up there, dressed darkly and staring down like a priest on his congregation.

She tried to smile again but couldn't bring the corners of her mouth up. Something didn't feel right. It was the change of plans. The switch. She realized then how much she wanted to go up and how much she was going to miss the charge it would put in her blood. She knew then it was really about her, not Max. She wasn't being protective of Max. She was being selfish. She wanted that charge one last time.

'Anything happens,' Max said, 'I'll see you when I see you.'

Now she frowned outright. That had never been part of the ritual, a good-bye like that. A negative like that.

'Max, what's wrong? Why are you so nervous?'

Max looked down at her and hiked his shoulders.

''Cause it's the end, I guess.'

He tried a smile, then touched her cheek and leaned down. He kissed her on the cheek and then quickly moved over to her

4

lips. He reached a hand down beneath the table where nobody could see and ran his finger up the inside of her leg, tracing the seam of her jeans. Then, without another word, he turned and left the lounge. He started walking through the casino toward the elevator alcove and she watched him go. He didn't look back. That was part of the ritual. You never looked back.

1

The house on Lookout Mountain Road was set far in from the street and nestled against the steep canyon embankment to the rear. This afforded it a long and flat green lawn running from the wide front porch to the white picket fence that ran along the street line. It was unusual in Laurel Canyon to have such an immense lawn, front or back, and one so flat as well. It was that lawn that would be the key selling point of the property.

The open house had been advertised in the real estate section of the *Times* as starting at two P.M. and lasting until five. Cassie Black pulled to the curb ten minutes before the starting time and saw no cars in the driveway and no indication of any activity in the house. The white Volvo station wagon she knew belonged to the owners that was usually parked outside was gone. She couldn't tell about the other car, the black BMW, because the little single-car garage at the side of the house was closed. But she took the missing Volvo to mean that the owners of the home were out for the day and would not be present during the showing. This was fine. Cassie preferred they not be home. She wasn't sure how she would act if the family was right there in the house as she walked through it.

Cassie remained in the Boxster until two P.M. and then grew concerned, her mind jumping to the conclusion that she had gotten the time wrong or, worse yet, the house had already been sold and the showing canceled. She opened the real estate section on the passenger seat and checked the listing again. She had been correct. She looked at the FOR SALE sign posted in the front lawn and checked the broker's name against the name in the advertisement. They matched. She got her cell phone out of her backpack and tried to call the realty office but couldn't get a connection. This didn't surprise her. She was in Laurel Canyon and it always seemed impossible to get a clear cell transmission in any of L.A.'s hillside neighborhoods.

With nothing to do but wait and control her fears, she studied the house that stood behind the FOR SALE sign. According to the advertisement, it was a California Craftsman bungalow built in 1931. Unlike the newer homes on either side, it was not only set back off the street into the hillside rising behind it, but it also seemed to possess a good deal of character. It was smaller than most of the neighboring homes, its designers obviously putting a premium on the large lawn and the openness of the property. The newer houses in the neighborhood had been built to every lot line, under the philosophy that interior space was premium.

The old bungalow had a long, sloping gray roof from which sprouted two dormer windows. Cassie assumed that one belonged to the bedroom shared by the couple and the other was the girl's room. The sidings were painted a reddish brown. A wide porch ran the length of the front of the house and the front door was a single-light French door. Most days the family lowered a set of blinds over the door's glass but today the blinds over the door and the front picture window were up and Cassie could see into the living room. An overhead light had been left on.

The front yard was definitely the play area. It was

always neatly cut and trimmed. Built along the left perimeter was a wooden swing set and jungle gym. Cassie knew that the girl who lived in the house preferred to swing with her back to the house and facing the street. She had often thought about this, wondering if there was something about this habit that could be read as some sort of psychological clue.

The empty swing hung perfectly still. Cassie saw a kick ball and a red wagon sitting motionless in the grass, also waiting for the attention of the girl. Cassie thought the play area might be one of the reasons the family was moving. All things being relative in Los Angeles, Laurel Canyon was a pocket of reasonable safety in the sprawling city. Still, it wasn't desirable in any neighborhood to have your children playing in the front yard so close to the street, the place where harm could befall them, where danger could come to them.

It didn't say anything about this potential problem with the yard in the advertisement. Cassie looked down and read it again.

> BRING ALL OFFERS!
> 1931 Classic Calif. Craftsman
> 2/2, spacious living/dining, huge wooded
> lot.
> Highly motivated and anxious!
> Reduced and priced to sell!

Cassie had noticed the FOR SALE sign on the property during a routine drive-by three weeks earlier. The sighting had thrown her life into turmoil, which was manifested in insomnia and inattention at work. She had not sold a single car in the three weeks, her longest absence ever from the sales tote board.

Today's showing was the first open house as far as she

knew. So the wording of the ad struck her as curious. She wondered why the owners would be so anxious to sell that they would already have reduced the price after only three weeks on the market. That did not seem right.

Three minutes after the open house was scheduled to begin, a car Cassie didn't recognize, a maroon Volvo sedan, pulled into the driveway and stopped. A slim, blond woman in her mid forties got out. She was casually but neatly dressed. She opened the trunk of her car and removed an OPEN HOUSE sign, which she carried toward the curb. Cassie checked her hair in the visor mirror, reached to the back of her head and pulled the wig down tight on her scalp. She got out of the Porsche and approached the woman as she set up the sign.

'Are you Laura LeValley?' Cassie asked, reading the name off the bottom of the FOR SALE sign.

'I sure am. Are you here to look at the house?'

'Yes, I'd like to.'

'Well, let me open it up and we'll go from there. Nice car you've got there. Brand new?'

She pointed to the dealer blank in the front license plate holder of the Porsche. Cassie had taken the plates off in the garage at her home before driving to the open house. It was just a precaution. She wasn't sure if brokers took down plate numbers as a means of tracing leads or backgrounding potential buyers. She didn't want to be traced. It was the same reason she was wearing the wig.

'Uh, yes,' she said. 'New to me but used. It's a year old.'

'Nice.'

The Boxster looked pristine from the outside but was actually a repo with almost thirty thousand miles on it, a convertible top that leaked and a CD player that habitually skipped when the car hit the slightest bump in the road. Cassie's boss, Ray Morales, was letting her use it while he dealt with the owner, allowing the guy until the end of the month to come up with the money before putting the car onto the lot. Cassie expected that they would never see a dime from the guy. He was a deadbeat through and through. She'd looked at the package. He'd made the first six payments, late every time, and then skated on the next six. Ray had made the mistake of taking the guy's paper after he'd gotten no takers from the outside loan companies. That was the tip-off right there. But the guy had talked Ray into taking the paper and turning over the keys. It really bugged Ray that he had been beaten. He'd personally gone out on the rig when they hooked up the Boxster outside the deadbeat's hillside box overlooking Sunset Plaza.

The real estate woman went back to her car and removed a briefcase, then led Cassie up the stone walkway to the front porch.

'Are the owners going to be home?' Cassie asked.

'No, it's better when no one's home. Then people can look where they want, say what they want. No hurt feelings. You know, people's tastes are different. One person will think something is gorgeous. Somebody else will call it hideous.'

Cassie smiled to be polite. They got to the front door and LeValley removed a small white envelope from her briefcase and took out a key. As she opened the door she continued the patter.

'Are you being represented by a broker?'

'No. I'm just kind of in the looking stage at the moment.'

'Well, it helps to know what's on the market. Are you currently in ownership?'

'Excuse me?'

'Do you own now? Are you selling?'

'Oh. No, I rent. I'm looking to buy. Something small like this.'

'Children?'

'Just me.'

LeValley opened the door and called out a hello just to make sure no one was home. When there was no answer, she waved Cassie in first.

'Then this should be perfect. It's just two bedrooms but the living spaces are large and very open. I think it's just darling. You'll see.'

They walked into the house and LeValley put her briefcase down. She then offered her hand and introduced herself again.

'Karen Palty,' Cassie lied as she shook the broker's hand.

LeValley gave a quick description of the attributes and assets of the house. From her briefcase she took out a stack of printed fliers containing information on the house and gave Cassie one as she talked. Cassie nodded occasionally but was barely listening. Instead she was intensely scrutinizing the furnishings and the other belongings of the family who lived in the house. She stole long glances at the photos on the walls and on tables and chests. LeValley told her to go ahead and browse while she set up the sign-in sheet and information packets on the dining room table.

The house was very neatly kept and Cassie wondered how much of that was due to the fact that it was being shown to potential buyers. She moved into a short hallway and then up the stairs that led to two bedrooms and bathroom above. She stepped a few feet into the master bedroom and looked around. The room had a large bay window that looked out on the steep rock hillside at the rear of the house. LeValley called from below, seemingly knowing exactly what Cassie was looking at and thinking.

'Mudslides are not a problem. The hillside out there is extruded granite. It's probably been there for ten thousand years and, believe me, it's not going anywhere. But if you are seriously interested in the property, I would suggest you get a geological survey done. If you buy it, it will help you sleep better at night.'

'Good idea,' Cassie called down.

Cassie had seen enough. She stepped out of the room and crossed the hall to the child's bedroom. This room, too, was neat but cluttered with collections of stuffed animals, Barbie dolls and other toys. There was a drawing easel in one corner holding a crayon drawing of a school bus with several stick figures in the window. The bus had pulled up to a building where a red truck was parked in a garage. A firehouse. The girl was a good artist.

Cassie checked the hall to make sure LeValley had not come up and then stepped over to the easel. She flipped over some of the pages containing prior drawings. One drawing depicted a house with a large green lawn in front of it. There was a FOR SALE sign at the front of the house and a stick figure of a girl stood next to it. A bubble coming from the girl's mouth said *Boo Hoo*. Cassie studied it for a long time before breaking away and looking around the rest of the room.

On the left wall there was a framed movie poster for an animated film called *The Little Mermaid*. There were also large wooden letters spelling the name JODIE SHAW, each letter painted a different color of the rainbow. Cassie stood in the middle of the room and silently tried to take it all in and commit it to memory. Her eyes fell on a photo which stood in a small frame on the girl's white bureau. It showed a smiling girl standing with Mickey Mouse amidst a crowd at Disneyland.

'Their daughter's room.'

Cassie almost jumped at the voice behind her.

She turned. Laura LeValley stood in the doorway. Cassie had not heard her on the steps. She wondered if the broker had been suspicious of her and intentionally sneaked up the stairs to catch her stealing or doing something else.

'Cute kid,' LeValley said, giving off no sign of suspicion. 'I met her when I first took the listing. I think she's six or seven.'

'Five. Almost six.'

'Excuse me?'

Cassie quickly pointed to the photo on the bureau.

'I would guess. I mean, if that photo's recent.'

She turned and raised a hand, taking in the whole of the room.

'I also have a niece who is five. This could be her room.'

She waited but there were no further questions from LeValley. It had been a bad slip and Cassie knew she was lucky to have gotten away with it.

'Well,' LeValley said, 'I want to get you to sign in so we have your name and number. Are there any questions I can answer for you? I even have an offer sheet with me if by any chance you're ready to do that.'

She smiled as she said the last line. Cassie smiled back.

'Not just yet,' she said. 'But I do like the house.'

LeValley headed back to the stairs and down. Cassie moved toward the door to follow. As she stepped into the hallway, she glanced back at the collection of stuffed animals on a shelf above the bed. The girl seemed partial to stuffed dogs. Her eyes then went back to the drawing on the easel.

Down in the living room LeValley handed her a clipboard with a sign-in sheet on it. She wrote the name *Karen Palty*, the name belonging to an old friend from her days dealing blackjack, then made up a phone number with a Hollywood exchange and an address on Nichols Canyon Road. After she handed it back LeValley read the entry.

'Karen, you know, if this house isn't what you are looking for, there are several others in the canyon I'd be more than happy to show you.'

'Okay, that would be fine. Let me think about this one first, though.'

'Oh, sure. You just let me know. Here's my card.'

LeValley offered a business card and Cassie took it. She noticed through the living room's picture window a car pulling to the curb behind the Boxster. Another potential buyer. She decided it was time to ask questions while she still had LeValley alone.

'The ad in the paper said the Shaws were anxious to sell the house. Do you mind me asking how come? I mean, is there something wrong here?'

Halfway through her question Cassie realized she had used the name of the owners. Then she remembered the letters on the wall of the girl's room and knew she was covered if LeValley noticed the slip.

'Oh, no, it has nothing to do with the house at all,' LeValley said. 'He's been transferred and they are anxious to make the move and get settled in their new place. If they sell it quickly they can all move together, rather than him having to commute back and forth from the new location. It's a very long trip.'

Cassie felt she needed to sit down but stood still. She felt a terrible dread engulf her heart. She tried to remain steady by placing her hand on the stone hearth but was sure she was not hiding the impact of the words she had just heard.

It's a very long trip.

'Are you okay?' LeValley asked.

'Fine. I'm fine. I had the flu last week and ... you know.'

'I know. I had it a few weeks ago. It was awful.'

Cassie turned her face and acted as though she were studying the brickwork of the fireplace.

'How far are they moving?' she asked, as casually as was possible considering the fears welling up inside her.

She closed her eyes and waited, sure that LeValley knew by now she wasn't here because of the house.

'Paris. He works for some kind of clothing import business and they want him working on that end of things for a while. They thought about keeping the house, maybe renting it out. But I think realistically they know that they probably won't be coming back. I mean, it's Paris. Who wouldn't want to live there?'

Cassie opened her eyes and nodded.

'Paris . . .'

LeValley continued in an almost conspiring tone.

'That's also the reason they would be very interested in any kind of an offer. His company will cover him on anything below appraisal value. Anything within reason. So a quick, low bid might really be able to turn this. They want to get over there so they can get the girl into one of those language schools this summer. So she can start learning the language and be fairly integrated by the time school starts.'

Cassie wasn't listening to the sales pitch. She stared into the darkness of the hearth. A thousand fires had burned there and warmed this house. But at the moment the bricks were black and cold. And Cassie felt as though she were staring at the inside of her own heart.

In that moment she knew that all things in her life were changing. For the longest time she had lived day to day, carefully avoiding even a glance at the desperate plan that floated out on the horizon like a dream.

But now she knew that it was time to go to the horizon.

2

On the Monday after the open house Cassie got to Hollywood Porsche at ten as usual and spent the rest of the morning in her small office off the showroom going down her list of call-backs, studying the updated inventory list, answering Internet inquiries, and running a search for a customer looking for a vintage Speedster. Mostly, though, her thoughts remained concentrated on the information she had learned during the open house in Laurel Canyon.

Mondays were always the slowest days in the showroom. Occasionally there were leftover buyers and paperwork from the weekend but as a rule very few first-visit car buyers came in. The dealership was located on Sunset Boulevard a half block from the Cinerama Dome and sometimes it was so slow on Mondays that Ray Morales didn't mind if Cassie walked over and caught a flick in the afternoon, just as long as she had her pager on and could be recalled if things started hopping. Ray was always cutting Cassie a break, starting with giving her the job without her having any valid experience. She knew his motives weren't entirely altruistic. She knew it would only be a matter of time before he came to her to collect the return. She was surprised he hadn't made the move yet; it had been ten months.

Hollywood Porsche sold new and used cars. As the newest person on the six-member sales force, it fell to

Cassie to work Monday shifts and to handle all Internet-related business. The latter she didn't mind because she had taken computer courses while at High Desert Institution for Women and had found she enjoyed the work. She had learned that she preferred dealing with customers and salesmen from other dealerships over the Internet rather than in person.

Her search for a Speedster of the quality her customer sought was successful. She located a '58 convertible in pristine condition on a lot in San Jose and arranged to have photos and the particulars overnighted. She then left a message for the customer saying he could come in the next afternoon and look at the photos or she would send them over to his office as soon as she got them.

The one test drive of the day came in shortly before lunch. The customer was one of Ray's so-called Hollywood hard-ons, a name the fleet manager had come up with himself.

Ray religiously scoured the *Hollywood Reporter* and *Daily Variety* for stories on nobodies becoming overnight somebodies. Most often these were writers who were snatched from penniless obscurity and made rich and at least known for the day by a studio deal for a book or screenplay. Once Ray chose a target, he tracked down the writer's address through the Writers Guild or a friend he had in the voter registrar's office. He then had the Sunset Liquor Deli deliver a bottle of Macallan Scotch whisky with his card and a note of congratulations. A little more than half the time it worked. The recipient responded with a call to Ray and then a visit to the showroom. Owning a Porsche was almost a rite of passage in Hollywood, especially for males in their twenties – which all the screenwriters seemed to be. Ray passed these customers on to his salespeople, splitting the commission on any eventual sale, after the cost of the whisky.

The test drive Cassie had on Monday was a writer who had just signed a first-look deal with Paramount for seven figures. Ray, fully aware that Cassie had not sold a car in three weeks, gave the 'up' to her. The writer's name was Joe Michaels and he was interested in a new Carrera cabriolet, an automobile that would price out at close to $100,000 fully loaded. Cassie's commission would cover her draw for a month.

With Joe in the passenger seat, Cassie took Nichols Canyon up to Mulholland Drive and then turned the Porsche east on the snaking road. She was following her routine. For it was up on Mulholland that the car and power and sex all blended in the imagination. It became clear to each customer what she was selling.

The traffic as usual was light. Other than the occasional pack of power bikers, the road was theirs. Cassie put the car through the paces, downshifting and powering into the turns. She glanced at Michaels every now and then, to see if he had the look on his face that said the deal was done.

'You working on a movie right now?' she asked.

'I'm doing rewrite on a cop film.'

That was a good sign, his calling a movie a film. Especially a cop movie. The ones who took themselves too seriously – meaning they had money – called them films.

'Who's in it?'

'It hasn't been cast. That's why I'm doing rewrite. The dialogue sucks.'

To prep for the test drive Cassie had read the story in *Variety* about the first-look deal. It said Michaels was a recent graduate of the USC film school and had made a fifteen-minute film that won some kind of studio-sponsored award. He looked maybe twenty-five years old tops. Cassie wondered where he would get his dialogue from. He didn't look as though he had ever met a cop in his life, let alone any outlaws. The dialogue would probably come from television or other movies, she decided.

'You want to drive now, John?'

'It's Joe.'

Another bingo. She had called him the wrong name on purpose, just to see if he would correct her. That he did meant he was serious and ego-driven, a good combination when it came to selling and buying automobiles that were serious and ego-driven.

'Joe, then.'

She pulled into the overlook above the Hollywood Bowl. She killed the engine, set the brake and got out. She didn't look back at Michaels as she walked to the edge and put a foot up on the guardrail. She leaned over and retied her black Doc Marten work shoe and then looked down at the empty bowl. She was wearing tight black jeans and a sleeveless white T-shirt beneath an unbuttoned blue Oxford dress shirt. She knew she looked good and her radar told her that he was looking at her instead of the car. She ran her fingers through her blond hair, newly cut short so she could wear the wig. She turned abruptly and caught him looking at her. He quickly looked past her, out to the view of downtown in the pastel pink smog.

'So what do you think?' she asked.

'I think I like it,' Michaels said. 'But you have to drive it to know for sure.'

He smiled. She smiled. They were definitely moving on the same plane.

'Then let's do it,' she said, careful to keep the double entendre working.

They got back in the Porsche and Cassie sat in the passenger seat a bit sideways, so she was facing Joe. She watched as he brought his right hand up to the steering column and it searched for the ignition and keys.

'Other side,' she said.

He found the keys in the ignition on the dashboard left of the wheel.

'That's a Porsche tradition,' she said. 'From back when they made cars for racing. It was so you could start with your left hand and have your right already on the gear shift. It's a quick-start ignition.'

Michaels nodded. Cassie knew that little story always scored with them. She didn't even know if it was true – she had gotten it from Ray – but she told it every time. She knew Michaels was imagining himself telling it to some sweet little thing outside any number of pickup joints on the Sunset Strip.

He started the engine and backed the car out and then drove back out onto Mulholland, over-revving all the way. But after a few shifts he picked up on the nuances of the gearbox and was taking the curves smoothly. Cassie watched as he tried not to smile when he hit a straightaway and the speedo hit seventy-five in just a few seconds. But the look came over his face. He couldn't hide it. She knew the look and what it felt like. Some people got it from speed and power, some got it in other ways. She thought about how long it had been since she had felt the hot wire coursing through her own blood.

Cassie looked into her little office to check for pink phone slips on the desk. There were none. She moved on through the showroom, running her finger along the spoiler of a classic whale tail, and past the finance office to the fleet manager's office. Ray Morales looked up from some paperwork as she came in and hooked the keys from the Carrera she had used on the test drive on the appropriate hook on the fleet board. She knew he was waiting to hear how it went. After all, he had invested more than a hundred dollars in Scotch whisky.

'He's going to think about it a couple days,' she said without looking at Ray. 'I'll call him Wednesday.'

As Cassie turned to leave, Ray dropped his pen and pushed his seat back from his desk.

'Shit, Cassie, what is up with you? That guy was a hard-on. How'd you lose him?'

'I didn't say I lost him,' Cassie said, too much protest in her voice. 'I said he's going to think about it. Not everybody buys after the first test drive, Ray. That car's going to run a hundred grand.'

'With these guys they do. With Porsche they do. They don't think, they buy. Cassie, damn, he was primed. I could tell when I had him on the phone. You know what you're doing? I think you're psyching these guys out. You gotta come on to these guys like they're the next Cecil B. DeMille. Don't make 'em feel bad about what they do or what they want.'

Cassie put her hands on her hips in indignation.

'Ray, I don't know what you're talking about. I try to sell the car, I don't try to talk 'em out of it. I don't make them feel bad. And none of these guys even know who Cecil B. De Mille was.'

'Then Spielberg, Lucas, whatever. I don't care. There is an art to this, Cassie. That's what I'm saying and what I've been trying to teach you. It's finesse, it's sex, it's givin' the guy a hard-on. When you first came in here you were doin' that. You were moving, what, five, six cars a month. Now, I don't know what you're doing.'

Cassie looked down at his desk for a moment before

answering. She slid her hands into her pockets. She knew he was right.

'Okay, Ray, you're right. I'll work on it. I guess I'm just a little out of focus right now.'

'How come?'

'I'm not sure.'

'You want some time, maybe take a few days?'

'No, I'm cool. But tomorrow I'll be in late. I've got my see-and-pee up in Van·Nuys.'

'Right. No problem. How's that going? That lady doesn't call or come around anymore.'

'It's going. You probably won't hear from her unless I fuck up.'

'Good. Keep it that way.'

Something about his tone bothered her but she pushed it aside. She averted her eyes and looked down at the paperwork on his desk. She noticed that there was a fleet report on a stack of paperwork to the side of his work space.

'So we have a truck coming?'

Ray followed her eyes to the report and nodded.

'Next Tuesday. Four Boxsters, three Carreras – two of them cabs.'

'Cool. You know colors yet?'

'The Carreras are white. The Boxsters are coming arctic, white, black and I think yellow.'

He grabbed the report and studied it.

'Yeah, yellow. Be nice to have these locked in before they get here. Meehan already has a contract on one of the cabs.'

'I'll see what I can do.'

He winked at her and smiled.

'Thattagirl.'

There was that tone again. And the wink. She was getting the idea that Ray was finally getting around to wanting to collect on all of his goodwill. He'd probably been waiting for her to hit a drought so she'd feel she had less choice in the matter. She knew he would make his move soon and that she should think about how to handle it. But there were too many other things that were more important on her mind. She left him in the office and headed back to her own.

3

The offices of the California Department of Corrections, Parole and Community Services Division, in Van Nuys were crowded into a one-story building of gray, precast concrete that stood in the shadow of the Municipal Court building. The nondescript design features of its exterior seemed in step with its purpose: the quiet reintegration of convicts into society.

The interior of the building took its cue from the crowd control philosophy employed at popular amusement parks – although those who waited here weren't always anxious to reach the end of their wait. A maze of roped-off cattle rows folded the long lines of ex-cons back and forth in the waiting rooms and hallways. There were lines of cons waiting to check in, lines waiting for urine tests, lines waiting to see parole agents, lines in all quadrants of the building.

To Cassie Black the parole office was more depressing than prison had been. When she was at High Desert, she was in stasis, like a character in those sci-fi movies where the journey back to earth is so long that the travelers are put into a hibernation-type sleep. That was how Cassie saw it. She was breathing but not living, waiting and surviving on hope that the end of her time would come sooner rather than later. That hope for the future and the warmth of her constant dream of freedom got her past all the depression. But the parole office was that future. It was the harsh reality of getting out. And it was squalid and crowded and inhuman. It smelled of desperation and lost hope, of no future. Most of those surrounding her wouldn't make it. One by one they would go back. It was a fact of the life they had chosen. Few went straight, few made it out alive. And for Cassie, who promised herself she would be one of the few, the monthly immersion into this world always left her profoundly depressed.

By ten o'clock on Tuesday morning she had already been through the check-in line and was nearing the front of the pee line. In her hand she held the plastic cup she would have to squat over and fill while an office trainee, dubbed the *wizard* because of the nature of her monitoring duty, watched to make sure it was her own urine going into the container.

While she waited Cassie didn't look at anybody and didn't talk to anybody. When the line moved and she was jostled she just moved with the flow. She thought about her time in High Desert, about how she could just shut herself down when she needed to and go on autopilot, ride that spaceship back to earth. It was the only way to get through that place. And this one, too.

Cassie squeezed into the cubicle that her parole agent, Thelma Kibble, called an office. She was breathing easy now. She was near the end. Kibble was the last stop on the journey.

'There she is . . . ,' Kibble said. 'Howzit going there, Cassie Black?'

'Fine, Thelma. How about you?'

Kibble was an obese black woman whose age Cassie had never tried to guess. There was always a pleasant expression on her wide face and Cassie truly liked her despite the circumstances of their relationship. Kibble wasn't easy but she was fair. Cassie knew she was lucky that her transfer from Nevada had been assigned to Kibble.

'Can't complain,' Kibble said. 'Can't complain at all.'

Cassie sat in the chair next to the desk, which was stacked on all sides with case files, some of them two inches thick. On the left side of the desk was a vertical file labeled RTC which always drew Cassie's attention. She knew RTC meant *return to custody* and the files located there belonged to the losers, the ones going back. It seemed the vertical file was always full and seeing it was as much a deterrent to Cassie as anything else about the parole process.

Kibble had Cassie's file open in front of her and was filling in the monthly report. This was their ritual; a brief face-to-face visit and Kibble would go down the checklist of questions.

'What's up with the hair?' Kibble asked without looking up from the paperwork.

'Just felt like a change. I wanted it short.'

'Change? What are you, so bored you gotta make changes all'a sudden?'

'No, I just . . .'

She finished by hiking her shoulders, hoping the moment would pass. She should have realized that using the word *change* would raise a flag with a parole agent.

Kibble turned her wrist slightly and checked her watch. It was time to go on.

'Your pee going to be a problem?'

'Nope.'

'Good. Anything you want to talk about?'

'No, not really.'

'How's the job going?'

'It's a job. It's going the way jobs go, I guess.'

Kibble raised her eyebrows and Cassie wished she had

just stuck to a one-word answer. Now she had raised another flag.

'You drive them fancy damn cars all the time,' Kibble said. 'Most people that come in here are washin' cars like that. And they ain't complaining.'

'I'm not complaining.'

'Then what?'

'Then nothing. Yes, I drive fancy cars. But I don't own them. I sell them. There's a difference.'

Kibble looked up from the file and studied Cassie for a moment. All around them the cacophony of voices from the rows of cubicles filled the air.

'A'right, what's troubling you, girl? I don't have time for bullshit. I got my hard cases and my soft cases and I'll be damned if I'm gonna have to move you to HC. I don't have time for that.'

She slapped one of the stacks of thick files to make her point.

'You won't want that, neither,' she said.

Cassie knew HC meant High Control. She was on minimum supervision now. A move to HC would mean increased visits to the parole office, daily phone checks and more home visits from Kibble. Parole would simply become an extension of her cell and she knew she couldn't handle that. She quickly held her hands up in a calming gesture.

'I'm sorry, I'm sorry. Nothing's wrong, okay? I'm just having ... I'm just going through one of those times, you know?'

'No, I don't know. What times you talkin' about? Tell me.'

'I can't. I don't know the words. I feel like ... it's like every day is like the one before. There is no future because it's all the same.'

'Look, what did I tell you when you first came in here?

I told you it would get like this. Repetition breeds routine. Routine's boring but it keeps you from thinking and it keeps you out of trouble. You want to stay out of trouble, don't you, girl?'

'Yes, Thelma. But it's like I got out of lockdown but sometimes I feel like I'm still in lockdown. It's not . . .'

'Not what?'

'I don't know. It's not fair.'

There was a sudden outburst from one of the other cubicles as a convict started protesting loudly. Kibble stood up to look over the partitions of the cubicle. Cassie didn't move. She didn't care. She knew what it was, somebody being taken down and put in a holding cell pending revocation of parole. There were one or two takedowns every time she came in. Nobody ever went back peaceably. Cassie had long ago stopped watching the scenes. She couldn't worry about anyone else in this place but herself.

After a few moments Kibble sat back down and turned her attention back to Cassie, who was hoping that the interruption would make the parole agent forget what they had been talking about.

There was no such luck.

'You see that?' Kibble asked.

'I heard it. That was enough.'

'I hope so. Because any little mess-up and that could be you. You understand that, don't you?'

'Perfectly, Thelma. I know what happens.'

'Good, because this isn't about being *fair*, to use your word. Fair's got nothing to do with it. You're down by law, honey, and you're under thumb. You're scaring me, girl, and you should be scaring yourself. You're only ten months into a two-year tail. This is not good when I hear you getting antsy after just ten months.'

'I know. I'm sorry.'

'Shit, there's people in this room with four – and five – and six-year tails. Some even longer.'

Cassie nodded.

'I know, I know. I'm lucky. It's just that I can't stop myself from thinking about things, you know?'

'No, I don't know.'

Kibble folded her massive arms across her chest and leaned back in her chair. Cassie wondered if the chair could take the weight but it held strong. Kibble looked at her sternly. Cassie knew she had made a mistake trying to open up to her. She was in effect inviting Kibble into her life more than she was already into it. But she decided that since she had already strayed across the line, she might as well go all the way now.

'Thelma, can I just ask you something?'

'That's what I'm here for.'

'Do you know ... are there any, like international treaties or agreements for parole transfers?'

Kibble closed her eyes.

'What the hell are you talking about?'

'Like if I wanted to live in London or Paris or something?'

Kibble opened her eyes, shook her head and looked astonished. She shifted forward and the chair came down heavily.

'Do I look like a travel agent to you? You are a *con*vict, girl. You understand that? You don't just decide you don't like it here and say, "Oh, I think I'll try Paris now." Are you listening to yourself talking crazy here? We aren't running no Club Med here.'

'Okay, I was just—'

'You got the one transfer from Nevada, which you were lucky to get, thanks to your friend at the dealership. But that's it. You are stuck here, girl. For at least the next

fourteen months and maybe even further, the way you're
acting now.'

'All right. I just thought I'd—'

'End of story.'

'Okay. End of story.'

Kibble leaned over the desk to write something in
Cassie's file.

'I don't know about you,' she said as she wrote. 'You
know what I oughta do is I oughta thirty-fifty-six you for
a couple days, see if that clears your mind of these silly
ass ideas. But –'

'You don't have to do that, Thelma. I—'

'– we're full up right now.'

A 3056 was a parole hold – an order putting a parolee
in custody pending a hearing to revoke parole. The PA
could then drop the revoke charge at the time of the
hearing and the parolee would be set free. Meantime, the
revisit to lockdown for a few days would serve as a
warning to straighten up. It was the harshest threat
Kibble had at her disposal and just the mention of it
properly scared Cassie.

'I mean it, Thelma, I'm fine. I'm okay. I was just
venting some steam, okay? Please don't do that to me.'

She hoped she had put the proper sound of pleading
into her voice.

Kibble shook her head.

'All I know is that you were on my A list, girl. Now I
don't know. I think I'm gonna at least have to come
around and check up on you one of these days. See
what's what with you. I'm telling you, Cassie Black, you
better watch yourself with me. I am not fat old Thelma
who can't get off her chair. I am *not* someone to fuck
with. You think so, you check with these folks.'

She raked the end of her pen along the edges of the
RTC files to her left. It made a loud ripping sound.

'They'll tell you I am not someone to be fucked with or fucked over.'

Cassie could only nod. She studied the huge woman across from her for a long moment. She needed some way to defuse this, to get the smile back on Kibble's face or at the very least the deep furrow out of her brow.

'You come around, Thelma, and I have a feeling I'll see you before you see me.'

Kibble looked sharply at her. But Cassie saw the tension slowly change in her face. It had been a gamble but Kibble took the comment in good humor. She even started to chuckle and it made her huge shoulders and then the desk shake.

'We'll see about that,' Kibble said. 'You'd be surprised by me.'

4

Cassie felt a weight lifting off her as she came out of the parole offices. Not simply because the monthly ordeal was over. But because she had caught a glimmer of understanding about herself while inside. In her struggle for an explanation of her feelings to Kibble she had arrived at an essential conclusion. She was marking time and she could do it their way or her own way. The open house in Laurel Canyon was not the cause of this. That was simply an accelerant; it was gasoline on an already burning fire. Her decision was clear now and in that clarity were feelings of both relief and fear. The fire was burning strongly now. Inside she began to feel the slight trickle of melt water from the frozen lake that for so long had been her heart.

She walked between the municipal and county court-houses and through the plaza fronting the LAPD's Van Nuys station. There was a bank of pay phones near the stairs leading up to the police station's second-floor entrance. She picked one up, dropped in a quarter and a dime and punched in a number she had committed to memory more than a year earlier while in High Desert. It had come on a note smuggled to her in a tampon.

After three rings the phone was answered by a man. 'Yes?'

It was more than six years since Cassie had heard the

voice but it rang true and recognizable to her. It made her catch her breath.

'Yes?'

'Uh, yes, is this ... is this D. H. Reilly?'

'No, you have the wrong number.'

'Dog House Reilly? I was calling—'

She looked down and read off the number of the phone she was standing at.

'What kind of crazy name is that? No Dog House here and you've got the wrong number.'

He hung up. Cassie did, too. She then turned around and walked back into the plaza and took a seat on a bench about fifty feet from the pay phones. She shared the bench with a disheveled man who was reading a newspaper so yellowed that it had to be months old.

Cassie waited almost forty minutes. When the phone finally started to ring, she was in the midst of a one-sided conversation with the disheveled man about the quality of the food service in the Van Nuys jail. She got up and trotted to the phones, the man yelling a final complaint at her.

'Sausage like fucking Brillo pads! We were playing hockey in there!'

She grabbed the phone after the sixth ring.

'Leo?'

A pause.

'Don't use my name. How you doing, sweetheart?'

'I'm okay. How are—'

'You know, you been out now like a year, am I right?'

'Uh, actually—'

'And all that time and not even a hello from you. I thought I'd hear from you before now. You're lucky I even remembered that Dog House Reilly schtick.'

'Ten months. I've been out ten months.'

'And how's it been?'

'Okay, I guess. Good, actually.'

'Not if you're calling me.'

'I know.'

There was a long silence then. Cassie could hear traffic noise coming from his end. She guessed he had left the house and found a pay phone somewhere on Ventura Boulevard, probably near the deli he liked to eat at.

'So, you called me first,' Leo prompted.

'Right, yeah. I was thinking . . .'

She paused and thought about everything again. She nodded her head.

'Yeah, I need to get some work, Leo.'

'Don't use my name.'

'Sorry.'

But she smiled. Same old Leo.

'You know me, a classic paranoid.'

'I was just thinking that.'

'All right, so you're looking for something. Give me some parameters? What are we talking about here?'

'Cash. One job.'

'One job?' He seemed surprised and maybe even disappointed. 'How big?'

'Big enough to disappear on. To get a good start.'

'Must not be going too good then.'

'It's just that things are happening. I can't . . .'

She shook her head and didn't finish.

'You sure you're okay?'

'Yes, I'm fine. I feel good, actually. Now that I know.'

'I know what you mean. I remember the time when I decided for good. When I said fuck it, this is what I do. And at the time, hell, I was only boosting air bags out of Chryslers. I've come a long way. We both have.'

Cassie turned and glanced back at the man on the bench. He was continuing his conversation. He hadn't really needed Cassie to be there.

'You know, don't you, that with these parameters, you're probably talking Vegas. I mean, I could send you down to Hollywood Park or one of the Indian rooms but you're not going to see a lot of cash. You're talking fifteen, twenty a pop down there. But if you give me some time to set something in Vegas I could push the take.'

Cassie thought a moment. She had believed when the bus to High Desert pulled out of Las Vegas six years before that she would never see the place again. But she knew that what Leo was saying was accurate. Vegas was where the big money was.

'Vegas is fine,' she said abruptly. 'Just don't take too long.'

'Who's that talking behind you?'

'Just some old guy. Too much pruno while in lockup.'

'Where are you?'

'I just left the PO.'

Leo laughed.

'Nothing like having to pee in a cup to make you see life's possibilities. Tell you what, I'll keep an eye out for something. I got a heads up about something coming up in the next week or so. You'd be perfect. I'll let you know if it pans out. Where can I reach you?'

She gave him the dealership number. The general number and not her direct line or her cell phone number. She didn't want those numbers written down and in his possession in case he took a bust.

'One other thing,' she said. 'Can you still get passports?'

'I can. Take me two, three weeks 'cause I send out for them, but I can get you one. It will be fucking grade A, too. A passport will run you a grand, a whole book twenty-five hundred. Comes with DL, Visa and Amex. Delta miles on the Amex.'

'Good. I'll want a whole book for me and then a second passport.'

'What do you mean, two? I'm telling you the first one will be perfect. You won't need another with –'

'They're not both for me. I need the second for somebody else. Do you want me to send pictures to the house or do you have a drop?'

Leo told her to send the photos to a mail drop. He gave her the address in Burbank, then asked her who the second passport was for and what names she wanted used in the manufacture of the false documents. She had anticipated the questions and had already picked the names. She offered to send the cash with the photos but Leo told her he could front it for the time being. He said it was an act of good faith, seeing that they were going back into business together.

'So,' he said, returning to the main business at hand. 'You going to be ready for this? Been a long time. People get rusty. If I put you out there, I'll be on the line, you know.'

'I know. You don't have to worry. I'll be ready.'

'Okay, then. I'll be talking to you.'

'Thanks. I'll be seeing you.'

'Oh, and sweetheart?'

'What?'

'I'm glad you're back. It'll be like old times again.'

'No, Leo. Not without Max. It will never be the same again.'

This time Leo didn't protest her use of his name. They both hung up and Cassie walked away from the phones. The man on the bench called after her but she couldn't make out what it was he had said.

She had to walk up to Victory Boulevard to get to the Boxster. It was the closest she had been able to get to the criminal justice complex. Along the way she thought about Max Freeling. She remembered their last moments together; the bar at the Cleo, the beer foam in his mustache, the tiny scar on his chin where no whiskers grew.

Max had made a toast and she repeated it now silently. *To the end. To the place where the desert is ocean.*

Thinking about what happened afterward left her depressed and still angry, even after so many years. She decided that before she went to the dealership she would drive by Wonderland Elementary and catch the lunch recess. She knew it was the best way possible to chase the blues away.

When she got to the Boxster she found it had been ticketed after the two hours on the meter expired. She pulled the citation off the windshield and tossed it onto the passenger seat. The car was still registered to the deadbeat it had been repossessed from. So when the ticket went unpaid, the bill from the city would go to him. He could deal with it.

She got in the car and drove off. She took Van Nuys Boulevard south to the 101. The boulevard was lined with new-car dealerships. Sometimes she thought of the Valley as one big parking lot.

She tried listening to a Lucinda Williams compact disc but the stereo was so jumpy that she had to pop it out and just listen to the radio. The song playing was an old one. Roseanne Cash singing about a seven-year ache.

Yeah, Cassie thought. Roseanne knew what she was talking about. Seven years. But the song didn't say anything about what happened after seven years. Did that ache go away then? Cassie didn't think it ever would.

5

In the following days, while she waited for word from Leo, Cassie Black found herself dropping into the rhythm of preparation that was both familiar and comforting to her. But most of all it was exciting, putting a thrill into her life she had not felt in many years.

The preparation was also a solitary time of introspection. She studied her decision repeatedly and from all angles. She found no cracks, no second thoughts, no intruding guilt. The hurdle had been in making the choice. Once decided upon, it only brought her relief and a great sense of freedom. There was the excitement of danger and anticipation in her that the years of incarceration had robbed from her memory. She had forgotten how truly addictive the charge of adrenaline could be. Max had simply called it outlaw juice because he could not put his feelings into words. In those days of preparation she came to realize that the true essence of incarceration was aimed at removing that charge, of washing it from memory. If so, then five years in lockdown had failed her. The charge of outlaw juice was boiling in her blood now, banging through her veins like hot water through frozen winter pipes.

She began by changing her body clock, dramatically shortening her sleeping hours and pushing them well into the morning. She offset the sleep deprivation with a regimen of energy-enhancing vitamins and an occasional late-afternoon nap on her living room couch. Within a week she had dropped from seven to four hours of sleep per night without a noticeable impact on her alertness or productivity.

At night she started taking long drives on the dangerously curving Mulholland Drive so that she could sharpen her sustained alertness. When home she moved about her house without lights on, her eyes adjusting and becoming reacquainted with the contours of night shadows. She knew she would have the option of night-vision goggles when the job came up but she also knew it was good to be prepared for any eventuality.

By day, when she wasn't working at the dealership, she started gathering the equipment she might need and making the tools she would use. After carefully making a list of every conceivable thing that would help her overcome any obstacle on a job, she memorized its contents and destroyed it – such a list in her possession was enough in itself to violate her parole. She then spent an entire day driving to a variety of hardware stores and other businesses, gathering the items on the list and spreading her cash purchases across the entire city so that the various parts to her plan could never be construed as the whole.

She bought screwdrivers, iron files, hacksaw blades and hammers; baling wire, nylon twine and bungee cords. She bought a box of latex gloves, a small tub of earthquake wax, a Swiss Army knife and a painter's putty knife with a three-inch-wide blade. She bought a small acetylene torch and went to three hardware stores before finding a small enough battery-powered and recharge-able drill. She bought rubber-tipped pliers, wire cutters and aluminum shears. She added a Polaroid camera and a man's long-sleeved wet suit top to her purchases. She bought big and small flashlights, a pair of tile worker's knee pads and an electric stun gun. She bought a black leather backpack, a black fanny pack and belt, and several black zipper bags of varying sizes that could be folded and carried inside one of the backpack's pockets. Lastly, in every store she went to she bought a keyed padlock, amassing a collection of seven locks made by seven different manufacturers and thereby containing seven slightly different interior locking mechanisms.

In the small bungalow she rented on Selma near the 101 Freeway in Hollywood, she spread her purchases out on the scarred Formica-topped table in the kitchen and readied her equipment, wearing gloves at all times when she handled each piece.

She used the shears and the torch to make lock picks from the baling wire and hacksaw blades. She made a double set of three picks: a tension spike, a hook and a thin, flat tumbler pick. She put one set in a Ziploc bag and buried it in the garden outside the back door. The other set she put aside with the tools for the job she hoped would be coming from Leo very soon.

She cut half a sleeve off the wet suit and used it to encase the drill, sewing the sound-deadening rubber tightly in place with the nylon twine. From the rest of the wet suit she created a roll-up satchel in which she could quietly carry her custom-made burglary kit.

When her working tools were ready, she rolled them up in the satchel, secured it with a bungee cord and then hid it in the hollow of the Boxster's front right fender, attaching it to the suspension struts with more bungee cords. Her fingerprints were on nothing. If the tool satchel were ever discovered by Thelma Kibble or any other law enforcement officer, Cassie would have a degree of deniability that might keep her out of lockdown. The car was not hers. Without prints on the tools or evidence of her having purchased and made them, it ultimately could not be proved that they belonged to her. They could hold her and sweat her but they would eventually have to let her go.

The seven padlocks Cassie used for practice. She locked them onto a wooden clothing hanger and dropped the keys into a coffee cup in a kitchen cabinet. At night she sat in the dark in her living room and blindly worked the extra set of picks into the padlocks. The nuances of finessing a lock open came back to her slowly. It took her four days to open all seven padlocks. She then hooked them back on the hanger and closed them. She started over, this time wearing latex gloves. At the end of two weeks she was regularly timing herself and she could open all seven locks in twelve minutes with gloves on.

She knew all along that what she was doing was as much mental preparation as anything else. It was getting back into the rhythm, the mind-set. Max, her teacher, had always said the rhythm was the most important preparation. The ritual. She knew it was unlikely she would have to pick a lock on the job Leo would find for her. Most of the hotels in Las Vegas and elsewhere had gone to electronically programmed card keys in the last decade. Subverting electronic protection was another matter altogether. It required inside help or a skill at *soshing* – short for social engineering, meaning the con at the front desk or the finesse moves with the housekeeper.

The prep time brought her close to memories of Max, the man who had been both her mentor and lover. These were bittersweet memories because she could not think of the good times without remembering how they had all ended so badly at the Cleopatra. Even still, she often found herself laughing out loud in the darkness of her house, the hanger full of padlocks on her lap, her hands sweating inside tight latex gloves.

She laughed hardest as she remembered one soshing trick Max had pulled to perfection at the Golden Nugget. They needed to get into a room on the fifth floor. Spying a night service maid's cart outside a room down the hall, Max went into a service alcove and took off all his clothes. He then ruffled his hair and walked down the hall to the maid's cart, cupping his privates in his hands. After startling the woman, he explained he had been sleeping and got up to go to the bathroom and in his sleepy confusion had inadvertently stepped through the wrong door and out of his room, the door closing and locking behind him. Not wanting to prolong her encounter with a naked man, the housekeeper quickly handed him her pass key. They were in.

What made the story so funny in memory to Cassie was that once Max was in the room he had to dress and return the key to the maid in order to complete the trick. But his clothes were hidden down the hall in the alcove. So he put on a set of the mark's clothes. The man they had targeted was slightly shorter than Max and rail thin. He weighed at least fifty pounds less. He was also openly gay and his clothes announced this to the world. Max walked back down the hall to the maid in a flamingo pink shirt open to the navel and black leather pants so tight he couldn't bend his knees.

Each night when she had finished practicing and was ready for sleep, Cassie reburied the second set of picks and put a heavy winter coat on the hanger holding the padlocks. She zipped the coat closed, hiding the locks, and returned it to a hallway closet. Ever aware that Thelma Kibble might make good on her threat to make an unscheduled appearance, she left no outward appearance in her home or activities of what she was planning and preparing for.

But she never saw any sign of Kibble's presence. The

parole officer apparently didn't even make a follow-up call to Ray Morales to check on Cassie's behavior and work status. Cassie believed the woman was simply overrun with too many cases. Despite the stern words to Cassie, Kibble probably had dozens of hard cases that were more deserving than Cassie of a field visit.

As Cassie waited for the call from Leo she kept her old routines as well. Each morning she went running at the Hollywood Reservoir, circling the lake and crossing the Mulholland Dam twice. The run was penance for her earlier morning ritual: stopping at the farmers' market on Fairfax for doughnuts and coffee at Bob's. She would take her breakfast in the car, driving up into the hills of Laurel Canyon and stopping, if parking was available, near the fenced playground outside the Wonderland School.

As she ate her glazed doughnuts and gulped steaming black coffee, she watched the children being dropped off by parents and playing in the schoolyard before the morning bell. Her eyes would solemnly scan the fenced playing ground until she found the grouping of the kindergarten girls, usually gathered closely around their teacher – a woman who looked very caring and kind. Cassie's eyes would move into the pack and search out the same face each morning: the girl who wore the backpack with the *Have a Nice Day* smiley face on it. She would watch as the bright yellow backpack bobbed and moved in the crowd. Cassie would not lose sight of the girl until the bell rang and the children were herded inside to the classrooms. Only then would she crumple the doughnut bag and start her car to head to the reservoir to work her body and mind to near exhaustion before the day had barely begun.

6

Fifteen days after Cassie Black made contact with Leo, she got the return call. She was sitting in her office, going over the figures on a trade-in sheet with Ray Morales, when the phone rang. Her mind on the work at hand, she grabbed the phone and punched the line without thinking about it.

'This is Cassie Black, can you hold?'

'Sure.'

She recognized the voice with that one word. She paused as a cold finger slid down her spine, then she hit the hold button. A palpable excitement rose in her chest.

'You okay?' Morales asked.

'Sure, fine. I have to take this, though.'

'Go ahead.'

'I mean alone. It's personal.'

'Oh. Okay.'

Ray looked a little rejected and maybe even annoyed. To him *personal* probably meant a new boyfriend was calling. Cassie had gently rebuffed him two days earlier when he had asked her out to dinner after work. Now that he had finally made his move, he was too late. Cassie was waiting on Leo and wasn't going to complicate things with Ray. If things went the way she was planning, she would be doing him a favor by not getting involved with him. He'd have no secrets to hide when the cops came to talk to him.

Ray said he would be in his office if she wanted to finish going over the trade-in report. He moved out of her small office and closed the door without Cassie's having to ask. She leaned forward to look over the desk at the bottom of the doorjamb. She could tell that Ray was standing just outside the door, hoping to hear her conversation.

'Ray?'

He didn't respond but Cassie watched the feet move away. She clicked the hold button on the phone.

'Hello?'

'What, did you go for a test drive or something?'

'Sorry.'

'Well, I got something for you.'

Cassie didn't respond at first. The trilling of adrenaline in her blood was strong. Outlaw juice. She felt a sense of being at the edge of a cliff. It was time to go over. Now or never. Those people who got in padded barrels and floated over the falls had nothing on this.

Leo spoke into the silence, breaking the spell.

'I'm not sure you're going to like it, though.'

Cassie swallowed back a catch in her throat.

'How come?'

'We'll talk about it when I see you.'

'When and where?'

'Just come here. But make it soon. Either tonight or tomorrow first thing. This has to go down by tomorrow night or we lose it.'

'All right, tonight after work. You still in the same place?'

'Always. One last thing. I'm turning on the memo button on the phone machine here so I have this on tape. Kid, you know I love you but it's been a long time. Don't get insulted, because this is just a precaution. Ever since

49

Linda Tripp and Monica Lewinsky, it's standard operating practice around here. Here goes. Are you currently working with any law enforcement agency at this time?'

'Leo . . .'

'Don't say my name. Just answer the question. I'm sorry but this is a precaution I have to take. People been settin' traps right and left out there.'

'No, Leo, I'm not. If I wanted to set you up I could have done it back before I spent the nickel at High Desert. Everybody and their brother wanted me to make a deal then. But I didn't.'

'You sure didn't and you know I appreciated it. Didn't I take care of you when I could? What about that PI you wanted to hire – that cost me five grand, you know.'

'You took care of me, Leo. I won't forget.'

'I wish you'd forget using my name.'

'Sorry.'

'Okay, good enough. The tape's off. We're good to go. I'll see you in a little while. Take—'

'Did you get the passports?'

A pause.

'Not yet. Next time I'm out I'll make a call to check on that. Okay?'

'Okay, but I need them. Soon.'

'I'll deliver the message. See you soon. Take all usual precautions.'

After she hung up Cassie's eyes traveled up the wall next to the door. Her eyes held on the poster taped on the wall and facing her. It showed a woman in a string bikini walking on a sun-drenched beach. The word TAHITI! was scrawled in the sand behind her, just out of reach of the surf's wash.

'To the place where the desert is ocean,' she said out loud.

7

Cassie drove west on Sunset. She had the top down on the Porsche. She loved the thrum of the engine coming through the seat and the deep, guttural tones she heard on the curves. At Beverly Glen she turned the Boxster north and followed the winding canyon road over the hill and down into the Valley.

Leo Renfro lived in Tarzana in the flats north of Ventura Boulevard on a street fronting the 101 Freeway. His house was a small, postwar ranch house without any real defining design or style. It was like every other house in his neighborhood and that was exactly the way Leo wanted it. Leo had survived by being nondescript, by blending in.

She drove by the house without braking and then up and down the surrounding blocks, studying every parked vehicle she passed and looking for the telltale signs of a surveillance vehicle: vans with mirrored windows, cars with more than one antenna, pickup trucks with camper shells on the back. One vehicle caught her attention. It was a plumbing repair van, according to the sign painted on the side panel. It sat at the curb in front of a house one block from Leo's house. Cassie passed it without stopping but then turned around and headed back, pulling to the curb and parking a half block from the van. She sat there watching the vehicle and looking for movement behind the glass, a shifting of the suspension as people moved around inside, any indication of life within. Nothing happened but Cassie maintained her vigil for almost ten minutes before she saw a man in a blue jumpsuit come out of the house and approach the van. He opened the side door and climbed inside. A few moments later he carefully lowered a heavy pipe-snaking machine to the road. He then got out, closed and locked the van's door, and pushed the machine toward the front door of the house. He seemed legit to Cassie. She restarted the Porsche, made one more circuit through the neighborhood and then returned to Leo's house. She parked at the curb out front and reminded herself not to buy into Leo's constant paranoid sensibility. She remembered all the rules and precautions he used to lay on her and Max before a job. Don't bet black before a job, don't eat chicken before a job, never wear a red hat and so on and so on. It was all *step on a crack, break your mother's back* stuff as far as Cassie had been concerned.

Until that last night at the Cleopatra.

When Cassie got to the front door she looked up at the joists of the roof overhang and saw the old bullet camera was still in place. She was wondering if it still worked and got her answer when Leo answered the door before she knocked. She smiled.

'Guess it still works.'

''Course it does. Had that there goin' on what, eight years now. Person put it there guaranteed it for life and I believed her. Nobody knew her shit better than her.'

He smiled.

'How are you, Cassie? Come on in.'

He stepped back to let her in. Leo Renfro was in his early forties, with a trim, medium build. He had thinning hair that was already gray. It had been gray when Cassie met him almost a decade earlier. He'd told her then that it was from having to grow up too quickly. He'd practically raised Max, his stepbrother, after their mother died in a drunk-driving accident. Leo's father was an unknown but Max's wasn't. He was in Nevada State doing ten to twenty-five for armed robbery.

Cassie stepped into the house and Leo pulled her into a fast, tight bear hug. It felt good to her. It felt comforting, like home.

'Hey, kid,' he said with a somber and loving tone.

'Leo,' she said and then pulled back with a concerned look on her face. 'I can say your name now, right?'

He laughed and pointed toward the back and started leading the way to where she knew he kept his office in a wood-paneled den off the pool.

'You look good, Cassie. Real good. Like the short hair. Is that sort of a butch thing left over from High Desert? What was it I heard they call the lamb choppers up there, the High Dee Hoes?'

He glanced back at her and winked.

'You look good, too, Leo. Still the same.'

He looked back again and they exchanged smiles. It had been years since Cassie had seen him but Leo had barely changed. Maybe a little less hair but still deeply tanned and trim. She assumed he must still be following his regimen of yoga and then morning lap swimming to stay in shape.

In the living room they had to step around a couch that was oddly placed at an angle facing the corner of the room rather than the fireplace. This caused Cassie to look about and she noticed all of the furnishings of the room were positioned strangely, as if the fireplace – the obvious center of the room – were not there.

'Remind me to get your interior designer's number before I leave,' she said. 'What style is this – postmodern break-in?'

'Hey, I know. I just had the place feng-shuied and this is the best I can do with it. For now.'

'Feng what?'

'Feng *shui*. The Chinese art of harmonic placement. Feng shui.'

'Oh.'

She thought she remembered reading about feng shui. Something about it being the latest cottage industry in L.A. among the cosmically enlightened.

'This place is doomed,' Leo was saying. 'Bad vibes in all directions. I feel like Dick Van Dyke – comin' in the door and tripping over the furniture. I should just get out of here. But I've been here so long and I have the pool right here and everything. I don't know what I'm gonna do.'

They came to the office. Leo's desk was at one end, next to the row of sliding glass doors that looked out on the pool. Lined along the opposite wall were dozens of cases of champagne. Seeing the stacks of boxes gave Cassie pause. In the past, the Leo Renfro she knew and had worked for would never have stolen property in his own home. He was a middleman who set capers into motion and arranged for the fencing of the merchandise afterward but he almost never came into physical proximity with it unless it was cash. Seeing the champagne right in his office made Cassie question what she was doing there. Maybe things had changed with Leo since Max. She stood in the doorway to the office as if afraid to enter.

Leo went behind his desk and looked back at her. He didn't sit down.

'What's the matter?'

She gestured toward the lineup of boxes completely covering one wall. There must be fifty cases, she guessed.

'Leo, you never kept the swag in your own house. It's not only dangerous but stupid. You –'

'Relax, would you? It's all totally legit. I bought it – ordered it through the distributor. It's an investment.'

'In what?'

'The future. You watch. The millennium celebration is gonna liquidate all stores of champagne. Around the whole fucking world. What's left will sky-rocket in value and I'll be sitting pretty. Every goddamn restaurant in town will be coming to me. You should see my garage. I'm hoarding five hundred cases of this stuff. Six thousand bottles. I double my wholesale price and take home a couple hundred K minimum. You want to buy in on it? I've got investors.'

She came into the room and looked out through the doors at the glimmering surface of the pool. It was lighted from beneath the surface and glowed like blue neon in the night.

'I can't afford it.'

She could see the automatic vacuum slowly moving across the bottom, the water tube trailing behind it and the debris bag rising, undulating in the water like a ghost.

She could hear the background hiss of the nearby freeway. It was the same at her house in Hollywood. She wondered for a moment if it was a coincidence that they both had places so close to the freeway. Or was it something about thieves. They needed to know the escape route was close.

'You'll be able to buy in after we do this thing here,' Leo said. 'Come on, sit down.'

He sat down and opened the middle desk drawer. He took out a pair of half-cut reading glasses and put them on. There was a manila file waiting on the desk. Leo was all business. He could just as well have been preparing to go over a tax return with a client as the details of a hot prowl burglary. He actually had studied accounting at UCLA until he realized he wanted to manage money that was his, not somebody else's.

Cassie came over and sat down in the padded leather chair at the desk opposite Leo. She looked up at a string of red coins that was hanging from the ceiling directly over the desk. Leo caught her stare and waved up at the coins.

'That's the cure. The remedy.'

'Cure for what?'

'For the feng shui. They're I-Ching coins. They make up for the lack of harmony. That's why I have them hanging right here. Where I do my work is the most important spot in the house.'

He gestured to his desk and the open file.

'Leo, you were always paranoid but I think you're finally wigging out.'

'No. I believe it. And it works. Another thing is the stars. I consult the stars now before making a plan.'

'You're not instilling confidence in me. You mean you're asking some astrologer for a blessing on your moves? Leo, don't you –'

'I don't ask or tell anybody anything. I do it on my own. See?'

He turned and pointed to a row of books held between bookends on the credenza behind him. They all had titles that appeared to be taken from astrological circumstances. One title was *Calendar of Voids* and another book was called *Investing in the Stars*.

'Leo, you used to just quote your Jewish grandfather who said things like "Never pick up a penny that is heads down." What about him?'

'I still believe in him. I believe in it all. The important thing is to believe. Not to hope, but to believe. There is a difference. I believe in these things and so that helps me do what I have to do and accomplish what it is I want to accomplish.'

Cassie thought it was a philosophy that could have come from nowhere else but California.

'That's the beauty of it,' Leo was saying. 'I'm covered from all directions. It's good to have any edge you can get, Cass. Max used to say that, remember?'

Cassie nodded somberly.

'I remember.'

A long pause of uneasy silence and sad memories went by. Cassie looked out at the pool. She remembered swimming with Max one night after they thought Leo was asleep. Then the pool light came on and they were naked.

She finally looked back at Leo.

He had opened the file on the desk. There was a quarter-inch-thick stack of hundred-dollar bills in the file along with a page of neatly printed but indecipherable notes torn from a yellow legal pad. One of Leo's precautions. He always kept notes in a coded language that only he knew. He was studying the notes on the yellow paper.

'Now, where do I begin?' he said to himself.

'How about with the reason you said I won't like this one.'

Leo leaned back in his chair and studied her for a long moment.

'Well,' Cassie finally said, 'are you going to tell me or is it written in the stars somewhere for me to read?'

He ignored the jab.

'This is the deal. It's in Las Vegas, which I already warned you about. It's a lot of cash, I am told. But it's a contract job and—'

'With who?'

'Some people. That's all you need to know. Everybody has a part. Nobody knows everybody else. Not even me. We got a guy watching the mark right now and he's just a voice on the phone that tells me things. I have no idea who he is. He knows me by phone but he doesn't know about you. See? It's safest that way. Different players hold different pieces of the same puzzle. Only nobody sees the whole puzzle, just the piece they hold.'

'That's fine, Leo, but I'm not talking about the bit players. You *know* who it is you're setting this up for, right?'

'Yeah, I know them. I've done business with them in the past. They're good people. In fact, they're investors.'

He pointed to the wall of champagne cases.

'Okay,' Cassie said. 'As long as you vouch for them. What else won't I like about this?'

'What else? The big what else is that it's the Cleo.'

'Jesus Christ!'

'I know, I know.'

He raised his hands as if surrendering in an argument. He then leaned back in his chair and took off his glasses. He put one of the ear hooks in the corner of his mouth and let the glasses dangle.

'Leo, you expect me to go back into that place, let alone Las Vegas, after what happened?'

'I know.'

'I'm never going to set foot in that goddamn place again.'

'I know.'

She got up and stood with her face just inches from one of the sliders. She looked out at the pool again. The vacuum was still moving. Back and forth, back and forth. It reminded her of her own existence.

Leo put his glasses back on and spoke to her in a calming and measured tone.

'Now can I say something?'

She gestured for him to go on though she still didn't look at him.

'Okay, let's remember something here. You called me, I didn't call you. You asked me to set up a job. You said you wanted it big and you wanted it soon. And you wanted it to be cash. Have I got all of that right?'

He waited for an answer but she didn't say anything.

'I'll take your silence as a yes. Well, Cass, this is that job.'

She turned to face him.

'But I didn't say—'

He held up his hand, silencing her.

'Let me finish. All I'm saying is that I brought this to you for consideration. You don't want it, fine. I'll make some calls and I'll go with someone else. But, girl, you were the best I ever knew of on the hot prowl. You are a true artist, if ever I knew one. Even Max would have admitted that. He was the teacher but the student got smarter. So when these guys came to me and told me about this thing, I started thinking it was you all the way. But, hey, I'm not forcing you to do anything. Something else will come down the pipe and I'll call you then. I don't know when that will be, but you'll still be first on my list. You will always be first, Cassie. Always.'

She slowly came back to her chair and sat down.

'You're the artist, Leo. A great bullshit artist. That speech is your way of saying I should do it, isn't it?'

'I didn't say that.'

'You don't have to. It's just that, Leo, you believe in your stars and your I-Ching coins and all your other things. The one thing I have to believe is that that place, that night . . . that there was just a ghost or something in the mix. A jinx. And it was either on us or on that place. For six years I've been saying that it wasn't us, that it was that place. And now you ... you want me to go back there.'

Leo folded the file closed. Cassie watched the stack of money disappear.

'I only want you to do what you want to do. But I have to make some calls now, Cass. I need to set this up with somebody else tonight because the job has to be tomorrow night. The mark's supposed to check out Thursday morning.'

Cassie nodded and felt this awful sense that if she passed on this job there wouldn't be another. She didn't know if this was because Leo wouldn't trust her or because of something else. It was just a premonition. Her mind flashed on the scene of a beach and the surf coming up and wiping out letters drawn in the sand. They were gone before Cassie could read them but she knew what they spelled. *Take the job*.

'What's my end if I do it?'

Leo looked at her and hesitated.

'You sure you want to know?'

She nodded. He opened the file again and slid the yellow page out from beneath the stack of currency. He spoke while looking down at his notes.

'Okay, this is the deal. We get the first hundred off the top and forty points on the rest. They've been watching this guy. They think he's got about five hundred K, all cash. In a briefcase. That pans out, that comes to two-sixty for us. I'd cut it sixty/forty, you on the big end. Better than a hundred and a half for you. I don't know if it's enough to disappear on permanently but it's a fucking A start and not bad for a night's work.'

He looked up at her.

'Not bad for them, either,' she said. 'Two-forty for doing nothing.'

'Not nothing. They found the mark. That's most

important. They also have somebody on the inside who will make things very easy for you.'

He paused for a moment to let the money and the details sink in.

'You interested now?'

Cassie thought a moment.

'You don't know when the next one will be coming, do you?'

'Never do. Right now, this one's all I got. But to be honest, I wouldn't count on the next one being this kind of money. Probably take two, three jobs to put this kind of bread together. This is the big one. This is the one you want.'

He leaned back in his chair, looked over his glasses at her and waited. She knew he had played it just right. He'd let her run out with the line but now was slowly reeling it back in. She was hooked and she knew it. A job with a potential payoff of more than a hundred and fifty thousand dollars didn't come along often. The most she and Max had ever pulled on a caper was sixty thousand dollars they took off an assistant to the sultan of Brunei. It was pocket change to the sultan but she and Max had celebrated until dawn at the Aces and Eights Club in North Vegas.

'All right,' she finally said. 'I'm interested. Let's talk about it.'

8

Leo leaned over the counter where he was working and spoke without looking at his notes or at Cassie.

'The mark is registered under the name Diego Hernandez. He's a pro, a TexMex out of Houston. His game is baccarat. Far as anyone knows he plays clean. He's just good at it. Spends a few days at each casino and moves on, that way he isn't taking too much out of one place and raising eyebrows too high. They tracked him from the Nugget to the Stardust and now the Cleo. Cleaned up every place he went.'

They were in the kitchen of Leo's house. Cassie sat at the kitchen table while Leo stood at the counter and made them peanut butter, honey and banana sandwiches. It was his specialty. He used seven-grain bread.

'Each night he takes his winnings in cash and keeps it all in a briefcase. If he leaves the building he takes the case with him. Locked to his wrist. The only time he doesn't have it with him is when he's down in the casino playing. What he does is take it to the front desk and have them hold it in the vault for him while he's playing, then he picks it up when he goes up to bed. Whenever he's carrying the case he's got a security escort. He doesn't take chances.'

'So what you are saying is that the only time to get it is to go in while he's asleep.'

'Exactly.'

Leo came over to the table and put down two plates with two sandwiches each on them. He then went to the refrigerator and came back with two bottles of Dr Pepper. He sat down and opened the bottles as he talked.

'In the room he probably transfers the cash from the case to the closet safe as an added precaution. That's not for sure but we have to expect it. You want a glass with that?'

'No. What is the safe? I don't remember from before.'

Leo looked down and studied his notes.

'It's a Halsey Executive five-button. Sits on the floor in the closet beneath the clothes rack. Bolted to the floor from the inside. You can't move it. You have to go in and open it – while the guy is right there in the room.'

Cassie nodded and picked up half a sandwich. Leo had cut them into triangles. He always did it that way and she remembered he once got annoyed when she had made a sandwich and cut it lengthwise. She took a bite and immediately smiled.

'*Gawd*,' she said, her mouth full of peanut butter and moving slowly. 'I forgot how good these are, Leo. I remember you makin' them for Max and me after we drove all night to get back here after jobs.'

'Made these sandwiches for him since he was six years old. Always his favorite. It always hits the spot.'

Mentioning Max robbed her of the smile. Cassie turned back to the business at hand.

'The Halsey has a front-mounted keypad. I can do it with one camera – two to be safe if there's time. I'll have to know if the mark's right- or left-handed. I'll get that when I see him on the floor.'

She was primarily talking to herself. Seeing the job in her mind. Then a question for Leo came up.

'You ask your man about the paint?'

Leo nodded.

'Swiss Coffee. The room was painted two months ago but it's a smoking room. Our guy smokes cigars.'

'That'll help with the smell.'

She committed the paint color to memory. She decided she'd pick up a pint and a pump bottle at Laurel Hardware in the morning before leaving.

'I'm also told he's a fat fuck,' Leo said. 'A snorer. Makes it a little easier.'

'Nothing's easy, Leo. Not in Las Vegas.'

That made her think about going back to the Cleopatra again and a foreboding came over her.

'If he's leaving Thursday, why don't we wait and see where he goes and hit him at the new place? Why does it have to be the Cleo?'

'Because we don't know if he's going anywhere else. He might be going back to Texas, for all we know. His briefcase might be full and he's going home. Besides, we have the inside man at the Cleo. Who knows if we'll get lucky like that if he moves on.'

Cassie nodded. She knew Leo had thought about all of this and had decided that hitting the mark at the Cleopatra was the only way.

'I read that the Cleo's for sale,' she said, just to be saying something that would take them away from her thoughts.

'Yeah, three thousand rooms and half of them empty on any given night. Big white elephant is what it is. Seven years old and already for sale. I heard Steve Wynn took a look at it but then took a pass. You know something must be fucked up there if he didn't see a way to turn it around. He touches something, it's gold.'

'Maybe the place never got over the bad publicity – you know, with Max.'

Leo shook his head.

'Old news. The problem is they made that place as

cheap as Mother Hubbard's flophouse and now it's falling apart and nobody wants to stay there. Too many other nice places on the Strip for the same dough. You got the Bellagio now, the Venetian. The Mandalay Bay down at the end.'

He was naming places that hadn't even existed the last time Cassie had been to Las Vegas. She finished her first sandwich and immediately moved on to the next after taking a swig of cold soda from the bottle. She went back to laying out the plan, talking with her mouth full.

'Unless things have changed, the Cleo is on magnocards. That means I have to get over there early tomorrow to work on the maid. I finesse my way into the room, set things up and come back at night through the air-return vent – just like last time.'

She gulped down a mouthful and felt it hit her stomach with a thud.

'I don't know, Leo. They might have changed the design of those ducts after me and Max used them.'

She looked over at him. He was looking over his glasses at her and smiling.

'What?'

'You're not listening to me,' he said. 'I told you the spotter is an inside man. Forget the ducts. And the maid, too. No soshing on this one. You'll have a complete package waiting for you at the VIP desk.'

He looked down at the notes.

'Under the name Turcello. You'll have everything you –'

'Why Turcello? Who's that?'

'That's you. Who cares why? It's just the name the spotter gave me. In the package will be everything you'll need. You'll go in through the front door to the room because you'll have a pass key. And you'll also have a room nearby. So you can set up and watch. Also there'll be a pager. You put it on and you'll get a buzz the minute the mark starts cashing out for the night.'

'A pass key only gets me halfway there. I'll need to change out the deadbolt. It's been so long I can't remember the make. Did you get –'

'Got it right here. Relax. I told you, I've got everything. This isn't amateur hour.'

He referred to his notes.

'The deadbolt is a Smithson Commercial. Same as last time. That a problem?'

'I won't know until I get there. Like you said, when they built that place they went cheap in the places you can't see. They used half gears in all the deadbolts. I guess using halves instead of wholes in three thousand locks saved a nice piece of bread. The question is, did they go back and change them all out after that night with Max?'

'What if they did?'

'Then it's trouble. It means I'll have to take out the whole and cut it in half.'

'In the room?'

'No. I'll have to leave and come back. I'll bring a cutting torch with me and leave it in the trunk. But if I have to go down to use it, I'll have to find a place out of sight. Meantime, the guy could go up to the room and end of story.'

'What about the other room? You could take the gear out of that lock, cut it and then take it into the mark's room.'

Before Cassie could say he was right, Leo shook off the possibility that the locks had been changed.

'I tell you, don't worry about it. That place has been losing money since the day it opened its doors. They wouldn't have gone out and changed three thousand deadbolts because one guy – who wasn't going to be doing it again – finessed a lock. Forget about it.'

'Easy for you to say. You're staying here.'

Leo let that go and reached into the file. He pulled out the stack of money and put it down next to Cassie's plate.

'Our partners are serious people. They know there are equipment costs. That's ten grand there. For camera shopping and whatever else you need.'

'I've already spent close to nine hundred on the basics.'

'Let me ask you something, how up to date are you on all of the cameras and stuff? You know what you want?'

'I'll go see my guy at Hooten's. If he's still there. It's been a long time.'

'Sure has.'

'If he's not, I'll go to Radio Shack. I've kept up. I'll make it work, Leo. Don't worry about that part.'

Leo studied her over his eyeglasses again.

'So what happened, Cass? Why'd you wait so long to call me? I had given up hope of you ever turning up again.'

'I don't know, Leo. I guess at first I just thought I was going to make a run at it, you know?'

Leo nodded.

'The straight and narrow,' he said. 'But it wasn't there for you.'

'One day everything changed.'

'Well, welcome back. We could use you on our side.'

He smiled. Cassie shook her head.

'Leo, this is a one-shot deal. I mean it. I'm not on your team. I'm going to disappear after this.'

She knew the money wouldn't be enough. It would only be a start. But that was all she wanted, the promise of a new start.

Leo nodded and looked down at the yellow page of notes.

'Well, this little caper should get you to wherever it is you want to go.'

'Did you make that call on the passports?'

Leo raised his eyes to hers without raising his face.

'I did. I'm told they're on the way. I'll check the drop later. I like going late, after the counter's closed.'

'Good. Thanks for doing that.'

'No problem. I want you to get to where you want to go, Cassie.'

She picked up the money and stood up.

'I guess I better get it in gear if it's going to be tomorrow. I have to –'

'Wait. One more thing. This is important.'

He pushed his plate aside although his second sandwich was uneaten. From the rear pocket of his pants he pulled an appointment book. It was the size of a checkbook but thicker. He took a rubber band off it and opened it to a page marked with a pink Post-it sticker. Cassie could see it was the current month's calendar. Many of the blocks denoting the days were filled with Leo's printing. Leo ran his finger along the blocks until he found what he was looking for. He spoke without taking his eyes off the page.

'I want you to humor me on something when you're over there.'

'Fine. What?'

'Promise me.'

'I'm not going to promise you anything until I know what you're talking about. What is it, Leo?'

'Okay, this is it. Whatever you do, no matter what happens, don't be in that guy's room between three twenty-two and three thirty-eight in the morning. Okay? That's Wednesday night going into Thursday morning. Write it down if you think you'll forget.'

Cassie felt a bemused, questioning smile come across her face.

'What are you talking about?'

'It's a void moon.'

'A void moon . . .'

'This is my astrological calendar, okay? I work with those books I showed you in the office and I chart things, including the moon.'

'Okay, so you chart the moon. What's a void moon?'

'It's an astrological situation, okay? See, when the moon is moving from one house to another up there in the constellations, it sometimes is in no house at all. When that happens it means it is "void of course" until it finally gets into a house. It's a void moon. And like I said, on Wednesday night going into Thursday morning there's a void moon for those, what, sixteen minutes. It's hanging out there between Cancer and Leo. It's void of course from three twenty-two until three thirty-eight. I worked it all out here.'

He closed the calendar and held it up to her as if it were something sacred.

'And so?'

'And so it's a bad luck time, Cass. Anything can happen under a void moon. Anything wrong. Just don't make your move during that time.'

Cassie studied him for a moment and registered his look as completely sincere. Leo had always been a true believer in whatever it was he chose to believe in.

'It's going to be tough,' she said. 'It all depends on when the guy goes down. I need to go two hours into the sleep pattern. At least two hours to be sure.'

'Then go in after the void. I'm not fucking around here, Cass. You know Lincoln, McKinley and Kennedy were all inaugurated during a void moon? All three of them and look what happened to them. Clinton, too, and he might as well've been shot, what happened with him.'

He nodded very somberly and held the calendar up again as if it were proof of something itself. To Cassie there was something endearing about his fervent belief. Maybe it was because she wasn't sure she believed in anything anymore.

'I mean it,' Leo said. 'You can look this stuff up going back as far as you want.'

Cassie took a step toward the table and reached for the book. But as Leo offered it, she pulled her hand back. She wanted to ask something but wasn't sure she wanted the answer.

Leo read her. He somberly nodded.

'Yeah,' he said. 'I looked it up. That night six years ago with Max, he had a void moon, too.'

She just looked at him.

'Remember what you said before about there being a jinx? It was the void moon, Cass. That was the jinx.'

At the door Leo wished her good luck and said he would see her after the job was completed. Cassie hesitated on the front steps. The discussion of the void moon and Max had put a somber veneer over everything now. She rolled her shoulders as if catching a chill.

'What is it?' Leo asked.

She shook her head as if to dismiss the question and then asked her own.

'Leo, do you think about Max?'

Leo didn't answer at first. He stepped through the open door and looked up at the night sky. The moon was pale and hung like an egg in the sky.

'It will be full in a couple days. Nice and bright.'

He continued to stare for a moment and then looked down at Cassie.

'Not a single day goes by that I don't think about him,' he said. 'Not a day.'

Cassie nodded.

'I still miss him a lot, Leo.'

'Me, too, Cass. So you be careful over there. I don't want to lose you that way, too.'

9

By noon on Wednesday, after making a few last stops for paint and supplies, Cassie Black was crossing the desert, the sun gleaming off the silver skin of the Porsche and heat waves rising off the pavement in front of her. Though the highway was reasonably clear and she was driving a car capable of cruising smoothly at 110 mph or better, she kept the Porsche at a steady two miles under the limit. It was tantamount to holding a thoroughbred race horse at a canter but she had good reason. The moment she had left Los Angeles County she was in violation of her parole. Drawing a traffic stop from the highway patrol could result in her immediate incarceration.

As soon as she crossed the county line she knew that the stakes were high and her life was now at risk. Any interaction with law enforcement would probably result in her returning to lockdown. She had been paroled five years into a seven-to-twelve-year sentence for manslaughter. If she got hooked up she'd be returned to prison for a minimum two years but probably even longer.

She put a Lucinda Williams compact disc in the car stereo and listened to it over and over during the drive. The music rarely skipped badly on the smooth freeways. She liked the outlaw spirit of the songs, the sense of yearning and searching for something the singer put in every song. One of them made Cassie cry each time it

came up on the disc. It was about a lost lover who had
gone back to Lake Charles to die.

> Did an angel whisper in your ear
>   hold you close and take away all your fear
>   in those long, last moments

For Cassie the question posed in the song was a ghost
that haunted her all the time. She hoped an angel had
come to Max.

The sharp-edged outlines of the casino resorts were
visible ahead by three and she felt an unmistakable mix of
excitement and trepidation. For many years she had
believed she would never again see the place where she
had grown up, where she had met and lived with Max.
She had comfortably reconciled that and put Las Vegas
behind her. Returning now made her think of pain and
regrets and ghosts. But she also couldn't help but marvel
at the genius of the place. If ever something had been
made out of nothing, Las Vegas no doubt was it.

As she cruised the Strip she found the changes made in
her absence to be remarkable. On every block there rose
a new resort, a new testament to greed and excess. She
drove by a faux New York skyline, the colossal MGM
Grand and the new Bellagio. She saw re-creations of the
Eiffel Tower and Venice's Piazza San Marco. They were
places and things she had never seen. But now here they
were on the Las Vegas Strip. She remembered something Max had once said. 'Everything and everybody will
eventually come to Las Vegas. It will take away any
reason to go anywhere else.'

Then they went to islands and they knew there was at
least one place that couldn't be counterfeited or corrupted.

She came to the Cleopatra and her attention was

immediately drawn to the side-by-side Tigris and Euphrates Towers. Her eyes drew along the mirrored glass of the top floor of the Euphrates Tower and held momentarily on one window.

Her eyes dropped to the rising triangular form of the glass atrium that covered the sprawling casino twenty floors below. The reflection of the sun was as sharp as a diamond on the side of the mirrored glass uprising. The complex was set almost a hundred yards off the Strip and the entrance drive took the visitor past a series of reflecting pools at graduated levels and from which fountains rose in a choreographed water dance. Set in the reflecting pools were pure white statues of children at play – all under the benevolent eye of Cleopatra, who sat in a throne at the edge of the highest pool. Behind her, an Egyptian motif was integrated into the modern design of the sand-colored exterior of the hotel and casino.

Cassie drove by and waited with the traffic to turn onto Flamingo and head out into the industrial warrens on the west side of the city. She couldn't help but think about Max. About their times here. About the end. She had not expected such biting pain and regret upon her return. The landscape of Las Vegas was always changing, reinventing itself. She had not expected a place that was essentially just a facade to have such a nostalgic resonance. But it was there and it burned. She had not been with another man since Max and she was sure she never would be. Perhaps, she thought, this pain was all she would ever have. That she should embrace it. But then she remembered there was more. There was the plan out on the horizon.

Hooten's Lighting & Supplies was located in an industrial complex near an elevated section of the freeway. It had been there for almost forty years, though its business had changed markedly over that time. Originally a wholesaler of lighting equipment to the casinos, its business had evolved more into the arena of electronics. It was no longer simply a supplier but a manufacturer as well. HLS now built and sold much of the sophisticated surveillance equipment employed in the casinos in Nevada as well as in gaming rooms on Indian reservation land throughout the West.

What the operators of HLS and the casinos that purchased the equipment were not aware of was that inside the company there was at least one person who made the same technology available – for a price – to those intent on circumventing the casino security systems the company installed.

Cassie parked the Boxster in the fenced rear lot, where the installers parked their trucks at night, and went in through the back door. Once inside she stood still for a moment as her eyes adjusted to the dim interior. When she could see clearly, her attention was drawn to the long counter that ran the length of the right side of the no-frills equipment-and-catalog room. Behind the counter were a half dozen men working with customers or working the phones. Most of them had copies of the thick HLS catalog open in front of them and were writing down orders. Cassie noticed that not much in the place had changed. The same slogan that had been painted along the wall behind the counter seven years ago was still there.

IN GOD WE TRUST
ALL OTHERS WE MONITOR

It took Cassie a few seconds to spot Jersey Paltz. He was working on the phone at the far end of the counter.

He had a beard now and more gray hair. But he still had the ponytail and the silver loop earring. It was him.

Paltz hung up just as Cassie stepped up to the counter but he didn't look up at her. He finished writing notes on the top page of an order book. Reading upside down, Cassie could see the order was from the Tropicana. She spoke while he was still writing.

'So, Jersey, too busy to say hello to an old friend?'

Paltz finished the line he was on and then looked up smiling. The smile faltered a little and his face showed the slow register of recognition.

'Cassie Black?'

Cassie nodded and smiled.

'Hey, girl, sure been a long time. When did you ... uh ...'

'Ten months ago. I just haven't been around. After High Desert I moved to California. I like it out there. Where I live the temperature only hits trips a few times a year.'

Paltz nodded but there was hesitation there. Cassie could easily read him. He was realizing she wasn't there to make old acquaintances – there had never been anything but a business relationship between them in the first place. She glanced around to make sure their conversation was private and then leaned over the counter, her elbows on his open catalog and order book.

'I need a kit. Full rig, at least three cameras, and one has to be green.'

Paltz put the pencil he'd been using behind his ear and shook his head once without looking directly at her.

'I'm going to need a pair of NVGs and a roll of Conduct-O tape, too,' Cassie added. 'I stopped at Radio Shack on the way over and they don't sell the tape anymore. The rest of the tools I brought with me.'

'Well, that might be a problem,' Paltz said.

'The goggles or the tape?'

'No, all of it. We don't ... I mean, I just don't get involved in that sort of –'

'Look, Jersey. Don't you think that if I was going to set you up I would've done it six years ago when it could have done me some good? I mean, Max and me, we made you a lot of money back then. You remember that, don't you?'

He nodded his head once, reluctantly.

'It's just that things are different now in this town. You cross a line and they come after you. I mean they really come after you.'

Cassie straightened up.

'You don't have to convince me of that. Or Max.'

'Sorry. I know that.'

He nodded once more and put his hands flat on the counter.

'So what do you think, Jersey? I've got cash and I'm ready to rock and roll.'

She casually swung her backpack under her arm and flipped up the top flap, exposing the stack of hundreds Leo had given her. She knew that loyalty and trust were one thing in the outlaw world, but showing the cash was another.

'I gotta know now 'cause if you're not going to help me I've gotta find somebody else.'

Paltz nodded. She could tell, the money had turned him.

'Tell you what,' he said. 'I might be able to do something for you. What time are we talking about?'

'We're talking right now, Jersey. Tonight. I'm here. I gotta job to do.'

He looked up at her, maintaining his hands-on-the-counter pose. His eyes moved around to make sure they were still talking in private.

'All right. . . . I'm working till five. How about Aces and Eights at six?'

'That old dump's still in business?'

'Oh, yeah. Always.'

'I'll see you at six.'

She started to step away from the counter but Paltz made a low whistling sound with his mouth and she turned back to him. Paltz took the pencil off his ear and wrote something on a scratch pad. He tore the page off and handed it to her.

'You'll need to have that with you.'

She took the page and looked at it. It had a price on it.

$8,500

She thought it was high. She had read enough about the current technology to know the costs for what she needed should be in the range of five thousand dollars, including a nice profit for Paltz. Before she could say anything Paltz apparently read her.

'Look,' he whispered, 'you're gonna pay high end for this stuff. What we make here is proprietary. You take a bust with this stuff on you and they'll trace it right back here. Now sellin' it to you ain't illegal per se, but they could get me on an aiding-and-abetting bit. They throw conspiracy charges around now like confetti. On top of that, I'd lose my job. So you gotta pay high to cover my exposure here. Take it or leave it, that's the price.'

She now realized she had made a mistake showing him the cash before they had a deal.

'Okay, fine with me,' she finally said. 'I'm on an expense account.'

'See you at six, then.'

'Yeah, six.'

10

Cassie had two hours to kill before her meeting with Jersey Paltz. She thought about going to the Cleo and picking up the package waiting for her at the front desk but decided against it because it meant she would have to leave to make her meeting and then come back. That would mean two extra trips under the cameras. She didn't want to give the people on the other side of those cameras two extra chances at making her.

Instead she stayed away from the Strip. She first stopped at a nail salon in a strip mall on Flamingo and had the manicurist cut her nails as short as possible. It wasn't very stylish but the manicurist, who was Asian, probably Vietnamese, didn't ask any questions and Cassie tipped her nicely for it.

She then drove east on Flamingo out past UNLV and into the neighborhood where she had lived until she was eleven. On the drive from L.A. she had convinced herself that she wanted to see it one last time.

She passed the 7-Eleven where her father took her to get candy and the bus stop where she was let off after school. On Bloom Street the little house her parents had owned was still painted pink but she could see that some changes had been made in the two decades since they had left it. The swamp cooler on the roof had been changed out with a real air conditioner. The garage had been converted into living space and the backyard was now fenced, just like all the other houses on the block. Cassie wondered who lived there now and whether it was the same family that had bought it at auction after the foreclosure. She had the urge to go knock on the door and see if she could be allowed a quick look at her old room. It seemed that the last time she had ever felt completely safe had been in that room. She knew how nice it would be to have that feeling again. The image of her room as it had been back then made her momentarily think of Jodie Shaw's room and the collection of stuffed dogs on the shelf over the bed. But she quickly dismissed that image and moved back to her own memories.

Staring at the house, she thought about the time she came home from school and saw her mother crying while a man in a uniform tacked a foreclosure notice on the front door. He told her it had to be in public view but as soon as he left her mother tore the papers off the door. She then grabbed Cassie and they got in the Chevette. Her mother drove with reckless abandon toward the Strip, finally pulling to a stop with two wheels up on the curb in front of the Riviera. Yanking Cassie along by the hand, she found Cassie's father at one of the blackjack tables and shoved the foreclosure papers into his face and down the front of his Hawaiian shirt. Cassie always remembered that shirt. It had topless hula dancers on it, their swaying arms covering their breasts. Her mother cursed her father and called him a coward and other things Cassie could no longer remember, until she was pulled away by casino security men.

Cassie could not remember all of the words but she vividly remembered the scene as through the eyes of a child. Her father just sat on his stool and kept his place at the gambling table. He stared at the woman screaming at him as though she were a complete stranger. A thin smile played on his face. And he never said a word.

Her father didn't come home that night or any of the nights after. Cassie saw him only one more time – when she was dealing blackjack at the Trop. But by then he was deep inside the bottle and didn't recognize her. And she didn't have the courage to introduce herself.

She looked away from the house and again images from the house on Lookout Mountain Road intruded. She thought of the drawing on the easel in Jodie Shaw's bedroom. The little girl in the picture was crying because she was leaving her home behind.

Cassie knew exactly how she felt.

11

Traffic into North Las Vegas was a miserable crawl. By the time Cassie got to the Aces and Eights Club she was fifteen minutes late. But before going in she still took the time to sit in the car and put on the wig she had bought for the Lookout Mountain Road open house. She flipped down the visor and used the mirror to style the wig and then used an eyebrow pencil to darken her eyebrows to match. She added a pair of pink tinted glasses she had bought at a Thrifty drugstore.

The Aces and Eights was a locals bar and up until six years ago Cassie had been a regular. Most of the patrons made their living off the casino trade – legally or otherwise – and if there was anyplace where she might be recognized, even after a six-year absence, it was the Aces and Eights. Cassie had almost told Jersey Paltz to choose another spot for the rendezvous but she'd gone along with his choice so as not to spook him. She also had to admit to herself she was a bit nostalgic. She wanted to see if the old hangout had changed.

After checking herself once more in the mirror, she got out of the Boxster and went inside. She carried her backpack over one shoulder. She saw several men at the bar and could tell by their uniforms or the colors of their dealer's aprons what casinos they worked for. There were a couple of women in short dresses and heels with their pagers and cell phones on the bar – hookers waiting for jobs and not worried about being obvious about it. Nobody cared at the Aces and Eights.

She saw Paltz in a circular booth in the rear corner of the dimly lit bar. He was leaning forward over a bowl of chili. Cassie remembered that the chili was the only thing on the menu that the regulars dared to eat. But she'd never eat it again, here or anywhere else, after having to eat chili every Wednesday for five years in High Desert. She walked up and was sliding into the booth when Paltz began protesting.

'Honey, I'm waiting for—'

'It's me.'

He looked up and recognized her.

'Little early for Halloween, isn't it?'

'I thought there might be people in here who'd remember me.'

'Shit, you haven't been around in six years. In Vegas that's ancient history. You know, I was just about to give up on you but figured, hey, you haven't been here in six, seven years. You don't know how bad traffic's gotten.'

'I just learned. I thought L.A. was bad but this is . . .'

'Makes L.A. look like the fucking Autobahn. They need about three more freeways here, all the building they been doin' around here.'

Cassie didn't want to talk about traffic or the weather. She got right to the point of the meeting.

'Did you bring me something?'

'First things first.'

Paltz slid around in the booth until he was right next to Cassie and moved his left hand under the table and started patting and feeling her body. Cassie immediately stiffened.

'Always wanted to do this,' Paltz said with a smile. 'Ever since I saw you that first time with Max.'

His breath was chili and onions. Cassie turned away and looked out into the bar.

'You're wasting your time, I'm not—'

She stopped when he brought his hand up her torso to her breasts. She pushed his arm away.

'Okay, okay,' Paltz said. 'You just can't be too careful these days, you know? You got eighty-five bumblebees in that bag?'

She looked out of the booth and across the bar to make sure no one was watching. They were clear. If people were noticing their serious looks, they were dismissing it as a pointed negotiation between a big-haired hooker and a john. No big deal. Even the pat-down could be seen as part of the negotiation; these days a buyer had to be sure of the quality and gender of the product.

'I brought what you told me to bring,' she said. 'Where's the kit?'

'In the truck. You show me what I need again and we'll take a walk.'

'We already did this once,' Cassie protested. 'Move back.'

Paltz slid back to his spot. He scooped some chili into his mouth and took a long pull on a bottle of Miller High Life.

Cassie moved the backpack across her lap and put it down on the seat between them. She pulled the flap back halfway. Her rubber tool satchel was now in the bag. On top of it was the sheaf of currency. Hundred-dollar bills – or bumblebees, as some of the longtime locals called them. It was Vegas slang dating back several years to a time when thousands of counterfeit hundred-dollar chips had flooded the Vegas underworld. They were perfect counterfeits of the black-and-yellow hundred-dollar chips used at the Sands. They were called bumblebees.

The fakes were so good that the casino had to change the colors and design of their chips. The Sands was long gone now, demolished and replaced by a new casino. But the underworld code of calling a hundred-dollar bill or chip a bumblebee remained. Anyone who used the term had been around a while.

Cassie made sure Paltz got a good look at the money and then flipped the backpack closed just as a barmaid came to the table.

'Can I get you something?' she asked Cassie.

Paltz answered for her.

'No, she's fine,' he said. 'We're just gonna go outside and then I'll be right back. I'll need another beer then, sweetheart.'

The barmaid walked away and Paltz smiled, knowing that what he had just said would leave the waitress thinking that they were going outside to complete a sexual transaction. This didn't bother Cassie because it played into her cover. But what did annoy her was his calling the waitress 'sweetheart.' It always bothered Cassie when men called women they did not know by endearing names they didn't mean. She bit back on an urge to call Paltz on it and started sliding out of the booth.

'Let's do it,' she said instead.

Once they were out the door Paltz led the way to a van parked at the side of the bar. He unhooked a set of keys from his side belt loop and unlocked the sliding door on the passenger side. The van was parked so that the open door was only a few feet from the side wall of the bar. No one could look into the van without coming right up to it. Cassie understood this to be good and bad. Good if Paltz was going to be legit with her. Bad if this was a rip-off.

Paltz climbed into the van and signaled Cassie to

follow. The front cab was partitioned off with a wall of plywood. In the rear of the van two bench seats faced each other across a work area. Various tools hung on hooks protruding from punch boards on the walls and five-gallon buckets contained more tools, equipment and rags. Cassie hesitated in the open door. She was carrying close to ten thousand dollars in cash in her backpack and was being beckoned into a van by a man she had not seen, let alone dealt with, in more than six years.

'Well, you want it or not? I don't have all night and I thought you didn't either.'

Paltz pointed to a medium-sized American Tourister suitcase that was on the floor. He picked it up and sat down on a bench seat with it on his lap. He opened it, raising the lid against his chest so that Cassie could see the equipment displayed in foam cushioning in the case.

Cassie nodded and climbed into the van.

'Close the door,' Paltz said.

She slid the door closed but kept her eyes on Paltz as she did it.

'Let's do this quick,' she said. 'I don't like being here.'

'Relax, I'm not going to bite you.'

'I'm not worried about getting bit.'

Now that she was closer, Cassie looked at the case again. Pieces of electronic surveillance equipment were placed in cutouts so they would not move during transport. Cassie recognized most of the pieces from prior use or from electronics magazines and catalogs. There were pinhole cameras, a microwave transmitter, a receiver and several pieces of related equipment. There was also a pair of night-vision goggles.

Like a door-to-door salesman, Paltz waved his arm in front of the display and started his spiel.

'You want me to go over everything or you think you've got a handle on it?'

'Better show me everything but the NVGs. It's been a while.'

'All right, then, let's go from image capture to picture delivery. First, the cameras.'

He pointed to the upper half of the case. Four small black squares with open circuitry and circular centerpieces were displayed in the foam rubber.

'You've got four chip cameras here – should be enough for any job. When we spoke before you didn't say if you needed color but –'

'I don't need color. I don't need audio. I need clarity. I need to read numbers.'

'That's what I figured. These are all black and white. The first three you see here are your standard pinhole board cameras. When I say standard, I mean Hooten L&S standard. Nobody puts together a better board right now. With these you get four hundred lines resolution from a linear electronic iris. Very clear. Runs four to six hours on a dime battery. How's that work for you, timewise?'

'Should be fine.'

Cassie felt herself getting excited. Keeping up through electronics magazines was one thing, but actually seeing the equipment was dipping the hot wire into her blood. She could feel the blood pounding in her temples.

Paltz went on with his show.

'Okay, then this fourth board is your green camera. It's called the ALI – like Muhammad Ali. That's why we call it the "greatest little camera of all time" in the catalog.'

'Ali?'

'A-L-I. Ambient Light Iris. With this one you have vision with lights on or off. With infrared you sometimes get exposure blooms on your LED screen when lights are on. So we developed this. It operates with what light is in the room and gives you enough picture to see what you have to see – shapes, shadows, movement. Green field of vision, as usual. Tell you what, t'night's supposed to be a full moon. If you—'

'A void moon, too.'

'A what?'

'Never mind. Go on.'

'I was just saying that if you can get some moonlight into the area you are filming, then that'll be all you need for this camera to work.'

'Okay, sounds good.'

Cassie only needed to be able to see enough to confirm the mark's location in the darkness of his room. The ALI seemed to be all she needed.

'Good, then moving on, you can take any of these boards and use them in any of the shells contained here.'

He removed a false smoke detector and showed it to her. There was a small drill hole in the cowling. On the inside he showed her where the board camera would fit, aligning the lens with the drill hole.

'Now if you need a lower angle . . .'

He next removed a phony electric wall socket plate. The board camera could be installed behind the upper socket. He handed it to Cassie and she marveled at how small it was.

'This is great.'

'But a little risky. Guy could try to plug something into it and – bingo – he finds a fucking camera in his room. So if you use this one, put it in a spot where it's not likely the guy will want to plug in his computer or shaver or whatever.'

'Got it.'

'Okay, good. So what you do is connect your cameras to the batteries like so.'

Paltz plugged tiny round batteries into cradles attached by wires to the board cameras.

'Then install. You then have to hook the cameras to the transmitter. This is all going to be short run, right?'

Cassie nodded.

'Right. Eight, ten feet at the most, probably less.'

He pulled out a roll of what looked like Scotch tape and held it up.

'Conduct-O tape. You used to use this, right?'

'Yeah, toward the end . . . on a few jobs.'

Paltz went on with his explanation as though Cassie had said the opposite.

'It's your magic tape, man. It's got two conductors in it, one for video and one for ground. You connect to the camera and then run it to your transmitter. Just remember, keep it short. The longer the run, the more image distortion. You don't want that if you're readin' numbers.'

'Right. I remember.'

Sweat was running out of Paltz's hairline and down both of his cheeks. Cassie didn't think it was warm enough inside the van to create such a response. She watched him raise his arm and wipe his face.

'Something wrong?'

'Nothing,' Paltz said as he reached into the suitcase. 'It's getting toasty in here, that's all. This is a four-channel transmitter.'

He pulled a flat square box about the size of a cell phone out of its place in the foam. It had a six-inch stub antenna.

'This is omnidirectional – it don't matter what angle you place it at. Just get it close to your cameras for the clearest signal. You notice this is not disguised in any way. Since it ain't a camera, you can hide it just about anywhere – under a bed or in a drawer or a closet or wherever. It, too, has a battery – lasts about as long as the cameras. Okay?'

'Got it.'

'Now what this transmitter does is send your captured image to your remote. This little baby.'

He pulled from the case the largest piece of equipment. It looked like a small laptop computer. Or maybe a space-age lunch box. Paltz flipped open a screen and folded up another stub antenna.

'This is your microwave receiver/recorder. You can set this up to two hundred yards from your transmitter, depending on the knockdown, and still pull in a decent picture.'

'What's the knockdown?'

'Nothing you'll probably have to worry about. Water mostly. Tree sap is a killer too. You're not going to be working near a forest, right? Those trees just send a signal into the dirt.'

'There a forest in Las Vegas, Jersey?'

'Not that I know of.'

'Then no forest. No trees, no sap.'

She was getting annoyed with his manner and his nervousness. It was getting contagious. She realized that without any windows in the back of the van she had no idea whether there would be someone waiting outside for them – or for her – when they opened the door. This rendezvous had been a mistake.

'What about the pool?' Paltz asked.

The question took Cassie out of her thoughts. She thought a moment and remembered the pool at the Cleopatra was at ground level.

'No pool.'

'Good. Steel, concrete, all of that is no problem. Just stay inside with it and it should work perfect.'

Paltz started working the buttons on the receiver/

recorder. He turned it on and the screen came up full of static snow. He tapped a red button on the right side of the mini-keyboard.

'That's your record there. You can record everything or just watch it. You can quarter the screen and watch up to four cameras at once.'

He hit a series of buttons and the screen split twice. It was still four views of snow.

'We won't get a picture because we don't have the cameras connected. But I've got your four camera freeks already loaded on here and it's good to go.'

'Okay. It's a great kit, Jersey. You got anything else to show me? I gotta go.'

'That's it. Now if you pay me what we agreed on, you can get out of here and I can go back to my chili – though it's gotta be cold by now.'

Cassie pulled her backpack around to her lap.

'You working this one alone, Cassie?'

'Yup,' she answered without thinking.

She pulled open the flap just as Paltz closed the suitcase and raised his other arm, revealing that he was holding a pistol pointed at Cassie's chest.

'What are you doing?'

'Stupid, girl,' he said.

Cassie started to stand but he raised the weapon and nodded her back down with it.

'Look, man, I'm going to pay you. I have it right here. What's the matter with you?'

Paltz switched the gun to his other hand and lowered the suitcase to the floor of the van. He then reached out for the backpack.

'I'll take that.'

He roughly grabbed the backpack out of her hands.

'Jersey, we had a deal. We—'

'Just shut the fuck up.'

Cassie tried to remain calm while she waited for him to go for the money. Without flinching a muscle she took all the weight off her left foot and raised it slightly off the ground. Paltz was sitting directly across from her, his knees a foot apart. She spoke in a calm, measured tone.

'Jersey, what are you doing? Why put the kit together if you were just going to rip me off?'

'I had to make sure you were working this alone. Make sure you didn't go and get a replacement for Max.'

Now Cassie began to feel the rage blooming inside her. This guy had played her. All along he had seen her as a victim. Someone he could rip off if she was alone.

'And you know what?' Paltz said, almost giddy now that he had the bag with the money. 'Now that I think of it, maybe I oughta grab me a blow job for good measure. Get some of that stuff Max was keepin' to himself. I bet five years in stir, you could prob'ly use some practice sucking cock.'

He grinned.

'You're makin' a mistake, Jersey. I'm here alone but I'm working for people. You think I just blew into town and picked a target at random? You jack me and you jack them. They won't like that. So why don't we just make the deal. You take the money, I take the kit. I forget about that gun and what you just did. And what you just said.'

'Bullshit.'

Keeping his eyes on Cassie, Paltz began reaching into the backpack for the money. Immediately there was an electronic snapping sound and Paltz let out a yelp. His hand recoiled from the bag and in the same instant Cassie's left leg shot out and she drove her thick-soled Doc Marten shoe into his crotch. Paltz doubled over with a loud grunt and pulled the trigger on the pistol.

The gun fired and the sound was deafening in her ear. Cassie felt a slight tug on her wig as the bullet tore through her false tresses. She felt the sting of burning gunpowder and discharge gases singe her neck and cheek. She leapt onto Paltz and grabbed the gun with both hands. She turned her body into his until she was almost sitting on his lap. She yanked his gun hand up to her face and bit down viciously on the top of his hand. It wasn't fear that charged her actions. It was rage.

Paltz screamed and let go of the gun. Cassie grabbed it and spun away from him. She pointed the gun – which she quickly looked down at now and determined was a 9 mm Glock – at Paltz's face from two feet away.

'You stupid piece of shit!' she yelled. 'You want to die? You want to fucking die here in this van?'

Paltz was gasping for air and waiting for his testicles to recover. Cassie brought a hand up to her face and ran it along her skin looking for blood. She was sure the shot had missed but had always heard that sometimes you didn't even know it when you'd been clipped.

She took her hand away and looked at it. No blood. She cursed loudly anyway. Paltz's ill-conceived decision to try to jack her complicated everything. She tried to think clearly but her ear was ringing and her neck was tingling with the surface burn.

'Lie down on the floor!' she commanded. 'Get down! Fucking rapist! I oughta shove this gun up your ass!'

'I'm sorry,' Paltz whined. 'I was scared. I—'

'Bullshit! Just get on the floor. Face down. Now!'

Paltz slowly got down to his knees and then onto the floor.

'What are you going to do?' he whimpered.

Cassie stood over him, a foot on either side of his body, leaned down and pressed the muzzle of the gun into the back of his head. She palmed the cock back and the sound of it snapping back made Paltz's shoulders shudder.

'Hey, Jersey, what do you think, you want me to suck your cock now? You think you could get it up for me?'

'Oh, God . . .'

Cassie looked around the van and at the buckets of equipment and tools. She grabbed a plastic snap cuff used for bunching cables out of one of the buckets and told Paltz to put his hands behind his back. He did as ordered and Cassie noticed that one of the terminals from the stun gun had left a burn mark in the top of his hand. She wrapped the plastic strip around his wrists and through the lock, pulling it tight, to the point it was cutting into his skin. She then put the gun down on the floor of the van and grabbed more cuffs to bind Paltz's legs and ankles.

'I hope you had enough chili, asshole. It's going to be a while before seconds.'

'I have to take a piss, Cassie. I drank two beers waitin' for you.'

'I'm not stopping you.'

'Oh, man, Cassie, please don't do this.'

Cassie grabbed a rag out of one of the buckets and abruptly dropped her knees onto his back and leaned over close to his ear.

'Keep in mind that it was you who made the play, asshole. Now I'm going to ask you a question and you better give me a straight answer because it could mean your life. You understand?'

'Yes.'

'When I open this door, is there going to be somebody out there waiting for me? Like one of your buddies you brought in on the jack?'

'No, nobody.'

She picked up the gun and pushed the muzzle hard against his cheek.

'You better be straight. I open the door and see anybody, I'm going to empty this into your fucking head.'

'There's nobody. It was just me.'

'Then open wide.'

'Wha—'

She shoved the rag into his open mouth, cutting him off. She looped two snap cuffs together and wrapped them around his head and across his open mouth, holding the gag in place. Paltz's eyes grew wide as she tightened the cuffs.

'Through your nose, Jersey. Breathe through your nose and you'll be okay.'

Cassie unhooked the van's keys from the belt loop on his pants. She then got off him and went to her backpack, removing and unfolding a black gym bag. She started transferring the camera equipment from Paltz's suitcase to the bag.

'Okay, this is the deal,' she said. 'We're taking your van and I'm gonna go do this thing.'

Paltz tried to protest but his words were mumbles into the gag.

'Good, I'm glad you agree, Jersey.'

Once she had everything transferred, she hooked the backpack over one shoulder and moved to the sliding door. She reached up and turned the van's overhead light off and then opened the door with one hand while holding the gun ready with the other.

It was clear. She climbed out of the van, grabbed the gym bag and then locked and closed the door. She came around to the driver's side, still holding the gun up and ready. The parking lot was crowded with cars but she saw nobody waiting in any of them or watching from nearby.

She unlocked the driver's door and opened it. Before getting in she ejected the Glock's clip and thumbed out the bullets, letting them drop onto the asphalt. She then ejected the last round from the chamber and threw the gun and the clip onto the flat roof of the Aces and Eights.

She got into the van, started it and headed out of the parking lot. She noticed that the dashboard radio had a hole torn in it. The bullet Paltz had fired had gone through the plywood partition and into the radio. It reminded her of the burning sting on her neck and cheek. She turned the overhead light on and checked herself in the mirror. Her skin was red and blotchy. It looked as if it had a poison ivy rash.

She checked her watch next. Paltz's play had put her behind schedule. She turned off the light and drove toward the neon Strip, the glow of which she could see in the distance.

12

Koval Road ran parallel to Las Vegas Boulevard and offered easy access to the parking garages behind the grand resorts fronting the always crowded boulevard, better known as the Strip. Cassie passed by the Koval Suites, the monthly apartment building where she and Max had once kept a safe house, and turned into the multi-level parking garage attached to the Flamingo Casino and Resort. The casino garage was centrally located to the casinos on the mid-Strip, the key being never to park at the target hotel. She parked Paltz's van on the roof of the eight-story garage because she knew there would be fewer cars up there and a lesser chance that her bound and gagged passenger would be discovered. She skipped the elevator in favor of the stairs down to the walkway leading into the casino.

Carrying her black bag over one shoulder and the gym bag down at her side, she went in the rear entrance of the Flamingo and walked through the casino to the front door, stopping briefly along the way in one of the lobby shops to buy a pack of cigarettes, in case she had to set off a fire alarm, and a souvenir pack of playing cards with which to pass the time while waiting for her mark to fall asleep. Once she stepped out the front doors, she crossed Las Vegas Boulevard and then walked the two blocks to the Cleopatra.

Cassie was carried past the reflecting pools on a

moving sidewalk that delivered gamblers to the casino entrance. She noted that there was no automatic ride that took gamblers away from the casino after they were done losing their money.

The casino entry walls were lined with hieroglyphics that showed ancient Egyptian figures in headdresses playing cards and throwing dice. Cassie wondered if there was any historic precedent for these depictions but also realized that it was not a necessity because there was no historical precedent for anything about Las Vegas.

Farther past the drawings, the walls were dedicated to Cleo's Club – photographs of the big slots winners over the past year. Cassie noticed that many of the winners posed in front of their winning machines were smiling in a way that suggested they were hiding missing teeth. She wondered how many of the winners used the money to see a dentist and how many dumped it right back into the machines.

When she finally got to the casino floor, she paused and tried to take it all in without raising her face toward the cameras she knew were overhead. A visceral sense of dread took hold of her heart. Not for the job that was ahead this night. But for the memory of the last night she had been in the Cleopatra Casino. It was the night that all things in her life had changed with the permanency of death.

The casino looked no different to her. The same setup, the same interchangeable gamblers chasing desperate dreams. The cacophony of money and machines and human voices of joy and anguish was almost deafening. She composed herself and pressed on, weaving her way through a football field of crowded slot machines and blue felt gaming tables. She was also aware that every move she made was now being recorded from above and kept her head level, if not slightly turned down. She pulled the wide brim of her hat down tight over her brow. The drugstore glasses completed her camouflage. Her scalp was warm and damp under the wig but she knew she had hours to go before there would be any relief from it.

As she passed through the cards and dice gaming aisles she saw many men and a few women in the blue-blazer uniform of casino security. They seemed to be posted at every column and at the end of every row of dealers' tables. She saw signs leading to the lobby and followed. She glanced upward at one point but without raising her chin.

The ceiling rose in a three-story-high glass atrium above the gaming tables. When it first opened its doors seven years before, the Cleopatra had been called the 'Crystal Cathedral of Casinos,' a reference to its borrowing of the atrium and other design elements from a California house of God that was prominent on religious television programming. Below the partial glass ceiling iron standards stretched from wall to wall and held up banks of lights and cameras. The Cleopatra was like no other casino in Las Vegas in that it allowed natural light to enter the gaming room. It also made no effort to hide the cameras that watched over everything. Other casinos favored contained environments of artificial lighting and placement of cameras behind mirrored walls and ceiling globes, even though not a single player below doubted that every move that he or she made – as well as the money on the tables – was being closely watched.

Cassie's eyes were drawn upward to the balcony that extended like two joined arms out and above the crowded gaming tables. The hands of the arms formed a cup – the crow's nest from which a craggy-faced man looked down upon the gaming floor. He had white hair and wore a dark suit, not a blue blazer. She guessed he had to be one of the men in charge, maybe the man himself. She couldn't help but wonder if he had stood in the pulpit six years earlier on the last night she had been in the casino.

Once past the tables Cassie got to the lobby and went to the far end of the long desk, where she saw the sign for INVITED GUESTS AND VIPS. There was no one in line. She approached the counter and a woman wearing some sort of white tunic that was only vaguely Egyptian smiled at her.

'Hello,' Cassie said. 'There is supposed to be a package for me here. The name is Turcello.'

'One moment.'

The woman stepped away from the counter and retreated to a door behind her. Cassie felt her breathing slow as thief's paranoia rose in her chest. If this was all a setup, then now would be the time for the men in blue blazers to come back through that door to get her.

But it was the woman in the tunic who came back out. She carried a large manila envelope bearing the Cleopatra symbol – a line drawing of a woman's face in profile, wearing a headdress of a rising serpent – and handed it to her with a smile.

'Thank you very much,' she said.

'No, thank you,' Cassie said.

She carried the envelope without looking at it to a nearby alcove of pay phones. There was no one using any of them. She went to the phone in the corner and huddled close to it, using her back to shield what she was doing from the view of any person or camera.

She tore open the envelope and dumped the contents on the marble counter under the phone. A black pager with a digital readout slid out of the envelope along with an electronic card key, a photograph and a note torn from a Cleopatra scratch pad. She quickly glanced at the pager and hooked it onto her belt. She then slipped the card key into the back pocket of her black jeans and looked at the note. Four lines were printed on it.

EUPHRATES PENTHOUSE
His: 2014
Yours: 2015
Return envelope with *all contents* to the VIP desk

She studied the first line and felt a turning in her stomach. She leaned her head against the phone. The penthouse of the Euphrates Tower was familiar to her. It was the place where dreams and hopes had ended for her. It was one thing to come back to Vegas, another to return to the Cleo. But to go back to the penthouse . . . Cassie fought the urge to cut and run. She reminded herself of all that was at stake. She had gone too far to turn around at this point.

She tried to change her thoughts. She looked at the note again and picked up the card key. One key for two rooms meant she was holding a pass key. That explained the last line of instructions on the note. The key had to be returned because all pass keys probably had to be accounted for. If any investigation followed the crime she was about to commit, pass keys would be inventoried.

She slowly crumpled the note in one hand and looked at the photo. It showed a baccarat table where there was only one player: an obese man in a suit with a large stack of chips in front of him. Diego Hernandez. The photo had a date-and-time stamp on the corner – it had been taken that afternoon. It was obvious to Cassie that the photo had come from a casino surveillance camera. The pass key and the photo told Cassie that the spotter Leo's partners had was deeper inside than she had thought.

She committed the image of the fat man to memory and then put the photograph and the crumpled note back into the envelope. She folded it twice and shoved it into a zippered pocket on her backpack. She then headed back to the casino floor.

Without raising her head she scanned the table signs in the casino until she saw the one over the baccarat salon. She took the long way, skirting the edge of the gaming area until she came to the railing that ran along the perimeter of the baccarat salon. She put an elbow and an arm along the railing, nonchalantly leaned back against it and looked out across the casino. Her eyes encountered no one looking at her. She was cool. Slowly she turned, as if noticing the baccarat salon behind her for the first time, and shifted her position so that she was looking into the room.

He was still there. The mark. Diego Hernandez. The man was short but obese, the girth of his stomach making him appear to be sitting away from the table. He was overdressed in a baggy dark suit and tie. As Cassie watched, she noted that he played with an economy of physical movement, his eyes constantly scanning the table but his head not moving. On the table in front of him were several stacks of hundred-dollar chips. Cassie estimated that he had at least ten thousand dollars on the table.

Cassie watched a few deals but never held her eyes on Hernandez for more than a few seconds. At one point he suddenly looked up and out toward the railing. She quickly looked away. When she surreptitiously glanced back, his eyes were back on the table. He apparently had paid little mind to her.

She needed only one thing from Hernandez before

going up to the penthouse. She focused her attention squarely on his hands as they moved chips and handled his cards. It took less than a minute for her to decide that he favored his left hand. The clincher was when the right cuff of his suit coat caught on the edge of the table's elbow pad and drew back to expose his watch. Cassie had what she needed. Hernandez was left-handed. She stepped away from the railing and proceeded, head down, in the direction of the elevator alcove of the Euphrates Tower.

As Cassie entered an elevator in the Euphrates Tower, she saw that a card key had to be inserted in the panel before the penthouse button could be engaged – a security measure that had been added since the last time she had been in the hotel. She pulled the pass card from her back pocket and engaged the button. She stayed close to the doors and averted the impulse to look up at the lighted numbers over them, assuming there was a camera somewhere above her. She looked at her watch and saw it was already almost nine o'clock. She needed a minimum of an hour in the room and knew she was now pushing it.

On the twentieth floor Cassie came out of the elevator alcove, looked both ways in the hall and found she might already be riding a piece of luck. There was no housekeeping cart in the hallway. It was apparently after VIP turn-down service. The only thing in the hall was a room service table topped with a white tablecloth and the detritus of a candlelight dinner, including an empty champagne bottle floating upside down in a silver ice bucket.

She went to her right to find room 2015 but as she first passed by the door to room 2001 she gave it a wide berth, moving all the way to the left side of the hallway and averting her eyes from the door and the memory behind it. She said a silent prayer, calling on Max to be with her tonight.

The hallway was dimly lit by wall sconces to the left of every door. She found rooms 2014 and 2015 directly across from each other near the end of the hallway and the emergency exit. That was a good break. In case something went wrong, the stairs were right there. Cassie knocked on the door of room 2014 and also pushed the glowing button to the left of the door frame. She heard a soft chiming sound from the other side of the door and she waited.

As expected, no one answered the door. She took the card key out of her back pocket again, looked up and down the hall once more, and then used it to open the door.

As she stepped into the room she felt the immediate jangling of adrenaline coursing through her veins. It felt like a flooding river inside her, powerful enough to take anything in its path.

13

Cassie used an elbow to close the door and turn on the light switch. She dropped quickly to her knees, putting her hat and the gym bag on the floor and then swinging her backpack down in front of her. From the small front pocket of the backpack she took a pair of latex gloves and pulled them on, making sure they were tight around her fingers and short-cut nails.

She quickly removed and untied the rubber satchel that contained her tools. She unrolled it across the carpet and dragged a finger across the tools, making sure she had everything. She then pulled the Polaroid camera out of the gym bag, got up and began a survey of the suite.

It was a VIP accommodation, the kind given to comped guests of the casino. It was one large living room with double doors leading to the bedroom to the right. The furnishings were plush and Cassie knew that in most of the hotels the VIP suites were refurbished annually to keep them looking pristine and their inhabitants thinking they were among the few who got the privileges of the comped.

She became aware of the heavy odor of cigar in the air – Hernandez was helping her without even knowing it. She moved into the bedroom, for it was where she would do all of her work. She flicked on the light, revealing a large room containing a king-size bed, a bureau and a small writing desk in addition to the floor-to-ceiling television cabinet. She noted that the turn-down maid had already been in the room. The bedcovers had been folded back neatly and there was a foil-wrapped mint on the pillow next to a morning room service checklist to be hung outside the room on the door handle.

There was an alcove to the right with an open door to the bathroom on one side and a double set of louvered doors on the other. Cassie opened these to reveal a wide and deep closet. This action also revealed that when the doors were opened an interior light automatically went on. Cassie bent down and saw the room safe anchored to the floor, partially obscured beneath a sport coat and several long, flowing shirts Hernandez had placed on hangers.

Before touching anything in the closet, Cassie stepped back, aimed the Polaroid and took a photo of the clothes. She then squatted down and took a second photo of a pair of shoes and a pile of dirty clothes lying on the floor of the closet.

Cassie stepped back into the bedroom and put the developing photos on the bed. She then began photographing the entire bedroom, covering every angle of the room with the remaining eight photos in the Polaroid cartridge.

When she was confident she had thoroughly documented all areas of the suite she would possibly be disturbing, she went back to the closet, shoved the clothing to the side and looked down at the safe. The information from Leo's spotter was on the money. It was a Halsey five-number combination safe. The five-digit electronic LED screen said LOCKD but she reached down and checked it anyway. It was locked.

As she backed out of the closet and into the bedroom her eyes moved over the walls and up to the ceiling. There was one smoke detector. It was located on the wall directly over the headboard of the bed. She decided that a second one in so large a room would not seem too unusual. She fixed on a spot on the wall just above the entry to the bathroom/closet alcove. Locating a camera there would give her a full view of the bedroom and it would mean only a short run with the Conduct-O tape into the closet.

Having decided on the installation plan, she went back to searching the suite, looking in drawers and on shelves for any weapons or other protection devices that Hernandez might have brought with him. On a shelf above the wet bar in the living room she found a doorknob alarm – a cheap electronic gizmo that is hooked on a doorknob and sounds an ear-splitting alarm if a clip squeezed into the doorjamb is disturbed.

Cassie knew that the alarm was so painfully loud that most users of the device never checked them before inserting the clip into the doorjamb. Instead, they relied on the red signal light that indicates a battery has juice. She used a small screwdriver to remove one screw and then unsnap the outer casing. With pliers she snipped the conductor and ground wires, then pruned a quarter inch of rubber sleeve off each wire and wound them together, closing the circuit usually closed by the clip when it was slid into the doorjamb.

She turned the device on and the signal light came on, indicating good battery. No alarm sounded although the clip was not in place. She turned it off and returned it to the place she had found it on the wet bar shelf.

Cassie went back to the suite's entrance hallway and sat down on the floor. From her backpack she pulled the pair of knee pads, which she strapped on over her black jeans. She then knelt in front of the door and went to work. She picked the drill up off the tool display, put in a Phillips bit and began removing the screws from the cover plate of the interior door handle and deadbolt. The homemade drill cowling dampened its sound considerably. Cassie figured someone would have to actually be listening on the other side of the door to notice the noise.

When she had the cover plate off she put a penlight in her mouth and pointed it into the interior of the lock apparatus while she used a screwdriver to pop the lock washer off the bolt axle. She then gripped the bolt switch with a pair of rubber-tipped pliers and pulled it out of the apparatus, using both hands. She leaned in and looked closely at the interior mechanism.

Cassie took the light out of her mouth and exhaled in a low whistle of relief. Leo had called it correctly. The lock mechanism relied on a half gear to drive the bolt home. Despite knowing this was a problem six years ago, the managers and security providers of the hotel had chosen to avoid the expense of changing every deadbolt in the 3,000-room hotel. The decision made back then would allow Cassie to stay in the room and complete the installation. If a full gear had been installed in the lock's mechanism, she would have had to remove it and take it someplace – maybe the bathtub in the room across the hall – and cut it with the acetylene torch. It was only at that moment of relief that she realized how lucky she was not to have to use the torch; she had forgotten about it and left it in the trunk of the Boxster back at the Aces and Eights.

Cassie put the penlight back in her mouth. She pushed the screwdriver into the barrel slot and used it to turn the half gear forward, to the right, a quarter turn. She then checked her work with the flashlight and slid the bolt axle back into place. She turned the lock and looked into the doorjamb. The bolt extended outward but came just shy of the receiver plate on the other side of the jamb. By turning the half gear forward she had reduced the number of gear teeth driving the bolt home by half. Therefore it crossed the half-inch space of the doorjamb but did not lock the door. The only way for Hernandez to realize this would be to get down on his knees and look into the doorjamb crack. That was unlikely.

Cassie got up and looked through the peephole to make sure the hall was empty. She then opened the door. The bolt barely scraped the jamb but still made a slight noise. She looked out into the hallway to make sure it was empty and then quickly went back to her tools. She grabbed the steel file and quickly ran it back and forth along the scrape line the bolt had made in the jamb plate. She then dropped the file, checked the hall again and once more closed and reopened the door. There was no scraping sound this time.

After closing the door she went to work on the flip-over lock. She used the drill to remove the four screws that attached the flip-over arm to the doorjamb. Once the arm was removed she changed bits and ran the drill into each of the screw holes to widen them. She dug the tub of earthquake wax out of her bag and used a dab of it on the back of the lock's anchor plate to glue it back into place. She then used more of the quick-drying wax to hold the screws back in place in the loosened screw holes.

Cassie sat back on her heels and looked at the door. There was no outward sign that she had tampered with the locks. Yet with the card key she had in her back pocket she would be able to enter the room despite Hernandez's use of the additional locks and his portable alarm.

The first step toward preparing the suite was completed. Cassie checked her watch and saw that it was almost nine-thirty. She rolled her tool satchel up and carried it along with her black bags into the bedroom. She placed everything down in the middle of the floor and set to work. She removed the Conduct-O tape and the ALI camera, snapping the latter into place inside one of the smoke detector cowling shells. She then connected a battery to it, closed it and removed the adhesive backing. She pulled the chair out from the desk and used it to step up and reach the wall over the entry to the closet and bathroom alcove. She pressed the smoke detector camera onto the wall, about a foot below the ceiling line.

The roll of Conduct-O was as small as a roll of household tape. It was clear, with two thin copper wires imbedded in the adhesive and running the length of the tape. She wrapped one end of the tape on the connector posts and then closed the detector cover. She ran the tape down the wall to the lower alcove ceiling and then ran the tape along the ceiling to the wall over the closet. She then ran it down over the door frame and into the closet, where she ran it straight down to the floor alongside the door and then along the baseboard to a position behind the safe.

Cassie removed the transmitter from one of the bags and put it in place behind the safe, where it was unlikely Hernandez would have reason to look. She cut the Conduct-O tape and wrapped it around one of the transmitter's receiving terminals. Cassie turned on the transmitter and went back out to her equipment. She pulled out the receiver/recorder and opened it on the floor. She turned it on and studied the strip of masking tape Paltz had placed below a line of frequency buttons. She pushed the button marked ALI (1) and a view of the room, herself sitting on the floor, appeared on the monitor screen. The image was clear and took in almost the entire room. The important thing was the bed. She had a full view of the bed. She got up and went to the door and turned off the lights, dropping the room into darkness except for the bleed of exterior light – the spotlights thrown on the Cleopatra's towers at night – from around the curtains.

She came back and looked closely at the screen. The outline of the bed was barely visible in the green-tinged image. It wasn't as good as Paltz had claimed it would be but she knew it would have to do. She got up again and went to the curtains, pulling them open just an inch or so and letting a sliver of light into the center of the room.

The added light was enough. The details of the room took on a more defined look on the screen. Cassie now had to hope that Hernandez wouldn't notice the slight opening in the curtains and close them before going to bed.

Cassie turned the light back on and returned quickly to the closet. She had to first make sure that during the hot prowl she would be able to get into the closet where the safe was without the interior light automatically going on and possibly waking the mark and exposing her. She could not simply loosen the bulb in the ceiling of the closet. Hernandez might notice that and have it replaced or, worse yet, become suspicious. She also needed the light working for the cameras she planned to set inside the closet to record Hernandez opening the safe.

The twin louvered doors to the closet slightly overlapped, with a strip of wood edging on the left door covering the joint between the two doors. This meant she could open the left door without opening the right. But if she attempted to open only the right she would pop the left open a few inches because of the overlapping strip. The problem was that the auto-switch for the light was inside the frame of the left door. A small button dropped out of the top frame when the door was opened just an inch, completing the electric circuit that fed juice to the light.

Cassie went to the desk, opened the drawer and looked for something to write with. She found a pencil with a sharp point and went back to the closet. On the exterior trim of the door frame she drew an up-and-down line at the spot where the auto-switch button was located.

From her tool collection she removed the painter's putty knife. She closed the closet doors and reached up with the flat tool to the spot on the exterior trim marked with pencil. She slid the putty knife in and brought pressure upward against the door frame. With her other hand she opened the left door a few inches and then opened the right all the way, the door swinging free of the overlap trim. She then closed the left side, removed the putty knife and stepped into the closet through the right side.

She had entered the closet without turning on the light. But she knew she had no time to celebrate. She opened the left door again and the closet light went on. She leaned over the front of the safe as if to open it with her left hand. She then looked back to her right and put her finger on the wall on a spot where she believed a camera would have the best view of the combination pad. She marked the spot with the pencil and then went back out to the equipment bag, from which she pulled the wall socket cover and one of the board cameras.

She quickly set the camera inside the fake socket plate, attached a battery and Conduct-O tape to the terminals and used the drill to mount it on the spot on the wall with the center screw. She adjusted the plate so that it was level, then ran the tape down the wall to the baseboard and back around the safe to the transmitter.

Back out of the closet she checked the receiver/recorder. She pushed the camera buttons until she had the socket camera on the screen. The location and focus of the camera was perfect. She was looking right at the combination pad and could read the numbers on it. It was perfect. She felt the stirring of excitement inside but it was quickly cut short by the vibration of the pager against her belly.

Cassie caught her breath and froze. She pulled the pager off her belt and looked at the digital display.

CASHING OUT – ON HIS WAY

'Shit!' she exclaimed in a loud whisper. She threw the pager into the backpack rather than put it back on her belt.

The page changed everything. She abandoned her plan to put a second camera in the closet – this one overhead – and quickly backed out of the closet area. The page meant Hernandez had cashed out and left the baccarat table, but he still had to go to the front desk and retrieve his briefcase. That gave her time to finish.

From the gym bag she removed the Ziploc bag containing the small pump spray bottle of paint and the aerosol can of deodorizer. She stepped back into the closet alcove and looked up at the ceiling while shaking the paint bottle. She then sprayed the paint up onto the Conduct-O tape. It wasn't a perfect match but it was close. She started spraying the paint in a large back and forth arc, covering the tape but most of the ceiling as well. She then followed the tape down the wall to the frame of the closet door. Inside the closet she sprayed the tape line running from the false electric socket down to the baseboard and left it at that. She then grabbed the deodorizer and sprayed healthy bursts into the closet and alcove, then throughout the rest of the suite as she hurriedly moved through it.

After quickly packing her equipment in the two bags, Cassie grabbed the Polaroids off the bed and went back to the closet. Using the photos as a guide, she moved the clothing and shoes back into the same positions they had been in when she first entered the suite. She was careful not to allow the clothing to rub on the rear wall of the closet where there was wet paint.

As she slid the hangers back into place on the clothing bar, something heavy and hard in the pocket of a large sport coat banged against her. She reached into the pocket and brought out a gun. It was a Smith & Wesson 9 mm pistol with a black finish. She ejected the clip and found it was full. She paused even though she knew time was critical. Should she leave it or take it? Should she unload it? Too much was happening for her to think through the possibilities and come up with the right answer. She remembered something Max had always said about the ripple effect.

Remember the ripple effect. If you change something in a room it changes the universe of the job. It creates ripples.

She knew the answer then. You take the gun, the mark may notice and the job is finished. You unload the gun and the mark may notice and it is finished. No action means no ripples, no change in the universe.

She shoved the gun back into the pocket of the jacket and backed out of the closet, checking her work against the Polaroid one last time. Time was up. In her mind she saw Hernandez having already retrieved his briefcase and riding up in the elevator.

She grabbed the two bags, hoisting the straps over her shoulders, and headed out of the bedroom. As she stepped into the living room she glanced backward and froze.

She had left the desk chair pulled out from the desk. No ripples, she thought, as she quickly moved back into the room and put the chair back in its place. She glanced around and everything now seemed right – she had no time for a Polaroid check of the bedroom. She went back to the living room and to the suite's front door, picking her hat up off the floor.

She turned the light out and looked through the peephole. She saw an empty hallway. She turned her head and listened. She heard no footsteps or any other sound. She put her hat on, then opened the door and stepped out into the hall.

As Cassie pulled the door closed she heard the chime signaling the arrival of an elevator car in the alcove down the hall. She quickly pulled the card key out of her back pocket and crossed to room 2015.

She opened the door and stepped in. She had made it.

14

The hallway was empty but she waited. Cassie stood against the door inside room 2015 and pressed her left eye close to the peephole. Her hat tipped off her head and fell to the floor behind her. She heard voices in the hallway and began to believe she was mistaken, that it was not Hernandez but a couple returning to their room.

But then there he was. His huge form moved into her field of vision and the convex lens of the peephole made Hernandez appear even wider. He bent slightly to insert a card key into the door with one hand, the briefcase held at his side with the other. Trailing just behind him and almost out of view through the peephole was another man. Cassie noted the blue blazer with the Cleopatra insignia on the breast pocket. The security escort. She turned away from the peephole and moved close to the doorjamb so that she could listen.

'You want me to check for you, sir?'

'No, I'm fine. I appreciate it, though.'

'Then good night, sir.'

'Good night.'

Cassie heard the door across the hall opening. She switched back to the peephole. The security man was gone and Hernandez was moving into the open doorway. He suddenly stopped and stepped back into the hall.

'Oh, Martin?'

Cassie felt her heart skip a beat. *What did he see, what*

did I miss? She tried to quickly review her hurried exit from room 2014 but she could not think of anything. She looked down at the two bags at her feet and started running an inventory through her mind. But she had barely begun when Hernandez began to speak and she moved her ear to the doorjamb.

'I almost forgot. This is it for me. I'll be leaving tomorrow. Can you hold on a second? I'd like to give you something for watching out for me these last few days.'

Martin's voice returned, very close to Cassie's door.

'That's not necessary, Mr Hernandez. You can just thank Mr Grimaldi. He wants all our guests to feel secure and, besides, it's against house policy for me to accept—'

'Who's gonna know? Vincent Grimaldi won't unless you tell him. Hold on a second.'

There was the sound of a door closing and Cassie returned to the visual. The security man called Martin stood in the hallway, his hands clasped in front of him. He looked up and down the hall, as if worried somebody – maybe the Vincent Grimaldi who was mentioned – would see him taking a gratuity. He then turned and looked right at the peephole through which Cassie was watching him. She froze. She thought that if she moved away he might see a change in the light behind the glass and then know he was being watched.

The door behind Martin opened and Hernandez appeared.

'You know, if you don't mind, come in here and check this out,' Hernandez said. 'There are fumes or something in here.'

Cassie pressed against the door harder and balled her hands into fists. She watched as Martin entered the room, leaving the door open behind him.

She could only see a door-wide slice of the suite. Hernandez and Martin both walked out of sight to the left and then after a few moments crossed her field of vision in the direction of the bedroom. Cassie heard talking and moved to the doorjamb and listened but could not make out what was being said. She moved back to the peephole and in a few moments Martin, followed by Hernandez, appeared again and headed toward the door. Their discussion became clearer as they got closer to Cassie's position.

'. . . in the smoking rooms,' Martin was saying. 'It's pretty much industrial-strength stuff that they use. See, you can't open the windows. No hotel in Vegas has windows that open. Too many jumpers.'

'Well, I guess it's been building up. This is my third day. I've smoked a few in here.'

He guffawed.

'Yes, sir,' Martin said. 'But if it is going to bother you I could check with the desk and see about moving you into another suite. I'm sure we'd have something available.'

Nooooo, Cassie felt like yelling. But it was Hernandez himself who rescued her.

'No, that's not necessary. I'll just have to light one up and see which one is stronger.'

He laughed again and this time Martin joined him.

'Okay, good night, sir. Have a good trip home.'

'I will. Oh, and here. Almost forgot.'

Hernandez held out his hand and Martin raised his. Cassie heard the click of casino chips being dropped into the security man's hand. There must have been a lot of them and they were of high value. Martin's exclamation of thanks came through the door loud and clear.

'Mr Hernandez, thank you! *Thank you!*'

'No, thank you, Martin. Have a good one.'

'With this I'll have more than one!'

Hernandez laughed and closed his door after hooking a DO NOT DISTURB sign on the handle. Martin disappeared from Cassie's point of view. She heard Hernandez turn the deadbolt and then there was the metallic click of the flip-over lock being slapped closed. She stood motionless and not breathing for five seconds. Nothing happened. She knew her work on the door had gone unnoticed.

Cassie turned and leaned against the door and then slid down to the floor. She quickly unzipped the black gym bag and pulled out the receiver/recorder. She opened the screen and raised the antenna, then quickly hit the button that put the view from the bedroom smoke detector camera on the screen.

The bedroom became visible, though the screen was largely in shadow because the only light came from the slight break in the curtains.

She waited.

The door opened and the light came on. Hernandez stepped into the room, the briefcase still at his side. Cassie leaned in close to the screen and saw that the case was attached to his wrist with a handcuff. It put a little shiver of excitement in her. Leo's spotter knew how to pick them.

Hernandez was smoking a fresh cigar and blowing clouds of smoke toward the ceiling while he stood in the center of the room and looked around, never once looking up at the camera. He then stepped beneath the camera and into the alcove leading to the closet and the bathroom.

Cassie switched screens to the closet cam and waited. The screen wasn't completely dark. Light from the bedroom slashed through the slats. In a moment she saw Hernandez's legs through the slats and then the door opened. Cassie hit the record button in case Hernandez opened the safe.

But he didn't. He apparently rustled through his clothes, though Cassie couldn't see this because of the camera angle, then stepped out of the closet. Cassie thought of the gun and retraced her actions with it. She was sure she had returned it to its place in the jacket pocket exactly the way she had found it.

She returned to the bedroom cam and just caught a glimpse of Hernandez going through the door to the living room. She immediately lamented not setting up a camera in the living room. But she just as immediately dismissed the regret as Monday morning quarterbacking. The fact was that if she had installed a camera there, she might not have had the time to install the bedroom or closet cameras, which were necessities.

Getting up quickly, Cassie moved with the receiver/ recorder to the table in her suite. Spread on the table were tourist magazines, hotel information and room service folders, a pad and pencil, and a bottle of chardonnay from Robert Long Vineyards with a generic welcome card on it. She pushed everything aside so she would have room to work.

She checked the screen again and saw Hernandez was back in the bedroom. He had placed the briefcase on the bed while he worked a key into the cuff and detached it from his wrist. Once free of the encumbrance he reached over and picked up the foil-wrapped mint that had been left on the pillow as part of the turn-down service. He ate it in one bite, returned the cigar to his mouth and then turned toward the closet alcove, reaching into the inside pockets of his suit coat and removing thick sheaves of money as he approached.

Cassie switched screens to the closet camera and hit

the record button. This was it. All her work had been to put her in this position.

On the screen the light came on in the closet and Hernandez's big left arm followed by part of the upper portion of his body dropped into the picture. He reached down to the combination and started tapping the numbers. But before he was done his right arm swung through the picture and he put his hand on the top of the safe to support himself.

SHIT NO! Cassie wanted to yell. But instead she brought a clenched fist up to her mouth.

Hernandez opened the safe's door, dropped to one knee and reached inside. He brought out a two-inch stack of currency and placed it on top of the safe, then put down the equally thick stack he had just removed from his pocket. He reached into the side pockets of his jacket and took out two more wads of cash. He combined all of the currency into one thick stack he could barely hold in one hand. He hefted it. Cassie could not see his face because of the angle of the camera but she knew he was smiling.

Hernandez put the cash into the safe and closed it, then got up and closed the closet door, extinguishing the overhead light.

As Cassie watched she wondered about the briefcase. It appeared that it was too large to fit into the safe. But why hadn't Hernandez taken the cash that must be in it and placed it in the safe?

She switched to the bedroom camera but there was no sign of Hernandez. The briefcase was lying flat on the bed. Her question about the case and Hernandez's decision not to put its contents into the safe did not hold her attention long. There was a more important question she had to answer. She switched the receiver/recorder to the playback program and began watching the recording of the closet camera. She grabbed the hotel pad and pencil and hit the slow-motion button just as Hernandez's hand dipped into the picture.

'Come on, baby.'

The numbers could clearly be seen on the screen. Hernandez's finger hit 4–3–5 but then his right arm, reaching for support on the safe, swung through the frame and obscured the final two numbers. Cassie reversed the recording and replayed it with the same result. She was short the final two numbers of the combination.

'Son of a bitch!'

She got up from the table and paced across the room to the curtains. She pulled them open and looked out, the view going across the Strip to the dark outlines of the mountains far from the city of neon. She looked up and saw the moon.

She knew she couldn't go in with just three numbers and hopes of trying various combinations of the final two to open the safe. The Halsey safes had built-in tampering devices. If three successive erroneous combinations were entered on the keypad, the locking mechanism would freeze. It would then take a visit from security and an electronic device called a D-Lock to open the safe. The D-Lock was usually kept under lock in the hotel manager's safe.

There was only one alternative, Cassie decided. A fire drill.

15

Cassie watched the screen and waited. The alarm was blaring in the hallway and she could smell the smoke. But Hernandez showed no sign of moving from his room. He was fully clothed and lying propped on a pile of pillows on the bed. He was watching the television but the angle of the smoke detector camera prevented Cassie from seeing what was on the screen.

She dialed his room and watched as Hernandez lazily reached for the extension on the bedside table.

'Yes?'

'Mr Hernandez, this is hotel security. We have an alarm and a report of smoke on your floor. We are going to need you to evacuate immediately.'

'A fire? I heard the alarm.'

He sat up abruptly.

'We're not sure yet, sir. We have people coming up. But other guests are reporting smoke on the twentieth floor. Please, sir, gather your valuables and evacuate down the emergency stairs until we can evaluate what is happening.'

'Okay, bye.'

As Hernandez jumped up from the bed Cassie was surprised at the big man's agility and speed. As he was putting his shoes on, Cassie switched screens to the closet camera and hit the record button. She waited.

In a few moments the door opened and this time

Hernandez knelt in front of the safe instead of leaning over it. He reached to the combination pad and hit the buttons, in full sight of the camera. Cassie could tell the last number was 2 and wrote it on the hotel pad.

As Hernandez quickly pulled the money from the safe and started stuffing his pockets, Cassie blew out her breath excitedly and hit the playback program on the receiver/recorder. She once more played the opening of the safe in slow motion.

This time she got it. She wrote the last missing number down on the pad.

4–3–5–1–2

She took no time to celebrate. She switched back to the live feed from the bedroom cam. Hernandez was standing at the desk, locking the briefcase onto his wrist. Cassie picked up the phone and called his room. Hernandez grabbed the phone quickly.

'Yes?'

'Mr Hernandez, this is security. We have isolated the problem and there is no risk. You do not have to evacuate your room.'

'What was it?'

'We think someone left a cigarette on a room service cart near a smoke detector. It set off the alarm.'

'Well, can you turn it off now?'

'We're working on it, sir. Sorry for the incon—'

'Did Vincent tell you to call my room?'

Cassie was momentarily taken aback.

'Excuse me?'

'Vincent Grimaldi.'

'Uh, no sir. We're just following standard practice. Good night, sir.'

She hung up. It was the second time in the past half

hour that the name Vincent Grimaldi had been mentioned. Cassie was sure she had heard it before. As she was thinking about it, the alarm from out in the hallway was finally turned off.

She went to the suite's door and listened at the jamb. She heard men talking from far down the hall. She could not make out the words but she assumed they had found the cigarette she had left burning on a room service cart under a smoke detector.

Now all she needed was for Hernandez to go to sleep.

She switched the receiver back to the bedroom cam and saw Hernandez had stripped to boxer shorts and a T-shirt. He was back on the bed watching television. All the lights were off except for the glow from the television. Cassie checked her watch; it was almost midnight. She thought about the name Hernandez and the security escort had used. Vincent Grimaldi. It had a resonance but she couldn't place it.

Cassie picked up the phone, dialed the hotel operator and asked to be connected to Vincent Grimaldi. A moment later the connection had been made and the call was picked up after one ring.

'Security,' a man's voice said. 'Mr Grimaldi's office.'

'Oh,' Cassie said. 'I think I have the wrong number. I wanted to see about getting a line of credit in the casino. Does Mr Grimaldi handle that?'

The man at the other end of the line chuckled.

'Well, you could say he's in charge of all of that but he doesn't handle applications. He runs the casino, ma'am. He's the director of all casino operations. So what you need to do is just go down to the casino and apply for credit at the big cashier's station next to the Sphinx. They'll take care of you.'

'Okay, I'll do that. Thanks.'

Cassie hung up as she now remembered the name Vincent Grimaldi and who he was. Six years earlier, his name had been in all of the papers in the days following Max's last caper. He had been part of the cover-up.

She remembered that at the time Grimaldi was identified as the chief of casino security at the Cleo. In the six years since, he had moved up the ladder to director. Maybe it was what had happened with Max that had sent him on his way.

Hernandez's having dropped Grimaldi's name did not seem unusual to Cassie. It seemed legit for a high-rolling, comped guest of the casino to know the casino's director by name. Cassie tried to dismiss the whole thing but remained troubled by the memories the name Vincent Grimaldi conjured in her mind.

Needing a distraction, she put the receiver/recorder on the floor next to the chair where she sat, then opened the front pocket of her backpack and took out the deck of cards she had bought at the Flamingo. She removed the jokers from the deck and put them back into the box and off to the side.

She began running through her old warm-up routine – one-handed deck cuts followed by spread and rolls and then up-and-down shuffling. The shuffling felt clumsy through the latex gloves and at one point the cards exploded in her hands, several falling to the floor. She stripped off the gloves and picked the cards up. She then began dealing blackjack to five nonexistent players at the table and to herself, the house.

As she played she went through the dealer's patter in her head as she turned cards over. *Man with an axe, boy meets girl, jack takes five . . .*

But soon her mind traveled and she remembered the first time she met Max. She would always remember it as the random collision of matching souls. Something that didn't happen often in the world, something that surely would never happen to her again.

She had been dealing Caribbean poker at the Trop on a slow midnight shift and he had taken the number two seat. She had one other player, an old Asian man in the seven seat. Max was a beautiful man. He had a presence and Cassie couldn't help watch the way he handled his cards, cupping them and opening them in a tight spread, then quickly laying them flat and making his bet.

But he bet recklessly and soon it became apparent that he wasn't a schooled gambler. He lost money but didn't seem to mind. After a dozen hands Cassie surmised that he wasn't at the table to gamble. He was there to watch the other player. Max was on a con of some sort and that made him all the more intriguing.

When she went on break she waited near the cashier's window and watched Max watch the Asian gambler. Eventually, the mark slid off his stool and called it a night. After a few moments, Max followed suit and started trailing the Asian. He turned off after watching the Asian step onto an elevator.

And that's when Cassie made her move. She walked right up to him.

'I want in,' she said.

Nonplussed, Max just looked at her.

'I don't know what it is you're doing but I want to learn it. I want you to teach me. I want in.'

He looked at her for a few more minutes and then a small smile curved his mouth.

'My name's Max. You want to get a drink or is that against the rules for the dealers here?'

'It's against the rules but I just quit the rules.'

Now his smile widened into a grin.

As she dealt the cards on the table Cassie periodically

checked the screen on the receiver/recorder. When she checked at one o'clock the glow of the television still lit the room. But Hernandez was sprawled across the bed and under the covers with his face turned away from the screen. She noticed that the light from the screen was steady. There was no flickering from changing images. She knew that he was asleep and the pay movie he had been watching was over. On the television screen was probably just a blue screen or the unchanging movie menu.

She checked her watch. She figured that by two forty-five Hernandez would be in the deepest part of the sleep cycle. She decided she would go in at three. That would leave plenty of time for her to be in and out before Leo's void moon began.

She slid the playing cards back into their box and returned it to her bag. She decided to do something she knew put her at unneeded risk and that Max would have never done. But she felt she needed to do it. For Max and for herself.

16

Cassie made her way through the still crowded casino to the cocktail lounge off the hotel lobby. It was crowded here as well but the table she wanted was empty. She sat down and looked out across the gaming room but no longer was really seeing it. She was remembering Max and the run they had had, how the *Sun* and the *Review-Journal* had called them the 'high-roller robbers' and the Las Vegas Casino Association had put a reward up for their arrest and conviction. She remembered how after a while it hadn't even been about the money. It was about the charge it put in their blood. She remembered how they could stay up the rest of the night making love after a job was finished.

'Can I help you?'

Cassie looked up at the cocktail waitress.

'Yes. A Coke with a cherry in it and whatever you have on draft.'

The waitress put down napkins, one in front of Cassie and the other opposite her spot at the small round table. She smiled in a world-weary sort of way.

'Is somebody coming or is the second drink to keep the hitters away?'

Cassie smiled back and nodded.

'I just want to be alone tonight.'

'I don't blame you. It's a mean crowd tonight. Must be the moon.'

Cassie looked up at her.

'The moon?'

'It's full. Didn't you see it? It's burning brighter than any of the neon they've got around here. A full moon always adds an edge to things around here. I've been here long enough. I've seen it.'

She nodded as if to cut off any debate on the subject. Cassie nodded back. The waitress left then and Cassie tried to ignore what she had said and concentrate her thoughts on remembering the night six years before when she had sat in the same spot at the same bar. But no matter how hard she thought of Max's beautiful face she could only focus on the bad that followed. She still marveled at how a moment of wonderful joy then could be the same moment that incited so much pain and dread and guilt now.

She was pulled out of her reverie by the cocktail waitress, who was putting the drinks down on the napkins. The woman put down a piece of paper and left. Cassie turned it over and saw she owed four dollars. She pulled a ten from her pocket and put it down.

Cassie watched the bubbles floating up through the beer and forming a half-inch layer of foam at the top of the glass. She remembered the foam in Max's mustache that night. She knew deep inside that what she was going to do this night was as much about Max as about anything else. She had come to believe that somehow there would be a lightening of her guilt, a redemption for all that had gone before if she did this thing right. It was a crazy thought but it was one she had secretly grabbed on to and now seemed to have placed as high as all others. The thought was that if she did this right she could reach back across the tide of time and make up for things, even for just a moment.

She picked up her Coke and looked around to make

sure no one was watching. She caught a woman staring at her but then quickly realized that she was looking at her own face in the mirrored wall at the back of the lounge. Because of the wig and the hat and the glasses she had momentarily not realized who she was looking at.

She quickly looked away. She picked up her glass, reached across the table and tapped it lightly on Max's glass of beer.

'To the end,' she said quietly. 'To the place where the desert is ocean.'

She took a sip and tasted the small hint of cherry. She then put her drink down and got up from the table. She left the lounge and walked back through the casino to the elevators.

She followed the ritual. She didn't look back.

17

At 3:05 A.M. Cassie Black opened the door to room 2015, looked both ways, and came out into the hallway with the desk chair. Her disguise was now gone. She wore black jeans and a tight black sleeveless T-shirt. Around her waist was the small fanny pack with the tools she would need. She placed the chair beneath the wall sconce next to the door of room 2014 and stepped up on it. After licking her gloved fingers she reached over the lip of the sconce and turned the light bulb until it went out. She then moved the chair to a spot below the sconce next to 2015 and turned that bulb out as well. She returned the chair to her room and came back to the hallway with an empty black pillow case and the night-vision goggles hanging from a strap around her neck.

She closed her door against the flip-over lock so it would not close all the way and then stepped across to Hernandez's door. She unhooked the DO NOT DISTURB sign and lowered it to the floor. She raised the card key, checked the time on her watch, and then slid the card through the electronic reader. The little green light on the door handle's face plate glowed. She silently turned the handle and began pushing the door open.

There was a slight click and then the earthquake wax made a sucking sound as it gave way and the flip-over lock came off the doorjamb. Cassie's fingers came through the opening crack and grasped it before it could fall or rattle against the door. At the same moment she heard the clip from Hernandez's electronic alarm fall from the doorjamb, the alarm silenced by Cassie's tampering. She swung herself around the door and then carefully and silently pushed it closed. She unhooked the flip-over bar and placed it down on the carpet. She stood up and held still a moment as her eyes adjusted to the darkness of the suite and she felt the rush run through her. It had been a long time but she remembered the feeling well. The adrenaline was searing through her blood. She felt its soft and welcome finger move down her spine. It seemed as though all the fine blond hair on her arms was standing with the electric current.

Finally, she moved into the suite and scanned the living room. She found it empty as expected and focused her attention on the double doors leading to the bedroom. One of them had been left open and from the room beyond came the sound of deep and heavy snoring. Leo had been on the money again, Cassie thought. Hernandez was a snorer. It was like having an early-warning system built into the caper.

Cassie went through the open door and stepped into the blue glow of the bedroom. She saw that she had been right, the television had reverted to the blue menu screen after the movie Hernandez had been watching had ended. It cast enough light into the room that she decided she would not need to use the goggles.

Cassie could see the shape of Hernandez's great, round body slowly rising and falling in the blue light. His snoring was deep and resonant. Cassie wondered if he was married and if his wife could even sleep in the same room with him.

Beyond him on the bed table the numbers of the clock glowed red. She had plenty of time. Next to the clock she saw Hernandez's watch and wallet – and the gun.

Hernandez had apparently removed it from the jacket in the closet to keep it at the ready. She moved around the bed to approach the bed table. Hernandez groaned and started to move. She froze.

Hernandez lifted his head and dropped it, opened his mouth and closed it, and then adjusted the position of his body. He was lying on his back, covered to the neck with the bedspread. The bedsprings protested under the redistribution of his weight but then he finally found comfort and stopped moving.

After a long moment of remaining still, Cassie took the last three steps to the bed table and reached for the gun. She slowly unfolded the pillowcase and put it inside. She put the wallet in next and picked up the watch. She turned it over in her hand, careful to prevent its metal band from chinking. She ran her thumb over the wrist plate and found it to be smooth stainless steel. There was no variation in the feel as there should have been from the Rolex seal stamped on the plate. The watch was a counterfeit. She silently put it back down on the bed table and slowly backed away from the bed.

She had to fight the urge to immediately go to the safe, grab the cash and run. But she knew she had to retrieve the cameras. The equipment was proprietary. It could be traced to Hooten L&S. If it could be traced there it could possibly be traced to Jersey Paltz. From him the trail could lead back to her and Leo.

She pulled the chair away from the desk, positioned it under the smoke detector camera and slowly stepped up onto it. She opened the casing and with a small pair of wire snips taken from the pack on her belt she cut the connection to the Conduct-O tape. She then carefully closed the cover and pulled the smoke detector off the wall, its adhesive strip making a *snick* sound as it came free. She turned on the chair and looked down at the bed. Hernandez didn't move.

Climbing down, Cassie almost shouted when she caught a glimpse of herself in the full-length mirror on the back of one of the doors and mistook it for someone else in the room. She shoved the smoke detector into the pillowcase and put the chair back in its place. Turning her back to the bed she brought her wrist in close to her chest and pressed the illumination button on her watch. It was now 3:11 and she had only the closet and safe remaining.

From the fanny pack she removed the painter's putty knife. She clicked on the night-vision glasses and pulled them up in front of her eyes. She spotted the pencil mark on the door frame and slid the blade of the tool into the crack. Following the same procedure as before, she opened the closet without the interior light being activated. Once she was inside and the doors were closed, she carefully and silently slid Hernandez's clothes to one side, then stepped up onto the safe and reached to the bulb overhead. She unscrewed it and left it on the shelf next to the extra pillow.

She crouched on the floor and used a screwdriver to remove the electric socket plate containing the second camera. She snipped the tape as well. Last came the transmitter. She reached behind the safe, grasped the antenna and pulled it out of its hiding place. She cut the tape connections and secured it in the pillowcase with the rest of the equipment.

Now the safe. She took a deep breath, reached to the keypad and carefully typed in the combination of 4-3-5-1-2 she had committed to memory. The safe came open, making a soft *phump* sound like that of a can of fresh tennis balls being opened. She froze and waited, her left ear next to the door slats. Hernandez's snoring continued uninterrupted.

Cassie carefully pulled the safe's door open all the way, then shifted her position so that her body mass was between the opening and the bedroom behind her. She pulled the goggles down around her neck and took the small penlight from the pack. She reached it into the safe before turning it on.

The light illuminated the thick stack of currency she had watched Hernandez put together. Next to the money was a keychain with four keys on it. And nothing else.

Cassie flicked the light out and sat still for a moment thinking about this. Where were the contents of the briefcase? Where was the half million dollars in cash Leo's partners had promised?

She reached back into the safe and grabbed the stack of money, bringing it out and spreading it on her lap. She flicked the light on for a second and saw the currency appeared to be all one-hundred-dollar bills. Her rough estimate was that she had close to a hundred thousand dollars in her lap. A lot of money to be sure – more than she had ever had or stolen. But it wasn't as much as she expected and had been told to expect. Something was wrong. *Where was the briefcase?*

She realized she had not seen it while moving through the other rooms. She would now have to go back into the suite and find it. Perhaps Hernandez had grown lazy and decided not to open the case and transfer its contents to the closet safe. Perhaps, with his gun and his door alarm, he believed he and the case were safe.

Cassie put the stack of cash into the pillowcase, closed the safe and stood up. She carefully wrapped the loose end of the pillowcase around her right hand, drawing it tight so that the contents would not rustle against each other. She pushed open the right door and was stepping out of the closet and into the blue glow of the room when the phone on the bed table rang.

Cassie jerked herself back into the closet and silently pulled the door closed.

The phone rang a second time and she heard Hernandez stirring. She realized she had made a mistake. Rather than having retreated to the closet she should have moved, gotten out of there with what she had, and retreated to the room across the hall.

Now she was stuck. It was probably going to be security on the phone – they had discovered that someone had entered the room across the hall!

The bedsprings sighed as Hernandez moved on the bed. He answered the phone on the fourth ring.

'Hello?' he said in a scratchy voice.

Cassie just closed her eyes and listened. She was helpless.

'The fuck you doing?' Hernandez said angrily. 'What time is it?'

Cassie opened her eyes. She remembered the gun and wallet. If Hernandez put on the light he would surely see them missing and then come directly to the closet to check the safe.

'Three hours' difference, you moron.'

Cassie reached into the pack and wrapped her fingers around the stun gun. While it was still inside the pack she switched it on, then carefully and quietly pulled it out. She realized as soon as she had it out that the red light indicating that the device was on was not on. She flicked the switch off and on again but didn't get the light. The device was dead. She realized she hadn't turned it off after hiding it in her backpack for her meeting with Jersey Paltz. Leaving it on and the jolt that had been delivered to Paltz had sapped the stored charge. It was useless.

She looked through the door slats and in the blue light saw the hulking form of Hernandez sitting on the side of the bed. She then lowered the pillowcase to the floor and reached inside it.

'Yeah, well, call me then. I don't care how nervous he is, what am I going to do about it at a quarter after three in the goddamn morning?'

She pulled the gun out.

'Yeah, yeah, later. Good-bye.'

Cassie heard him slam down the phone.

'Fuck!' he called out.

The blue glow from the television was extinguished, dropping the closet into complete darkness. Cassie heard the bedsprings move as Hernandez tried to get comfortable and return to sleep. She was pulling the goggles up into place when Hernandez let out another expletive.

'Fuck!'

A light in the bedroom was turned on. Cassie heard the bed protesting and then heavy footfalls on the carpet, coming closer. Hernandez was coming toward the closet. She slowly backed as far into the closet as she could and raised the gun in a two-handed, elbow-locked grip. She told herself that she would not shoot. She would only back him off until she could escape.

Hernandez's wide shadow eclipsed the light coming through the slats. Cassie braced herself.

But then the shadow was gone and the closet doors didn't open. Cassie dropped her aim and took a step toward the door. In a few moments she heard the toilet seat bang against the tank, then came the sound of Hernandez urinating. She lowered the gun all the way and fought the urge to cut and run, to grab the pillowcase and go for the door. She could be on the stairs before Hernandez figured out what was going on. And she would have the gun. He could do nothing but call security. This time of night it would be a skeleton crew. She'd be out of the hotel before anyone could react.

But she stayed in the closet and waited. She knew the best escape was the undetected escape. But that wasn't her reason. The briefcase was the reason. She wanted that case. She needed it.

After the toilet was flushed another long period passed and then Hernandez finally walked back past her viewing point and got back into the bed. The light went out without his noticing that the wallet and gun were missing from the bed table.

Cassie slowly moved down to the floor and sat with her knees up and her back against the safe. She brought her wrist up and pressed the button that lighted the face of her watch. It was now 3:20 and she felt a searing sense of loss. She folded her arms on her knees and put her head down. She knew she wasn't going to leave the closet until well after the void moon began. She couldn't risk it.

Cassie thought about Leo. She wondered if he was awake this late and if he was thinking about the void moon, if he was checking his watch. He had called it a bad luck time. But to Cassie, the bad luck had come before the void moon had started. It was that phone call to Hernandez. That was the bad luck. She would have to tell Leo that. Explain it. Surely he would understand. And if he didn't, Cassie would make him.

18

At 3:46 A.M. Cassie Black opened her eyes in the bedroom closet of the man she was trying to steal from. That man had finally started to snore again and Cassie knew it was time to make her final move. She slowly stood up and pushed the closet door open. She pulled the goggles up over her eyes and looked at the bed. She could see Hernandez under the covers with his head propped up on two pillows. If he opened his eyes he would be staring right at her, but his deep breathing and the guttural pitch of his snoring indicated he was down deep into sleep. It didn't matter to Cassie anymore if he awoke. She was tired of waiting. It was time for her to find the briefcase and get out of the suite and out of Las Vegas for good.

She stooped down and massaged her left calf. It had cramped up while she waited. When she was ready she wrapped the pillowcase around her hand and again slowly pushed the closet door all the way open.

For a moment Cassie stood motionless in the bedroom and studied the sleeping hulk on the bed. It was always the strangest part of a job, to observe the mark sleeping. It was like knowing a secret you weren't supposed to know. She began a sweeping look around the room in search of the briefcase but it was nowhere in sight.

She backed into the alcove and checked the bathroom.

Nothing. She came back into the bedroom, got down on the floor and reached the penlight under the bed. She flicked it on, revealing the space to be empty save for an assortment of dust balls and a room service menu.

Cassie got up and went into the living room, where she surveyed every square foot of the room but found nothing that even hinted at the location of the briefcase. She started panicking and thinking about her decision earlier to go down to the bar for a cherry Coke and to rekindle memories of her last moments with Max. During that time had Hernandez possibly gotten up from bed, left the suite and stashed the briefcase, only to return and go right back to sleep? It seemed ludicrous, except for the fact that she could not find the briefcase.

Suddenly she remembered the safe. Hernandez's keys had inexplicably been inside it. Cassie tried to determine what this could mean and quickly came to a conclusion. The keychain held keys that opened the briefcase and the handcuffs. To put those keys in the safe rather than to take measures safeguarding the case and its contents would be done only if those measures *had* been taken in some other way. If Hernandez had not left the suite, how else other than with use of the safe could he safeguard the case?

Cassie moved back into the bedroom and surveyed the bed. She visualized what she had seen through the peephole when Hernandez had opened the door. The briefcase had been attached to his right hand. She came around the right side of the bed and gently pressed her hands down on the rumpled bedcovers, careful to stay away from formations created by Hernandez's body. She didn't breathe as she did this. It was the closest she had ever come to a mark. It was too close and every one of her senses was focused on the bed and the huge body that snored beneath the covers.

Her hand eventually came down on something flat and hard and she knew she had found the briefcase. She slowly began lifting the bedspread until she had uncovered the case and the handcuff link to Hernandez's right wrist.

Realizing she needed the keys to remove the case, she went back to the closet and reopened the safe. As she did this she noticed that she had left the gun sitting on top of the safe. She grabbed it, opened the safe and carefully removed the keys. In the green vision of the goggles she studied them. There were four keys and Cassie had had enough experience with handcuffs to know the little key with a round barrel went to the handcuffs. She detached it from the others so that she could work with it without causing the others to jangle and left the closet once more for the bedroom.

Hernandez hadn't moved. Cassie put the gun down on the bed and silently worked the key into the cuff attached to the steel handle of the case. She turned it and the cuff came open with a metallic clicking sound. She started to remove it just as Hernandez, possibly alerted by the sound, began to stir.

Cassie quietly removed the handcuff and straightened up, taking the briefcase off the bed. She reached down and grabbed the gun. Hernandez let out a sigh and started kicking his legs beneath the covers. He was waking up.

Cassie raised the gun. She told herself she could do it if she had to. She could blame it on the bad timing of a phone call, on the void moon or on simple fate. It didn't matter. But she could do what she needed to do. She held the gun straight out and pointed it dead center at the moving mass on the bed.

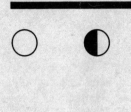

19

The first thing Jack Karch noticed as he walked through the Cleopatra Casino was that the crow's nest was empty. He knew Vincent Grimaldi wouldn't be up there right now because he knew exactly where Grimaldi was. But the custom and practice of the casino since the day it opened had been always to have somebody up in the nest. That was twenty-four hours a day, seven days a week. If it wasn't Grimaldi, then it was usually somebody else. Karch knew it was all imagery. Sleight of hand. The illusion of security created security. But right now nobody was watching from above and that told him the thing Vincent had called him in to handle was big and important. This realization juiced Karch's blood a lot better than the twenty-two-ounce cup of 7-Eleven coffee he had gulped down on the drive.

As he cut between the gaming tables and weaved around drunken, all-night gamblers who crossed blindly into his path, Karch kept his eyes on the door behind the pulpit, half expecting someone to come hustling out of security, maybe adjusting his collar or his tie as he took his position. But nobody ever came and Karch finally dropped his eyes when he got to the Euphrates Tower elevator alcove.

The alcove was empty except for one woman who was holding her plastic change cup and waiting. She looked at Karch's severe face and then turned away, putting her free hand over the top of her cup as if guarding its contents. He casually stepped over to the sand jar beneath the call button and brought his foot up onto the edge of it, bending over as if he were about to tie his shoe. He did this so his back was to the woman. Instead of tying his shoe he dipped his finger into the black sand, which had been freshly cleaned of cigarette butts and smoothed. He cut his finger through the sand until it found what he knew would be there. He withdrew the card key and straightened up just as an elevator chimed its arrival.

After following the woman into the elevator, he blew the dust off the card key and used it to engage the PH button after the woman had pushed the six button. Standing next to her Karch could glimpse between her splayed fingers and into her cup. It was about half full of nickels. She was the smallest of the small-timers and either didn't want him to know it or she actually thought there was something suspicious about him. She was about his age, with big hair. He guessed she had come to Las Vegas from somewhere in the south. She stood with her face cast downward but he knew she was keeping an eye on his reflection in the polished wood veneer of the door. Karch knew he had the kind of face that made people wary. His nose and chin were sharply drawn, his skin was always sallow despite a life beneath the desert sun, and his hair was as black as a limousine. These features all took a backseat to his eyes. They were the color of puddle ice and looked just as dead.

Karch reached into his pocket and pulled out his smokes. Holding the four fingers of his right hand together as a blind to the reflection, he shook two cigarettes out, palming one while passing the second to his left hand. He half expected her to protest the very sight of a cigarette but she said nothing. He then expertly performed the ear-to-mouth trick his father had taught him so many years ago. Holding the second cigarette at the end of all four fingers and the thumb of his left hand, he created the illusion of pushing the cigarette into his ear and then using his right hand to pull it out of his mouth and into place between his lips.

He watched her reflection and could tell she had seen the gag. She turned slightly as if she was about to say something but then caught herself. The door opened and she stepped out on six. As she turned to the left to leave the alcove and the elevator doors began to close, Karch called out to her.

'Made you look.'

He then laughed to himself as the doors closed on his vision of the woman turning back toward him.

'Next time take your nickels to Branson,' he said after the elevator began its ascent again.

Karch shook his head. The Cleo had once had such promise. Now it was the destination of the nickel-and-dimers, a place where the carpets were worn thin and the pool was crowded with men wearing sandals and black socks. One more time he wondered what he was doing, how and why he had ever sold out to Vincent Grimaldi.

Ten seconds later he stepped out on the twentieth floor. He stepped into the hallway and found it empty except for a room service cart somebody had shoved into the hallway. It smelled rancid as Karch walked around it and headed down the hallway to the right.

He looked up at the first door he passed and saw it was 2001. He remembered that room from a long time before. It was in that room that he had made his first play to Vincent Grimaldi. It seemed to Karch to have been so long ago and so the memory annoyed him. How far had he come since then? Not far, he knew. Not far at all. Perhaps he, too, was a nickel-and-dimer in a nickel-and-dime palace. His thoughts jumped to the empty pulpit down in the casino and he imagined what the view of the gaming room was like from there.

He came to room 2014 and used the card key to open the door.

As he stepped in he saw Vincent Grimaldi standing at the floor-to-ceiling window of the suite's sitting room. He seemed to be staring out across the city toward the expanse of desert lying before the chocolate-brown mountains that edged the horizon. It was a clear, bright day out there.

Grimaldi apparently had not heard Karch's entry and did not turn around. Karch came down the entrance hallway and into the suite. He noticed the bedroom doors were closed. The place smelled of old cigars, disinfectant and something else. He tried to place it and then his heart moved up a gear. Burned gunpowder. Maybe Vincent really needed him this time.

'Vincent?'

Grimaldi turned away from the window. He was a short man with a harsh and overtanned, V-shaped face with skin that looked as though it had been stretched too tight across the cheekbones. His iron-gray hair was slicked back perfectly and he wore an impeccable Hugo Boss suit. He always dressed as though the casino and hotel he ran was the Mirage. But he was the mirage. The Cleopatra was second tier, moving toward the third. Its location on the Strip was the only thing stopping that for the moment. But there was no doubt that Grimaldi was the captain of an old river barge in a sea of new luxury liners with names like Bellagio, Mandalay Bay and the Venetian.

'Jack! I didn't hear you. Where you been?'

Karch ignored the question. He looked at his watch. It was 8:10, only forty minutes since he had gotten

Grimaldi's page with the 911 emergency code added at the end. Forty minutes wasn't bad, especially in light of Grimaldi's refusal to tell him what the problem was over the phone.

'What's up?'

'What's up is that we have a big fucking problem here.'

He stepped over and held his hand out for the card key Karch still held in his hand. Karch gave him the key and thought about lighting his cigarette but decided to wait.

'You indicated that on the phone, Vincent. Now I'm here. What am I supposed to do, guess what the problem is or are you finally going to tell me?'

'No, Jack, I'll show you. Check it out.'

He pointed to the bedroom door with his chin. It was a typical gesture with Grimaldi, who always employed an economy of physical movement as well as words.

Karch looked at him a moment, awaiting further explanation, but none came. He turned and went to the bedroom door. He opened it and stepped into the room.

The bedroom was dark save for a slice of sunlight that cut through the inch-wide break in the closed curtains. The light cut diagonally across the bed, where the body of an overweight man lay face up. The dead man's right eye was gone, obliterated when a bullet was fired almost point blank through the socket and into his brain. The wood headboard and wall behind the bed were splattered with blood and whitish-gray brain matter. Six inches above the headboard there was a bullet hole in the wall.

Karch came around the front of the bed and looked down, studying the corpse. The dead man was wearing a white T-shirt and a pair of pale blue boxer shorts. Karch saw that a pair of handcuffs had been attached to his right wrist – both cuffs around the same wrist. Also on the bed, a handgun was lying between the dead man's legs. Karch bent down and studied it. It was a Smith & Wesson 9 mm with a satin finish.

Grimaldi came to the bedroom doorway but didn't come in.

'Who found him?' Karch asked, his eyes still on the corpse.

'Me.'

Karch looked over, his eyebrows raised. He had expected the answer to be that a maid had found the body, though it seemed kind of early for that. Still, not the director of casino operations. That was out of left field. Grimaldi picked up on the vibe and offered an explanation.

'I had a seven A.M. breakfast with him. Rather, I was supposed to have one. When he didn't come down, I called. When he didn't answer, I checked. This is what I found. I called you.'

Now things were getting curious, Karch thought.

'Who was he, Vincent?'

'Just a courier. From Miami. Name is – was – Hidalgo, though we had registered him under an alias.'

Karch waited. Grimaldi said nothing else.

'Look, Vincent, you want to take me in and tell me what's going on or am I supposed to bring up Seymour the Psychic from the lounge to guess for me every step of the way?'

Grimaldi blew out his breath. Karch was enjoying the moment. The old man was in a jam and needed him. Karch already knew one fact for sure. He planned to milk this thing, whatever the fuck it was, for all he could get. And if that included finally putting Vincent Grimaldi back on his heels, then Karch would do that in a heartbeat. He thought about the crow's nest downstairs. He could see himself up there. Watching the money. Watching everything.

'Yeah, I'm going to tell you.'

Grimaldi stepped into the room and looked down at the body.

'It's money, Jack. The fat fuck had two and a half million dollars with him. It's not here now and he can't exactly say what happened to it, can he?'

'Two and a half? For what? I assume he didn't bring it to put down on a blackjack table.'

Karch saw a vein high on Grimaldi's temple start to tick. The old man was angry. Karch knew how dangerous he was when he was angry. But he was like a little boy standing at the Christmas tree with a broomstick. He had to see how fragile those glass balls really were.

'He came to make a drop,' Grimaldi said. 'This morning. That's what the meeting was about.'

He gestured toward the body.

'I come up this morning and find this. The fucking mutt brought somebody in here and now the money's gone. We have to get that money back, Jack. It's spoken for, know what I mean? We need to get it quick. We—'

Karch shook his head, took the unlit cigarette from his mouth and cut in.

'Spoken for by who?'

'Jack, some things you don't need to know. You just need to get on this and find out who—'

'Take it easy, Vincent. And good luck with this.'

Karch waved a hand and headed toward the door. He got all the way to the living room and was heading to the suite's front door when Grimaldi caught up with him.

'Okay, okay, hold on, Jack! I'll tell you, okay? I'll tell you the whole thing, you think you need to know.'

Karch stopped. He was still facing the door with Grimaldi behind him. He noticed that the door's flip-over lock was missing. He reached up and touched the unpainted square on the door frame where it had been fastened. There was a grayish, waxy material in the screw holes. He rubbed some of this between his finger and thumb, thinking he had seen it before. He turned back to Grimaldi.

'Okay, Vincent, from the beginning. If you want my help on this you have to tell me everything. Don't leave anything out.'

Grimaldi nodded and pointed to the couch. Karch stepped back into the room and sat down. Grimaldi went back to his position by the room's glass wall. From Karch's angle, he was completely framed in bright blue sky. He was the dark, angry cloud in the middle of that sky. Karch took the unlit cigarette out of his mouth and put it in his coat pocket with the one he had used during the elevator gag.

'All right, this is the story,' Grimaldi said. 'Two weeks ago I got the word from somebody that there was going to be a problem with the transfer. Something came up on the background. What they call an association problem.'

Karch nodded. He wasn't as far inside the loop as Grimaldi, but his job gave him more than a general understanding of what was going on. The Cleopatra Resort and Casino was for sale. A Miami entertainment consortium called the Buena Suerte Group was lined up to buy. The Investigations Unit of the Nevada Gaming Commission had been working on a background inquiry of the buyers for twelve weeks and would soon submit a final report making a recommendation to the commission to approve or disapprove the sale. The commission – an appointed board – almost always followed the investigative branch's lead, making the report the key element in any bid to buy or open a casino in Nevada.

'What happened?' he asked. 'From what I heard, Buena Suerte was gonna come up clean.'

'It doesn't matter what happened. What matters is the money, Jack.'

'Everything matters. I have to know everything. What came up?'

Grimaldi waved his hands in frustration and surrender.

'A name came up, okay? They found a connection between one of the directors and a man named Hector Blanca. Now, you'll ask, who is Hector Blanca. Suffice it to say that he's a silent partner who was supposed to have remained silent. And that's all I'm saying on him.'

'Let me guess, Vincent. La Cuba Nostra?'

Karch said it in an I-told-you-so voice. He and Vincent had talked about the mob hybrid before. Transplanted Mafia soldiers from the northeast teaming with Cuban exiles in Miami to take control of organized crime in South Florida. The word in criminal intelligence circles was that the group had secretly bankrolled a failed gambling referendum in Florida a few years before. It stood to reason that if they couldn't get casinos into Florida, they would look elsewhere to invest their money.

That elsewhere most likely would include Nevada, where you didn't need a referendum approval to set up gambling operations; you just needed to get by the Gaming Commission and the short-term memory of the current city fathers. The fact that Las Vegas was born of a mobster's dream and run for decades by like-minded and associated men was being lost in the community's collective amnesia. Las Vegas had been reborn as the All-American city. It was pirate ships and half-scale Eiffel Towers, waterslides and roller coasters. Families welcome. Mobsters need not apply. The problem was, every time a new subdivision was approved and cut farther into the desert, the backhoes of progress came perilously close to digging up the reminders of the city's true heritage. And some of the sons and grandsons of those forefathers – even some of the ones buried out in the desert – could not let the old place go.

'We're not going to talk about La Cuba Nostra,' Grimaldi said, seemingly putting both an Italian and Cuban accent on the words. 'My ass is on the line here and I don't give two shits about how smart you think you are.'

'Okay, Vincent, then let's talk about your ass being in the crack. What happened?'

Grimaldi turned and gazed out the window as he spoke.

'Like I said, I got wind there was a problem. It was brought to my attention and I was informed that the problem could go away, could be cleaned up, for the right price.'

'Why you?'

'Why me? Because I had the connection. You might not think I'm worth a shit, Jack, but I've been working this city for forty-five years. I was already here a lifetime before your old man got his first gig. I've seen a lot. I know a lot.'

He glanced over his shoulder and looked pointedly at Karch as he said the last sentence. Karch took it as a reminder of what Grimaldi knew about him. Karch looked away and immediately wished he hadn't.

'Okay, Vincent. How much was this little cleaning operation going to cost?'

'Five million. Two and a half up front, the rest after the commission vote.'

'And I guess you stepping in and brokering the deal was going to solidify your position here under the new ownership.'

'Something like that, Jack. It would have solidified yours, too. Anybody with me would be along for the ride. I was going to get kicked up to GM. I would've been able to pick my own man in casino ops, put whoever I wanted up in the nest.'

'What about Hector Blanca? He'd want his own man up there.'

'Doesn't matter. The deal I made gave me the choice.'

Karch got up and joined Grimaldi at the window. They spoke while both looked out across the desert to the mountains beyond.

'So the guy on the bed – Hidalgo – came out here with payment number one and got ripped off. It sounds like their problem, Vincent. Not yours. Not ours.'

Grimaldi responded in an even tone. His words were measured, severe. The histrionics were gone and Karch knew this was when he was most dangerous. Like a dog with a broken tail. You try to pet it and you still might get your hand bitten off.

'It is my problem and that makes it yours,' Grimaldi said. 'I set up the transaction. The second that Hidalgo stepped off the plane at McCarran he and the money were in my care. That's the way Miami looks at it, so it's my ass that is on the line.'

Karch raised his eyebrows.

'You already told Miami about this?'

'I talked to Miami right before I called you. Not an enjoyable call to make. But the picture was made real clear to me. The courier is no great loss. But the money, that's different. They're holding me responsible for it.'

He paused for a moment and when he began again there was a note of desperation and maybe even pleading in his voice. It was a small note but it was there. It was a tone Karch had never heard coming from Vincent Grimaldi in the many years they had known each other.

'I have to get the money back, Jack. The GCIU report goes to the printer on Tuesday. After that it's too late to change. I have to get the money back and make the payment or the sale goes down the toilet. That happens and Miami will be sending people out.'

He used his chin again to point, this time out toward the desert.

'That's where they'll take me. Out with the rest of them who didn't go the distance in this town. Breathing sand.'

Grimaldi shook his head once, a quick, tight back-and-forth.

'I'm sixty-three years old, Jack. Forty-five fucking years in this town and that's what I'll get.'

Karch let a delicious ten seconds slide by before responding.

'We can't let that happen, Vincent. We won't.'

Grimaldi nodded and his mouth turned up into a humorless smile.

'Good old Jack of Spades. I knew I could count on you.'

20

Karch began with the body, studying its position and the pattern of blood spatter on the headboard and wall. The fat man had obviously been sitting upright on the bed when he took the bullet. The shooter had been standing at the foot of the bed.

'A lefty,' he said.

'What?' Grimaldi asked.

'The shooter. He was left-handed. Most likely.'

He stood in the position the shooter would have stood and extended his left arm. He nodded. It was likely that if Hidalgo had been hit in the right eye by a bullet from a gun held by someone facing him, then that person held the gun in his or her left hand.

His eyes traveled up from the body to the headboard and wall. Back at the office he had a couple of books on blood spatter – how to read the meanings of elliptical versus circular blood drops and so on. But he had never gotten past the introductory chapters because the stuff was so deadly boring and rarely usable in his line of work. What was to be read of significance from this tableau? Not much. The guy was alive and then he was dead. That was all.

'Anybody report a shot?' he asked.

'No,' Grimaldi said. 'But I wanted him isolated. So none of the rooms on either side or across were occupied. Also, I don't know if it connects up but there was a fire alarm on this floor last night.'

Karch looked at him.

'About eleven,' Grimaldi said. 'Somebody left a cigarette on a room service cart and parked it in the service alcove, right below a smoke detector.'

Karch nodded at the dead man.

'Was he evacuated? Did he leave his room?'

'Not that we know of. I have somebody pulling together the tapes so we can look at everything.'

Karch nodded but was unsure how the fire alarm could have played into things. He looked at the body again.

'I think what you have here is a half-assed attempt to make this look like a suicide. But –'

'This was no suicide. This was a fucking rip-off.'

'I know, Vincent, I know. Listen to me. I said an *attempt* to make it look that way. A *lousy* attempt at that. Just listen to me before you start going off.'

He decided to discontinue his running commentary. He'd let Grimaldi figure out things for himself. What bothered him most about the scene was the handcuffs. He didn't understand why they weren't removed.

'Vincent, I take it you searched this place top and bottom for the money?'

'Yes, it's gone. The case, too.'

'What about his keys?'

'Keys?'

'Keys.' He pointed to the dead man's wrist with the two cuffs on it. 'The key to the cuffs, where is it?'

'I don't know, Jack. I didn't see any keys. Whoever took the money, took the keys, I guess. But they'll get a surprise.'

'What surprise?'

'The key to the briefcase won't be on there. Fat boy here didn't have it. Mr Bla – uh, his boss didn't want him opening it, maybe going down to the tables with a piece of the cash. So he sent the key to me and I would open the case at the drop meeting this morning. I have the key but no fucking briefcase to open. The case has electronic protection – like a stun gun. Somebody tries to open it without the key, they'll get knocked on their ass good. Ninety thousand volts.'

Karch nodded and took a small notebook and pen from his pocket. He jotted down a note about the key and the briefcase.

'What are you writing, Jack?'

'Just a couple notes, so I can keep things straight.'

'I don't want any of this information getting into the wrong hands.'

Karch turned and looked at Grimaldi. It backed him down.

'I know, Jack. You'll be discreet.'

Karch came around the bed and looked at the watch on the night table. It looked like a Rolex. He hooked the pen through the metal band and lifted it, holding it so that he could look at the wrist plate.

'Whoever it was who did this was smart enough to know this is a phony.'

'Anybody on the con would know that, Jack. They sell those things for fifty bucks on the sidewalk outside of any place on Fremont. Whoever it was was smart enough to know what they wanted was the goddamn money and that was it.'

Karch nodded and put the watch back down. He stepped over to the closet and opened it and looked down at the safe. The door was open and it was empty.

'Tell me about this guy, Vincent. When did he come into town?'

'Three days ago. I wasn't sure when the drop would take place. The guy we were paying was calling the shots on that. We just had to be ready with the cash. Hidalgo came in Monday and we waited.'

Karch squatted on his haunches and closed the door to the safe but not all the way. He studied the combination pad.

'He stay in the room the whole time?'

'No, he spent a lot of time on the floor. I gave him a draw and the fuck started cleaning up on me. Christ, I thought if we didn't get this drop taken care of soon he was going to bankrupt us down there.'

Karch turned and looked up at Grimaldi.

'How much did he win, Vincent?'

'I gave him fifty bees out of the cage on Monday. By last night he had turned that into a hundred K and change. He was doing good. He was tipping hundred-dollar bills around like it was toilet paper.'

Karch looked back at the safe and swung the door open. He looked into its emptiness but was not really seeing anything. He was thinking, brooding on what Grimaldi had just said.

'You see what you did, Vincent? You brought this on yourself.'

'The fuck you talking about?'

'You gave the guy money and he turned it into more money. And he was showing it to the world. This town, that was like putting blood in the water, Vincent. It drew a shark to your fat man.'

'What are you saying, that whoever did this did it for the hundred, not the two and a half million?'

'I'm saying that whoever did this came in for the hundred and then found the rest. Luckiest fucking day of his life.'

'That can't be, Jack. That—'

'Who knew about the money? I mean, that it was here and who had it. Who knew?'

'Only me.'

'What about Miami? Could there have been a leak from there?'

'No, only one person knew.'

'Maybe the courier told somebody.'

'It's unlikely, Jack. He worked directly for the source. If the money was taken he knew they'd look at him.'

'Unless he ended up dead. What about the guy getting the drop?'

'He knew it was here somewhere but he didn't know who had it or where exactly it was. Besides, why steal what we're givin' him?'

'Exactly. So if nobody knew it was here, it goes to prove my point. This was a hot prowler, Vincent. Somebody who picked up on this guy winning a hundred grand and went after it. And he hit the fucking jackpot.'

From his crouched position Karch looked up at the closet. He studied Hidalgo's clothes, all pushed to the side so that the thief could work around the safe. His eyes caught on something on the wall behind the safe. It looked like peeling paint. He moved forward onto his knees and looked behind the safe. He looked closer and saw it was not paint that was peeling, but painted tape. He reached down and grabbed the tab and pulled it up. The tape went along the baseboard of the closet, up alongside the door, over the door frame to the wall over the closet and then out and along the alcove ceiling. It finally ended on the wall above the alcove entrance.

'What the fuck is that?' Grimaldi asked.

'Conducting tape. This was a pro who did this, Vincent. He was watching this guy.'

'You mean cameras?'

Karch nodded and returned to the closet. He scanned the ceiling again and then the walls. He saw the small drill hole on the right-hand wall and found more tape. He pulled it off the wall and it led to the rear of the safe.

'Two cameras. One in the room to watch the mark. The other right here to pick up the combo. This was good.'

'I haven't heard about anybody using cameras since . . . since that last time. Max Freeling.'

Karch looked at Grimaldi.

'I haven't either. But we know that Max didn't do this, don't we?'

'You're right about that.'

Karch left the closet and went back through the suite, his eyes scanning the ceiling and upper walls. He came to the front door and opened it. He squatted down again and studied the locking mechanism.

'What about prints?' Grimaldi said from behind.

'There won't be any.'

He turned the deadbolt and saw the bolt come only halfway out. He closed the door with the bolt extended. He nodded. He admired a job well done. He stood up, closed the door and looked at Grimaldi. Karch couldn't help but smile.

'What's so fucking funny?' Grimaldi demanded.

'Nothing,' Karch said, his smile broadening. 'I just get a rise out of a worthy opponent, that's all. I'm really glad you called me in on this, Vincent. I'm going to enjoy it.'

'Listen, this isn't about you getting a rise. It's about me getting the money back.'

Karch let Grimaldi have the rebuke. It didn't bother him. He could already see how he was going to use this job to his advantage, to get what he had always wanted.

'Vincent, you have a problem.'

'I know that! Why do you think I reached out for you?'

'I mean a problem within a problem. Look at this.'

Karch stepped back so he could show Grimaldi the door's locking mechanism.

'He gaffed the lock. The fat man thought he was locked up tight in here but the deadbolt and the flip-lock were gaffed. So was this Radio Shack piece of shit he added himself.'

Karch jerked the electronic door alarm off the door-knob and tossed it onto the floor.

'But, see, all of this only worked on the in-room protections. The main lock wasn't gaffed. That means—'

'He had a key.'

Karch nodded.

'You're real good, Vincent,' he said in a tone that implied the opposite. 'He had a key. That means he had somebody who got it for him. An insider.'

Grimaldi looked down at the floor and Karch watched as the older man's color deepened again. Karch didn't wait for the wave of anger to subside.

'My guess is our guy also had a key to one of these empty rooms around here so he could set up and watch his cameras and make his move when the time was right.'

'You want to take a look?'

'Oh, yeah.'

The first room they checked was directly across the hall, Suite 2015, and Karch immediately said upon entering that they had found the spot where the thief had waited for the mark to go to sleep.

'How do you know?' Grimaldi asked.

Karch pointed to the table. The magazines, the room service menu and hotel information binder were stacked and pushed to the side along with the bottle of welcome wine.

'This is where he waited.'

Karch looked around the suite but wasn't expecting much. This guy was good and the chances of a mistake were almost nothing. The bedroom looked undisturbed. He poked his head into the bathroom and saw nothing unusual. If the perpetrator had used the toilet he had even put the seat back down when he was finished.

He walked back into the living room, where Grimaldi was standing in the middle of the room with his arms folded. Karch was trying to think of something to say that would twist the knife a little bit but then noticed something beneath the table by the curtains. He stepped over and got down on his knees to crawl under the table.

'What've you got, Jack?'

'I don't know.'

He reached under the curtain and lifted it up. On the floor was a playing card. The ace of hearts. Karch looked at it a moment, considering it. He noticed that two opposite corners had been clipped – an indication it was from a casino souvenir pack. After use in the casino the cards were clipped and then sold in the casino gift shop. The clipping was done to make sure nobody tried to slip one back into play at a casino table.

'What is it?' Grimaldi asked from behind him.

'A card. The ace of hearts.'

Karch suddenly thought of his old man and what he used to say about the ace of hearts. The money card, he called it. Follow the money card, he would say.

'The ace of hearts?' Grimaldi said. 'What do you think it means?'

Karch didn't answer. He reached to the card and picked it up, his thumb and forefinger holding it by the edges. He crawled out from under the table, holding the card out. When he was standing again, he turned his wrist so he could see the top of the card. It had a design of two pink flamingos with their necks entwined and forming the outline of a heart.

'From the Flamingo,' he said.

Grimaldi stared at the card.

'What does it mean?'

Karch shook his shoulders.

'Maybe nothing. But our guy had to have been in here watching the cameras for a while. Maybe he was playing a little solitaire to pass the time.'

'Well, if he dropped the ace of hearts, then he never fucking won.'

'Very perceptive, Vincent.'

Grimaldi exploded.

'Look, Jack, are you going to help me out here or are you going to spend your time playing word games and trying to make me look stupid? Because if that's what you're about, then I'll reach out for somebody else who can do the job without giving me the grief.'

Karch waited a long moment before responding in a calm tone.

'Vincent, you reached out for me because you know there isn't anybody else who can handle this like I can.'

'Then let's stop talking and get it handled. The clock is ticking.'

'All right, Vincent. Whatever you say.'

Karch looked down at the card he still held by the corner. He knew he could call in a favor from Iverson over at Metro and run the card for latent prints. But that would bring Iverson into something that Karch expected was going to get dirty. He decided to keep the idea as a last alternative. He went over to the table and opened the folder containing the hotel information packet. There were envelopes and writing paper inside one of the pockets. He slipped the playing card into an envelope and put it into his inside jacket pocket.

'Prints?' Grimaldi asked.

'Maybe. I'll try a few other things first.'

They went back across the hall to 2014 and took a

final look around while they discussed their options. Grimaldi said Miami didn't care what became of the courier and so that left things open. They could back out of the room and let things run their course when the housekeeping maid discovered the body. Or they could bring a laundry cart to the room, put the body in it and take it down the service elevator to the loading dock and a waiting van. Any trace of the courier's stay in the hotel could be wiped off the computers and tapes and his body could then be planted out in the desert after nightfall.

'It will take four guys to lift that sack of shit,' Grimaldi lamented.

'You widen the circle of people who know about this and you widen your exposure,' Karch said.

'But if we let things go, that means Metro comes in, and talk about the hotel getting a black eye. I can't remember the last hotel homicide we had in this town. They'll go after this like Tyson went after Evander's ear.'

'That's true. But maybe that sort of pressure on our guy will be useful. Maybe force him into a mistake.'

'Yeah, and what if Metro Homicide gets to him before you?'

Karch just looked at Grimaldi with an expression that said the idea was absurd.

'You call it, Vincent. We're wasting time. I want to look at the tape downstairs and get on with it.'

Grimaldi nodded.

'Okay, no Metro. I'll have some people come up and take care of things here.'

'Good call, Vincent,' Karch said, but in a way that might make Grimaldi wonder if he really meant it. 'Let's go watch the tape.'

They both backed out of the room then, leaving the dead man behind on the bed. Grimaldi made sure he hooked the DO NOT DISTURB sign on the door handle.

21

On numerous prior occasions Karch had been in Grimaldi's office on the second level of the casino. He held a secret security consulting contract with the Cleopatra – no records, payments in cash – and as such he most often met with Grimaldi in his office, even though the tasks he was given normally had little to do with anything that went on in the casino below. Karch was most often involved in what Grimaldi liked to call ancillary security issues and problems. Karch liked his outside status all right. He knew he would never be the kind of man who could willingly wear a blue blazer with the profile of the Queen of Egypt emblazoned on the breast pocket.

The office was large and opulent, with a desk area, a sitting area and a private bar. The entrance was through the casino's huge security center, where dozens of video techs sat in rows of booths watching the screens of video tubes showing the ever-changing views of the hundreds of cameras focused on the casino floor. This room was dimly lit and never warmer than 65 degrees because of the delicate electronics. Most of the techs wore sweaters beneath their standard blue blazers. In Las Vegas, when you saw somebody wearing a sweater to work in the summer, you knew he worked inside, watching tubes all day.

One wall of Grimaldi's office had windows looking out

into the security center. Another wall had windows viewing the casino. And located directly behind Grimaldi's desk was the door leading out to the crow's nest. It could be reached only through Grimaldi's office and he had never once invited Karch out for a view of the casino floor. This was something that bothered Karch and his frustration was compounded because he believed Grimaldi knew.

As they entered the office, Karch noticed a man sitting behind Grimaldi's desk and working the control board of the multiplex video station to the right of the desk.

'What have you got?' Grimaldi said as he turned to lower the blinds on the windows viewing the security center.

'I gotta surprise is what I got,' the man behind the desk said without looking up from the four screens he had active on the video station.

'Tell us.'

The word *us* made the tech look up from the screens. He nodded once to Karch and then cast his eyes back down.

'Well, looks to me like this guy mighta been ripped off by a woman,' he said.

Grimaldi came around the desk and looked over the tech's shoulder at the screens.

'Show us.'

Karch remained on the other side of the desk but could see the screens. He glanced past the two other men and out the glass door that led to the crow's nest. Grimaldi did not bother to introduce the technician to Karch.

For the next five minutes the tech used tapes taken from several overhead cameras to intermittently show Hidalgo's last night in the casino. It was called a video trail. There were enough cameras over the casino floor –

any casino floor in Las Vegas – to never lose sight of an individual once he entered the so-called video net. The best techs had the quadrants of the net memorized and with fingers flying across a keyboard could jump from one camera to another to follow a target.

Grimaldi's tech did that now, only it wasn't live action. He had pieced together Hidalgo's video trail from the night before. He showed Hidalgo playing baccarat and blackjack, even a couple of spins on the roulette wheel. Whatever game he was playing, he seemed to do it with a minimum of conversation with fellow players and casino employees. Finally, when the counter showed the time on the tape to be 10:38 P.M. they watched as Hidalgo headed to the VIP desk and retrieved the brushed-aluminum briefcase from the vault. He was met at the desk by a security escort who then walked with him to the elevators.

'Who's the escort?' Karch asked.

'His name's Martin,' Grimaldi said. 'He's a shift supervisor. Been here a couple years, coming over from the Nugget. I had him escorting the fat man all week.'

'We'll have to talk to him.'

'I don't know what it will get you but it will be no problem.'

The tech pointed to a new screen where Hidalgo's trail continued. It showed the fat man and the blue-blazered Martin stepping onto an elevator. Hidalgo took his card key from his pocket and Martin took it and plugged it into the control panel before hitting the penthouse button. Though the tape did not have audio it was clear that the two men were not engaged in conversation.

'And that's the last we see of him,' the tech said.

'No hallway cameras, right?' Karch said.

'Nope. We lose him once he's off the elevator in the penthouse.'

'What about when the fire alarm went off later?' Grimaldi asked. 'Any sign of him then?'

'Nope,' the tech said. 'I checked all elevator and stairwell cams. He didn't evacu—'

'Wait a minute,' Karch suddenly said. 'Go back. Back the elevator tape up.'

The tech looked at Grimaldi, who nodded. He backed the tape up until Karch said he had gone far enough and then replayed it. They watched silently. It was clear Martin said something to Hidalgo, who then reached into his pocket and produced his card key. Martin then used it to engage the penthouse button.

'Vincent, you said Martin's a shift super?'

'Right.'

'Wouldn't he have a key to the penthouse?'

Grimaldi was silent for a moment as he computed what they had just seen on the tape and the meaning of Karch's question.

'Son of a bitch. He used Hidalgo's card when he could've used his own.'

'Because maybe he didn't have his on him.'

'Because maybe he gave it – where's this woman you're talking about?'

The tech hit some memory codes and the tape on one of the screens reversed to a preset point. On the screen was a wide view of the baccarat salon. One table was in use and Hidalgo was the only player. Using a roller ball built into the console the tech moved the image forward a few frames at a time. He pointed to the bottom of the screen, his finger tapping it just below the image of a woman leaning on the railing that separated the salon from the rest of the casino.

'Her,' he said.

'What about her?' Grimaldi asked.

'She's trying not to show it but she's watching him.'

He continued to move the roller and the image moved forward. The three men watched the screen in silence. The woman on the screen appeared to be resting or maybe waiting for someone. She had a small backpack over one shoulder and a black gym bag gripped in one hand. She looked as though perhaps she had just checked in and was waiting for someone, perhaps a husband who had stopped to play a few hands of blackjack before they went up to their room. But twice she glanced into the salon and her eyes seemed to fall directly on Hidalgo. Each time her eyes held for what seemed to be more than a passing glance would call for. It was curious to Karch, but not enough.

'He's the only guy playing,' he said. 'Who else is she going to look at?'

'That's true. But I put her trail together, too.'

He ejected a tape from the console and put another one in. Grimaldi came up closer behind him to look at the screen. Karch put his hands flat on Grimaldi's desk and leaned over for a better view. The tape showed the woman with the two bags entering the casino at 8 P.M. and proceeding to the VIP desk, where she was given an envelope.

'That's got to be the key,' Grimaldi said. 'Martin's fucking key!'

Karch was thinking the same thing but did not say as much. He was also thinking the dark flowing curls that framed – and concealed – the woman's face had to be a wig. He watched as she huddled against a phone in the lobby and probably opened the envelope away from any camera's view. She then turned and started moving toward the casino floor. She moved without hesitation, with a strong purpose. The bags she carried appeared heavy but she held them steady.

After her stop at the baccarat salon, the video trail followed her through the casino and onto an elevator in the Euphrates Tower.

'She was damn good,' the tech said. 'Never looked up once. We've got nothing. That hat and that hair, she might as well been walkin' under an umbrella.'

Karch smiled as he watched. The tech was right. She was good, and already knowing what she had done upstairs, Karch found himself enthralled by the woman on the video screen. She was disguised but he was able to draw a sense of her from the videotape. Young, maybe early thirties, the skin beneath her chin taut, the jawline beneath the brim of the hat set with determination. No earrings, no rings or other jewelry that he could see. No distractions. Nothing but drive toward her goal. Karch wished he could see her eyes because he knew they'd be something to see.

On the screen the woman in the elevator used a card key from her back pocket to engage the penthouse button.

'There's the key all right,' Grimaldi said.

Karch wished he would shut up and just observe but didn't say anything.

'Okay,' the tech said while typing in a new command on the keyboard. 'So she gets off the elevator on twenty. But then we see her two more times.'

'Twice?' Grimaldi said.

'Yes, sir. First time she came back down to meet somebody but they never showed up.'

He pointed at the screen and the video trail continued. The three men watched silently as video snippets showed her moving through the casino to the lounge, picking an empty table and ordering from a waitress. The trail jumped in time twelve minutes and showed the woman sitting alone but with two drinks on the table.

'What the fuck?' Grimaldi said. 'I thought you said nobody showed.'

'Nobody did,' the tech said. 'She ordered the drinks but nobody ever came.'

'Let's just watch, okay?' Karch said, annoyed by their banter.

On the screen the woman casually glanced around herself as if to make sure no one was watching and then picked up the glass in front of her. It looked like a Coke to Karch. The woman reached across the small round table and tapped it on the glass of beer. Karch leaned in closer to the screen and watched her lips as she obviously spoke out loud.

'I think you've tailed the wrong person,' Grimaldi said, his voice rising in frustration. 'This broad's sitting there talking to herself. We don't have the time to be –'

'Wait, sir, check this out. She goes back to the elevators now and goes back up to twenty.'

He fast-forwarded the tape.

'And then we don't see her again until four. She comes back down, and take a look at what she's carrying. She went up originally with two bags and she comes back down with two. But something's different.'

The woman appeared again on the casino floor, moving quickly through the thin crowd of die-hard gamblers. Right away Karch saw that the tech was right. Things were different. She had the backpack strap over one shoulder but the gym bag was gone. Instead she carried a large black canvas bag with two hand straps. The tech hit a key and froze the image. The second bag contained an object that was rectangular, its dimensions clearly showing through the canvas. It was the mark's briefcase.

'That little bitch,' Grimaldi said calmly. 'She's got my money.'

'You follow her out?' Karch asked.

The tech hit a key starting the video again and simply pointed at the screen. The cameras tracked the woman as she made her way completely across the huge casino floor to the VIP desk. From the canvas bag she removed an envelope and left it on the counter without speaking to anyone. She then proceeded to the south exit. It was not the main casino entry and exit point. Karch also knew that it did not lead to a parking lot or drive-up circle. Rather, it led to the sidewalk which took pedestrians to Las Vegas Boulevard.

'She didn't go out the front door, Vincent,' he said.

There was enough urgency in his tone to draw Grimaldi's eyes away from the video console. The older man raised his eyebrows, picking up on the tone but not knowing the significance of it.

'She didn't park here because she didn't want the cameras to see her vehicle,' Karch said. 'So she parked somewhere else and walked in.'

Karch pointed at the screen even though it was now blank.

'The south exit,' he said. 'She was heading to the Flamingo.'

Impressed, Grimaldi nodded.

'Ace of hearts. You have someone there?'

Karch nodded.

'No problem.'

'Then go.'

'Wait a minute, Vincent. What about Martin? We should start with him.'

'I'll take him. You follow the money, Jack. The money's the priority and we're on a fucking clock.'

Karch nodded. He guessed Grimaldi was probably

correct in his thinking. He thought about the ace of hearts he'd found upstairs. Follow the money. Follow the money card.

'Well, what are you waiting for?'

Karch broke away from his thoughts and looked at Grimaldi.

'I'm on it.'

He glanced once out the door to the crow's nest and then headed toward the office exit. He stopped at the door.

'Vincent, you might want to send somebody back up to the second room up there to check the AC vents.'

'What for?'

'She went up with two bags, a backpack and a gym bag. She came back down with the backpack and the briefcase inside a black canvas bag. Where's the gym bag?'

Grimaldi paused for a moment while he thought about this. He smiled, impressed that Karch had picked up on the missing bag.

'I'll have it checked. You stay in touch. And remember, Jack of Spades, the clock is ticking.'

Karch shot him with a finger and went out the door.

22

Karch followed the same route out of the Cleopatra that he had watched the woman take on the video screen a few minutes before. As he wound his way around the tables and circumnavigated the idiots who lazily walked into his path, his mind became preoccupied by thoughts of the woman on the video. She had come close to pulling off a perfect caper. One glance too many and too long at the mark while at the baccarat railing. Her only mistake. Otherwise they'd probably still be scratching their heads. Still, he had to admire her. He was looking forward to the moment he would meet her. And he had no doubt that moment would come. She was good but he was better. Their time would certainly come.

He gruffly pushed by a man in shorts who had slowly shuffled into Karch's path while absentmindedly looking up through the glass panels of the atrium.

'Well, pardon *you*,' he protested as Karch went by.

Karch looked back at him without slowing his stride.

'Fuck you, dipshit. Go back to losing your money.'

'Hey!' the man called after him.

Karch stopped and turned back toward the man. The man quickly realized he had overstepped and started shuffling away in the opposite direction. Karch watched him go until the man glanced back and their eyes locked. Karch was smiling, letting the man know he had made him run away like a boy.

Karch followed the River of Nile hallway to the exit the woman had used and soon was on the Strip walking toward the Flamingo, a block away. He realized as he got to the venerable and many times expanded and renovated casino that he needed some cash. He silently chastised himself for not asking Grimaldi for expense funds and thought about going back but knew the delay would probably set Grimaldi off. Instead he looked around inside the Flamingo until he found a cash machine and then withdrew the three-hundred-dollar maximum his account would allow. Usually, Don Cannon charged him five hundred for a trail but the three would have to do. He didn't think Cannon would be a problem. The money came out in hundreds, unlike any machine found outside of a casino. While still standing at the machine, Karch folded the three bills twice so that they could easily be palmed. He creased the bills and put them in the palm of his right hand. He closed it slightly and let it hang naturally at his side. He thought about Michelangelo's hands. The master. He envisioned David's right hand hanging loosely at his side. Or the casual repose of the hands of the figure portraying Dusk at the tomb of Lorenzo de' Medici. Karch's father had gone as a young man to Italy to study the hands of the master. The son didn't have to bother. There was a full-scale replica of Michelangelo's David in the shopping rotunda at Caesar's Palace.

Karch went to the telephone alcove off the lobby area and picked up a house phone. He asked for Don Cannon in security and the call was transferred to an intermediate, who asked who was calling. Karch was then put on hold once more and this time waited more than a minute. He used the time to think about what he would say. Cannon was a shift supervisor in the tube room. Karch had met him on a missing-person case five years earlier and he had been cooperative – for a price – ever since. In a dozen years working the Strip Karch had made connections like Cannon in almost all of the casinos. They were all legitimate except for his relationship with Vincent Grimaldi. But now, one way or the other, he was seeing a way out of Grimaldi's grasp.

A voice barked on the other end of the line.

'Jack Karch!'

'Don? Howzitgoing?'

'Keepin' my powder dry. What can I do you for?'

'I'm working a case and could use a little help from your cameras.'

'You want a little electronic magic, huh? What's the case?'

'Pretty basic. Guy at the DI got ripped off by a hooker. He calls me because he's trying to keep it low profile, if you know what I mean. No coppers, no official record. But the broad took some jewelry – a watch and a ring – that've got sentimental value. You know, inscriptions and bullshit like that. He can't replace them on short notice and if he goes back to Memphis tomorrow without this stuff, he's going to have a hard time explainin' it to the wife.'

'I get the picture. What's it got to do with the Flamingo?'

'I think she parked in your garage – the one fronting Koval. My guy met her at the bar in Bugsy's last night, then they cabbed it to the DI. She ripped him after he passed out. I trailed her through the Desert Inn Casino to the sidewalk and I think she was heading here. This was about four in the A.M. today.'

'You said *here*. You're here now?'

'Downstairs.'

'Why didn't you say so? Come on up.'

He hung up before Karch could say anything else.

Karch walked to the elevators and took a ride up to the second floor. As he rode he took a handkerchief out of his back pocket, balled it and stuffed it into the breast pocket of his suit jacket. He pushed it down so that it could not be seen but still served to hold the pocket open about an inch. He then checked his pocket for change and came up with a quarter and a dime. They were both recently minted and very shiny. He bent down and slid the quarter into one shoe and the dime into the other. One at a time he shook his feet to move the coins below the arches. He hoped Cannon wasn't watching him on one of his cameras.

Out of the elevator he went left to the security complex entrance and rang the buzzer to the left of the steel door. There was a two-way speaker mounted on the wall above the buzzer but it remained silent. After five seconds the door buzzed and he went in.

Don Cannon was a big and burly dark-haired man with a full beard and glasses. It was likely he had been hired for his size and what he could do with it when necessary on the casino floor. But over the years he had graduated to inside work, and the only parts of the casino he usually saw these days were on the video screens he and his minions monitored in the so-called tube room. He was waiting for Karch in a small anteroom on the other side of the steel entrance door. They shook hands as they always did and the folded hundred-dollar bills were seamlessly passed from one right hand to the other. As with most hotels on the Strip, it was the Flamingo's policy not to accept any remuneration to itself or its personnel for help given on criminal investigations. However, Karch knew the value of a gratuity and how it would keep that steel door's lock buzzing for him the next time he called.

'I'm a little light today,' Karch said in a low voice. 'I'll have to catch you later on that, if that's okay.'

'No problem. I loaded the four o'clock chip while you were on the way up. Come on back.'

Pocketing the currency as he moved, Cannon led Karch into the tube room, which was not unlike the casino security center at the Cleo. Video techs sat at rows of twelve-screen multiplex consoles, their eyes endlessly moving from screen to screen and using keyboards and joysticks to choose and manipulate camera angles and magnifications. They watched over everything, but most of all the money. It all came down to the money.

Cannon stepped up onto a stage at one end of the room where a lone console was situated so that as shift supervisor he could monitor cameras and video techs at the same time.

'You said she came in from the DI, right? Did she walk?'

Cannon slid into a seat on rollers and then pulled it close to the console. Karch stood behind him.

'Looks like it. A little after four.'

'That's a long walk. Okay, let's see. We'll try the north entrance first.'

His fingers started flailing across the keyboard as he typed in search commands. He continued talking.

'We went digital since I think you were last in here. It's a blast.'

'Great.'

Karch didn't know what going digital meant but it wasn't important to him.

'Okay, here's the door starting at four. I'll put it on double time until you see something.'

He pointed to the large master screen directly in front of him in the console. It was divided into a matrix of twenty-four different camera angles. He moved the joystick and an arrow moved across the screen to one of the small squares. He hit the enter button and the image on the small square took over the entire screen. The image was from a camera showing an angled overhead shot of a set of automatic glass doors. The image was moving quickly. Cars seen in the distance through the doors sped by and people passing by on the sidewalk seemed to move at a quick trot. Karch stared intently at the screen and at the figures occasionally entering and leaving through the doors.

'There!' he said after nearly three minutes. 'I think that was her. Back it up.'

'All right.'

Cannon moved the digital image until the figure that had gone by so quickly reappeared going backward out the door.

'There.'

The image was frozen and then replayed on slow motion. The automatic doors opened and the woman Karch had watched on the video tubes at the Cleo entered carrying her backpack and the canvas bag containing the briefcase.

'That's her.'

'Not bad-looking for a hooker. Too much hair, though. Wonder what she charges.'

'Five bills minimum, my guy told me.'

Cannon whistled.

'There's your rip-off right there. I don't care what a woman looks like, no piece of ass is worth five bills.'

Karch laughed dutifully.

'She take the guy's luggage, too?'

'Yeah. But he doesn't care so much about that. He just wants that watch and ring.'

'I don't know, she's holding that one bag like it's got Fort Knox jammed into it.'

Karch started to perspire. He had hoped Cannon would run the video trail for him without being too interpretive.

'Well, let's see where she goes,' he said, hoping to get Cannon to stop analyzing what he saw and just move through the video.

It seemed to work. Cannon grew silent and he trailed the woman through the matrix of camera angles until she left the casino building through the rear entrance and entered the eight-story self-parking garage at the rear of the property on Koval Road.

'That's gotta be a wig she's wearing, but even so, she looks new to me,' Cannon finally remarked after five minutes of silence. 'If you want, we can check our hooker bin for her.'

'Hooker bin?'

'That's what we call it. We've got most of the working girls in town on computer file. Might be able to come up with a name if we can match her photo. Trouble is, she hasn't so much as looked up a single time. We don't have a clear shot of her so far.'

And you're not going to get one, Karch thought.

'Well, let's see what she does and then worry about that after,' he said instead.

In the garage the woman took the elevator to the eighth floor. She then walked to a blue unmarked van that was backed into a space in the corner farthest from the elevator. This time of night the upper floors of the garage were nearly empty. There was not another vehicle within twenty spaces of the van.

'No plate,' Cannon said. 'Looks like this girl takes precautions. You sure she's a hooker, Jack? Like I said, she doesn't look all that familiar to me and, besides, mosta these girls use drivers. Especially your five-hundred-an-hour variety.'

Karch didn't answer. He was intently watching the screen. The woman opened the driver's door with a key, then loaded in the bags and climbed in. The lights came on as she started the van. Before putting it in gear the woman reached back and knocked on the partition between the front and the rear cargo area. Karch watched her lips move as she said something. Someone was obviously in the back of the van.

'Don, show that part again, will you?'

'No problem.'

Cannon reversed the digital image and showed the woman knocking on the partition again. He froze it and went through some computer commands in an effort to clean up the picture. He then switched to the roller ball and slowly advanced the recorded image again.

'She said something,' Cannon said. 'I don't . . . it looks like maybe, "How are you doing?" or "How's it going?" Something like that.'

'How's it going back there,' Karch said.

'Damn, Jack, I think you're right. You're good, man. We could use you up here.'

'I'd go stir-crazy inside a week. You going to be able to get a rear shot of the van?'

'As soon as she drives out.'

Cannon went back to the matrix – now displaying only garage cameras – and followed the van down the seven levels until it went out the exit to Koval. As it passed through the exit, the van's rear end was recorded by a ground-level camera focused at the average height of a license plate.

The van's rear plate was missing as well.

'Damn!' Karch cried out, surprised by his own outburst.

'Wait a sec,' Cannon said.

He reversed the image and replayed it in slow motion.

He then froze the picture and magnified it. Karch looked at him and then at the screen and then finally understood what he was doing. The van's plates were gone but there was a parking sticker on the left side of the bumper. Cannon expertly moved in on it and expanded it. The larger letters and numbers became almost clear. Karch could see the current year on the sticker and was trying to make out the letters when Cannon whistled.

'What?'

'It looks like HLS to me.'

'Me, too. What's that?'

'That's Hooten Lighting and Supplies. Their logo. You know, the company that makes all of this shit.'

He indicated the console with his hand.

'Okay.'

Karch didn't know what else to say. The discovery was making the cover story he had told Cannon seem more and more of a stretch. For the first time he realized how cold it was in the tube room. He folded his arms across his chest.

'I don't get it,' Cannon said. 'A hooker driving herself in a van from Hooten's. You sure this, uh, client of yours told it to you straight?'

He looked up at Karch, who decided he had to extricate himself from this situation.

'Nope. But that's what I'm going to go find out before I take another step on this thing. If the guy's lying, I'm flying. Thanks for your help, Don. I better get back over there to the DI and talk to this guy.'

'Yeah, it sounds kind of hinky to me. You want to look through the hooker bin anyway? Got some real beauties in there.'

Karch frowned and shook his head.

'Nah, maybe later. Let me talk to this guy first and see

what's what. Oh, and I'll catch you later with the rest of what I owe you for the trail.'

Karch nodded at the video console.

'Forget about it. Anyway, looks like I opened more holes for you than I closed. The only thing I want from you is a little sleight of hand. You got something to show me?'

Karch went into his act, feigning that he had been caught off guard by Cannon's request.

'Well . . .'

He patted his pockets for change.

'You got some change? A quarter or something?'

Cannon leaned back in his seat so he could work his hand into his pocket. He finally came up with a palm full of change. Karch pulled the sleeves of his jacket halfway up to his elbows and then chose a recently minted and shiny quarter, taking it off Cannon's palm with his right hand. He then performed a variation on the classic French Drop with an added toss-away vanish devised by J. B. Bobo. It was a sleight-of-hand trick he had been practicing since he was twelve years old. It was one he could do in his sleep. He expertly accomplished it with fluid motions and a practiced ease.

With his right hand palm up and chest high he held the quarter by its edges between his thumb and four fingers, tilting it forward slightly so that Cannon could see its face. He then brought his left hand over the top of the coin as if to take it away. As his left hand closed over the coin he let it drop down into his right palm, completing the fake take.

Karch closed his left fist and held it out toward Cannon. He started manipulating the muscles and balling his fist as if he were pulverizing the coin supposedly held within it to dust. At the same time he moved his right hand in a flat circular motion above his closed left fist. He never took his eyes off his left hand.

'To powder it goes, where it ends up nobody knows.'

He made the circle with his right hand wider and wider until suddenly he snapped his fingers and opened both hands, palms out to Cannon. The coin was gone. Cannon's eyes quickly moved from hand to hand, then a broad smile cracked across his face. It was the usual response. The trick was a double misdirection. The skeptical viewer believes the coin never left the right hand but is baffled when the coin shows up in neither hand.

'Fantastic!' Cannon cried. 'Where'd it go?'

Karch shook his head.

'That's the problem with this one. You never know where that coin's going to turn up. That part I never got a handle on. I guess you can add two bits to what I owe you.'

Cannon laughed loudly.

'You're cool, Jack. How'd you learn that one, your father?'

'Yeah.'

'He still around?'

'Nah, he's gone. Long time ago.'

'And he used to work the Strip, right?'

'Yeah, here and there. In the sixties. One week he opened for Joey Bishop, who opened for Sinatra at the Sands. I have pictures of the three of them.'

'Cool! The Rat Pack. The good old days, huh?'

'Yeah, some of them were good.'

Karch had a vision of seeing his father coming home from the hospital after the incident at Circus, Circus. Both hands bandaged white. It looked like he was holding two softballs. His eyes looked like they were staring at something far, far away.

Karch realized he had lost his smile and looked at Cannon.

'Anyway, I better hit the road and get on this thing. Thanks for the help, Don.'

He offered his hand and Cannon took it.

'Anytime, Jack.'

'I'll find my way out.'

He turned toward the steps and started walking away. But then he stopped and leaned on the railing.

'What the . . . ?'

He raised his left foot and worked the shoe off. Without even glancing at Cannon but knowing he was being watched, he looked inside the shoe and then shook it. Something rattled inside and he turned the shoe upside down, dropping the quarter he had planted earlier into his other hand. He held it up and looked at Cannon. The big man banged a fist on his console and started smiling and shaking his head.

'Son of a gun, I told you,' Karch said. 'Never know where the damn thing'll go.'

He flipped the coin to Cannon, who caught it in his fist.

'I'm saving this one, Jack. It's fucking magic.'

Karch saluted and headed down the steps and out of the tube room. He waited until he was out of the Flamingo and away from the view of Cannon's cameras before reaching into the breast pocket of his suit coat and removing the handkerchief and the quarter he had dropped into it while circling his hand during the trick.

He would get the dime out of his shoe later, when he had time to sit down.

23

Ninety minutes later Karch was standing outside the fenced employee lot of Hooten's Lighting & Supplies with a cell phone in his hand. Parked directly on the other side of the fence was the blue van that had been recorded driving out of the garage at the Flamingo about six hours earlier. Only now there was a license plate attached to the rear bumper. Karch was pacing a little bit, anxious as he waited for a call-back. The small tickle of an adrenaline rush was beginning to caress the back of his skull. He was getting close. To the money, to the woman. He cocked his head back and that seemed to accentuate the trilling up his spine and into his brain.

The phone rang and his thumb was already poised on the button.

'This is Karch.'

'This is Ivy. I got it.'

Ivy was a Metro detective named Iverson who ran plates for Karch for fifty bucks a shot. He'd do other things for other prices, using the power of his badge to generate two incomes. Karch was always circumspect about his requests, even on totally legitimate jobs. He had learned over the years to treat all Metro cops – and Iverson more than others – with the same caution and distance as the prostitutes, pawnbrokers and casino sharps he regularly dealt with on his cases.

Karch tilted his head and hooked the phone in the crook of his neck while he got out his notepad and pen.

'Okay, what've you got?'

'Plate comes back to a Jerome Zander Paltz, forty-seven years of age. Address is three-twelve Mission Street. That's North Las Vegas. I ran him on NCIC for you and he's got a clean ticket. I threw that in for free, by the way.'

Karch had stopped writing after the last name. He knew Jerome Paltz. Or at least he was pretty sure he did. He knew a Jersey Paltz who worked behind the counter at Hooten's. He realized he had always thought the name Jersey referred to where Paltz had come from. He now realized it was apparently a play on his first and middle names.

'Hey, boss, you there?'

Karch came out of his thoughts on Jersey Paltz.

'Yeah. Hey, thanks, Ivy. This clears something up for me.'

'Really? What?'

'Oh, just this thing I'm working on. It's a surveillance outside a construction site. The Venetian. This van's showed up a few times and I was kind of suspicious. But Paltz is on the list of vendors. He works for Hooten's L and S and they're putting in the cameras. So scratch that.'

'What do they have over there, a theft problem?'

'Yeah, construction supplies mostly. This Paltz guy's van isn't marked so I thought I'd check it out.'

'Back to square one, huh? Looking for a wheelbarrow thief.'

Karch guessed Iverson was smiling on the other end of the line.

'You got it. But thanks, man. This'll save me some time.'

'Catch you later.'

Karch closed the phone and looked through the fence at the blue van while he tried to think about his next move. The trace coming back to Paltz put a curve on things.

Finally, he opened the phone again and called information and got the general number for Hooten's Lighting & Supplies. He called and asked for Jersey Paltz, who picked up after a half minute.

'Jerome Paltz?'

There was a pause.

'Yes, who is—'

'Jersey Paltz?'

'Who is this?'

'It's Jack Karch.'

'Oh. What's with the Jerome? Nobody ever—'

'It is your name, right? Jerome Zander Paltz. That's where the Jersey comes from, right?'

'Well, yeah, but nobody ever—'

'I need you to come outside. Right away.'

'What are you talking about?'

'I'm talking about you coming outside right away. I'm waiting for you. Come out through the employee lot. I'm parked on the shoulder. Right on the other side of the fence from your van.'

'Tell me what's going on. I don't—'

'I'll tell you when you get here. Come out now. I can probably still help you but you've got to work with me and come out *right now*.'

Karch closed the phone before Paltz could respond. He then walked over to his car and got in. It was a black Lincoln – a Towncar with the old styling and the big trunk. The windows were tinted an impenetrable black. He liked the car but the tank drained too quickly and he was often mistaken for a limo driver. He adjusted the rearview mirror so he could slouch in the driver's seat and keep an eye on the parking lot entrance thirty yards behind him. He opened his jacket and pulled the Sig Sauer nine out of his holster. He then reached under the seat and up into the springs, feeling around until his fingers closed on the silencer he had taped up there. He tore it loose, snapped it on to the end of the Sig and put the weapon down at his side between his seat and the car door.

After five minutes of waiting Karch saw Jersey Paltz enter the mirror's field of view and start heading toward the Lincoln. He was smoking a fresh cigarette and walked with a deliberate, if not angry, stride. Karch smiled. He was going to have fun with this.

Paltz got into the front passenger seat all blustery and with onion bagel breath.

'This better be good, goddammit. I'm on the fucking clock.'

Karch looked over at him and waited for eye contact before responding.

'I hope so.'

That was all he said. Paltz waited a few moments and then erupted.

'Well, what the fuck do you want?'

'I don't know. What do *you* want? You called me.'

'What are you talking about. You just called me and—'

Karch burst out laughing, which shut Paltz up with confusion. He turned the key and started the car. He quickly dropped it into drive and looked over his left shoulder in preparation for pulling out onto the road. He heard the door locks automatically engage upon the transmission being moved into drive.

'Hey, wait a fucking second here,' Paltz protested. 'I'm on the clock, man. We're not going any—'

He tried to open his door but the auto-lock prevented

it. While he started looking around for a button that would disengage it, Karch gunned the engine and pulled out onto the roadway.

'Relax, you can't unlock it while the car's in drive. It's a safety feature. I was thinking, Ted Bundy should've driven a Lincoln.'

'Goddammit,' Paltz said, throwing his hands up in disgust. 'Where are we going?'

'We've got a problem, Jerome,' Karch said calmly.

He turned west on Tropicana. He could see the crests of the mountains rising above the build-up line.

'What are you talking about? We don't have a problem. I haven't talked to you in a year and don't fucking call me that.'

'Jerome Zander Paltz . . . Jerry Z . . . JerZEE. What name do you want on the stone?'

'What stone? Would you just—'

'The stone they put on your fucking grave.'

Paltz was finally silenced. Karch looked over at him and nodded.

'It's that serious, fuckball. They saw your van. Last night. Got it on tape.'

Paltz started shaking his head as if he were trying to shake himself awake from a nightmare.

'I don't know what you're talking about. Where are we going?'

'Some place private. Where we can talk.'

'We're not talking, man. You're talking and I don't know anything about what you're saying.'

'Okay, then, we'll talk when we get there.'

Ten minutes later they were past the industrial warrens and the city sprawl was thinning out as they approached open desert. Karch glanced over at Paltz and saw the man was beginning to get the proper feel for his predicament. They usually did as the desert started closing in. He reached down for the Sig and brought it up and onto his lap, the muzzle pointing at Paltz's torso.

'Ah, shit,' Paltz said when he saw the gun and fully understood his situation. 'That fucking bitch.'

Karch smiled broadly.

'Who is she?'

'Name's Cassie Black,' Paltz said without delay. 'Fuck her, man. I ain't protecting her.'

Karch squinted his eyes as he tried to think. Cassie Black. The name was vaguely familiar but he couldn't place it at the moment.

'She was the one with Max Freeling six years ago.'

Karch looked sharply at Paltz.

'No lie, man. Don't you remember?'

Karch shook his head. It didn't make sense.

'She was a spotter, a lookout, not the one who went inside.'

'Well, I guess Max must've taught her a thing or two.'

'But they nailed her. She went to High D. For killing him.'

'Manslaughter, Karch. She's out now. She said she's been living in California. In L.A.'

Karch thought about this. He checked his watch. It was three hours since he had met Grimaldi in 2014 and he already had a name and a history. He rolled his shoulders, savoring the excitement building in his chest. He then returned his thoughts to the person and problem at hand.

'You know, Jerome, I thought we had a deal. I thought that anytime something came your way that had *anything* to do with the Cleo, you were going to give me the heads up. And you know I check my messages two, three times a day if I'm not in my office. And it's funny, 'cause I didn't get a call from you this week or last week or anytime that I can remember.'

'Look, man, I didn't know it was going to be the Cleo and I couldn't have called anyway. I was fucking *detained*, man.'

'Detained? In what way were you detained?'

'Tied up in the back of the van.'

Paltz spent the next ten minutes anxiously telling Karch his version of the night before. Karch listened silently and kept a mental list of all the incongruities and conflicts in the story.

'I couldn't have called you,' Paltz said in summation. 'I would have and I was planning on it but she had me in the back of the van all night. Look at this, man.'

He turned and leaned across the seat. Karch raised the gun and Paltz held his hands up, palms out. He then pointed to the corners of his mouth, where there were matching cuts that looked fresh and painful.

'That's from the fucking snap cuff she used to gag me. I'm telling you the truth, man.'

'Sit back.'

Paltz moved back to his side. They drove in silence for a minute while Karch thought about Paltz's story.

'You're not telling me everything. Did she know you snitched them off to me last time?'

'Nope. Nobody knew that except you.'

Karch nodded. There had never been any trial so he had never had to tell his story in public. Only to the cops – and one of the leads was Iverson.

'Who was she working with this time?'

'She was by herself. She just showed up at the counter yesterday and it went from there. I never saw anybody else.'

Still, Paltz's story didn't make complete sense.

'You're not telling me everything. You did something to her. You try to rip her off?'

Paltz didn't say anything and Karch took that as confirmation.

'You did. You saw she was alone and you tried to hijack her. Only she was ready for it and got the drop on *you*. And that's why she couldn't cut you loose until she finished the job.'

'All right, so I did. So fucking what?'

Karch didn't answer. They were well out from the city now. Karch liked it out here, especially in the spring before it got too hot.

'What was she doing in L.A.?' he asked.

'Didn't say and I didn't ask. Look, where are we going? I told you everything I know.'

Karch didn't answer.

'Look, Karch, I know what you're doing. You think I walked out of there without telling anybody exactly who I was going to see out in the lot?'

Karch glanced over at him, a bemused look on his face.

'Yeah, Jersey, that's exactly what I think you did.'

It was hardly a bluff worth calling. Karch knew that the relationship he and Paltz had shared over time dictated that Paltz would tell his fellow countermen that he was stepping out for a smoke, nothing more.

He turned the big Lincoln left on an unmarked road he knew was called Saddle Ranch Road on the county plat books. It was part of a subdivision that had been platted and surveyed three decades before. A few roads had been put in but the plan went bust and no houses were ever built. The city, spreading as quickly as it was, was still a decade or so away from catching up. Then the houses would come. Karch hoped he wouldn't be around for that.

He stopped the car in front of an old and abandoned sales office. The windows and door were long since gone. Bullet holes and graffiti marked every wall inside and out and the floor inside was covered with broken glass and beer cans. The morning sun caught on a silvery spider web that hung in the open doorway. Karch looked past the structure to the Joshua tree growing about ten yards behind it. He had planted it many years before to simply mark a spot. He was always surprised to see how full it had grown in such a desolate place.

He killed the engine and looked at Paltz. The blood seemed to have drained from his passenger's face.

'Look, man, now I've told you everything I fucking know about the bitch and what happened. There's no need for—'

'Get out.'

'What, here?'

'Yeah, out.'

He held the Sig up as a reminder and Paltz tried to open the door. It was still locked. Karch looked on with amusement as his passenger's hands scrabbled over the door, looking for the unlock button. He finally found it and opened the door. He got out of the car and Karch followed him out from his side.

Karch came around the front of the car toward Paltz. He held the Sig at his side.

'What are you going to do?' Paltz asked, holding his hands up in surrender.

Karch ignored the question and looked about their surroundings.

'This place . . . I've been coming out here for years. Since I was a kid. My father used to drive out here at night so we could see the stars. In the winter we'd sit on the hood of the Dodge and the heat from the engine would keep us warm.'

He turned and looked back in the direction of the city.

'Man, at night he could look back at the Strip and pick out the casinos just based on the color and glow of the neon. The Sands, the DI, the Stardust ... I loved this place then. Now it's just ... bullshit. Amusement parks and bullshit. No class anymore. Sure, the bent nose bunch ran the place back then but it had class. Now it's just ...'

He didn't finish. He looked at Paltz as though he had just noticed him for the first time.

'How much did she pay you?'

'Nothing.'

Karch started to advance on him and Paltz blurted out a new response.

'Eight grand. That's it. But that was for the equipment. She didn't cut me in on anything. She just gave me the eight and cut me loose.'

It occurred to Karch that it was odd that Cassie Black had let Paltz go – and had even paid him – after she had not let Hidalgo live. It was a pattern conflict that he would have to think about. Something had happened in that hotel room and there was probably only one person who could tell him what it was.

'Where's the eight grand?'

'In a strongbox in my house. Let's go. I'll show you. I'll give it to you.'

Karch smiled without humor.

'She tell you about the job when she cut you loose?'

'She didn't say jack to me. She just cut me loose and got out of the van. I found the eight grand on the front seat with the keys.'

'What about the briefcase?'

'What briefcase?'

Karch paused for a moment and decided to let it go. He doubted she would have shared knowledge of the briefcase with Paltz. She had probably recognized the case as being electronically trapped and hadn't even opened it at that point anyway.

Karch concluded he had all he was going to get from Paltz – except maybe the eight thousand in his house.

'Come over here,' he said, pointing to the hood of the Lincoln. 'Put your wallet down on the hood. And your keys.'

Paltz did as instructed, standing at the front of the car while Karch stood to the side by the left fender.

'You people stole from the wrong people. And she shot the wrong man.'

Paltz dropped his mouth open but then quickly recovered.

'I don't know what the fuck you're – I didn't steal anything. I—'

'You helped and that makes you just as guilty. You understand that?'

Paltz closed his eyes and when he spoke his voice was a desperate whine.

'I'm sorry. I didn't know. Please, I need a break here.'

Karch looked past him at the surrounding scrub land. His eyes lingered again on the Joshua tree and then moved on. The desert was truly beautiful in its desolation.

'You know why I come out here?'

'Yes.'

Karch almost laughed.

'No, I mean to this place. This specific spot.'

'No.'

'Because thirty years ago when they charted this place and started selling lots to the suckers they had the whole place graded so it would look like it was ready to go, that they'd start building your house as soon as they got your money. It was part of the scam and it worked real well.'

Paltz nodded as though he found the story interesting.

'My old man bought a lot . . .'

'That's why you come out, huh?'

Paltz's conversational tone was forced and desperate. Karch ignored the question.

'Thirty years is a long time. The ground's pretty hard again but you go anywhere else out here and start digging and you got about a foot of top sand and then after that it's like digging through solid rock. People think it's like digging at the beach. But it isn't close. The earth below the top sand hasn't been touched in a couple million years. The fucking shovel bounces off it.'

He looked at Paltz.

'So I like it here. I mean, don't get me wrong, it's still hard work but you got about three feet of earth you can deal with. That's all you really need.'

Karch offered a knowing smile. Paltz suddenly took off as Karch knew he probably would. He ran around the sales office and then past the Joshua tree, attempting to use them as a blind. This also was not new to Karch. He stepped away from the Lincoln and calmly walked out to the left of the office to improve his angle. As he moved he unsnapped the silencer from the Sig because it was no longer needed and would affect his accuracy. He trained on the range with the gun without the silencer.

Paltz was about thirty yards away, moving right to left, his feet kicking up little clouds of sand and dust as he desperately ran in a zig-zag pattern. Karch dropped the silencer into his coat pocket and stopped. He spread his feet, raised the Sig in a standard two-handed range grip and traced Paltz's movement. He aimed carefully and fired once, leading the target by about two feet. He lowered the weapon and watched as Paltz's arms started to windmill and he went down face first into the sand. Karch knew he had hit him in the back, maybe even the spine. He waited for movement and after a few moments he saw Paltz kicking in the sand and rolling over. But it was clear he wasn't getting up.

Karch looked around for the ejected shell and found it in the sand. It was still hot to the touch when he picked it up and put it in his pocket. He went back to the Lincoln and used the key remote to pop the trunk. He took his jacket off and folded it over the bumper, then reached in for his jumpsuit. He stepped into the legs and worked his arms into the sleeves and then pulled the zipper up to his neck. The jumpsuit was baggy and black, chosen for night work.

He then reached in for his shovel and headed over to the spot where Paltz had fallen. There was a bloom of maroon blood at the center of Paltz's back. His face was caked with sand and dirt. Blood was on his lips and teeth. It meant the bullet had ripped through a lung. He was breathing quickly and hoarsely. He wasn't trying to speak.

'All right, that's enough,' Karch said.

He leaned down and tucked the muzzle of the Sig under Paltz's left ear. With his other hand he held the shovel by its neck and positioned the blade so that it would block the blow-back of blood. He fired one shot into Paltz's brain and watched him go still. The shell ejected from the Sig clanked off the shovel and fell into the sand. Karch picked it up and put it in his pocket.

Karch opened the front of the jumpsuit, put the Sig back into his holster and looked up at the sky. He didn't like doing this during the day. It wasn't just being in a black jumpsuit under the desert sun. Sometimes when things backed up at McCarran the airliners were put into low holding patterns out this way.

He started digging anyway, hoping that wouldn't happen and wondering if this would be the time of coincidence, when his spade would strike bone already in the ground.

24

Karch stood in front of the practice mirror adjusting the tie on his fresh suit. It was a Hollyvogue that had belonged to his father, with Art Deco spirals on it. He was wearing it with the two-tone gabardine Hollywood jacket and pleated pants he had picked up at Valentino's in downtown.

His pager sounded and he picked it up off the bureau. He recognized the call-back number as Vincent Grimaldi's. He deleted it, hooked the pager on his belt and finished adjusting his tie. He wasn't going to call Grimaldi back. He planned to drop by in person to inform him of the progress he had made.

When he was done with the tie he went back to the bureau for his guns. He holstered the Sig and snapped the safety strap over it. He then picked up the little .25 popper. It was a Beretta he could fit in his palm. He turned back to the mirror and held his hands loosely at his sides, the .25 hidden in his right hand. He made a few moves and gestures, always sure to keep the pistol hidden from view. David's right hand, he thought. David's right hand.

He then went on to practice the finish, moving his apparently empty hands as if in conversation and then suddenly producing the gun pointed right at himself in the mirror. When he had practiced this enough he put the little gun back into the black silk magician's pocket that he'd had a downtown tailor sew onto the inside rear belt line of his pants – every pair of pants he owned. He then held his hands palms out to the mirror and then brought them together as if in prayer. He bowed his head and backed away from the mirror, end of show.

On his way to the garage Karch stopped in the kitchen and took a mason jar out of one of the cabinets. He took the top off and dropped the two bullet shells from the desert into it with the others. He then held the jar up and looked at it. It was almost half full of shells. He shook the jar and listened to the shells rattle inside. He then put it back in the cabinet and took out a box of Honeycombs cereal. He was famished. He hadn't eaten all day and the physical exertion in the desert had sapped his strength. He started eating the cereal right out of the box, handfuls at a time, careful not to get any crumbs on his clothes.

He stepped into the garage, which had been illegally converted into an office, and sat down behind his desk. He didn't need an office in a commercial building like most private investigators. Most of his work – on the legitimate side – came in from out of state on the phone. His specialty was missing persons cases. He paid the two detectives who ran Metro's missing persons unit five hundred dollars a month to refer clients to him. As a matter of policy, Metro could not act on a routine report of a missing adult until forty-eight hours had elapsed since the time of the report. This practice had originated because most missing people were missing on purpose and often turned up on their own a day or so after supposedly disappearing. In Las Vegas this was most often the case. People came on vacation or for conventions and cut loose in a city designed to knock down inhibitions. They shacked up with strippers and hookers, they lost their money and were too embarrassed to go home, they won lots of money and didn't want to go home. There were endless reasons and that was why the police had a wait-and-see attitude.

However, the forty-eight-hour policy and the reasons behind it did not placate the concerned and sometimes hysterical loved ones of the supposedly missing. That was where Karch and a legion of other private investigators came in. By paying off the cops in the MPU, Karch made sure his name and number were often suggested to people who reported missing persons and didn't want to wait the required forty-eight hours before a search was begun.

The five hundred Karch deposited each month into a bank account the two cops had access to was a bargain. He drew as many as a dozen calls a month on missing persons cases. He charged four hundred dollars a day plus expenses, with a two-day minimum. He often located the supposedly missing person inside an hour with a simple credit card trace but he never told the clients that. He just had them wire payment to his bank account before he revealed their loved one's location. To Karch it was all another form of sleight of hand. Keep things in motion with misdirection. Never reveal what is in your palm.

His office was a shrine to a Las Vegas long gone by. The walls were a collage of photographs of entertainers from the fifties and sixties. There were numerous shots of Frank and Dean and Sammy, some individual and some as a group. There were photos of dancers and framed fight cards.

There were postcards depicting casino resorts that no longer existed. There was a framed collection of gambling chips – one from every casino that opened its doors in the fifties. There was a large blowup photo of the Sands crumbling to the ground after being dynamited to make way for the new era of Las Vegas. Many of the photos were autographed and inscribed, but not to Jack Karch. They were inscribed to 'The Amazing Karch!' – his father.

At center on the wall Karch faced while seated at his desk was the largest frame on any of the walls. It was a blowup photo of the huge neon-gilded headliner sign that had stood outside the Sands. It said

Now Appearing
FRANK SINATRA
JOEY BISHOP
THE AMAZING KARCH!

Karch looked at the photo across from him for a long moment before getting down to work. He had been nine years old when he saw his father's name on the big sign. His father took him with him one night to watch the show from the side of the stage. He was standing there watching his father perform an illusion called The Art of the Cape when he was tapped on the shoulder and looked up to see Frank Sinatra. The man who was the living embodiment of Las Vegas faked a punch off his chin and asked with a smile if he had an exclamation point at the end of his name, too. It was the most indelible memory of his childhood. That and what happened to his father a few years later at Circus, Circus.

Karch looked away from the photo and checked the message machine on the desk. He had three waiting messages. He hit the playback button and picked up a pencil, ready to take notes. The first message was from a woman named Marion Rutter from Atlanta who wanted to hire Karch to look for her husband, Clyde, who hadn't come home from a kitchenware convention in Las Vegas. She was very worried and wanted someone to start looking for Clyde right away. Karch wrote down her name and number but wouldn't be calling back because for the moment he was booked.

The next two messages were both from Vincent Grimaldi. He sounded annoyed. He demanded that Karch check in with him right away.

Karch erased the messages and leaned back in his leather padded desk chair. He grabbed another handful of cereal and studied the two stacks of cash on his desk while he ate. He had gone to Jersey Paltz's apartment after the desert and used the dead man's keys to go in, open the strongbox he found in a closet and take the money. One stack was $8,000 in one-hundred-dollar bills. The other stack was $4,480 in twenties. Karch figured the $8,000 belonged to Grimaldi. Minus the $550 Karch had accumulated so far in expenses – $500 to Cannon for the Flamingo video trail and $50 to Iverson for the plate run. Make it an even $600 to cover gas and other incidentals, he decided. The other stack Karch was going to keep free and clear. It had not been part of the caper at the Cleo. It had apparently been Paltz's own savings.

He put what was his into one of the desk drawers, which he then locked with a key. He took out a preprinted and generic invoice form and wrote out a receipt for the $7,400 he would be returning to Grimaldi. He did not put his name anywhere on the form. When he was finished he folded the money inside the receipt and put it in an envelope he then slid into the inside pocket of his coat.

He sat motionless at the desk for a few moments wondering if he should have deducted more money to cover the trip he knew he would be making to Los Angeles. He finally decided against it and got up and came around the desk to the row of file cabinets beneath the blowup photo of the Sands going down. He unlocked a drawer with a key, looked through the files until he found the one he wanted and then went back to the desk with it.

The file was labeled FREELING, MAX. Karch opened it on the desk and spread the contents out. There were several police reports and handwritten pages of notes. There was also a packet of carefully folded and yellowed newspaper clippings. He opened these and read the one with the largest headline. It had been on the front page of the *Las Vegas Sun* six and a half years before.

'HIGH-ROLLER ROBBER' PLUNGES TO DEATH

BY DARLENE GUNTER
Sun Staff Writer

A man authorities believe to have been responsible for a string of hotel room burglaries of high rollers at Strip casinos jumped to his death early Wednesday when faced with certain capture in a penthouse suite at the Cleopatra Resort and Casino.

The man's body crashed through the casino's signature atrium ceiling, sending glass showering on players at 4:30 A.M. The body landed on an unused craps table and the incident caused a momentary panic among those in the casino. However, authorities said no one was hurt in the incident other than the man who fell.

Metro police spokesmen said the suspect, identified as 34-year-old Maxwell James Freeling of Las Vegas, fell twenty floors after crashing through the window of a penthouse suite when he was confronted by a Cleopatra security agent who had set up a sting operation to nab him.

It was unclear late Wednesday why Metro police were not involved in the sting operation. Also unclear was why Freeling chose to jump through the window in a fatal effort to avoid capture.

Vincent Grimaldi, the casino's chief of security, was close-lipped about the incident but expressed relief that it occurred during a time when the casino was at its least crowded.

'We were just lucky it happened when it happened,' Grimaldi said. 'There weren't many people in the casino at the time. If it had happened during a high-occupancy period, who knows what could have resulted.'

Grimaldi said the casino would stay open while repairs were made to the atrium ceiling. He said a small portion of the playing area would have to be roped off during the repairs.

After Freeling's death a 26-year-old woman was taken into custody at the hotel and turned over to police officers. She was arrested when she ran to Freeling's body in the casino after his fall. Authorities said that it became obvious by her reactions that she was 'involved' with Freeling in some capacity.

'If she had just split we probably wouldn't have ever known about her,' said Metro detective Stan Knapp. 'But she ran to the guy and gave herself away.'

The woman, whom police declined to identify until charges are filed, was being questioned throughout the day Wednesday at Metro headquarters.

Police said that Freeling is believed to have been the highly skilled thief who struck eleven times in the last seven months at casino hotels on the Strip. In each case, a casino guest was robbed of cash and jewels in his or her hotel room by a thief who entered while they slept.

The thief was dubbed the 'High-Roller Robber' by police because the targets were all 'players' – hotel guests who wagered and won large amounts of cash. The estimated take from the eleven capers was in excess of $300,000, according to police sources.

The thief apparently used several different means of entering the hotel rooms – from air-conditioning vents to gaining room keys from unsuspecting house-keepers and front-desk employees. None of the victims ever saw the thief, who came in after they had gone to sleep. A police source said the thief may have monitored his targets through hidden cameras but would not elaborate.

Karch stopped reading. Because it was the first article on the incident, it had the least information, the writer having woven several paragraphs out of a handful of facts. He went on to the next day's story.

ACCOMPLICE CHARGED IN 'HIGH-ROLLER' DEATH

BY DARLENE GUNTER
Sun Staff Writer

A woman police say was the lookout for the so-called High-Roller Robber was charged Thursday with homicide in his death from a fall from the penthouse of the Cleopatra Resort and Casino.

Cassidy Black, 26, of Las Vegas, was charged under Nevada's felony-homicide law, which holds anyone who takes part in a criminal enterprise responsible for any death that occurs during the commission of the crime.

Although Black was waiting for Max Freeling in the lobby of the Cleopatra when he crashed through a penthouse window twenty stories above, she is still legally responsible for his death, said Clark County District Attorney John Cavallito.

Cavallito said Black, who was also charged with burglary and criminal conspiracy, could face 15 years to life in prison if convicted of the charges. She was being held without bail at the county jail.

'She was just as much a part of this incident and this crime spree as Freeling was,' Cavallito said at a press conference. 'She was a co-conspirator and deserves to be and will be hit with the full weight of the law.'

Freeling's death was ruled an accident and not suicide. He reportedly crashed through one of the windows of the penthouse suite in an effort to avoid capture.

More details on the dramatic events of early Wednesday morning were revealed by Cavallito and police investigators on Thursday.

The so-called High-Roller Robber had struck at Strip resorts eleven times in seven months, prompting the Las Vegas Casino Association to put up a $50,000 reward for the capture and conviction of a suspect.

Police said the thief had allegedly been targeting high rollers who took their winnings in cash with them to their rooms at the end of the day.

On Tuesday a private investigator hoping to claim the reward money contacted officials at the Cleopatra and told them he believed the High-Roller Robber was currently targeting a guest in the hotel and casino.

The investigator, Jack Karch, then agreed to serve as a decoy. When the target gambler, whose name was not released, retired for the evening, a switch was made and it was Karch – disguised as the gambler – who went to the penthouse suite.

Two hours after Karch turned out the lights in the suite and feigned sleep, Freeling entered the room through an air vent he had accessed through the ceiling of the penthouse housekeeping station. As Freeling entered the suite's bedroom he was surprised by Karch, who held him at gunpoint and used a two-way radio to call for help from hotel security agents waiting nearby.

'Before those agents could get to the room, Mr Freeling inexplicably made a run for the window,' Cavallito said. 'He threw his body into it and crashed through and fell.'

Cavallito said there was a small ledge below the window and Freeling may have believed that he could escape on it by moving along the facing of the building to a nearby cable used to lower a window-washing platform down the side of the building.

However, the momentum of Freeling's body going through the glass carried him past the narrow ledge and down. He crashed through the casino's signature atrium window, creating a panic among the few gamblers in the casino at the time. No one else was hurt.

Following Thursday's press conference Cavallito answered few questions, citing the ongoing investigation and prosecution of Black. He refused to reveal how it was that Karch, the private investigator, learned that Freeling was targeting a gambler at the Cleopatra.

Efforts to contact Karch for comment were unsuccessful and messages left on his office answering machine were not returned. As a young child Karch performed on occasion with his father, the now deceased magician known as 'The Amazing Karch!' who was a mainstay at Strip casinos and hotels from the '50s to the early '70s.

The younger Karch was called 'Jack of Spades'

because of an illusion in which his father placed him in a locked mail sack in a locked crate and he would disappear and be replaced by a playing card – the Jack of spades.

While Cavallito said Karch has been cleared of any wrongdoing in the death of Freeling, the district attorney did criticize the decision of Karch and Cleopatra officials to set up the sting operation without police involvement.

'We certainly wish that they had contacted the Metro Police Department before going ahead with this,' Cavallito said. 'Maybe then this whole incident could have been avoided.'

Vincent Grimaldi, chief of security at the Cleopatra, declined to comment on Cavallito's criticism.

A spokesman for the Casino Association declined to say whether Karch could claim the reward in light of the death of the suspected thief and arrest of his accomplice.

More details about Freeling were emerging yesterday as well. Authorities said the suspect had twice before been convicted of burglary and had previously spent a total of four years in state prisons. Freeling was said to have grown up in Las Vegas and, like Karch, was the son of a figure of note. Freeling's father was Carson Freeling, who was convicted in 1963 of taking part in a daring armed robbery of the Royale Casino, a caper which many locals believe was inspired by the film *Ocean's Eleven*, starring Frank Sinatra and other members of the so-called Rat Pack.

Maxwell Freeling was three years old at the time of his father's arrest. Carson Freeling died in prison in 1981.

Karch studied the photo that accompanied the story. It

was a mug shot of Cassidy Black taken on the day of her arrest. Her long blond hair was messy and her eyes looked red and sore from crying. He remembered that she had refused to say one word to the Metro cops, even through twelve hours of interrogation. She had stood up and Karch admired that.

During the investigation of the Freeling incident, Karch had never met her or even been in the same room with her. It was impossible to confirm that the woman in the photograph was the one he had watched on surveillance videos at the Cleo and the Flamingo but in his gut he knew it was.

He scanned through the remaining few clips until he got to the last story. This one had another photo of Cassidy Black running alongside the story. It showed her in a jailhouse jumpsuit and shackles being led from a courtroom by two bailiffs. There was something about the angle of her jaw and the focus of her eyes upward that he liked. It showed that she still carried her dignity, despite the cuffs and the jumpsuit and the situation she was in.

His eyes moved over to the story and he read it. It was the last story in the saga, the cleanup. It was short and had been buried inside the *Sun*.

HIGH-ROLLER ROBBER
BLACK ENTERS PLEA, GETS PRISON
BY DARLENE GUNTER
Sun Staff Writer

Cassidy Black, one of the so-called High-Roller Robbers, pleaded guilty Monday to charges relating to the crime spree that included the dramatic death of her partner two months ago. She was immediately sentenced to state prison.

In a plea agreement negotiated with the Clark

County District Attorney's office, the 26-year-old one-time blackjack dealer pleaded guilty to one count of manslaughter and one count of conspiracy to commit burglary. She was sentenced by Circuit Court judge Barbara Kaylor to serve five to fifteen years in prison.

Black, dressed in a yellow jumpsuit, said little during the courtroom hearing. She spoke the word 'guilty' after each charge was read by Kaylor and then told the judge she fully understood the ramifications of her plea.

Black's attorney, Jack Miller, said the agreement was the best Black could do, considering the overwhelming evidence of her involvement with Maxwell James Freeling in a seven-month crime spree that ended with her arrest and Freeling's plunge from a penthouse window at the Cleopatra Resort and Casino.

'This agreement still leaves her a chance to start over,' Miller said. 'If she keeps her nose clean in prison she can be out in five, six, seven years. She'll still be in her early thirties and that leaves her a lot of time to start over and be productive in society.'

Authorities said the evidence mounted against Black indicated she was Freeling's spotter and lookout on capers in which the hotel suites of high-rolling gamblers were burglarized while they slept.

Karch dropped the clip onto the others without reading it to the end. Cassidy Black's guilty plea had precluded a trial and allowed him to avoid having to testify about what happened in that suite with Freeling. Her conviction also allowed him to claim the reward, though he'd had to get a lawyer to sue the Casino Association for it. After attorney fees and taxes he had walked away with $26,000 in reward money and Grimaldi's leash around his neck. He had allowed himself to become Grimaldi's go-to guy for all the misdeeds and dirty work, the runs out to the desert with the full trunk.

All that is going to change, Karch said to himself. *Soon. Soon.*

Karch carefully refolded the newspaper clippings and closed the file. He then closed the box of cereal and took it back to the kitchen on his way to the front door.

At the front door he picked up the suit bag he had packed earlier and chose a porkpie hat from the rack. His traveling hat. He looked at the inside lining before putting it on. It was chocolate brown, a Mallory, the inside label said, *For Youthful Smartness*. He fitted it on and geeked the brim flat like an old jazz musician would, the way he had once seen Joe Louis wear a porkpie as the greeter at the front door of Caesar's. He stepped out the door into the brilliant white sunlight.

25

As Karch walked through the casino at the Cleo he felt eyes upon him and looked up under the brim of his hat to see Vincent Grimaldi staring back at him from the crow's nest. Grimaldi did not have to gesture for Karch to know he was angry and waiting. Karch looked away and made his way to the elevators, a little more speed in his step.

When he was ushered into Grimaldi's office two minutes later, Karch was met by a large man he knew was Grimaldi's chief in-house thug. Karch couldn't recall his name but remembered it ended in a vowel. It was Rocco or Franco or something close.

'He wants to see me,' Karch said.

'Yes, we've been reaching out to you all morning.'

Karch noted the use of the plural and the condescending smirk on the other man's face as he gestured toward the door that opened onto the walkway to the crow's nest.

As Karch made his way around Grimaldi's desk he saw that it was spread with tools and equipment: an electric drill, a Polaroid camera, a large flashlight and a small tub of earthquake wax. He picked up the drill and saw that it had been wrapped in black rubber sewn together with fishing line.

'We found all of this in the air vent in room—'

'Two-thousand fifteen,' Karch said. 'I know. I told him it would be there.'

He put the drill down and returned the condescending smirk to the man. He then stepped through the door to the walkway. He closed the door behind him, his eyes holding the other man's through the glass.

Grimaldi didn't turn to Karch as he came out. He stood with his hands gripping the railing and stared out at the sea of gamblers below. Karch had never been in the crow's nest before. He looked around and down upon the casino floor with a sense of awe and reverence. He glanced back and saw Grimaldi's thug standing at the glass door watching him. He turned and stepped right next to Grimaldi.

'Vincent.'

'Whereya been, Jack? I've been calling.'

'Sorry, Vincent, I had my hands full.'

'What, changing your suit? Who you supposed to be, Bugsy Siegel or Art Pepper?'

'I'm here, Vincent. What do you want?'

Grimaldi looked at him now for the first time with an expression of warning.

'You know, I wonder if I was right about putting you on lead on this. My ass is on the line and I have no idea what you're doing besides changing clothes and putting on hats. Maybe I should hand this off to Romero. I know he's good to go on it.'

Karch stayed cool. He had a pretty good idea that Grimaldi was only venting.

'If that's what you want, Vincent. But I thought you wanted the money back.'

'I *DO*, goddammit!'

A few gamblers at a craps table below glanced up at Grimaldi's outburst. They were playing at the table where Max Freeling had landed six years before.

Karch decided to stop playing games with Grimaldi.

'Look, Vincent, I've been working the problem, okay? I've made progress. I have the woman's name and I know where she is. I'd already be on my way if you hadn't been calling and paging me.'

Grimaldi turned to him, the excitement clearly showing on his face.

'You've got a name?'

'Yes.' Karch nodded down toward the craps table below. 'You remember the thing with Max Freeling, right? The high diver?'

'Of course.'

'Well, remember the girl they picked up? His lookout?'

'Yeah. She went away, got fifteen, I think.'

'Five to fifteen, Vincent. Must have been a good girl. Because she did the five and got out. It was *her* last night.'

'Bullshit. She was a lookout. You said yourself this morning that this was a pro, somebody who knew exactly what the fuck she was doing.'

'I know. And it's her. Believe me, it's her.'

'Tell me how you know this.'

Karch spent the next ten minutes detailing his tracing of Jersey Paltz and his questioning of the electronics dealer.

'Motherfucker,' Grimaldi said of Paltz. 'I hope you took care of him.'

'Don't worry about him.'

Grimaldi's sharp, dark face cracked into a smile, revealing beautifully white teeth.

'They don't call you Jack of Spades for nothing. The man with a shovel in the trunk.'

Karch let it go. He remembered something and tapped his jacket below the breast pocket.

'I've got the eight K she paid him for the equipment. Minus my expenses. I'll leave it on the desk.'

'That's good, Jack. And guess what, I've got something for you. We've got a name, too.'

Karch looked at him.

'Martin was the insider?'

Grimaldi nodded.

'He acted dumb but we eventually got it out of him. He gave us everything but the girl's name because he didn't know it. So with what you got we have the whole picture.'

'Which is what?'

'The thing was set up by a guy in L.A. named Leo Renfro. He connected with Martin and then he procured the girl for the job. He's the middle man on this thing.'

'How'd he know Martin?'

'He didn't. He was put in touch with Martin.'

'How?'

'That's where it gets dicey. Turns out Martin kept an eye out for Chicago. When he was at the Nugget a few years back he was Joey Marks's ear. When Marks and his crew got taken down by the bureau, things scattered and Martin left the Nugget and started here with a new slate. Of course, I didn't know any of this history when I hired him. Anyway, like I said, he didn't know this guy Renfro. But when he sees Hidalgo raking in the cash at the baccarat table and then going up to his room every night with that handcuff case, he figured there was a nice score to be made. He tipped Chicago and they put him together with this Leo Renfro to set it up.'

Karch was barely listening. The mention of Chicago, of the so-called Outfit's involvement in the caper, was causing blood to pound in his ears. His hands tightened into fists.

'Hey, Jack, you still with me?'

Karch nodded.

'I'm here.'

'Look, I know with what happened with your father and all ... I just wanted you to see all the cards, you know?'

'Thank you, Vincent. You sure Martin was only working off what he saw the mark win? He didn't know about the two and a half?'

Grimaldi stepped a little closer to him. There was a humorless smile on his face.

'Let's just say that we questioned him closely and extensively on that point. And the answer is he didn't know. Chicago didn't know. It was just a casino score. It was like you said, Jack. I made a mistake giving the guy a draw. He turned it into more money and it drew sharks. Martin and his Chicago people. Everybody involved in this thing works for Chicago.'

Karch just nodded and kept his lips tightly together.

'So if the girl's from L.A. now and Renfro's from L.A., then that's where the money is. You have to get over there and get it before they turn it over to Chicago.'

'They probably already have it by now, Vincent.'

'Maybe, maybe not. She killed the guy in his bed. Maybe they want to check the heat on it before they make any further moves. We have to get over there and be sure. Besides, even if they passed the money on, I want these people dealt with. Due diligence. You know the score.'

Grimaldi looked at his watch.

'But I think we still have a shot at the money. Six hours into this and we've already got the whole story. You get over there and get the money. You have a line on the girl?'

'Not yet. If she came in from L.A. that means she probably jumped parole. I could check to make sure but that would leave an official trail. I don't think you want that yet, Vincent.'

'I don't. So hold that as a last resort. Maybe you should start with Renfro, go from there.'

Karch nodded.

'You have an address for him?'

Grimaldi shook his head.

'We got a cell phone number. The name and number was all Martin had. You'll have to trace it from there. Romero has it on a piece of paper in the office. Also written on there is the name of a guy I know over there in L.A. You need help with anything – tracing the number, anything – you call him and bring him in. There will be no official record with him. He's good people and has a lot of connections he'd be happy to share.'

'All right, Vincent.'

'Now you go grab a plane and you'll be on the ground by three at the latest and—'

'I'm not flying, Vincent. I never fly.'

'Jack, time is of the essence here.'

'Then have your guy in L.A. handle it. I'm driving. I'll be there before five.'

'All right, fine. You drive. Maybe you could make another stop in the desert for me. You know, along the way.'

Karch just looked at him.

'I've still got fat boy and Martin in a laundry basket on the loading dock.'

'It's just sitting down there?'

'I've got Longo down there watching it. Nobody'll get near it.'

Karch shook his head.

'Then have Long-*O* and Romer-*O* take care of it. I'm out of here, Vincent.'

Grimaldi pointed a finger at him.

'All right, Jack, but I want to be kept informed this time. You understand me?'

'Perfectly.'

'Then go get the money, Jack.'

Before heading in from the crow's nest Karch took one last look across the casino. He liked the view from up here. He nodded to himself and walked to the glass door.

26

Cassie Black punched the buzzer on Leo Renfro's door at noon and almost doubled over when the simple action sent a charge of pain up through her sore arm. When Leo opened the door she pushed in past him with the briefcase. He checked the street and then turned back to her as he closed the door. He was holding a gun down at his side. She spoke before he could say a word, and before she saw the gun.

'We've got a big problem, Leo. This thing was – why do you have that out?'

'Not here. Don't talk at the front door. Come back to the office.'

'What, more feng shui bullshit?'

'No, John Gotti. Who the fuck cares? Come on.'

He led her through the house once more to the rear office. He was wearing a white bathrobe and his hair was wet. Cassie assumed he had been swimming laps – which was late for him, unless he needed to do it to relieve stress.

They stepped into the office and Cassie lifted the case with her right arm and banged it down on top of the desk.

'Jesus Christ! Take it easy, would you? I've been going nuts here. Where the fuck you been?'

'Flat on my ass on the living room floor.'

She pointed to the briefcase.

'The fucking thing tried to electrocute me.'

'What?'

'Built-in stun gun. I tried to open it and it was like getting hit by a bolt of lightning. It knocked me out cold, Leo. Three hours. Look at this.'

She leaned forward and used both hands to spread the hair on the top of her scalp apart. There was a surface cut and a swollen bump that looked painful.

'I hit the corner of the table when I went down. I think that knocked me out more than the bolt.'

Leo's look of anger over her lack of communication was immediately replaced with a sincere look of surprise and concern.

'Jesus, you sure you're all right? You better get that checked.'

'I feel like I have that baseball guy Nolan O'Brien's arm.'

'Ryan.'

'Whatever. It feels like it's dead. My elbow joint hurts worse than my head.'

'You've been lying on the floor of your house all this time?'

'Just about. I got blood on my carpet.'

'Jesus. I thought you were dead. I've been going nuts here. I called Vegas and you know what I was told? My guy said something's screwy over there.'

'What are you talking about?'

'The guy disappeared. The mark. It's like he was never there. He's not in the room and his name's off the computer. No record of him at all.'

'Yeah? Well, that's not the worst of it. Take a look.'

She reached for the briefcase's latches but Leo quickly reached for her arms to stop her.

'No, no, don't!'

She shrugged him off.

'It's okay, Leo. I got some heavy-duty rubber gloves – like the ones the guys who work on the power lines use. It took me almost an hour to work the picks with the gloves but then I got it open. I disconnected the battery. The case is safe but not what's in it. Look at this.'

She unlatched the case and opened it. It was lined side to side with stacks of hundred-dollar bills bundled in cellophane and marked with a '50' in thick black ink. She watched as Leo's mouth dropped open and then a look of dismay crossed his face. They both knew that seeing a case full of cash of high denomination was not immediate cause for celebration. It was not the pot of gold at the end of every thief's rainbow. Rather, it was cause for concern and suspicion. Like a trial attorney who never asks a question of a witness that he doesn't already know the answer to, professional thieves never steal blind, taking something they do not know the consequences for stealing. Legal consequences are not the issue. The concern is over consequences of a more serious kind.

It was a good ten seconds before Leo managed to speak.

'Fuck . . .'

'Yeah . . .'

'Fuck . . .'

'I know . . .'

'You count this?'

Cassie nodded.

'I counted the bricks. There are fifty of them. If that fifty on each one means what it looks like it means, then you're looking at two and a half million in cash. He didn't win this money, Leo. He *came* to Vegas with it.'

'Hold on, hold on a minute. Let's think about this for a minute.'

Cassie started unconsciously massaging her sore elbow.

'What is there to think about? They don't pay you at the cashier's cage in fifty-thousand-dollar bricks wrapped in plastic. He didn't win this money in Vegas. Period, Leo. He brought it with him. It's a payoff of some kind. Maybe drugs. Maybe something else. But we took it – I took it – before it was delivered. I mean this guy, the mark, he was just an errand boy. He didn't even have a key to the case on him. He was just going to deliver it and probably didn't even know what was in it himself.'

'He didn't have a key?'

'Leo, have you heard anything I've said? I got knocked on my ass trying to open this with picks. Would I do that if I had the guy's key?'

'Sorry, sorry, I forgot, okay?'

'I took the guy's keys. He had a key that opened the cuffs but none to the briefcase.'

Leo dropped into his chair as Cassie put her backpack on the desk and started digging through it. She took out four rubber-banded stacks of hundreds and put them down.

'This is what he won. A hundred and a quarter. And half of the info you got from the spotter or your partners was for shit.'

She snaked her hand back into the bag. She brought out the wallet she had taken off the bed table in room 2014 and tossed it to him.

'Guy's name isn't Hernandez and he isn't from Texas.'

Leo opened the wallet and looked at the Florida driver's license behind the plastic window.

'Manuel Hidalgo,' he said. 'Miami.'

'He's got business cards in there. He's a lawyer for something called the Buena Suerte Group.'

Leo shook his head in the negative but he did it too quickly. More like he was trying to shake the information off than deny knowledge of it. Cassie didn't say anything at first. She put her palms flat on the desk and leaned down, looking at him with a face that said she saw the move and wanted to know what he knew. Leo glanced out at his pool and Cassie followed his eyes. She could see the hose of the automatic vacuum moving slowly on the surface, the vacuum somewhere down below.

He looked back at her.

'I didn't know a fucking thing about this, Cass, I swear.'

'I believe you about the money, Leo. What about Buena Suerte? Tell me what you know.'

'It's big money. Cubans from Miami.'

'Legit money?'

Leo hiked his shoulders in a gesture that suggested the answer could go either way.

'They're trying to buy the Cleo,' he said.

Cassie dropped heavily into the chair opposite Leo.

'It was a payoff on the license. I stole a fucking payoff.'

'Let's just think about this.'

'You keep saying that, Leo.'

She laid her injured arm across her body.

'Well, what else are we going to do? We have to think this out.'

'Who were these people you did this for? You wouldn't tell me before. But you have to tell me now.'

Leo nodded but then stood up. He went to the sliding door and opened it, then moved out by the pool. He stood at the edge and looked down at the vacuum gliding silently along the bottom. Cassie came up behind him. As he spoke he never took his eyes off the water.

'They're from Vegas by way of Chicago.'

'Chicago. You mean the Outfit, Leo?'

Leo didn't answer but in his silence was the answer.

'How the hell did you get involved with the Outfit, Leo? Tell me.'

Leo started walking along the edge of the pool, his hands deep in the pockets of his robe.

'Look, first of all, I'm smart enough to know not to intentionally get involved with the Outfit, okay? Give me a little fucking credit, okay? I didn't have a choice in the matter.'

'Okay, Leo, I understand. Tell me the story.'

'It started about a year ago. I met these guys. I was at Santa Anita and saw Carl Lennertz over there, you remember him, right?'

Cassie nodded. Lennertz was a scout, always had an eye out for what he called a good book – a score. He sold tips to Leo, usually collecting a flat fee or ten percent of the gross taken out of Leo's end. Cassie had met him once or twice with Leo and Max several years before.

'Well, he was with these two guys and he made the introductions. They were just two guys who hung around the track and were looking to back a move here and there. They said they were venture capitalists.'

'And you just took them at their word.'

A truck with a bad muffler system roared by on the nearby freeway and Leo didn't answer the question until the noise had abated.

'I had no reason to doubt them and they were with Carl and he's good people. Besides, at the time things were drying up and I was scratching bottom. I needed setup money and here were these two guys. So I set up a meeting for later and we got together and I asked them to, you know, back me up on a couple things I had on my desk. They said sure, no problem.'

He stepped to the side of the pool where a surface net at the end of a ten-foot pole was hooked to a fence. He took it down and used it to skim a dead hummingbird out of the pool.

'Poor things, I don't think they can see water or

something. They dive right in. This is the third one this week.'

He shook his head.

'Dead hummingbirds are bad luck, you know.'

He flicked the dead bird over the fence into a neighbor's yard. Cassie wondered if maybe the three dead hummingbirds were really just the same one that the neighbor kept throwing back over the fence and into the pool. She didn't say anything. She wanted Leo to get back to the story.

Leo hooked the net back in place on the fence and came back around to Cassie.

'So that's how it started. I took sixty-five bones off them against a hundred when the jobs were paid out. I was thinking six weeks tops. One was diamonds and that's always quick. And the other was a warehouse – Italian furniture. I had somebody lined up in Pennsylvania on that and was probably looking at six weeks tops on the turnaround. My end was going to be about two and I'd owe these guys one. Not bad. Most of the money I needed from them was for the data. The people I was working with had their own equipment.'

He was wandering, telling too many details about the plans and not what happened.

'You can skip all of this, Leo. Just read me the last page.'

'The last page is that both jobs went to shit. The data on the diamonds was bullshit. A rip-off. I paid forty for it and the guy disappeared. And then the furniture turned out to have been made down in Mexicali. It was counterfeit designer stuff and the made-in-Italy tags were as bogus as most of the tits you see in this town. I didn't know it till I got the truck all the way to Philadelphia and my buyer took a look. Shit, what a fucking mess. I just had them abandon the truck on the side of a road in Trenton.'

He paused as if trying to remember some other detail, then waved a hand in a resigned, dismissive gesture.

'And so that was it. I owed these guys a hundred grand and I didn't have it. I explained the situation to them and they were about as sympathetic as a night-court judge to a hooker. But when it was all said and done I thought I had bought some time. Only they just said that and turned right around and sold my fucking paper to another party.'

Cassie nodded. She could finish the story herself now.

'These two new guys come around and say they represent the new holder of the paper now,' Leo said. 'They make it real clear that the new holder is the Outfit without actually having to say it. Know what I mean? They tell me that we have to work out a payment schedule. I ended up paying two grand a week just on the interest. Just to stay afloat. It was killing me. I still owed the hundred but I was never going to get out from under. Never. Until one day they show up with a proposition.'

'What was it?'

'They told me about this job.'

He pointed through the open slider at the briefcase sitting on the desk inside.

'They told me to set it up with their guy in Vegas and that if I did it, then they'd burn my paper and still give me a cut on the caper.'

Leo shook his head. He walked over to the table and chairs near the shallow end and sat down. He reached over to a hand crank on the umbrella pole. He started turning it and the umbrella opened like a flower. Cassie came over and sat down. She cupped her left elbow in her right hand.

'So they obviously knew what was in the case,' she said.

'Maybe.'

'No maybes. They knew. Otherwise, they wouldn't have been so fucking magnanimous with you. When are they coming for it?'

'I don't know. I'm waiting on a call.'

'Did they give you a name?'

'What do you mean?'

'A name, Leo. Whoever bought your paper.'

'Yeah, Turcello. Same name that was on the package at the desk for you. He's supposedly the guy who picked up the pieces after Joey Marks went down.'

Cassie looked away. She didn't know the name Turcello but she knew who Joey Marks had been. He had been the Outfit's brutal point man in Las Vegas – one in a long line of vicious enforcers. His real name was Joseph Marconi but he was universally known as Joey Marks because of the keepsakes he left on those of his victims he allowed to live. Cassie remembered how she and Max had spent a year living in fear of Marks, who wanted a piece of their action. After she was in High Desert she picked up a newspaper one day and read about how Marks had been killed in his limousine during a bizarre shoot-out with the FBI and police in a bank parking lot in Las Vegas. She had celebrated after reading the story – which in prison amounted to sipping a paper cup of applejack she'd bought with a pack of cigarettes.

She didn't know who Marconi's replacement, Turcello, was but she assumed he had to be just as viciously psychopathic as Marks had been in order to be named to the position.

'And now you've got me in the box with you and these people,' Cassie said. 'Thanks, Leo. Thanks for—'

'No, you're wrong. I protected you. They don't even know about you. I took the job and set it up. Like I told you before, nobody knows everybody in the caper. They don't know you and they never will.'

Leo's promise was not reassuring. Cassie could no longer sit down while it seemed her life was passing in front of her. She got up and walked to the pool's edge and looked down into the calm, clear water. Her left arm hung at her side like a dead weight.

'What are we going to do, Leo? If I have this right, the Chicago mob used us to steal a payoff these Cubans from Miami were making to a third party on the buyout of the Cleo. We're sitting in the middle of what's going to be a war. Do you see that? What do we do?'

Leo got up and came to her. He pulled her into a tight hug and spoke calmly.

'Nobody knows about you. I promise you. Nobody knows about you and nobody ever will. You don't have to worry.'

She pulled away from him.

'Of course, I do, Leo. Come back to reality, would you?'

The tone of her voice silenced Leo. He raised and dropped his hands in a gesture of surrender. He started banging a tight fist against his lips. Cassie paced along the side of the pool. After a long minute she spoke again.

'What do you know about Buena Suerte?'

'Like I said, nothing. But I'll make some calls about it.'

After another long silence, Leo shook his shoulders.

'Maybe we just give the money back and say it was a mistake,' he said. 'We find a go-between who will—'

'Then we have Chicago after us, Leo. This Turcello person. Think, would you? We can't do that.'

'I'll tell them that when you went into the room last night the briefcase wasn't there.'

'I'm sure they're going to believe that. Especially, since the mark has suddenly disappeared.'

Leo flopped back into his seat under the umbrella. A defeated look was overtaking his face. There was a long period of silence while neither looked at each other.

'Sometimes you can steal too much,' Cassie said, more to herself than Leo.

'What?'

'Max used to say that sometimes you can steal too much. We just did.'

Leo pondered the statement in silence. Cassie folded her arms across her chest. When she spoke her voice was resolute and strong. She now looked directly at Leo.

'Let's take the money. All of it. We split it and we run, Leo. One point three and change each. It's more than enough. Fuck Chicago and Miami. We take it all and run.'

Leo was shaking his head before she was finished speaking.

'No way.'

'Leo . . .'

'No fucking way. You think you can run from these people? Where are you going to run? Name a place where it's worth living and they can't find you. No place, that's where. They will hunt you down to the end of the fucking earth just to prove the point. Bring your hands back to Chicago or Miami in a shoe box and put 'em on display at the wise guys' Sunday buffet.'

'I'll take my chances. I've got nothing to lose.'

'Well, I *DO!* I'm set up here. I am dug in and the last thing I want is to spend the rest of my life changing my name every month and holding my Glock behind my back every time I open a fucking door.'

Cassie came over to the table and crouched next to

Leo's chair. She held the plastic armrest with both hands and looked up into his eyes but he quickly looked away.

'No, Cass, I can't.'

'Leo, you can take two million and I'll take the rest. It's still more than I'll need. Two days ago I was thinking I'd be lucky to get a couple hundred out of this. You take the two. It's enough for you to –'

He got up and walked away from her. He went back to the edge of the pool. Cassie leaned her forehead against the armrest. She knew she wasn't going to convince him.

'It's not the *money*,' Leo said. 'Aren't you listening to what I'm telling you? It doesn't matter if it's one million or two million. What's the difference if you aren't around to spend it? Let me tell you, there was a guy a few years back. They tracked him all the way to Juneau-fucking-Alaska. Went up there, gutted him like a salmon from the river. I think every couple years they have to make an example. To keep everybody else in line. I don't want to be an example.'

Still crouched like a hiding child, Cassie turned and looked at his back.

'Then what do you want to do? Wait until someone comes *here* and guts you? How is that different from running? At least if we run we have a chance.'

Leo looked down into the pool. The vacuum moved silently along the bottom.

'Fuck . . .' he said.

Something in his tone made Cassie look expectantly at him. She began to think maybe she had convinced him. She waited him out.

'Two days,' he finally said, still looking down into the pool. 'Give me forty-eight hours to see what I can do. I know some people in Miami. Let me make some calls, see what I can find out. And I'll check on things in Vegas and Chicago. Maybe I can talk our way out of this. Yeah, maybe make a deal and even keep a piece of this for ourselves.'

He was nodding to himself, getting himself ready for the biggest negotiation of his life – of their lives. He couldn't see Cassie shaking her head. She didn't believe they had a chance his way. But she stood up and came to his side.

'Leo, you have to understand something. Turcello isn't going to give you a cut of what's in the briefcase. He never was. You call his people and tell him you have it and you'll be saying, "Here I am, guys, come get me." You'll be this year's salmon.'

'No! I tell you I can get us out. I can negotiate with these people. Remember, it's all about money. As long as everybody gets something, we can get out.'

Cassie knew she wasn't going to convince him. She was resigned.

'Okay, Leo, two days. And that's all. After that we cut it up and we go. We take our chances.'

He nodded his agreement.

'Call me tonight. I might know something. Otherwise, do what you do. I can only reach you at the dealership?'

She gave him her cell phone number, telling him not to write it in his book.

'I'm going, Leo. What do we do with the money?'

'The usual. It's still the perfect spot.'

Cassie hesitated. She knew it was best for him to hold the money, but parting with it gave her pause. Then she remembered something that had completely slipped her mind amid the recent developments.

'Hey, did you get my passports?'

'All I can tell you is that I got word they're on their way. I'll check the drop again tonight. If they're not there tonight, they will be tomorrow. Guarantee it.'

'Thanks, Leo.'

Leo nodded. Cassie turned toward the sliding door.

'Wait a minute,' Leo said. 'Let me ask you something, what time was it when you went in the room?'

'What?'

'What time was it when you went in the guy's room last night? You must've looked at your watch.'

She looked at him. She knew what he wanted to know.

'It was five after three.'

'And what, it took five, ten minutes tops to do the job, right?'

'Normally.'

'Normally?'

'He got a phone call, Leo. I was in the closet with the safe. The phone rang and he talked to somebody. I think it was about the payoff. He was going to make it today. Then after he hung up he got up and went into the bathroom.'

'And you snuck out.'

'No. I stayed in the closet.'

'How long?'

'Until he was asleep again. Until I heard him snore. I had to, Leo. It wasn't safe. You weren't there. I couldn't leave until —'

'You went into the void moon, didn't you?'

'It couldn't be helped, Leo, that's what I'm trying to—'

'Oh, Jesus Christ!'

'Leo . . .'

'I told you. I only asked you to do one thing.'

'It couldn't be helped. He got the call – a phone call at three in the morning, Leo. It was just bad luck.'

Leo shook his head as if not listening.

'That's it then,' he said. 'We . . .'

He didn't finish. She closed her eyes.

'I'm sorry, Leo. I really am.'

A buzzing sound near her left ear caught her attention.

She looked around and saw a hummingbird suspended in air, its wings a blur.

It darted to the left and then swooped over to the pool, dropping to just a foot above the surface of the calm water. It seemed to be looking down at its reflection on the surface. It then dropped lower until it hit the surface. Its wings fluttered wildly but they were too heavy now for flight. The bird was trapped in the water.

'See what I'm saying,' Leo said. 'Dumb birds.'

He started around the pool to get to the net so he could try to save the tiny creature's life.

27

Just before getting to Los Angeles, Jack Karch pulled off the 10 Freeway at the Ontario airport exit and followed the signs to the long-term parking lot. He cruised up and down five long lanes of parked cars before he came upon a Towncar that was the same make and model as his, and with California plates. He double-parked behind the car and left the engine running while he got out with the battery-powered drill that was among the tools recovered by Grimaldi's thug from the air vent in room 2015.

The drill worked beautifully. Karch had the plates off the front and back of the Towncar in less than a minute. He shoved them under the front seat of his own car and drove toward the exit. He had been in the parking lot so briefly that the cashier at the pay booth told him he had made it under the ten-minute grace period and didn't have to pay a thing. He asked Karch if he had a spare smoke and Karch was happy to oblige.

He had made good time from Vegas, traveling at a steady 100 mph until he hit traffic close to L.A. The last fifty miles took him a frustrating hour to cover. He decided that people in Los Angeles drove the way people walk through casinos: oblivious to the fact that somebody else might be on the road and need to get somewhere. In downtown he branched off the 10 to the 101 and headed northwest toward the San Fernando Valley. Though it had been at least a couple years since the last time, Karch had been to L.A. plenty times enough to know how to get around. When it got down to specific streets and places, he had a Thomas Brothers map book in his briefcase on the seat next to him. It was a few years old but it would do. He was headed to the Valley because the cell phone number Grimaldi had retrieved from Martin as being the contact number for Leo Renfro had an 818 area code and Karch knew that covered the Valley, the city's northern suburban sprawl. It was his assumption that Leo would be found in the confines of his cell phone's area code.

He got off the freeway at the Ventura Boulevard exit and drove until he saw a gas station with a pay phone. He opened his briefcase on the passenger seat and withdrew the folded piece of Cleopatra Resort stationery with the name *Leo Renfro* and the cell phone number written on it. Below the fold was the name of the contact Grimaldi had in L.A. but Karch had no intention of calling the man. Under no circumstances did he plan to allow a perfect stranger – no matter who vouched for him – to have knowledge of his business and activities. That would just be stupid and he wasn't about to turn stupid. The same reasoning prevented Karch from using his law enforcement contacts to run traces on Leo Renfro and Cassie Black. This job had to be done without leaving a trail.

Surprisingly, the pay phone had an intact phone book. Karch pulled it up and started with the white pages on the unlikely chance that Leo Renfro was actually listed. He wasn't. Karch then turned through the commercial business pages until he came to the advertisements for cell phone service providers. Judging by the size and quality of their advertisements, he made a list of the bigger companies and their service numbers. He then used the edge of the shelf under the phone to crack open a roll of quarters he had bought at the change cage at the Cleo and made his first call.

The call was answered by a machine that offered a variety of pathway selections. Karch chose what he wanted and was transferred to billing inquiries, where he was put on hold for two minutes before a human voice picked up.

'Thank you for calling L.A. Cellular, how can I help you?'

'Yes,' Karch said. 'I've been called out of town indefinitely and I want to cancel service on my cell phone account.'

After listening to a sales pitch for out-of-the-area service, the phone representative got down to business.

'Name?'

'Leo Renfro.'

'Account number?'

'I don't have that handy at—'

'Cell phone number?'

'Oh, okay.'

Karch glanced down at the paper and read off the number Martin had provided during his interrogation by Grimaldi.

'One moment, please.'

'Take your time.'

Karch heard the sound of typing on the other end of the line.

'I'm sorry, sir, I'm not showing an account with that name or—'

Karch hung up and immediately dialed the number of the next company on the list. He repeated the story over and over and finally hit the right company on the seventh call. Renfro had his account with a company called SoCal Cellular. When the service operator pulled up the account information on her computer, Karch immediately went in for the final con.

'I'm going to need you to send the final bill to my new address in Phoenix, if you don't mind.'

'Not at all, sir. Let me first set up the close-out screen.'

'Oh, sorry.'

'No problem. It will just take me a second.'

'Take your time.'

Karch let a few seconds go by and then started in again.

'You know, I just realized I'll be back in L.A. at the end of next week for a few days to clear up some things. I may need the phone then. Maybe I should wait and do this after.'

'It's up to you, sir.'

'Uh ... tell you what, let's wait, then.'

'Okay, sir. Do you want to wait on the address change, too?'

Karch smiled. It always worked best when the victim prompted the con.

'No, let's do – tell you what, maybe I should wait. My mail's being forwarded from my old place anyway. But wait a minute, I forget offhand, which address does the bill go to? My home or office?'

'I don't know, sir. Four thousand Warner Boulevard, number five-twenty. Which is that?'

Karch didn't answer. He was writing the address down on the letterhead.

'Sir?'

'That's the office. So everything is fine. Let's leave it as is and I'll take care of it after next week.'

'Okay. Thank you for calling SoCal Cellular.'

He hung up the phone and went back to the car. He looked up the address in the index of the map book and learned he had been correct. The address was in the 818 area code. But it wasn't Los Angeles. It was Burbank. He started the Lincoln and checked the digital clock on the dash. It was exactly five o'clock. Not bad, he thought. He was getting close.

Fifteen minutes later the Lincoln was at the curb in front of a private mail drop and packaging shop at 4000 Warner Boulevard. He was not too disappointed. It would have been too easy and suspicious if the address he'd conned out of SoCal Cellular had led directly to Leo Renfro's front door.

He checked the business hours marked on the door. The shop closed in forty-five minutes but another sign on the door announced that clients had twenty-four-hour access to their boxes. Karch thought for a while about what to do and decided that Renfro was the type who probably checked his box after hours anyway to avoid becoming familiar to the people who ran the shop. It was in that thought that a plan suddenly sparked in his mind.

Karch entered the shop and saw that it was shaped like an L, with the counter at the end of one branch and the other branch lined with postal boxes. To the left of the door was a counter with a stapler, a tape dispenser and several plastic cups with pens and paper clips and rubber bands in them. Karch saw a man working on something on the floor behind the counter. Above him was a roll-down security fence that allowed for the business side of the shop to be closed and locked while still allowing customers with a key to the front door access to their mailboxes twenty-four hours a day.

Karch glanced to his left and noticed that the postal boxes were the kind with little windows through which holders could just glance in to see if they had mail. He walked into the box alcove and quickly found number

520. He had to bend down to look into it. He could see one envelope lying flat at the bottom of it. He glanced back to the right. There was a mirror positioned in the upper corner over the door that allowed the counterman to see into the mailbox alcove but he was still down behind the counter working on something.

Karch pulled a small penlight from his shirt pocket and turned it on. It lit up the interior of box 520 and he could read the writing on the front of the envelope. It was addressed to Leo Renfro. There was no return address on the upper left corner but there was a set of initials. He leaned closer to the glass to try to read them and realized they were numbers: 773.

Because there was already a piece of mail in the box, Karch thought for a moment about whether he needed to proceed with his plan. He decided to go ahead. His plan, if it worked, would still have the aspect of confusing the target, knocking him for a bit of a loop.

Karch walked around the corner to the counter. Behind it there was a man in his early twenties who was dumping little Styrofoam balls into a large box on the floor behind the counter. He spoke without looking up from his work.

'What can I do for you?'

This sort of impersonal service always annoyed Karch. He saw it all the time in Las Vegas but this time he was pleased because he didn't want the clerk to pay much attention to him.

'I need an envelope.'

'What size?'

'Doesn't matter. Normal size.'

'Number ten?'

The clerk left the box he was filling and walked to the wall at the rear of the service counter area. There were several boxes and envelopes of varying sizes mounted on the wall. Below them was the inventory arranged on shelves according to size. Karch scanned the envelopes and saw the number 10 size.

'Yeah, ten is fine.'

'Padded, unpadded?'

'Uh, padded.'

The clerk grabbed one off the shelf and came to the counter announcing in a high, whiny voice that Karch owed fifty-two cents including tax. Karch paid with exact change.

'Nice hat,' the clerk said.

'Thanks.'

Karch took the envelope to the counter by the door. It occurred to him that the clerk might actually have been making fun of his hat, but he let it go.

With his back shielding the clerk from viewing what he was doing, Karch reached into the pocket of his suit coat and took out the envelope containing the ace of hearts playing card he had found on the floor while searching room 2015 at the Cleo. He took the card out and slid it into the envelope he had just bought, then stapled it closed.

Using the thickest Magic Marker he could find in the plastic cups, he addressed the envelope to Leo Renfro and put down the postal box address and number. In large letters he then wrote DO NOT DELAY! and URGENT! on both sides. On the lines provided for a return address he wrote 773 and on the back he wrote Leo Renfro's cell phone number.

He went back to the service counter and saw the clerk was now taping shut the box on the floor. Again he did not look up. This time he didn't even ask what was wanted. Karch could see the name tag pinned to his shirt said STEPHEN.

'Excuse me, Steve, do you mind putting this into the proper box for me?'

The young man sullenly put down the tape and walked over to the counter. He took the proffered envelope and looked at it as though there was some question as to whether he could accomplish the request.

'I need it to go in there now because this guy always checks his box first thing in the morning.'

The kid finally decided he could handle the assignment and headed behind a partition that apparently led to the mail room.

'And it's *Stephen*,' he called back out to Karch.

Karch stepped away from the counter and went around the corner and down to box 520. He watched through the little glass window as the envelope he had just given the clerk was shoved into the box on top of the other piece of mail waiting for Leo Renfro.

Karch had left the shop before the clerk made his return to the counter. As he walked to his car, he said out loud, 'That'll be fifty-two cents . . . and it's Stephen.'

Once inside the Lincoln he said it again and again, working on the pitch and getting an approximation of the right sullen tone and whine into it. When he had it down close enough he started the car and pulled away from the curb.

To make the call he couldn't use an open pay phone with background traffic noise. He drove around Burbank for ten minutes looking for the proper venue. He finally spotted a restaurant called Bob's Big Boy and parked in the rear lot, backing into a slot next to a Dumpster.

Inside the restaurant he found a pay phone in the alcove leading to the rest rooms. He dropped in coins and called Leo Renfro's cell number. He realized the chance he was taking. Renfro's mailbox was a blind drop. Though it obviously was in his name, there was no way for Karch to know whether the operators of the shop would have Renfro's cell phone number. But his plan had a built-in contingency for that.

The phone at the other end of the line was picked up after two rings but no one said anything.

'Hello?' Karch finally said, his voice the best approximation of a high whine.

'Who's this?'

'Mr Renfro? This is Stephen at Warner Post and Pack It.'

'How'd you get this number?'

'It's on the envelope.'

'What envelope?'

Karch concentrated on his voice.

'That's what I am calling about. You got an envelope today. It's marked urgent and says do not delay. Your phone number is on it. I don't know, I thought I'd call you. We're closing up and since you didn't come in, I thought I should call you in case, you know, you were expecting some –'

'Is there a return address?'

'Yeah – I mean, no. All it says there is seven-seven-three.'

'Okay. Thank you. But do me a favor, don't ever call here again.'

Renfro abruptly hung up. Karch kept the phone to his ear as if giving Renfro the chance to get back on and ask more questions. Finally, he hung up. He thought it had worked. He felt confident. His impression of Renfro from the conversation was that he was a cagey guy. That meant it could be a long night ahead.

Back in the restaurant he went to the counter and ordered two hamburgers well done with ketchup on the side and two black coffees to go. While the order was being prepared he walked out to the parking lot. He got the stolen license plates out of his car and replaced the rear tag of his car with one. The Dumpster provided cover while he worked. He then got in the car, pulled out of the parking slot and pulled right back in forward.

He changed the front plate. Cassie Black's drill made the job a breeze. He decided he was going to keep the drill when the job was finished. The drill and a few other things.

28

One more dread added to an already dreadful day. Cassie
sat in the Boxster, the engine idling, at the curb across
the street from the house on Lookout Mountain Road.
The family had left the curtain behind the big picture
window open. She could see in through the living room
to the lighted kitchen where the three of them sat at the
table eating. She couldn't see it from this angle but
Cassie remembered from the open house that the chair
where the girl now sat had a phone book on it. She
probably thought of herself as too old for a booster chair,
yet she needed the extra inches.

She looked away from the window to the sign. A short
strip of painted wood had been hooked to the bottom of
the realty sign below the name of the Realtor.

IN ESCROW

Cassie had never bought a house before but knew that
the new sign meant an offer had been accepted. The
place was being sold and the family would move soon.
She gripped the wheel tightly. It made her elbow and
shoulder throb. She thought about Leo's plan to give the
money back. She knew there might not be time for
another job – and no job would have the kind of money
that had been in that briefcase. She found herself hoping

Leo would fail in his efforts. She couldn't help it. She wanted the money now. She wanted to run.

Her cell phone rang. She dug it out of her backpack and answered. It was Leo but he didn't say his name. The connection was horrible. She was surprised he had gotten through to her in the hills at all.

'How you feeling?' he asked.

'The same.'

'Well, you know those . . . you were waiting on? I just got a call. It looks like . . . and I'll pick them up tonight.'

She heard enough to be able to fill in the blanks.

'Good. But they won't do me any good if I don't have the money.'

'. . . ill working on that. I'm reaching . . . Maybe tomorrow I'll know something. One way or anoth—'

'What am I supposed to do in the meantime?'

'I didn't get that.'

'What am I supposed to do in the meantime?' she asked loudly, as if the force of her voice could improve the fragile connection.

'We talked about this, Cass. You go to wor . . . your thing. Everything normal until we get this figured . . .'

'Whatever. This connection sucks. I want to go.'

She sounded sullen and she didn't care.

'Look, sweetheart, we're almost there. I'm just waiting on—'

'I don't want to give it back, Leo. We're making a mistake. *You* are making a mistake. I have a really bad feeling about this. We need to go. Just *go*. Now!'

Leo was silent for a long time. He didn't even bother reminding her not to say his name. She was thinking that she had lost the connection when he finally spoke.

'Cassie, look,' he said in an overly calm voice. 'I'm getting . . . ibes, too. More than I usually get. But we have to ... and cover all the bases. It's the only way to be ...'

Cassie shook her head and glanced over at the realty sign once more.

'Sure, Leo. Whatever you say. Just be sure to call me and let me know when you figure out what to do with my life.'

She flipped the phone closed and turned it off in case Leo tried to call back. As she did it she had a sudden idea of creeping into Leo's house while he slept and getting to the money. She would take only her share, leaving the rest for Leo to do whatever he wanted with. As angry as she was with Leo, the idea filled her with guilt. She pushed the thought aside and looked back at the house.

She saw the husband standing up at the table and looking through the length of the house and out to the street. At her. She saw him put his napkin down and start coming around the table. He was going to come out to her, to see what she was doing in front of his house. She quickly dropped the Boxster into gear and drove off.

29

'Summer Wind' was the song. It always got to Karch. Every time it came up on the *Sinatra's Greatest Hits* CD he had to hit replay and hear it again. They were all good but none could touch 'Summer Wind.' It was the class of the class. Just like Sinatra.

Karch was on the fourth run-through of the CD, watching the front of Warner Post & Pack It from the crowded parking lot of a bar called Presnick's a half block away. It was exactly eleven o'clock when he noticed the brake lights flare on a car going by the shop. It was a black Jeep Cherokee about five years old. It was the second time it had gone slowly by the store. Karch turned the CD down and got ready. He was already wearing his black jumpsuit, though for a different reason this time. The sleeves were decorated with varying lengths of heavy-duty duct tape that he had cut in preparation. He reached into his open briefcase and removed the remote global positioning system receiver along with the cellular link box and antenna as well as the GPS antenna from the foam cushioning. He got the tools he would need ready and got out of the Lincoln after popping the trunk. From the trunk he took the Rollerboy Mechanics Helper – a cushioned creeper board on one-inch wheels – then locked the car and walked quickly across Warner Boulevard.

Warner Post & Pack It was a one-story stand-alone

building in a long line of stand-alone buildings, all of which were built to the property line, leaving anywhere from one to three feet of space between buildings. Karch slipped into the opening one storefront down from the mailbox business. It was about twenty inches wide and had primarily been used over time as a trash disposal point by pedestrians. Karch found himself almost knee high in debris – mostly bottles and crumpled bags of fast food. There was also the overpowering smell of urine in the cramped space. His entry into this dark crevice caused some unseen creature to loudly scramble through the debris and go back farther into the darkness.

Karch hung back about three feet from the opening, out of the direct light from the street, and waited. He was sure the Cherokee would come back and that it would be Leo Renfro driving. What Karch had to do next he had done many times before on other cases. But never as fast as he would have to do it this time. He figured he would have less than a minute to complete the installation. There could be no delays or mistakes.

The sound of an approaching car filtered into the hideaway. Karch crouched down and held the Rollerboy up as a shield. Even if Renfro was looking between the buildings, it was unlikely that he would notice Karch unless he completely stopped and shined a light into the darkness.

The car went by slowly and then Karch heard it stop in front of the mail drop business. He slowly moved toward the edge of the building he was leaning against. He glanced around the corner and saw it was indeed the Cherokee, sitting at the curb, still running and with its lights on. Karch pulled himself back into the crevice and waited. He knew he could step out and take Renfro right at that moment. But it was too risky to undertake out in the open and, more important, Renfro wasn't the goal.

The money was the priority. To achieve that he needed to follow Renfro to his home, to the place he felt safest. It was there that Karch knew he would find either the money or a line to Cassidy Black.

The Cherokee's engine cut off. Karch braced himself against the wall, ready to move. He felt the hard points of the stucco digging into his back. He bent forward to listen and heard the car's door open and then close. He heard steps moving quickly on the asphalt. He moved forward and looked once more around the corner. He saw a man in his mid forties and of trim build working a key into the front door of Warner Post & Pack It.

Once he had the door open the man looked up the street to the left and then back to the right. Karch ducked behind the corner. When he heard the door close he stepped out and crossed the sidewalk to the Cherokee. Crouching behind the car, he watched through the front window of the business as the man approached the wall of postal boxes. When he bent down in the area where box 520 was located, Karch knew he had his man. It was Leo Renfro.

Karch turned his penlight on and put it in his mouth. He then put the Rollerboy down and lay down on it face up. He grabbed the underside of the bumper and pulled himself completely under the car. He had done an installation on a Cherokee once before and was not anticipating a problem. It was tight quarters and hot; his chest rubbed the greasy undercarriage at several points and he had to keep his face turned to the side to avoid scraping it or even getting it burned on the hot pipes of the exhaust system.

He reached to his legs and removed the satellite receiver and CelluLink transmitter from the right cargo pocket of his jumpsuit. Both were small, square devices that had been lashed together with tape. A small stub antenna for the cellular connection was part of the bundle. The base of the receiver was a heavy-duty magnet. He reached up and attached the devices to the car's undercarriage frame directly below the driver's seat. Though the magnet appeared to hold firm, it was always Karch's practice to supplement to be sure. From his right arm he unwrapped two long pieces of duct tape and used them to lash the devices to the framework, further securing them to the underside of the car.

Using Cassie Black's silent drill he quickly attached the ground wire to the car's carriage pan, using a self-tapping screw. He then rolled to the curb and tried to look up and through the front window of the mail box business. But the angle was bad and he could not see Renfro or gauge how much more time he had.

He quickly pushed back to the middle and pulled down the electrical conduit that ran down the center of the carriage pan. Using an Exacto knife he slit open the plastic casing and quickly pulled out a bundle of wires. He combed through them until he found a red wire, the color indicating it was a full-time carrier of current from the battery to the rear of the car – most likely to a trunk light. The end of the power wire from the GPS receiver had a cut-in connector that he clipped to the red wire and then squeezed down on until he felt it cut through the rubber coating and into the live wire. He looked over at the receiver and saw the faint glow of the red power light beneath the duct tape.

He didn't have time to push the wires back into place. Instead he moved immediately to the last piece of the installation, the GPS antenna. He removed the small disk from his left cargo pocket and started unspooling the wire it was wrapped in. Just as he connected the wire to the receiver he heard the door to the shop open. He quickly turned the penlight around so that the lighted end was inside his mouth. He waited.

The door closed and Karch watched as Renfro's feet started moving around the car to the driver's door. Karch wanted to curse but knew he had to be silent. He continued unspooling the line from the antenna.

As Renfro opened the car door Karch used the sound as cover as he pushed himself down the length of the Cherokee. He was now directly below the rear bumper, the lower half of his body protruding from beneath the car. He reached the antenna up and wrapped the wire around the exhaust pipe just as the car started and he was hit with a blast of hot exhaust.

Karch stifled a cough and quickly brought the disk up and placed it on top of the bumper, where it would be in a direct line with the satellites above. He used the last piece of tape from his sleeve to tape the wire down and hold the antenna to the bumper.

It wasn't a finesse job but it would have to do, given the circumstances of the installation. He knew the GPS antenna would be spotted the first time Renfro looked at the back end of his car. But Karch was gambling that that wouldn't happen this night. What mattered was the next hour, maybe even less.

The Cherokee shuddered as it was put into drive. It started to move away from the curb. Karch let the bumper pass over his face and then quickly rolled off the Rollerboy and pressed himself to the curb. He kept his head down and listened for any hesitation in the Cherokee's engine. There was none. Renfro kept his foot on the gas and drove off. He never looked back. Or if he did, he was checking the road behind him, not the curb.

Karch finally looked up as the Cherokee receded from view. He smiled and got up.

*

As soon as Karch got to the Lincoln he took the laptop computer out of the briefcase, raised the antenna and booted up the QuikTrak software. With the receiver and the equipment he had just installed on Renfro's car, Karch would be able to track the Cherokee's movements with a global positioning system that took a signal transmitted from the car to a constellation of three satellites miles overhead and then back down. The satellites triangulated the precise location of the car and sent the data by cellular link to the cellular modem in Karch's computer. The QuikTrak software allowed him to follow the car's movements with real-time data displayed on street-level maps on the computer screen, or he could download historical data from the satellite that would show the car's entire movement over a selected time period.

Karch was first interested in making sure the installation had no flaws and he would be able to track the Cherokee by satellite. As a fallback he had committed the car's license plate number to memory and would be able to locate the car through the archaic means of a DMV trace in the morning, a move he hoped to avoid because it would leave an official trail of his activities.

He typed in the receiver code and frequency and waited. After what seemed like an interminable wait during which he could feel beads of sweat pop from his scalp, the lines of a map began to appear on the screen. After the street lines came the words *Los Angeles Region Map*. Then a pulsing red star appeared and began trailing a line. It was the Cherokee. The legend at the bottom of the screen gave the location.

RIVERSIDE DRIVE – WESTBOUND – 23:14:06

Karch smiled. He had him. The installation was

successful. He would be able to follow a map right to the treasure. He hoped.

'Fucking A,' he said out loud.

He decided not to follow the Cherokee's real-time movements in his own car at the moment. He figured that it was likely that Leo Renfro had opened the padded envelope in the mail shop or in the car. Either way, the playing card he found inside would be both confusing and threatening. It was Karch's guess – based on Leo Renfro's two drive-bys before finally stopping at Warner Post & Pack It – that his target would take a circuitous route to his next destination in an effort to carefully identify and then lose any surveillance. He typed in a command creating a file for historical data collection beginning immediately. He then closed down the program and put the laptop back into the briefcase.

Just after pulling down the zipper on his jumpsuit and opening the window to get some air, Karch heard a woman's sharp scream from the other side of the parking lot. He turned toward the sound but didn't see anything. He opened the door and got out and looked around. He put a cigarette in his mouth and lit it. He was about to get back into the Lincoln when he heard another shout and saw movement on the other side of a BMW parked about ten slots away.

Karch wasn't wearing his holster with the Sig Sauer. He had taken it off and left it under the front seat before putting on the jumpsuit. Rather than get the weapon now, he peeled off the top half of the jumpsuit and reached behind his back to remove the little .25 from the magician's pocket in his pants. He then tied the arms of the jumpsuit around his waist and went to investigate the screams.

Palming the small black pistol as he casually walked down the row of cars, he got to the BMW and heard the sounds of crying. He saw a couple standing at the front of the car. A young man and woman. The man had the woman bent backward over the front hood. He was leaning on her and kissing her neck while her head constantly rolled back and forth as if trying to get away from the rest of her body.

'Everything all right there?' Karch called.

The man looked over at him.

'We're fine. Why don't you just piss off?'

Karch started moving down the side of the car. The man suddenly stepped away from the woman and turned to Karch. He stood arms and feet wide apart and waiting.

'Why don't you leave her alone?' Karch said. 'It doesn't sound like she –'

'Why don't you fuck yourself? She's fine. She just likes to yell, okay?'

'No, not okay. Maybe you just like to make her yell. Makes you feel like you're in control of things.'

The guy suddenly leaped forward in a charge that Karch was expecting. Like an experienced bullfighter he quickly sidestepped the charging beast and used his hands to redirect his opponent's momentum into the side of a mini-van. The man hit the side door of the van headfirst, causing a dent in the door panel. As he was straightening up and turning around, Karch moved in. He dropped the .25 into place in his hand and brought it up under his opponent's chin, driving the muzzle deep into the soft underside of the jaw.

'You feel that? Feels small, right? It's a twenty-five, just a pop gun really. Very unreliable unless you get in close like this. I cap one off like this, the slug will go right up into your brain and it won't be strong enough to get out. It'll bounce around inside there a few times and cut everything up in there to mush. Probably won't kill you but you'll be wearing a slobber guard and riding a wheel chair the rest of your—'

'Hey, leave him alone,' the girl said from behind him. 'He didn't do anything.'

Karch made the mistake of not watching her.

'Shut up and back away. This guy—'

She grabbed Karch from behind then and he used his left arm to roughly shove her backward while keeping the gun pressed against the man's neck. He heard her hit the BMW hard and then fall to the pavement.

'Johnny!' she cried out.

'See what you did?' Johnny cried out. 'Big man. Look what you did to her. A knight in shining bullshit.'

Karch pulled back from him and stepped backward until he could keep his eyes on Johnny and see the girl as well. She was sitting on the pavement, her legs spread and looking a little dazed. Johnny ran to her and she grabbed him around the neck. She started crying again.

Karch turned and started walking quickly to his car. He was thinking *Why the fuck did I do that? I'm here for one reason only.*

He got into the Lincoln, backed out and drove away. He saw Johnny standing in the lot behind him, watching him go.

Karch pulled to a curb on Magnolia Boulevard, put on the dome light and got the National Law Enforcement Association frequency book out of the glove compartment. He had bought the book from Iverson for $500. It listed every federal, state and local law enforcement agency and the radio transmission frequencies assigned to them. Printed in large letters across the top of every page was 'Law Enforcement Use Only.' Karch laughed the first time he saw that.

He found the listing for the Burbank Police Department and punched in the three patrol frequencies assigned to the department on the scanner mounted below the dashboard. He then locked in a repeating scan on the three frequencies and waited and listened. If the couple he had just tangled with called in a report, he needed to know about it.

Things seemed quiet in Burbank for a Thursday night. A couple of domestic disputes went out to patrol units and then came a call to the parking lot at Presnick's bar. It had been reported as an assault and threat with a firearm.

'Shit!' Karch yelled loudly.

He banged his fist on the steering wheel. He looked at his watch. It was almost midnight. He knew he wasn't too far from Burbank Airport. He could go there and try to find another set of plates. But it was getting late and he knew he needed to get out of Burbank. He put the car in gear and drove until he reached a residential street. He turned onto the street and drove a block down before stopping. He killed the lights, reached under the seat for the car's proper license plates and got out with the drill. A minute later he got back in with the stolen plates in hand. He shoved them under the seat and put the car in gear. He drove a full block before putting the lights back on.

He drove west and didn't stop again until he was clear of Burbank and well into North Hollywood. He listened to a description of himself being broadcast on the Burbank frequencies and had to smile. The description that went out was fifty pounds too heavy and ten years too old. The rest was so generic it didn't matter. The tag number that went out accurately matched the plates now under his seat but the make of the car was off. It was described as a black Ford LTD. Karch lit a cigarette and tried to relax. Burbank was not going to be a problem.

It was now midnight and Karch thought that enough time had gone by for Leo Renfro to have gotten to wherever he was going. He pulled into the parking lot of a twenty-four-hour supermarket called Ralph's and stopped the car. He had just opened the QuikTrak receiver when his pager went off. He checked the number and saw the page was from Grimaldi. He decided not to call back and even turned the pager off. He didn't want it sounding again at an inopportune time.

The QuikTrak software booted up and Karch typed in a command asking for the historical data file on the movements of the transmitter beneath Leo Renfro's car. A map of northern Los Angeles appeared on the screen with a red line delineating the car's movements. Karch had been right. Renfro had gone on a long and convoluted drive around the Valley, driving in circles and making several U-turns. The computer showed the transmitter to be static for the last twelve minutes. Renfro had stopped. The computer placed the car on Citron Street in Tarzana.

'Here I come, Leo,' Karch said out loud.

He put the Lincoln in drive and nosed it out of the parking lot on his way to Tarzana.

30

The Cherokee was found easily enough. It was parked in a driveway in front of a small house on Citron. As Karch drove by he wondered why Renfro hadn't put it into the garage. He kept driving and continued around the block, looking for anything unusual or suspicious. He then pulled the Lincoln to the curb a half block away from the Cherokee. He worked his arms back into the sleeves of the jumpsuit and zipped up. He got his Sig out of its holster and attached the silencer. Leaving the Lincoln unlocked in case a quick escape was necessary, he headed down the street on foot.

Before approaching the house Karch got down on the pavement next to the Cherokee and reached underneath for his satellite equipment. He pulled it off the pan and jerked the wires free. He then went to the rear of the car to recover the disk antenna and put the equipment in the mailbox at the foot of the driveway. He planned to grab it later on when he headed back to the Lincoln.

Curious about Renfro's decision to park the car in plain sight, he walked to the garage and shined his penlight through one of the small windows on the door. The garage was completely filled with stacks and stacks of champagne cases. He assumed it was a stolen shipment and wondered if it would be worth his time and efforts later to have the shipment removed and sold. He could probably sell it all to Vincent Grimaldi for a nice profit.

He dismissed the idea and focused on the task at hand. He crossed the front of the house and moved down the left side, carefully looking for indications that Renfro had dogs. He wasn't concerned with alarms. People who worked the wrong side of the tracks rarely had alarms. They knew how easy they were to compromise, and they didn't want any kind of security system that could possibly bring the police to their door.

There was a wooden gate halfway down the side of the house. Karch easily scaled it and dropped over. He ran the light over the grass and in the shrub beds running down the side of the house. There were no dog droppings anywhere and no sign of any digging in the plants. He flicked the light off and continued down the side to the backyard. The moon was bright and he didn't need the light.

At the rear corner of the house Karch stepped out and saw the glowing blue surface of a pool. Just as he began moving along the back wall, he heard a sliding door open. He scrambled back to the corner and took a position giving him a view of the rear. A man stepped out through a sliding door and walked to the edge of the pool. It was the man from the mail drop. Renfro. He looked down at the pool and Karch saw an automatic vacuum moving slowly along the bottom. The man then looked up and seemed to be staring at the moon. Karch stepped out from his position and raised his gun.

Because of the background hiss from the nearby freeway Renfro never heard him. Karch put the cold end of the muzzle against the back of his neck. Renfro tensed but that was all. People in his line of work expected sooner or later to feel the cold muzzle of a gun against their neck.

'Nice clear night, eh?' Karch said.

'I was just thinking that,' the man said. 'Are you the ace of hearts?'

'That's me.'

'I looked but I didn't see you.'

'That's because I wasn't there. You're about a decade behind, Leo. I put a satellite bug on your car. I didn't need to follow you.'

'Live and learn.'

'Maybe. Let's go inside and talk. Keep your hands up where I can see them.'

Karch grabbed the back of Renfro's collar with one hand and held the gun against his back with the other. They headed back toward the house.

'Anybody else inside?'

'No, I'm alone.'

'You sure? I find anyone else in there I'll kill them just to make the point.'

'I'm sure you will. There's no one.'

They went in through the open sliding door into an office. Karch saw the desk at one end of the room. One entire wall was covered with more cases of champagne. Karch roughly pushed Renfro toward the front of the desk and let him go. He then reached back and closed the sliding door.

'Stay in front of the desk.'

Leo did as instructed. He kept his hands held up, chest high. Karch came around and went behind the desk. He noticed that sitting on the desk was the padded envelope he had left for Renfro at the mail drop as well as the envelope that had already been in the box. The flaps on both envelopes were torn open. Karch sat down in the chair behind the desk and looked up at Renfro.

'Been a busy man, Leo.'

'Oh, I don't know. Things are kind of slow.'

'Really?' He nodded in the direction of the wall of champagne. 'Looks like you're about to start celebrating something big time.'

'It's an investment.'

Karch picked up the padded envelope and shook it until the ace of hearts dropped out onto the desk. He tossed the envelope over his shoulder and picked up the playing card.

'Ace of hearts. The money card, Leo.'

He put the card into one of the pockets of his jumpsuit. He then picked up the other envelope and looked at it.

'I'm curious. What does the seven-seven-three mean? That some kind of code?'

'Yeah, it's a code. An area code.'

Karch shook his head.

'I should've known. Where?'

'Chicago. It's the new one.'

'Yes, that's right. You work for Chicago.'

'No, that's wrong. I don't work for anybody.'

Karch nodded but the smile on his face indicated he didn't believe Renfro. He picked up the other envelope and shook it. Two passports fell onto the desk. He picked up one and opened it to the photo page. Paper-clipped to one side was an Illinois driver's license and two credit cards. But Karch was more interested in the photo.

'Jane Davis,' he read out loud. 'Funny, that looks like Cassidy Black to me.'

He looked up at Renfro to catch his reaction. For a moment it was there. Surprise, maybe even shock. Karch smiled.

'Yes, I know a little more than you think.'

He picked up the second passport, expecting to find

Renfro's picture inside it. Instead, it was a photo of a little girl. The name below the photo was Jodie Davis.

'Well, maybe I don't know everything. Who have we got here?'

Renfro didn't answer.

'Come on, Leo, work with me here. We can't have secrets, you and I.'

'Fuck you. Do what you have to do, but fuck you.'

Karch leaned back in the chair and looked over Renfro as if appraising him.

'You Outfit guys think you're so untouchable.'

'I'm not with the Outfit, but fuck you anyway.'

Karch nodded as if amused by Renfro's protestations.

'Let me tell you a story about the Outfit. Long time ago in Las Vegas there was this magician. He'd been around a long time, worked all the casinos, never really caught on. Always the warm-up, never the headliner. Raisin' a son by himself on the side. Anyway, he had a gig in the Clown Room lounge at Circus, Circus. No big deal. Just a table act for chump change – tips mostly. And so one night he's dealing three-card monte to a table of these three guys and they keep telling him to do it again. You know, "Do it again and I'll get it this time." Only they never got it. They never picked the ace. And it went on and on and it got one of them hotter and hotter. Like he thought this magician was personally makin' a fool of him or something. So skip to the end of the night. The magician punches out and is in the back garage walking to his car. And guess who's waitin' for him but those same three guys from the bar.'

Karch paused but not for effect. The story always got to him at this point. Every time he thought about it or told it, the anger seemed to boil up in his throat like acid.

'And one of them, the boss of these three guys, had a hammer. They didn't say a word. They just grabbed the magician and bent him over the hood of his car. One of them used his tie to gag him. Then one by one the man with the hammer broke every one of the magician's knuckles. At some point he passed out and when they were done they just left him lying on the concrete next to his car. He never worked as a magician again. Couldn't even palm a quarter anymore. Every time he tried, it just dropped on the floor. I used to sit in my bedroom and hear him trying gags in the other room. I'd hear that quarter fall on that wood floor over and over again . . .

'He drove a cab for a living after that. Cancer finally killed him but he was dead long before that.'

Karch looked at Renfro.

'You know who the man with the hammer was?'

Renfro shook his head.

'That was Joey Marks. The Outfit's man in Vegas.'

'Joey Marks is dead,' Renfro said. 'And like I said, I don't work for the Outfit or anybody else.'

Karch stood up and came around the desk.

'I came for the money,' he said quietly. 'You stole from the wrong people and I've come to set it straight. I don't care if you're with Chicago or not. I'm not leaving here without the money.'

'What money? I sell passports. I invest in champagne. I don't steal money from people.'

'Listen to me, Leo. Your spotter's dead. So is your cameraman. You don't want to be like them, do you? So where's the money? Where's Cassie Black?'

Renfro turned so he was facing Karch and his back was to the sliding door. Behind him the pool glowed brightly in the dark. He lowered his chin as if looking inward and coming to a decision. He then nodded slightly to himself and looked back at Karch.

'Fuck you.'

Karch shook his head.

'No, Leo, this time it's fuck you.'

He lowered the barrel of the gun and calmly fired. The bullet blew out Renfro's left knee. It passed cleanly through the bone and tissue, hit the tile floor behind him and bounced up into the sliding glass door. The door shattered into large jagged pieces of glass that crashed down onto the floor and shattered again. Renfro dropped to the floor and grabbed his knee with both hands. His face was a mask of agony.

The breaking glass was more noise than Karch had planned on making. The door was shattered except for one large jagged piece of glass held in the bottom of the frame. He figured the house must have been built before safety glass was required. He looked out into the yard and hoped the freeway noise had covered the sound.

Renfro started gasping and moaning as he rolled over the glass, cutting himself on his arms and back. The floor was quickly becoming slick with blood. Karch stepped over and leaned down over Renfro.

'Give me the money, Leo, and I promise I'll end it quick and painless.'

He waited but got no response. Renfro's face was scarlet. His lips were pulled back, exposing teeth gnashed together.

'Leo? Leo, listen to me. I know you're in a lot of pain but listen to me. If you don't give me the money we're going to be here all night. You think it hurts now? You can't imagine what—'

'Fuck you! I don't have the money.'

Karch nodded.

'Well, at least we're making progress, right? We're now past the "What money?" stage. If you don't have it, then where is it?'

'I gave it to Chicago.'

The answer came too quickly for Karch. He looked closely at Renfro's face and decided he was lying.

'I don't think so, Leo. Where's the girl? Cassie Black, Leo, where is she?'

Renfro didn't respond. Karch stepped back a pace and calmly fired a bullet into his other knee.

Renfro let out a loud scream that was followed by a stream of epithets that dissolved into delirium and moans. He rolled over onto his chest, his elbows tucked in and his face in his hands. His legs were sprawled behind him, twin pools of blood leaking from his knees. Karch looked out the broken door, across the pool, and checked for lights or any indication that the neighbors had taken notice. All he heard was the freeway. He hoped it would keep him covered.

'Okay, okay,' Leo blubbered into his hands. 'I'll tell you. I'll show you.'

'Okay, Leo, that's good. Now we're getting somewhere.'

Renfro raised his head and pushed himself up onto his elbows. He started crawling forward, toward the shattered door, his dead legs dragging behind him and leaving a trail of blood.

'I'll tell you,' he choked out through pain and tears. 'I'll show you.'

'Then talk to me, Leo,' Karch said. 'Where are you going? You can't go anywhere. You can't even walk, for crying out loud. Just tell me where it is.'

Renfro moved another painful foot closer to the door. When he spoke his voice was ragged and was delivered through clenched teeth.

'See . . . you see . . . it was the fucking moon . . . the void moon . . .'

'What are you talking about? Where's the money?'

Karch realized he had gone too far. Renfro was

delirious with pain and blood loss. He was quickly becoming useless.

'The void moon,' Renfro said. 'It's the void moon.'

Karch took a step along with him.

'Void moon?' he said. 'What's that mean?'

Renfro stopped moving. He turned his face and looked up at Karch. The tightness had gone out of it. He almost looked relaxed.

'It means anything can happen, motherfucker.'

His voice was strong now. He suddenly raised himself off his elbows onto his hands. He raised himself up to full extension and lurched forward into the sliding door frame. His neck came down on the jagged piece of glass still held in the frame.

Karch realized what he was doing too late.

'No, goddammit!'

He reached down and grabbed Renfro's collar and jerked him up and off the glass. He dropped him to the floor and then grabbed his shoulder and turned him over.

He had acted too late. A deep, wide gash extended across Renfro's neck. He had cut his own throat. Blood was burbling out of the left side where the carotid artery had been severed.

Leo Renfro's eyes were bright as he looked up at Karch. A bloody smile formed on his face. Slowly he reached a hand up and used it to hold his neck together. His voice was a whispered croak.

'You lose.'

Leo dropped the hand and let the blood flow from his neck. He kept the smile on his face and his eyes on Karch.

Karch dropped to his knees and hovered over him.

'You think you beat me? Huh? Huh? You think you won?'

Leo could only answer with his smile. Karch knew it said *Fuck You!* He raised the gun and pressed the muzzle into Renfro's bloody mouth.

'You didn't win.'

He leaned back and turned his face away. He pulled the trigger. The shot blew out the back of Renfro's head and killed him instantly.

Karch pulled the weapon away and studied the dead man's face. His eyes were open and somehow he still had the smile.

'Fuck you. You didn't beat me.'

He leaned back on his heels and looked around himself. He saw a drop of blood spatter on the white instep of one of his two-tone Lite Tread spectator shoes. He used his thumb to wipe it off and then wiped his thumb on Leo's shirt.

He stood up and looked around the office. He sighed loudly. He knew he had a long night of searching ahead. He had to find the money. He had to find Cassie Black.

31

On Friday morning Cassie Black arrived at the dealership at ten and checked with Ray Morales to see what was what. He had taken her calls while she had been out the last few days. Ray said all was quiet but that he had a prospect coming in to test-drive a new Boxster at three. He had just been given a development deal at Warner Brothers that ran into seven figures. Ray had gotten it out of the *Hollywood Reporter* and expected it to be an easy sale. She thanked him for thinking of her with the prospect and was about to head to her office when he stopped her.

'You okay, kid?' he asked.

'Sure, why?'

'I don't know. You don't look like you've been sleeping much lately.'

Cassie brought her right hand up and cupped her left elbow, which still ached from the briefcase jolt.

'I know,' she said. 'Just been thinking about things. Sometimes it keeps me awake.'

'What things?'

'I don't know. Just things. I'll be in my office if you need me.'

She left him then and went to the sanctuary of her tiny office. She dropped her backpack into the foot well of the desk and sat down. She put her elbows up on the blotter and ran her hands through her hair. She felt like screaming I CAN'T DO THIS ANYMORE! But she tried to put her anxieties aside by reminding herself that one way or another her life would be changing very soon.

She picked up the phone to check her voice mail, even though on Tuesday she had left a generic outgoing message saying she would be off work for a few days and referring calls to Ray Morales until she got back. Four messages had been left for her anyway. One was from a body shop reporting a set of customized chrome wheels for a '58 Speedster she had sold were now ready. The second call was from one of Ray's prospects – a producer at Fox – from the week before. He wasn't calling about the car he had test-driven. He was just calling to tell her he had liked her style and wanted to know if she was interested in going with him to a premiere of a friend's picture the following week. Cassie didn't bother writing down the guy's private cell phone number.

'If you liked my style, why didn't you buy the car?' she said into the phone.

The third message was from Leo. There was an agitation in his voice she had not heard before. The message had come in at 12:10 A.M. that morning. She listened to it three times.

'Hey, it's me. What's wrong with your cell phone? I couldn't get through. Anyway, I just got back from my drop. I have those things you wanted but there's something else, something wrong. Somebody got the address somehow and dropped me something there. An ace of hearts from the Flamingo. I don't know what it means but it means something. Call me when you get this. Use all precautions and keep your head down. Oh, and erase this, okay?'

Cassie hit the three button on the phone, erasing Leo's recording before she went on to the fourth message. The last call had come in at seven-thirty that morning and it was a hang-up call. There had been no background noise, just a few seconds of someone breathing and then the hang-up. She wondered if it had been Leo.

She hung up the phone, reached down to the floor and pulled her backpack up onto her lap. She first dug through it until she found her cell phone. It had been turned off. She remembered doing it the night before after hanging up on Leo and deciding she didn't want him calling back.

She turned the phone on now and put it down on the desk. She then continued digging through the bag until she found the box containing the deck of cards she had bought in the gift shop at the Flamingo. She quickly opened it, turned the deck face up and started going through the cards one at a time looking for the ace of hearts. The closer she got to the bottom of the deck the greater the dread was that was building inside her. When she reached the last card without seeing the ace of hearts she cursed out loud and threw the deck across the small office. It hit the Tahiti poster and then cards exploded in all directions, coming down on the floor and the desk.

'Goddammit!'

She buried her face in her palms as she tried to figure out what to do. She snatched up the phone to call Leo but then thought better of it. *Use all precautions.* She thought of using her cell phone but dismissed that, too. She opened the desk drawer and grabbed a handful of change from a tray meant for pens and pencils and got up.

She opened the door and almost walked right into Ray Morales, who had apparently come to see what the commotion was about.

'Excuse me,' she said, making a move to go around him.

Ray looked past her into the office and saw the playing cards all over the place.

'What, you playing fifty-two pickup in there?'

'More like fifty-one.'

'What?'

'I'll be back in a few minutes, Ray. I have to take a walk.'

He silently watched her cross the showroom and go out the glass door.

Cassie walked a block down to the Cinerama Dome, where she knew there was a pay phone out front. She dialed Leo's cell phone number from memory and listened to ten unanswered rings before hanging up. Now questioning everything, she dialed it again in case she had messed up the first time. This time it went twelve rings before she hung up. The dread that had begun to rise in her while she looked through the cards had now gone several notches up the ladder to the level of panic.

She tried to calm herself by trying to think of reasons the call to Leo would go unanswered. The cell phone and Leo were attached like Siamese twins. If the phone had not been turned on, she knew her call would have been diverted to a message. She wouldn't have gotten the continuous ringing. So the phone was on but not being answered. The question was why.

The pool, she suddenly remembered. Leo swam laps in the morning. He'd have taken the phone out to the table next to the pool, but if he was in the middle of his laps he wouldn't hear it, not with the water sloshing around him and the freeway noise as well.

The explanation calmed her a bit. She called Leo's number once more and again it went unanswered. She put the phone back on its hook and decided to go back to the dealership. She would come back and try calling again in a half hour or forty-five minutes. She remembered Leo once told her he swam three miles a day. She had no idea how long that would take but figured that a half hour should be enough time.

Five minutes later she walked back into the dealership showroom and saw Ray and a man who wore a porkpie hat looking at the silver Carrera with the whale tail spoiler. Ray saw her and signaled her over with his fingers.

'Cassie, this is Mr Lankford. He wants to buy a car.'

The customer turned and smiled with embarrassment.

'Well, I want to look at a car. I mean, drive it. Then we'll see.'

He put his hand out.

'Terrill Lankford.'

She took his hand and shook it. His grip was firm, his hand dry as powder.

'Cassie Black.'

She looked at Ray. She didn't want to do this. Her mind wasn't on selling cars.

'Ray, is Billy in yet? Or Aaron? Maybe one of them would be—'

'Meehan's on a test and Curtiss isn't in till twelve. I need you to show Mr Lankford a car.'

Ray's tone indicated he was put out by her flaky behavior and that there was no debate allowed here. She turned her attention to Lankford. He was neat and well dressed in a set of retro clothes that went with the hat. Judging by his pasty complexion she guessed he'd be interested in a coupe. But that was okay because the Boxster didn't come in a coupe. That left only the higher priced Carreras.

'Which model are you interested in?'

Lankford smiled, showing off a perfect set of teeth.

Cassie noticed his eyes were sidewalk gray, an unusual combination with the man's jet black hair.

'A new Carrera, I think.'

'Well, I'll get a car ready. If you could give your driver's license and insurance card to Ray, he'll get it copied while I get a car ready.'

Lankford's mouth opened but he didn't say anything.

'You do have proof of insurance, don't you?' Cassie asked.

'Of course, of course.'

'Okay, then let Ray take care of that and I'll get the car. Cab or coupe?'

'Excuse me?'

'Hardtop or cabriolet – convertible?'

'Oh. Well, it's such a nice day, why don't we take the top off?'

'Sounds good to me. We've got one in stock and available. It's arctic silver. That sound good?'

'Great.'

'All right, come on out to the carport when you're done with Ray.'

She pointed to the glass doors at the opposite end of the showroom.

'I'll meet you there,' Lankford said.

While Ray took the prospect into the finance office where the copying machine was, Cassie went into his office and got the key to the silver cab off the board. She then went to her own office and grabbed her wallet out of her backpack. She looked around and saw the playing cards all over the place and realized that if Lankford wanted to make a deal, she'd have to stick him in Ray's office while she cleaned up. There wasn't time now.

She started out of the office and then remembered something. She grabbed her cell phone off her desk and clipped it onto her belt. Just in case Leo calls, she thought to herself.

She headed out to the side lot to the car. She got in, slid her wallet into a CD holder on the dash and then started the engine. She put the windows and top down, checked the fuel level and saw there was a quarter tank, then drove the car up to the showroom door just as Lankford was stepping out.

'Let me drive it until we get out of here,' she called over the sound of the engine that was over-revving as the car warmed up. 'Then you'll take over.'

Lankford smiled and gave her the okay sign and got into the passenger side. She pulled out onto Sunset and then turned north on Vine. At Hollywood Boulevard she took a left and went down to Cahuenga, which she took north toward the hills and Mulholland Drive.

They drove in silence at first. Cassie liked to let the prospects listen to the car, feel its power on the turns, fall in love with it, before there was any talking. She liked to hold back on the sales pitch and the particulars until the customer was behind the wheel. Besides, her thoughts weren't on Lankford and his interest in a $75,000 car. She kept thinking about Leo's call and the anxiety she'd heard in his voice.

The Carrera effortlessly climbed through the Mulholland curves from Cahuenga up to the crest of the Santa Monica Mountains. At the Hollywood overlook she pulled off the road, killed the engine and got out.

'Your turn,' she said, her first words since he had gotten in the car.

She stepped to the railing at the edge and looked down at the shell of the Hollywood Bowl far below. Her eyes moved out from the bowl across Hollywood toward the spires of downtown. The smog was heavy and had a pinkish-orange tint to it. But somehow it didn't look all that bad.

'Nice view,' Lankford said from behind her.

'Sometimes.'

She turned and watched as he got into the driver's seat. She went around and got in the passenger side.

'Why don't you keep going on Mulholland for a little ways. You'll get a good idea of how this handles. We can take Laurel Canyon down to the one-oh-one and take that back to Hollywood. You'll be able to open it up on the freeway a little bit, see how it does.'

'Sounds good.'

He found the ignition on the left side quickly and started the engine. He backed out of the parking slot, then dropped the transmission into first gear and pulled out onto Mulholland. He drove with one hand on the stick shift at all times. Cassie could tell immediately he knew what he was doing.

'I take it you've driven one of these before but I'm going to give you the pitch anyway.'

'That's fine.'

She started listing the attributes of the car, starting with the new water-cooled engine and transmission and moving toward the suspension and brakes. She then moved inside the cockpit and started going over the amenities.

'You've got cruise control, traction control, onboard computer all standard. You've got CD, automatic windows and roof, dual air bags. And down here . . .'

She pointed down between her legs to the front of her seat. Lankford glanced down there but then put his eyes back on the road.

'. . . you have a passenger-side cutoff for the air bag – in case you are traveling with a small child. You have kids, Mr Lankford?'

'Call me Terrill. And no, I don't have kids. You?'

Cassie didn't answer for a moment.

'Not really.'

Lankford smiled.

'Not really? I thought that was a yes or no question for a woman.'

Cassie ignored the statement.

'What do you think of the car . . . Terrill?'

'Very smooth. Very sweet.'

'It is. So what do you do for a living?'

He glanced over at her. The wind was threatening to blow his hat off. He reached up and cranked it down over his forehead.

'I guess you could say I'm a troubleshooter,' he said. 'I'm a business consultant. Have my own company. I take care of things. This and that. I'm a magician, really. I make other people's problems disappear. Why do you ask?'

'Just curious. These cars are expensive. You must be very good at what you do.'

'Oh, I am. I am. And cost is not a problem. I pay cash. Actually, Cassie, I expect to come into a large sum of money soon. Very soon, in fact.'

Cassie looked over at him and felt a sudden shiver of fear. It was instinctive more than intuitive. Lankford pressed the pedal a little harder and the Porsche started moving through the winding curves a little faster. He looked over at her again.

'Cassie. What is that short for? Cassandra?'

'Cassidy.'

'As in Butch? Your parents outlaw fans?'

'As in Neal. As in my father was always on the road. Or so I was told.'

Lankford frowned and hit the pedal a little harder.

'That's really too bad. My father and me, we were close.'

'I'm not complaining about it. You want to slow it down, Mr Lankford? I'd like to get back to the showroom in one piece, if you don't mind.'

Lankford didn't respond at first with his voice or his foot. The car powered through another turn, its tires protesting as they labored to hold the road.

'I said, do you—'

'Yes,' Lankford finally said. 'You do want to get back alive.'

Something about the tone in which Lankford delivered the line revealed that he was not talking about the possibility of a car accident. Cassie looked over at him and shifted in her seat so that her body was pressed against her door.

'Excuse me?'

'I said you want to make sure you get back alive, Cassidy.'

'Okay, pull the car over. I don't know what you think you're—'

Lankford slammed his foot down on the brake pedal and yanked the wheel hard to the left. The Porsche skidded and spun into a 180-degree turn as it stopped. He looked over at her and smiled, then dropped in the gear and popped the clutch out. The car lurched forward and he started speeding through the curves, back in the direction they had come.

'What the hell are you doing?' Cassie yelled. 'Stop the car! Stop the car right now!'

Cassie reached her right hand up and gripped the top of the windshield brace. Her mind was moving as fast as the car as she tried to come up with a plan, an escape.

'Actually, Lankford's not my name,' the man next to her was saying. 'I got it off a book I found on a shelf at

Leo Renfro's last night. It's called *Shooters* and I started taking a look at it. I thought it was about a guy in my line of work but it wasn't. But, hell, when your boss came up to me in the showroom and asked my name, it's all I could come up with on short notice, you know. My name is Karch. Jack Karch. And I've come for the money, Cassie Black.'

Through the terror building inside Cassie a thought pressed forward. *Jack Karch*, she thought. *I know that name.*

32

The Porsche was moving wildly through the Mulholland slalom. Jack Karch was going too fast for his skill now and the car was intermittently crossing the yellow line in the middle of the two-lane road and then rebounding by going off the road onto the shoulder. Karch was red-lining the tach but didn't want to take his hand off the wheel to pop the car into a higher gear. The engine roared and whined as the car went through the turns. Cassie gripped the windshield brace with both hands but was being thrown violently back and forth in her seat. Karch screamed over the din of the engine.

'I WANT THE FUCKING MONEY!'

She didn't answer him. She was too busy watching the road uncoiling in front of them and thinking for sure they would go off the shoulder and down the embankment.

'MARTIN IS DEAD! PALTZ IS DEAD! LEO IS DEAD!'

She turned to him at the mention of Leo's name. She felt her heart being pierced. Karch throttled back. He kept the car moving but the engine noise and wind abated.

'They're all dead,' he said. 'But I don't really want or need to hurt you, Cassie Black.'

He smiled and shook his head.

'In fact, I admire you. You do good work and I admire

that. But I came for the money and you're going to give it to me. You give me the money and we'll call it square.'

Cassie spoke slowly and sternly.

'I don't know what you are talking about, okay? Please pull the car over.'

A look of sincere disappointment crossed Karch's face and he shook his head.

'I spent all night at Leo's. I tore that place apart. I found a lot of champagne and I found the briefcase I was looking for. But I didn't find what was supposed to be in the briefcase. And I didn't find you until along about dawn when I found you sitting there right in front of me. Leo's cell phone. I hit redial and I got the dealership. I went through the direct extension directory and, lo and behold, I hear the name Cassie Black. I switched over just to hear your voice. "This is Cassie at Hollywood Porsche. I'm not at work for a few days but if you call back and ask for Ray Morales he can handle–" Blah, blah, blah, don't fucking lie to me. I don't like it. I WANT THE MONEY!'

'I SAID PULL THE CAR OVER!'

'Sure.'

Karch suddenly steered the car hard right and they turned violently onto a gravel road that cut through a stand of pine trees. Cassie thought it was a fire road or some kind of public utilities access road. Whatever it was, it was clear Karch was taking them away from other traffic, from potential witnesses.

When they were about two hundred yards down the road, Karch slammed on the brakes and the Porsche skidded to a halt on the gravel. Cassie was thrown forward, her body pressing against her shoulder harness, and then back. She had no sooner recovered from the jarring stop than Karch was leaning across the center console onto her and pressing the long dark barrel of a gun against her face. He brought his free hand up and locked it onto the underside of her jaw.

'Listen to me. Are you listening?'

He was squeezing her jaw and she was unable to speak. She nodded.

'Good. What you need to know is that the people I work for care about one thing at this time. The money. Nothing else. So don't be like your pals Leo or Jersey. It will only get you killed.'

Cassie just stared at him down the length of the gun. She could see it had a silencer attached to it.

'Don't think,' Karch said. 'Just talk.'

He relaxed the pressure slightly so she could speak.

'Okay,' she said. 'Don't hurt me and I'll tell you where it is.'

'You'll do more than that, sweetheart. You'll take me to it.'

'Okay. Whatever you—'

He cut her off by squeezing her neck.

'You get one chance. You understand?'

Cassie nodded. Karch slowly released his grip and took his hand away. He was leaning back toward his seat when he suddenly snapped his fingers and leaned toward her again. He reached up to her face and she flinched, but then his hand went past her face to her ear.

'I looked in your office in the showroom before you showed up. Playing cards all over the place. Like you were looking for something. This what you were looking for?'

He pulled his hand back and seemingly pulled something from her ear. He held it up in front of her face. It was the ace of hearts. He smiled.

'Magic,' he said.

And then it struck her. Magic. The name Karch. She remembered the newspaper stories. Reading them in

Metro detention before her arraignment. Jack Karch. He was the one.

He read something in her face.

'You didn't like that, huh? Well, I've got more. After we take care of business I'll show you a real disappearing act.'

He settled behind the wheel, his right arm still stretched across the console and poking the black gun into her ribs.

'Now, we're going to have to work together here, that okay with you? Put it in gear.'

He depressed the clutch pedal and she reached over and moved the shift into the first gear slot. He started the car moving. He turned it around and headed back up the gravel road to Mulholland. After he wound it out he called for second gear and she complied. He started talking again as though they were out for a Sunday drive.

'You know something, I gotta tell you, the way you did this thing, I . . . my hat's off to you. I think, you know, different circumstances . . . you and me, we could've . . . I don't know, done something.'

He took his hand off the wheel and pointed to the gear shift.

'See, we work good together.'

She didn't answer. She knew he was a psychopath, able to talk sincerely about doing things together with a woman he was holding at gunpoint. Cassie knew she had to make a move, to shift things. She knew this man was going to kill her. She would be part of the disappearing act he had promised. She couldn't help but smile sadly at the irony of her situation. She knew she could make the argument that this man had already killed her, six and a half years before.

'What's so funny?'

She looked at him. He had caught her glib smile.

'Nothing. The vagaries of life, I guess. And the coincidences.'

'You mean like fate, bad luck, that sort of thing?'

She casually moved her right arm so that her hand rested between her legs. Karch noticed and pushed the muzzle deeper into her side.

'Like the void moon?'

She turned sharply to look at him.

'Yeah, Leo mentioned something about it last night. Later on when I was looking around I read up on it in one of those books he's got. He was a big believer. Didn't do him any good in the end, did it? Where to?'

They were moving through the grove of pine trees, coming up to Mulholland. Cassie realized this might be her best chance. She took a deep breath and made her move.

'When you get up there you —'

She started raising her left arm as if to point out directions but then snapped her arm straight, knocking the gun away from her mid-section. She then grabbed the wheel with her left hand at the same time her right went down the front of her seat and engaged the air bag kill switch. She yanked the wheel hard right and the car lurched off the gravel road and directly into the trunk of a pine tree. It happened so fast Karch didn't have time to scream or fire his gun.

The driver-side air bag exploded from the steering wheel upon impact with the tree. It slammed Karch back against his headrest.

Cassie's shoulder harness stopped her forward trajectory before she hit the windshield. She was momentarily dazed but knew she had to move. She unfastened the seatbelt and frantically tried to open the door. It wouldn't budge. She didn't try it a second time. She hoisted herself up and jumped out of the car. Immediately, she started running downhill through the trees. She didn't look back at the Porsche.

Karch was more than momentarily dazed by the impact. The air bag hit him like a one-two punch to the chest and jaw. The tiny explosive used to propel it from the steering wheel also singed his face and neck. The impact knocked the gun out of his hand and onto one of the tiny rear seats. As the air bag began to deflate he came out of the daze and slapped it out of his face. He tried to jump up but his seatbelt held him secure. He quickly unfastened it and climbed up with his knees on the seat. He looked in all directions and then finally caught a glimpse of Cassie Black moving quickly away through the trees.

Instinctively he knew he would not catch her. She had a lead and she probably knew where she was going. It was her turf, not his.

'Fuck!'

He looked down into the rear of the car and found the Sig Sauer on the backseat. He reached down and grabbed it and then slipped back into his seat. He turned the key and tried to start the car again. Nothing happened. He turned the key back and forth several times but all he heard was a clicking sound.

'Fuck!'

He tried to open the door but it was jammed closed. The impact from the tree had apparently damaged the car body in such a way that the doors were sealed tight. He started climbing out of the seat again and as he did so he saw the little black wallet that Cassie Black had placed in the CD holder on the dashboard. He reached down for it and opened it. Behind a clear plastic window was a California driver's license. He studied the photo of

Cassie Black and then looked at the address. She lived on Selma in Hollywood.

Karch looked off into the woods. Cassie Black was long gone now. Still, standing on the front seat of the Porsche he held the wallet up as though she were in there someplace looking back at him.

'Look what I found,' he called out. 'You didn't win yet, sweetheart!'

He took the silencer off the Sig and fired the gun once into the air, just to let her know he was still coming.

As Cassie sprinted carefully down the hill she began to hear music and used its source as a beacon. Eventually she came out of the woods at a parking lot she recognized as being behind the Hollywood Bowl. She guessed that the Philharmonic must be practicing. She followed the access road down to Highland and then walked down to Sunset.

It took her twenty minutes to get back to the dealership. As she approached she saw two black-and-white police cars parked in the entranceway to the parking lot. There was also an unmarked car with a bubble light on the dashboard parked up on the curb in front of the showroom. Behind it an ambulance was parked but its rear doors were closed.

There were many people standing out on the sidewalk, including most of the dealership's sales and service staff. Cassie walked up to a salesman named Billy Meehan, who was staring into the showroom with a stricken look on his face.

'Billy, what happened?'

He looked down at her and his eyes grew large.

'Oh, thank God! I thought you were in there with them. Where have you been?'

Cassie hesitated, then decided on a lie that was not technically a lie.

'I was taking a walk. In there with who?'

Meehan put his hands on her shoulders and leaned down into her face as though he was breaking very bad news to her. He was.

'There's been a robbery. Somebody put Ray and Connie down on the floor in her office and shot them both.'

Cassie brought her hands up to her face and stifled a scream.

'They then stole the silver cab. We thought maybe, uh, you were a hostage or something. I'm glad you're okay.'

Cassie just nodded her head. Her history had been a guarded secret with Ray Morales. She realized that if other employees had known about it, they probably would have immediately suggested her as a suspect to the police. Maybe that was what Karch had been counting on.

She felt weak all of a sudden and had to sit down. She practically slid down Meehan's body and sat down on the curb. She tried to understand what had happened and could only conclude that Karch must have shot Ray and Connie because he didn't have a fake driver's license with the name Lankford on it. He knew there was no way he could leave a record with his real name on it. Not with what he had planned to do with her.

'Cassie, you all right?'

'I just can't believe – are they dead?'

'Yeah, both of them. I looked in there before the police came. It wasn't a pretty picture.'

Cassie leaned forward and vomited into the gutter. It was one deep heave that seemed to empty her totally. She wiped her mouth with her hand.

'Cassie!' Meehan cried as he watched. 'I'll go get one of the paramedics.'

'No, don't. I'm fine. I just . . . poor Ray. All he wanted to do was help.'

'What do you mean?'

She realized she had made a mistake giving her thoughts voice.

'I mean he was just a nice guy. Connie, too. They would have given up the keys or the money. Why'd he have to shoot them?'

'I know. It makes no sense. By the way, did you see someone?'

'No, why?'

'I noticed you said "he" when you were talking about it.'

'No, I've been gone. I was just saying it was a he because I just think it probably was. I can't think straight right now.'

'I know what you mean. I can't believe this is happening.'

She sat on the curb with her face in her hands, the guilt of the world weighing down on her. The words *I did this, I did this, I did this* kept running through her head. She knew she had to get away from this place and never look back.

She found her strength and stood up, grabbing Meehan's arm one time to steady herself.

'Are you sure you're okay?' he asked.

'Yes, fine. I'm fine. Thanks, Billy.'

'You should probably let the police know you're okay and you're here.'

'Okay, I will. Actually, could you tell them for me? I'm not sure I want to go in there.'

'Sure, Cassie, I'll go tell them right now.'

Cassie waited a few moments after Meehan walked

away, then walked down the sidewalk to the alley that ran behind the dealership. She followed the alley behind the service center to the other side of the dealership and walked into the sales lot. The silver Boxster that Ray had been letting her use was there. She always parked it in the sales lot in case a customer was interested.

The car was unlocked but her key was in her backpack in her office. She opened the door and pulled the front trunk release. She came around and opened the lid and took out the leather-bound owner's manual, then closed the trunk and got into the car. Behind one of the folds of the booklet was a plastic key for the eventual owner to put in a wallet as an emergency backup. She took it out, started the car and drove out of the lot into the alley. She kept a slow, deliberate speed until she had covered two blocks in the alley. She then cut up to Sunset and took a right, in a direction away from the dealership and toward the 101 Freeway.

Tears ran down her cheeks as she drove. What had happened at the dealership changed everything. Leo's death was awful and hurt her deeply. But Leo had been in the circle and knew the risks. Ray Morales and Connie Leto, the finance manager, were innocents. Their deaths signaled the lengths to which Karch was willing to go to recover the money. It meant there were no bounds anymore. To Karch, to her guilt, to anything.

33

Karch watched through the window of the taxi as it went by the Porsche dealership. He didn't care about the assemblage of police and television news vehicles surrounding the glass walls of the showroom. His eyes scanned the numerous people standing on the sidewalks. He was hoping to see Cassie Black but knew he was too late. His cell phone had failed to get a signal up in the hills. He'd had to hike up to Mulholland and then over to the Hollywood overlook, where he'd remembered seeing a pay phone earlier. It took him nearly an hour to cover the ground. Then it was another twenty minutes waiting for the taxi he called for to show up.

The taxi driver said something in very bad English about what had happened at the dealership but Karch paid no attention. The taxi continued another few blocks and turned onto Wilcox. Karch had him stop in front of a Hollywood memorabilia store. He paid and got out. After the taxi took off and had turned back onto Sunset he crossed the street to his Lincoln, which was parked at the curb. On its bumpers were a set of fresh plates he had picked up that morning in a long-term lot at LAX.

Karch got in and fired the car up. But before pulling out of the space he looked up Selma in the map book. He saw he was in luck. He was less than five minutes away.

There were no cars parked in front or on the driveway of

the bungalow on Selma where Cassie Black's driver's license said she lived. The house was on a dead end and Karch decided on a direct approach. He pulled right into the driveway and parked. Breaking and entering in daylight was not his idea of a wise move but he had to get into the house to see if Cassie Black had been there yet. He decided the safest way to go was straight in. He pulled into the drive, honked the Lincoln's horn twice and waited. Finally, he killed the engine, got out and went right up the front steps, spinning his key chain on his finger. When he got close to the door he bent over and raised his lock picks. He quickly went to work on the deadbolt, acting as though he were a man having trouble with his keys. He had no idea if he was being watched but he was putting on a good show.

He picked the lock in about forty seconds. He then turned the knob and walked in.

'Hey, Cassie?' he called loudly and for the benefit of any neighbor who might have been watching. 'Come on, I'm waitin' out here!'

He closed the door, pulled out his gun and quickly attached the silencer. He began a quick room-to-room check of the house.

It was empty. He began a second and slower sweep, looking around to try to determine if Cassie Black had been to the house in the time since she had escaped from him up on the hill. The home, though sparely furnished, seemed to be in neat order. He became convinced that she had not been there yet. He sat down on the couch in the living room and thought about what this could mean. Did she already have the money or did she not have the money? Had it been at Leo Renfro's and he had somehow missed it during his all-night search? Worse yet was another possibility that poked through: that

Renfro had been telling the truth when he claimed to have already given the money to his Chicago contacts.

Karch felt something lumpy beneath the spot where he was sitting. He moved down the couch and then pulled up the cushion. He picked up a clothes hanger with seven padlocks attached to it. It served to remind him of how formidable Cassidy Black had turned out to be. He decided in that moment that if he found out she had the money and was gone, he would chase her to the ends of the earth. Not for Grimaldi and definitely not for the faceless group that pulled strings from Miami. He would do it for himself.

He left the hanger on the coffee table and got up to start his third sweep of the house. This one would take the longest.

The bedroom was the logical place to start. Karch knew people liked to sleep with the things dear to them close by. The white-walled room was furnished with the basics, a four-poster bed, two bed tables, a bureau and a mirror. A framed poster of a beach scene from Tahiti was taped to a wall. He studied it for a moment and quickly realized it was a duplicate of the poster he had seen in Cassidy Black's office when he had stepped in while looking for her in the showroom. He had been looking at the poster when the manager had stuck his head in and asked if he could help.

Karch stepped over to the wall and studied the poster, wondering if it had any significance for his mission. The woman on the beach did not look like Cassidy Black. He finally decided he would have to worry about it later and turned to the nearby bed table and opened the top drawer.

The drawer contained a stack of *Popular Mechanics* magazines that looked as though they had been bought at a yard sale. They were all in poor condition and were several years old. Still, he flew the pages on every one of them in case there was a note or maybe a hidden address. He found nothing and dropped the last magazine back in the drawer and kicked it closed.

The bottom drawer of the table was empty except for a little net bundle containing cedarwood shavings and dried rosemary. He slammed that drawer closed and came around the bed to the other night table.

Before he opened the drawer he had a feeling he would have good luck here. This table had a lamp on it and the pillow on this side of the bed had an indentation from someone sleeping on it. He knew this was her side of the bed.

Karch sat down on the bed and put his gun down next to his thigh. With both hands he picked up the pillow and brought it to his face. He could smell her. Her hair. He wasn't good at identifying fragrances but he thought he could smell tea leaves, like when you first open a box of tea bags. He wasn't sure about it and put the pillow back down.

He opened the top drawer of the bed table and hit pay dirt. The drawer was crammed with personal items. There were books and hair bands and photograph albums. There was a still camera with a long lens and a video camera as well. Placed on top of everything was a small framed photograph. Karch picked it up and studied it. It showed Cassidy Black sitting on the lap of a man wearing a Hawaiian shirt. She was holding a pinkish-orange drink with a paper umbrella in it. Karch almost didn't recognize her because the smile on her face was so wide and bright.

However, he easily recognized the man in the photo. His was a face Karch would never forget. Max Freeling, the man who had permanently altered Karch's entire life in one moment of time. Karch knew he wouldn't be where he now sat if it had not been for Max Freeling and the decision he had made at the top of that hotel six years before. All these years, he had been under Grimaldi's thumb because of what happened in that room with Max Freeling.

He turned the picture over and hit the frame's glass harshly on the corner of the bed table. He heard the glass crack. He noticed something written on the cardboard backing of the frame. It said,

> I looked up and saw the outline of Tahiti and I realized this was the place I had been looking for all my life.
>
> *W. Somerset Maugham*

Karch turned the frame over and looked at the photo again. A spiderweb crack started on Cassidy Black's face and branched across the photograph. Karch tossed the frame into a wastebasket that was next to the bed table.

From the drawer he removed a thick photo album with a soft brown leather binding. As he opened it he expected to find more photos of Max Freeling but instead got a surprise. The album was full of photographs of a young girl. Almost all of them were taken from a distance – he glanced at the long-range camera in the drawer – and at the same location, a schoolyard.

He leafed through the book and found one picture of the girl dribbling a basketball. Painted on the wall of a building behind the playing area was the name Wonderland School.

He closed the album and pulled out another. It contained more photos of the girl, though these were not taken at the school. They depicted the girl playing in a yard in front of a house. In some she was pulling a wagon or kicking a ball, in others she was going down a sliding board or laughing on a swing. A grouping of photos in the back of the book but not yet placed in plastic windows showed the girl on a trip to Disneyland. One of the shots, again taken from afar, showed her embracing Mickey Mouse.

Karch realized something and reached into his coat pocket. He pulled out the two passports and opened the top one to the ID photo. It was the same girl from the photos in the albums. Jodie Davis, the name said.

Karch put the passports back in his pocket and let the photo album drop to the floor. He was having an epiphany, a moment when seemingly disparate memories and new pieces of information coalesced into a new truth. He now understood something that had tortured him for six years.

An idea started coming together, a plan for getting the money and Cassie Black, all at the same time. He closed the top drawer and opened the bottom. This one was less crowded. There was an electric hair dryer that didn't look as though it was ever used and a few old pieces of mail from inmates at High Desert Correctional Institution for Women. Karch opened one of the letters and saw it was just a howyadoin' from a former cellmate named Letitia Granville. Karch also threw these into the wastebasket and reached back into the drawer and underneath the hair dryer for a manila envelope that was address side down.

He turned it over and saw that it was addressed to Cassidy Black at High Desert Correctional. Whatever was in the envelope was something she had taken with her from prison. He ran his thumb under the return address and saw the preprinted envelope had been sent from Renaissance Investigations of Paradise Road, Las Vegas. Karch was familiar with the agency. It was mid-size, five or six investigators and an equal number of supposed specialties. He competed with them for the referrals from the Metro missing persons unit. Karch opened the envelope and pulled out a well-thumbed investigation summary. He was about to start reading the particulars when he was jarred by the screaming voice of someone in the doorway behind him.

'FREEZEITUPFUCKHEAD!'

Karch dropped the report and held his hands out in front of him. He slowly started to turn his head. What he saw further shocked him. Just inside the doorway of the bedroom was an enormous black woman. She stood in the classic Weaver stance taught at every law enforcement academy in the country. Feet spread, weight equally distributed, both hands up holding and bracing the gun, elbows slightly bent and pointed outward. Around her neck was a chain with a badge on it. She looked like no cop Karch had ever seen, but the 9 mm Beretta pointed at him won the debate.

'Take it easy now,' he said calmly. 'I'm on your side.'

34

Since getting the news at the dealership Cassie Black had felt as though she were under water, in some kind of surrealistic otherworld that had no bearing on her life. Deep down she knew it was an instinctive defense mechanism. It allowed her to continue, to move and do what needed to be done.

She now stood in the backyard of Leo's house staring at the dried blood streaking the jagged piece of glass standing in the bottom frame of the sliding door. Just seeing the glass confirmed what Karch had told her. She knew now that Leo was dead. If she went into the house she would find his body. And whatever way she found it would constitute an image she would never be able to remove from her memory.

She looked down into the pool at the vacuum standing motionless at the bottom. But almost immediately her eyes were drawn back to the door with the jagged glass. She knew she had to go in. Finally, she nodded once to herself and walked up to the door. And immediately she could see his body on the floor of the office. An eighteen-wheeler going by on the freeway behind the property drowned out the awful sighing sound that came involuntarily from her throat. She stepped over the glass and into the house.

Leo's body was sprawled face up to the side of the door. Blood seemed to be everywhere. Despite the horrible tableau the scene created, her eyes were drawn to what unmistakably appeared to be, if not a smile on his face, a look of satisfaction. Cassie crouched next to him and touched his cold cheek.

'Oh, Leo,' she said. 'What did I do?'

The tears started coming again. She tried to pinch them off by tightly closing her eyes and balling her fists.

Finally, when she opened her eyes again, she tried to study the body and the surroundings as maybe a detective would. She wanted to know what had happened. The fact that Karch had come to her and demanded the money meant Leo had stood up. She looked at the bloody drag marks on the tile floor and put it together. Leo had done it. He had gone to the glass. He had done it for her.

'Leo . . .'

She closed her eyes again and leaned her head down to his silent chest.

'I knew we should've run.'

She straightened back up with a new resolve. She would get away. She knew it was a selfish choice but she also knew that if she failed that Leo's noble death would be for nothing. That was Leo's hope in the end. His last prayer. That was what put the smile on his face. She would honor that.

She stood up and looked around the office. It had been completely destroyed by Karch's search. But he had been looking for two and a half million dollars, not for what she looked for now. She stepped over the body to the overturned desk and looked at the debris on the floor. Leo's astrology books and papers and notebooks were scattered about. The contents of the desk drawers had been dumped. Amidst the clutter she saw two envelopes on the floor, both addressed to Leo and with the same odd return address, just the numbers 773. She stooped down and picked them up. Both were empty. One was postmarked two days before in Chicago and then she knew. Karch had found the passports. He had them.

Cassie abruptly stood up and her head hit the red I-Ching coins that dangled from the ceiling and would have been directly over the upright desk. She looked up at them for a moment and then grabbed the desk chair and moved it over. She climbed up on the chair and unhooked the string of coins. She wanted something of Leo's to take with her. If not for luck, then just to remember him by.

As she got down she knew there was no point in going through the rest of the house. Karch had the passports and there was nothing else inside that she had wanted. She walked over to Leo's body and once more looked down on him. She thought of the song she had listened to so many times on the way to Vegas. She hoped there had been an angel to whisper in his ear.

'Good-bye, Leo,' she said.

She carefully stepped over the glass and through the broken slider out to the backyard. She walked to the pool's edge and looked down at the vacuum. Tracing its hose to a coupling in the wall, she walked around to the other side and then got down on her knees and reached into the water. She grabbed the hose and started pulling it up and out onto the pool's concrete skirt. It was heavy work and twice she almost toppled into the water. Eventually, the vacuum head and debris bag came to the surface and she wrestled it onto the concrete.

Water turned the white concrete dark and soaked the knees of her black jeans. She didn't care. She struggled with the collar of the debris bag but then saw the zipper running alongside the bag. She quickly zipped the bag open and spread it. Inside the bag was another bag, a heavy-duty white plastic bag with its mouth tied in a knot. She carefully lifted it out of the vacuum bag and then worked her fingers into the knot. It was too tight and she didn't have the fingernails for the job. She reached into her back pocket for the Swiss Army knife and used it to cut the knot off the bag.

Cassie looked inside. The bricks of hundred-dollar bills were there. Still wrapped in plastic and as dry as the day they were cut at the mint.

She closed the bag and looked across the pool at the broken sliding door. From this angle she could see the tops of Leo's shoes pointing upward. She silently said her thanks to him. He had said to her when he told where the money would be kept that the best hiding place was one in plain sight. He had been right.

Cassie looked down at the water. Her struggling with the vacuum had created a small current. Floating by her on the surface was a dead hummingbird, its tiny wings spread like an angel's.

35

Karch slowly stood up when ordered to by the woman with the gun.

'Who the hell are you?'

He nodded, hoping it would be a gesture taken as a sign of his full cooperation and compliance.

'My name is Jack Karch. I'm a private investigator. My license is in the inside right pocket of my jacket. May I get it out and show it to you?'

'Maybe later. A PI? What do you want with Cassie Black? And take two steps backward and lean against the wall.'

She was slowly coming further into the room. He did as he was told and leaned his shoulders against the wall as he spoke. He saw her eyeing the Sig, which was still on the bed.

'I'm on a case. A hot prowl in Vegas. A hotel room. A high roller was taken off for a lot of money. If you don't mind me asking, who are you?'

The woman was at the bottom of the bed. Keeping her eyes and the aim of her Beretta on Karch, she bent forward and reached her free hand for the gun.

'Agent Thelma Kibble, state parole.'

'Oh, yeah, Kibble. I was going to try to reach you today to talk about Black.'

'Since when does Nevada allow its PIs to run around with silencer-equipped weapons?'

Karch did his best to look surprised.

'Oh, you mean that? That's not mine. I found that in the drawer there. That's Cassie Black's. And you might be careful how you handle it. I think it's evidence.'

'Of what? You said it was a hot prowl.'

'They found the body of her old partner, a man named Jersey Paltz, in the desert. He was shot.'

Kibble looked down at the weapon in her left hand. Karch was about six feet away from her. He decided it was too risky to make a move from that distance.

'Tell you what, Mr Karch, why don't you very slowly open up your jacket for me?'

'Sure.'

Karch slowly opened his jacket, exposing the empty shoulder holster.

'I know what you're going to say,' he said quickly. ' "Empty holster, the Sig must be his." Not true. I have a license to carry a concealed weapon. But it's a Nevada state license. No good in California. If I had a weapon in this holster I would be breaking the law. My weapon is locked in its case in the trunk of my car. If you want to walk out with me I will show it to you.'

'I'm not worried about that. What I'm wondering is why you are here and not the Vegas cops. If there's a murder, why aren't the authorities involved? Why aren't they here?'

'Well, first of all they are involved. But, as you must know, the police are hampered by bureaucracy. I was hired by the Cleopatra Resort and Casino to investigate the room burglary. I have a staff and an expense account. I move faster. The police will be coming here and be in contact with you soon. In fact, I am working very closely with the Metro police. If you wish, I can give you the name and number of a detective who will vouch for me.'

If she bit, he would give her Iverson's number. He

could ad lib it. Karch would have to work something out with Iverson later with either a payoff or a bullet. But Kibble didn't bite.

'Even if someone vouched for you it wouldn't explain why you took it upon yourself to break into a suspect's home,' she said.

'I did not break in,' Karch said indignantly. 'The front door was wide open. Look, that's my car parked outside in the driveway. Would I park there if I was breaking in?'

'You seem to have an answer for everything, Mr Karch.'

'As long as they are true. Could you please stop pointing that gun at me now? I think I have sufficiently established who I am and what I'm doing here. Do you want to see my license now?'

Kibble hesitated but then lowered her gun to her side. Karch dropped his hands to his side without her protesting. He had hoped she would actually put the weapon away but nonetheless was pleased by what he saw. He decided to stay on the offensive.

'Now, can I ask *you* what you are doing here?'

Kibble hiked her sizable shoulders.

'I'm doing my job, Mr Karch. Just a routine home call. Checking up on one of my cases.'

'Seems a little too coincidental to me.'

'I had a conversation with her a couple weeks ago that didn't sit well with me. I put her on my list of field checks. Didn't get to it until today.'

'And you came here instead of visiting the dealership?'

'I called the dealership. She had a message on her line saying she wasn't in today. So I came here. Don't ask me any more questions, Mr Karch. I'm asking you the questions.'

'Fine.'

He waved his hands in surrender.

'You said there's a homicide in this? Well, I know Cassie Black probably better than anybody around here and I'll tell you right now there's no way she's involved in a homicide. No way.'

Karch thought of Hidalgo's body lying on the bed in the Cleo's penthouse.

'We'll have to agree to disagree on that, Agent Kibble. The evidence speaks for itself. And after all, remember, we're talking about an ex-con here, one who served time in Nevada on a murder conviction.'

'It was a manslaughter and we both know the circumstances. The law held her responsible for her partner's death but she was twenty stories below when he went out the window. Somebody may have pushed him, but it wasn't her.'

'Is that what she said? That somebody pushed him?'

'It's the way she had it figured. She said the casinos had to make an example of him. He got pushed.'

'That's bullshit, but never mind. How did she get out here?'

'She had her parole transferred. Once she got the job lined up with Ray Morales at the dealership it was a cinch. She had a lawyer petition and the parole transfer was approved. She knew Ray from Vegas when she was a dealer. Ray's an ex-con who made it in the straight life. He wanted to give her a shot at it. He probably also wanted something else but Cassie never complained.'

Karch had thought Morales was an ex-con. When he'd put him down on the floor of the finance office Morales had taken it with a certain dignity you never saw in citizens. The woman was like the rest of them. She started to whimper and was going to shout so he'd had to shoot her first.

'So did you get close to her?' Karch asked. 'Close enough to know what made her blood move?'

'You mean why she started ripping off high rollers in Vegas?'

Karch nodded.

'You ask me, I think it had something to do with her father. A degenerate gambler. I think she thought she was getting back at the casinos or something. I don't know.'

'I don't think you do. You mind if I sit down? I've got a bad back.'

He brought his arms up behind his back as if stretching the muscles. He kept talking the whole time.

'I'm on a pension from Vegas Metro. Partial disability. Wrecked my back chasing down a guy dusted on meth. He picked me up and *threw* me down a flight of stairs . . .'

None of it was true. It was all part of the sleight of hand. As he talked his left hand went under his jacket and picked the .25 out of the silk pocket inside his rear belt line.

'I have never seen that kind of power in a single human being . . .'

He brought his hands forward and clasped them together in an ad-libbed stretching motion during which he transferred the gun to his right hand. He then held it palmed at his side as he groaned and sat down on the bed. Kibble was now about four feet away and still holding her weapon at her side. She held the Sig by the barrel in her other hand and also at her side. Karch knew he had her. But he wanted to get more information from her first.

'Tell me about the kid she and Max Freeling had,' he said.

Kibble appraised him for a moment before answering.

'What kid and what's it got to do with a hot prowl in Las Vegas?'

Karch smiled and shook his head.

'She didn't come here because some guy offered her a job selling cars, Agent Kibble. She came because she and Max had a kid and that kid ended up out here.'

He looked up at her.

'But I think you know that, don't you?'

'I don't know anything about where the child is but, yes, you're right. Cassie was pregnant when she got arrested. Kept it a secret till it showed. By then she had pleaded out and was at High Desert Correctional. The child was born there. She nursed the baby three days and then it was given away. She put it up for adoption.'

Karch nodded. He hadn't known the details but had already figured out the main aspects of the story.

'You got kids, Agent Kibble?'

'Two of them.'

'Three days. That long enough to make a bond? A bond that nobody can break?'

'Three minutes is enough.'

'You know I'm tired –'

He leaped up off the bed and stuck the .25 into the collar of fat that was Kibble's neck.

'—of your sarcastic way of answering me, Agent Kibble. It is—'

He slapped the Beretta out of one of her hands and then reached over and took the Sig Sauer from the other.

'—*really* starting to bug me.'

Kibble froze and her eyes widened.

'What are you doing?' she asked.

'I'm sticking the short barrel of a twenty-five pop gun into your fat neck, Agent Kibble. I'm now going to ask you a few more questions and you're going to leave the bullshit out of your voice when you answer. Am I right about this?'

'Yes,' she whispered. 'Like I said, I got two kids. I'm all they got, so please don't –'

Karch sidestepped her and then pushed her down onto the bed. He put the .25 back into its pocket and pointed the Sig at her. He reached up and made sure the silencer was still properly attached. He waited until her frightened eyes looked up at him before he spoke.

'Well, if you want to see them again, you answer a few questions and without any of that fat lip anymore.'

'Okay, okay. What questions?'

'What else you know about the kid she had? The girl.'

'Nothing. Just the one time she told me about the birth and stuff. That was all she ever mentioned about it.'

'Why'd it come up?'

'I was showing her pictures of my boys and she just mentioned it. It was at the beginning and she had just come out from Nevada. I was trying to get to know her a bit and she seemed like a good girl.'

'What else she say? She didn't say her kid ended up out here?'

'Never mentioned it. She said she told Max she was pregnant on that last night – the night he went out the window.'

'That night?'

'That's what she said. She said it was going to be their last job. She told him she was going to have a baby beforehand and Max got all protective. He wouldn't let her do the hot prowl. So he did it.'

'What are you saying, that she was supposed to be the one who went up into that room?'

'You didn't know that?'

'How could anybody know? Max ended up splattered across a craps table and she never talked. She took a plea instead. Now I fucking know why.'

Karch winced. The pieces of that night were coming

together. He thought he understood everything now –
six years too late. He turned and stepped away from the
bed as if turning from a bad memory. In the mirror over
the bureau he saw Kibble's posture stiffen as though she
were going to make a move. Then she saw him watching
her in the mirror.

'Don't do anything stupid, Agent Kibble. Remember
those two kids of yours. What did Cassie Black say about
Max trying to fly that night?'

'She wouldn't talk about it, especially with me. There
was just this one time that she talked a little bit about it.
And she said Max had to have had some help going
through that window. That's all.'

'Yeah, well, she was right. But the help came from her,
nobody else.'

'What, you were there?'

Karch looked at her a long moment and he could see
fear rise in her eyes.

'I'm asking the questions now, remember?'

He paused to allow her to answer but she didn't.
Karch raised the aim of the Sig up her wide body, over
her face and to the wall behind her until he was pointing
at the woman walking on the beach in the poster.

'Tell me about Tahiti.'

'Tahiti?' She looked backward at the poster on the
wall. 'Tahiti was a dream.'

'Was?'

'She went there with Max once. Blew the take on one
of the jobs and went there for a week.'

Karch looked over at the wastebasket next to the bed
table. The photo of Cassie Black and Max and the
umbrella drink could be seen over the lip of the can. He
knew without a doubt then that it had been taken in
Tahiti.

'She thought that was where the baby got . . . you

know, conceived,' Kibble said. 'And the plan was for them to go back. After the baby was born. You know, retire from the hot prowl and live on an island or something in Tahiti. Live happily ever after and raise the child.'

'But all that went out the window with Max.'

Kibble nodded.

'They never made it,' she said. 'So Tahiti isn't a place anymore. Not for Cassie. It's a dream. It's all her plans. It's everything she never got with Max.'

Karch paused for a moment before responding. He looked down at the investigation report from Renaissance that was on the floor by Kibble's feet.

'It's almost everything,' he finally said, his eyes still on the report. 'But our Cassie Black has a plan, Agent Kibble. Something tells me she's the type who always has a plan.'

He was totally into his own thoughts. He quickly scanned through his theories and suddenly looked up at Kibble.

'Last question,' he said. 'What do I do with you now?'

36

Cassie pulled to the curb a block from the house on Selma and studied it for any indication that Karch might be there waiting for her. There was nothing obvious; no cars in the driveway, the front door wasn't kicked in. She watched for ten minutes but never picked up a warning vibe. Finally, she drove off to the street running parallel to Selma and one block over. She parked again, then got out and cut between two houses and climbed a fence into her backyard. She left the money locked in the front trunk of the Boxster. Her plan was to not leave the car for very long. She was only going in to get a single photograph, maybe some spare clothing if she wanted to push it. She dug the spare key out of the flowerpot on the back porch and quietly entered the house through the kitchen door.

Karch had been there. The place had not been searched and destroyed like Leo's house. But he had been there. The vibe was there. She could tell. There was something disturbed, something amiss. She stepped into the living room without making a sound and confirmed her instinct when she saw the hanger and seven locks lying on the coffee table. She hadn't worked the locks since before going to Las Vegas. She had not left them out in the open like that. He had.

She stood perfectly still and concentrated on the sounds of the house for almost two minutes. When she heard nothing else she retreated to the kitchen and took the largest knife she had out of a drawer. She carried it at her side as she entered the front hallway and slowly walked into her bedroom.

The first thing she saw was the poster. It hung askew on the wall and slashed across it was a large X that looked to her to have been painted with blood. It was a long moment before she could pull her eyes away from it to take in the rest of the bedroom. This room had been searched. Cassie did not have enough belongings to make the debris all over the floor seem to be much more than a minor mess. But she quickly dropped to the floor and grabbed her two photo albums. The idea that Karch might have handled them and looked in them repulsed her. She put the albums on the bed for taking even though she knew she didn't need them anymore. She then quickly began scanning the floor for the one photo that she did need, that was irreplaceable.

Finally, she saw it in the trash can, the glass over the photo shattered. She grabbed it out of the can and shook the glass out of the frame. The photo appeared to be undamaged and she let out a sigh of relief. It was the only photo ever taken of Max and her together. For five years it had been taped to the wall next to her bed at High Desert. She pulled it from the frame and placed it on top of the two albums on the bed. She looked at her watch and saw it was almost three. She needed to hurry. She grabbed a pillow off the bed and stripped off the case. She then put the albums and the photo of Max into it.

She went to the bureau next and shoved handfuls of underwear and socks into the pillowcase. She had no jewelry other than her Timex and one pair of earrings that she almost never wore – the silver hoops that Max had actually paid for and given her on a birthday.

She next went to the closet to grab extra pairs of jeans

and a few shirts. She opened the door with her eyes already angled up toward the string pull of the overhead light. So she didn't see Thelma Kibble until the light was on and she glanced down to see what her foot had just bumped into.

Her parole agent was lying on the floor of the walk-in closet with her back propped against the rear wall, her legs spread wide. Her head was tilted at an odd angle, her mouth was wide open and the front of the large, flowing dress she wore was a crimson mess. A hand came up and stifled a scream in Cassie's mouth. She jerked backward from it and then realized it was her own. The pillowcase dropped from her other hand and thumped on the floor.

The noise prompted Kibble to slowly open her eyes. It almost seemed that in all of that huge body the action of opening her eyes exhausted all her stores of strength. Cassie dropped to her knees between Kibble's outstretched legs.

'Thelma! Thelma, what happened?'

Without waiting for an answer she already knew, Cassie reached up and jerked one of the two dresses she owned off a hanger. She bunched it in her hands and moved in close to Kibble to use it as a compress. She saw a single bullet wound high on Kibble's chest. A tremendous amount of blood had leaked from the wound. So much that Cassie was stunned that Kibble was still alive. She pressed the dress over the wound and looked at Kibble's lips. They were soundlessly working as Kibble attempted to say something.

'Thelma, don't talk, don't talk. Was it Karch? A man named Karch?'

The mouth stopped working for a moment and there was a slight nod.

'Thelma, I am so sorry.'

'—ot me wi' my own gun . . .'

Her voice was no more than a rasp.

'Thelma, don't talk. I'm going to get help. You hang in there and I'll get help. Can you hold this?'

Cassie lifted the woman's left hand and put it over the bunched dress. When she released her hold the hand started to fall away. Cassie reached over to a plastic laundry basket and dragged it over. She overturned it and pulled it in tight against Kibble's side. She raised Kibble's left arm again and propped the elbow on the overturned basket. She then put the left hand back onto the makeshift compress. The weight of Kibble's huge arm kept her hand and the compress in place.

'Hang in there, Thelma,' Cassie ordered. 'There's no phone in the house. I have to go to my car. I'll call for help and be right back. Okay?'

She waited and saw Kibble's jaw start to tremble as she tried to say something.

'Don't answer! Just save your strength. Help will be here soon.'

Cassie started to get up but saw Kibble's mouth still working. She was determined to say something. Cassie leaned in close and turned so her left ear was close.

'He knows . . .'

Cassie waited but there was nothing else. She turned and looked at Kibble.

'He knows? He knows what?'

Kibble's eyes came up to hers and Cassie knew that what she was trying to say was important.

'Karch? He knows what, Thelma?'

She turned and leaned in again.

'Your daughter. He . . . has her picture.'

Cassie sprang back as if punched. She looked at Kibble with fearful and alert eyes. She then looked down at the pillowcase next to her as if it might contain a bomb set to go off at any moment. She grabbed the bag and turned it

318

over, dumping its contents. She grabbed up one of the albums – the one she called the school album – and opened it. The first photo was missing from the clear plastic window. Written across the window in a black marker was a message that froze her heart.

NO COPS
702–881–8787

Without a doubt she knew what the message meant.
'Go . . .'
Cassie looked up from the photo album to Kibble.
'Go now . . . go get her . . .'
Cassie looked at her a long moment and then nodded. She jumped up and ran from the closet, taking the photo album with the phone number in it and leaving everything else behind.

37

From a steady distance of three blocks Karch's Towncar trailed the white Volvo wagon as it left the Wonderland School. As Karch expected, the Volvo didn't go far. It stayed on Lookout Mountain Road until it almost crested the hill and then turned down a driveway next to a 1920's style home set well back from the road. Karch slowed and by the time he was abreast of the house he saw the woman and the little girl with the happy-face backpack heading toward the front door of the house. He went on by and turned around in a driveway a block farther up the street. He went back down the street and parked at the curb across the street from the driveway with the Volvo wagon parked in it. The woman and child were inside now.

Karch noticed the real estate sign on the property and the smaller hook-on sign announcing the property was in escrow. He thought another piece of the story was falling into place. He believed that if he ever got the chance to ask Cassidy Black, she would tell him that everything started with that sign. She saw that sign and put things into motion.

'And here we are,' he said out loud.

He had been doing that a lot lately – the audio commentary when no one was around to hear it but himself. But he wasn't worried about it. It ran in the family. He used to sit in the bedroom and listen to his father in the next room talking to himself in the mirror.

He'd do it while running quarters over his knuckles – both hands at once – and practicing coin and card gags. He always said the patter was as important in the art of the sleight as anything you did with your hands. Words could be part of the misdirection as well.

He heard a shout and looked over at the house. The girl had come outside. She had changed and was now wearing denim overalls over a long-sleeved T-shirt. She was kicking a ball with a ladybug design on it around the yard and finding something in the activity to yell about. Karch saw the woman standing just inside the open front door and watching over her. He waited and watched and eventually the woman stepped back into the house and out of sight. She apparently felt confident in the safety and sanctity of the yard.

Karch checked his watch and waited for her to come back to check on the girl. He wanted to get an idea of the time intervals and then he would know how much time he had. While he waited he thought some more about Cassidy Black. He believed he would soon have the high card in the game they were playing. And the last deal would be on his table, not hers.

The woman came back to the door to check on the girl after six minutes. Karch had also been counting the cars during that time. Only three had gone by. Traffic was beyond prediction but he figured, to be safe, he had between two and three minutes from getting out to getting back in.

He picked the Renaissance Investigations report off the seat next to him and checked the name once more. He then got out of the car and crossed the street, checking the surrounding houses for witnesses as he went. There were none that he could see. As far as he was concerned he had the green light. The plan was a go.

The girl looked up from her ball when he got to

within a few feet of the picket fence at the front of the property. The fence was a design flourish, not a safety measure. It was barely higher than Karch's knees. If needed he'd be able to reach over and grab her.

The girl didn't say anything. She just stopped her playing and looked at him.

'How do you do?' Karch said. 'You're Jodie Shaw, aren't you?'

The girl looked back at her house and didn't see her mother at the door. She looked back at Karch.

'You are, aren't you?'

She nodded and Karch took the last few steps to the fence. He had his hands in his pockets, a subliminally nonthreatening pose.

'I was hoping so. See, your daddy sent me over from the office to pick you up for the surprise party.'

'What su'prise party?'

Karch took his hands out of his pockets and stepped up to the little fence. He dropped into a baseball catcher's stance so he would be closer to her level. His face was still above the top of the fence. He looked over the girl's head at the front door. No sign of the woman but he knew he was on a clock. He turned his head and looked over both shoulders. No neighbors anywhere. No cars coming. He still had the green.

'The party he's having for your mommy. He doesn't want her to know about it. But it's going to be a lot of fun. With a lot of your friends there and there's even going to be a magic show.'

He reached over the fence to her right ear and seemed to grab a quarter out of thin air. When he had removed his hand from his pocket the quarter had been clipped between his third and fourth finger in the classic Goshman Pinch sleight. The girl looked at the coin and her mouth opened into a surprised smile.

'Hey!'

'And what about this side?'

He pulled another quarter out of her other ear with his other hand. The girl was grinning broadly now.

'How'd you do that?'

'If I told you I'd have to . . . uh, well, you know if you come with me now to see your dad, then I promise he and I will teach you how to do it. What do you say, Jodie? Okay? He's waiting for us, baby.'

'I'm not a baby. And I'm not supposed to go with strangers.'

Karch silently cursed to himself and checked the front door again. Still clear.

'I know you're not a baby. It's just a figure of speech I use, that's all. And the other thing is, I'm not really a stranger. I mean, you and I just met for the first time but I know your daddy and he knows me. Enough for him to pick me to come get you for the party.'

He checked the front door one last time. He knew he was going too long with this. He was way over time. The green light was now red.

'Anyway, your daddy really wants you there at the office so—'

He straightened up and reached over the fence.

'—you can yell "Surprise!" when your mommy gets there.'

He reached under her arms and lifted her up. He knew the key thing was to keep her quiet for thirty feet – from the fence to the car. That was all. After that, it didn't matter. He turned and walked quickly across the street toward the Lincoln.

'Mommy?' the girl said in a timid voice.

'Shhhh, shhhh,' he responded quickly. 'We don't want her to know about this, sweetheart. That would spoil the surprise.'

He got to the car, opened the back door and loaded her in. He then closed it and jumped into the front seat. He had done it, he realized. Grabbed her without incident or detection. He dropped the car into drive and started down Lookout Mountain.

'Is there going to be dancing at this surprise party?' Jodie said from the backseat.

Karch adjusted the rearview mirror so he would be able to watch the girl. The moment he did it he heard a scream in the distance. The windows were up in the Lincoln so the origin of the sound could not be pinpointed. Karch readjusted the rearview mirror and immediately saw the woman from the house run into the street fifty yards behind. Her hands were balled into fists and pressed against her temples as she stared at the retreating Lincoln. He quickly hit the button that turned on the stereo.

He checked the mirror again. The woman was still in the middle of the street screaming but the stereo was covering it in the car. It was Frank Sinatra singing 'That's Life.'

Karch started thinking about the license plates on the Lincoln. He doubted the woman had gotten a read off the back plate but he knew he needed to find a safe place to switch back to the originals. And he wasn't worried about having been seen himself. The windows were tinted too dark for that. He felt good. He was clear.

He remembered the girl had asked a question. He adjusted the mirror again and looked back at her.

'What did you ask?'

'Will there be dancing at the party for my mommy?'

'Sure, baby, plenty of dancing.'

'I'm not a baby.'

'Yeah? Who cares?'

38

The gears of the Boxster whined loudly as Cassie wound them out on the way into Laurel Canyon.

'Nine-one-one emergency, how can I help you?'

She had the phone on speaker.

'Listen to me, you have an officer down. An officer down!'

She gave the address of the house on Selma and the location within where Thelma Kibble could be found. She also described the wound she observed and told the operator to dispatch the ambulance.

'I am doing that by computer while we speak. What is your name, please?'

'Just send the paramedics, would you?'

She disconnected the call and immediately hit redial. At first she got a recording saying all 911 lines were busy but an operator picked up before the recording was completed.

'Nine-one-one emergency, how can I help you?'

At first Cassie thought it might be the same operator.

'Can I help you?'

She decided it wasn't.

'There's a man trying to abduct a little girl. You have to send someone.'

'What is the location, ma'am?'

Cassie looked at the dashboard clock. It was three-fifteen. She knew Jodie Shaw's schedule by heart and that she left Wonderland Elementary every day at three. If Karch hadn't already made his move he would have to do it at the house. She gave the operator the address of the house on Lookout Mountain Road.

'Hurry! Please!'

She disconnected the call. She caught the light at Hollywood and Laurel Canyon Boulevards and sped north into the canyon. She realized that she was probably closer than any LAPD patrol cruiser, unless there happened to be one already in the canyon or at Wonderland Elementary. She had to decide what to do if she got there first.

Traffic slowed as it winnowed to one lane and she found herself caught behind an old LTD that was meandering into the canyon.

'Come on!' she yelled, her hand pressed on the horn. 'Let's go! Let's go!'

She saw the man in the car in front of her looking at her in his mirror. She waved him to the side but he just raised the middle finger of his right hand to her and seemed to intentionally drive even slower. On the next turn she passed him, a dangerous maneuver that made an oncoming car pull off the road. The driver of that car and the man in the LTD serenaded her with long blasts of their horns. Cassie stuck her fist out the window and raised her finger to the LTD. She sped ahead.

She made the turn onto Lookout Mountain and sped up the hill. She slowed as she went by Wonderland Elementary. There were still children in the play yard and the street was crowded with double-parked cars as parents stopped to pick up their children. Cassie picked her way around but didn't bother looking for Jodie. She knew the schedule. She was at home – or already with Karch.

As she made the last curve before the Shaws' house her

heart jumped up into her throat. Up ahead was a police car, its lights flashing, parked in the street. Her hope was that it was there in response to her 911 call but her gut said that was impossible. She had made the call just three minutes earlier.

Cassie slowed the Boxster as she got to the house. She saw two police officers, a male and female team, standing on the lawn just inside the picket fence. They were looking at a woman whose face was so contorted and red that it was a moment before Cassie recognized her as Linda Shaw, the woman who had raised her child.

Tears were streaking her face. Her hands were white-knuckled fists held tight against her chest. The female cop was bending down a bit and looking into her face. She had one hand on Linda Shaw's arm in a comforting fashion. The other officer was speaking into a hand-held radio. Cassie knew she was too late.

All at once all three of them looked out into the street and at the Porsche, their attention drawn by the rumbling of the engine as Cassie powered it down.

The two officers checked the car for a few moments and turned their attention back to the woman between them. But Linda Shaw's eyes held on the Boxster. They pierced the windshield and looked right at Cassie Black. The two women had never met before. The adoption transfer had been handled blindly because of Cassie's incarceration and her desire at the time not to meet the people who would take her child.

But in that fleeting moment when their eyes met, Cassie felt something transmitted. They had connected on the cold plane where the worst fears of motherhood are hidden. In Linda Shaw's tortured and wet eyes Cassie saw that there could be no greater love for her daughter.

Cassie was the first to turn her eyes away. She kept the Boxster driving smoothly by. She knew she could take

Lookout Mountain up to Sunset Plaza and then back down into the city without having to go by the house again. That was what she would do, she decided.

And then she would go where he wanted her to go. Karch. They would play this out whatever way he wanted.

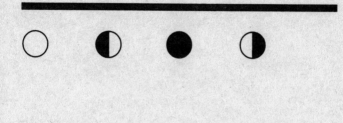

39

The desert sky was blue-black, the air cool and crisp. Karch loved the desert at night. He loved how peaceful it was and the memories it brought him. Even inside a Lincoln moving at ninety miles an hour he appreciated it. The desert was restorative. It was the city that took everything away.

He was halfway between Primm and Las Vegas and the glow of the Strip was lighting the horizon ahead like a distant wildfire. The 15 Freeway was wide open. He checked the dash clock and saw it was almost eight. He decided it was time to call Grimaldi. The old man was probably going nuts anyway, wondering and waiting. He turned the overhead light on and checked the girl once more. She was still lying across the backseat asleep. Just looking at her made Karch yawn. He hadn't slept in over thirty-six hours.

He shook it off and gulped black coffee from a to-go cup. He had bought it all the way back in Barstow and it was cold. He put it back in the dashboard cup holder and got the cell phone out of his jacket. He punched in Grimaldi's private office number and then turned the overhead light off. The call was picked up immediately.

'Yes?'

There was a lot of background noise. People noise, talking and yelling and clapping. Karch knew Grimaldi had picked up the extension in the crow's nest.

'Vincent, I need you to go to your computer.'

'Where the hell you been? I've been paging you since—'

'I've been trying to get your money back. Now can you—'

'All I want to know is if you have it, not that you're *trying* to get it. Trying doesn't mean anything without the other.'

Karch shook his head. He felt like yelling into the phone but knew it would wake up the kid. He kept his voice calm and even.

'It's coming, Vincent. But in order to collect it I'm going to need a little help. Now, can you check a room for me or not?'

'Of course I can check a room. Let me put you on hold while I get someone out here. Hold on.'

Grimaldi didn't wait for a reply. Karch was put on hold as the Lincoln steadily closed in on Las Vegas. After a good five minutes Grimaldi finally picked back up. The background noise was gone. He was in his office now. There was no banter. He got right to the point.

'What's the number?'

'The penthouse. Two-thousand-one. Like the space odyssey.'

'Wait a minute. That's the—'

'I know. Anybody in it?'

'I'm checking ... No, it's clear tonight.'

'Good, Vincent. Now block it off and reserve it under the name Jane Davis. You got a pen? I'll give you a credit card number.'

Karch took the passports out of his pocket and pulled an American Express card off the paperclip on the Jane Davis identification package. He turned the overhead light on and read Grimaldi the card number.

'Got it,' Grimaldi said. 'What else?'

The tone in Grimaldi's voice made Karch smile. It was so eager. Karch knew he was in control now. The trick would be to maintain it after this was all over. He spent the next ten minutes outlining his plan, looking over his shoulder twice to make sure the girl was still asleep and not listening. While he spoke the Lincoln passed the WELCOME TO LAS VEGAS sign that had adorned the city's outer perimeter for four decades. The neon-edged shapes of the Strip hotels came into view. Grimaldi badgered him during the telling with questions and voiced doubts. By the time he was finished the mood had shifted and he was exasperated.

'You sure this will work?' Grimaldi said.

'It is called synchronicity, Vin-*CENT*,' Karch said angrily. 'Have you ever heard the word? It will all fit together and you will have the money back. That is what you want, isn't it?'

'Yes, Jack, it's what I want.'

'All right then, we're in business. Better get things going. I'm almost there.'

He closed the phone and put it on the seat next to him. He checked the girl again and saw she was still out. He turned the light off just as the phone started to ring. He quickly grabbed it and opened it up before it woke the girl.

'What's wrong now, Vincent? You can't find *synchronicity* in your dictionary?'

'Who is Vincent?'

It was Cassie Black. Karch smiled, realizing he should have known it would not be Grimaldi because he didn't have the number.

'Cassidy Black,' he said quickly, hoping to cover. 'It's about time you checked in. Those were some nice moves you made today. But I think that if maybe we had been on my turf then things might have turned out—'

'Where is she?'

Her voice was a steely wire. Karch paused, his smile still fixed on his face. The moment was delicious. He had control and he was going to win this one.

'She's with me and she's doing fine. And that's exactly how she'll stay as long as you do *exactly* what I tell you to do. Do you understand that?'

'Listen to me, Karch. If that little girl gets hurt in any way . . . then it won't go by, you understand. I will make it my life's work to fuck you up. Do you understand *that*?'

Karch didn't answer for a while. He opened his window a half inch and got out a cigarette. He lit it off the dash lighter.

'Are you there, Karch?'

'Oh, I'm here. I'm just thinking to myself how ironic this is. I mean, I think it's irony – I never was very good in English class. Is it ironic when somebody whose plan it was to abduct a child complains about that very same child being snatched by somebody else first? Is that irony?'

Karch waited for her to answer but nothing came over the line. His smile broadened. He knew he was cutting her right to the bone. And the truth was always the best and sharpest knife to use for such a procedure.

'So tell me something, Cassie Black, what were you doing living in L.A.? Selling cars or watching the girl? And who was it you were going to take to Tahiti with you, seeing that Max can't exactly make the trip?'

He waited but there was only more silence on the open line.

'The way I figure it, I probably got to her maybe a half hour or an hour before you. So save the righteous indignation. I don't buy it.'

He thought maybe he could hear her crying but wasn't

sure. He felt some kind of strange closeness to her. Maybe it was from knowing her plan, from knowing what her secret dream was. It felt wonderful to be so intimately knowledgeable of the very thing another being lived for. It was almost like love.

'That's right,' he said quietly. 'I know all about you and your little plan. Keep an eye on the girl and wait out your parole – what did you have, a year or so to go? Then grab her and head off to paradise – Tahiti, the place you and Max had that wonderful, wonderful time so long ago. By the way, I have something of yours – and I don't mean the girl.'

He hooked the phone in the crook of his neck and picked the passports off the seat next to him. He opened one and looked at the photo of the woman he was now talking to on the phone.

'Jane and Jodie Davis,' he said. 'Isn't that nice? Whoever made these up for Leo did a really fine job. Too bad you didn't get the chance to try 'em out.'

Cassie was silent.

Karch kept sticking in needles.

'I guess when that For Sale sign went up you knew you were in trouble. Jodie told me the family was moving to *Pawis*, as she calls it, in a month. I bet that sure as hell shook you up and put a clock on your plan. You went to Leo for a job. And he put you into the Cleo again. Now here we are.'

'What do you want me to do, Karch? I have the money. Let's talk about the money and get this over with.'

'Where are you?'

'Where do you think, L.A.'

'That's bad. I guess that means you didn't get my little message until it was too late for Agent Kibble. Too bad. That'll be a big pair of shoes to fill at the parole office.'

Karch started laughing as he pulled into the exit lane for Tropicana Boulevard. He would be at the Cleo in ten minutes.

'You're sick, you know that, Karch? Thelma Kibble never did anything to you.'

'Honey, let me tell you something. Half the people I take out never did anything to me. Neither did Jodie Shaw – or should I say, Jodie Davis. I don't give a fuck, you understand?'

'You're a psychopath.'

'Exactly. So this is what you do. You listening? You bring that money back to Vegas as fast as you can. I don't care if you are flying or driving, but you get back here to the Cleo with it by midnight tonight. Back to the scene of the crime.'

He checked the dash clock.

'Four hours. That gives you plenty of time. When you get here you call me again and I'll have someone bring you up to me.'

'Karch, you—'

'Shut up! I'm not finished. I better hear from you by midnight or the Shaws will have to go back to High Desert to see if some other convict's got a bun in the oven they want to give away.'

'I didn't *want* to give her away!'

Karch held the phone away from his ear.

'I had no choice! I wasn't going to raise my daughter in a—'

'Yeah, yeah, same difference. You and Max must've thought along the same lines.'

There was silence on the line for a long time.

'What are you talking about? You killed him. I know it was you up there that night.'

'I was up there, but you got the rest wrong, lady. But I

gotta tell you I didn't even know for sure what happened until today. Until I found out about the girl.'

He paused and she said nothing.

'You want me to go on?'

He waited again. Finally, in a small voice, she told him to go on.

'See, I was in the bed like I was asleep. I let him go through the room and then go out into the second room, the living room. I then got up, got my gun from under the pillow and went out there. I confronted him. I had the gun and he didn't have shit. What else could he do but get down on the ground like I told him. But he didn't do it. I told him again and he just looked at me. Then he said something that's taken me all this time to figure out. Because, see, I didn't know about the baby, about you and him and what you told him that night before he went up to do the job.'

40

Cassie hated driving through the desert at night. It was like being in a tunnel with no end. What Karch was saying only made it worse. Tears began clouding her vision of the road in the lights of her car. She swallowed and tried to calm her voice.

'What did he say?' she said. 'Tell me what he said.'

She had the call on speaker. Karch's voice came to her out of the dark. Disembodied and carrying a slight echo, it sounded as though he was all around her and even inside her head.

'He said "Not again. Better none, than one in stir." Then he turned and ran right through that window. And I never knew what he meant until I found out from Kibble today what he knew that night. You told him he was a father, that you and him, you know. So he knew right then if he went with me he'd be in jail when that little kid was born and grew up. And that happened to him, remember? He grew up with an old man in stir. And he didn't want that for anybody.'

He stopped talking and Cassie had nothing to say. She wished she could just hang up, pull off the road and walk blindly into the desert night. She wouldn't care what was waiting out there in the darkness.

She believed Karch. She had no reason to but she knew in her heart that he was telling the truth about what Max had said. She realized then that telling him, surprising him with the news that night, had set things into a terrible motion. In her mind she suddenly saw Max's crumpled body on the casino table. She had run to him and cradled his head in her arms. They'd had to pull her away from him.

'So you see,' Karch suddenly said, 'if there's anybody you should blame it's you, not me. You had the kid in your belly and you told him the news. What do you think about that, Cassie Black?'

She didn't answer. She gripped the wheel so tightly her knuckles glowed white in the dim light from the dash gauges. She felt a deep-rooted tremble go through her. It started in her chest and then made her shoulders shake. It moved like a wave down her arms until control of the wheel was in question. Finally, it passed. She tried to put thoughts about Max aside, to be dealt with later. Jodie was the important thing. She had to concentrate on Jodie.

'You know something?' Karch said. 'Now that I understand what happened in that room with Max, the one thing I don't understand is what happened in the room with Hidalgo. I mean, why'd you do it?'

Cassie didn't understand why he asked such an obvious question.

'Why else? The money.'

'But why put the guy down unless you had to and it didn't seem to me that—'

'What are you talking about? Hidalgo? Hidalgo's dead?'

'You should know that better than—'

'No! I don't know what you're talking about!'

'It looked pretty cold-blooded to me. Guy sitting there in bed in his underwear, defenseless, and you pop him like that.'

As he spoke Cassie remembered her last moments in

the room. Hidalgo was restless, waking up. She stood at the foot of the bed and raised the gun. She had been ready and willing to do what was necessary. To cross the final line. Had she done it, had she crossed, and then blocked it from her memory? Impossible.

'Karch, listen to me. If he's dead somebody else did it.'

There was a pause and then Karch's voice came back.

'Sure. Whatever you say. It still doesn't change things. You're coming back here with the money and—'

'Karch?'

'What?'

'How do I know you even have her?'

He laughed in a fake way into the phone.

'That's just it. You don't.'

'I need to talk to her. Before I come there, I need to know you have her. And that she's alive. Please, Karch.'

'Oh, well, if you're going to be so polite about it . . .'

She listened. She thought she heard a horn honking and then Karch cursed at someone. She realized he was in a car and guessed it meant that he had pulled over and maybe cut someone off. She heard a rustling sound and then Karch's voice again, but not directed into the phone.

'Wake up, kid,' he said. 'Somebody wants to talk to you. Say hello.'

Cassie heard her daughter's breathing before her voice. Then she spoke one word that went through Cassie's heart like a diamond-tipped drill.

'Mommy?'

Cassie involuntarily drew her breath in and held it. She tried to halt the torrent of tears she knew was waiting to come down. She opened her mouth and tried to respond to the first word her daughter had ever said to her. But before she could form a sound, Karch's rude and gruff laugh loudly filled the inside of the car.

'Out of the mouths of babes, right?' he said. 'The Cleo by midnight, Cinderella, or your pumpkin gets smashed.'

He killed the connection and Cassie was suddenly riding in silence and darkness. In the tunnel.

She thought about calling Karch back but knew that all that was to be said had been said. She gazed out the windshield at the WELCOME TO LAS VEGAS sign as it passed. She had lied to Karch. She was coming in right behind him. It would give her a time advantage – a few hours to get ready – but little else. She had no idea what it was she would be getting ready for.

41

The girl sat up in the backseat of the Lincoln and took in the dazzling lights of the Strip.

'Where are we?' she asked.

'We're almost there.'

'I want my daddy.'

Karch turned the rearview mirror and looked back at her. It sounded like she was going to start crying again. Halfway from L.A. she had started crying and screaming for her mother and father. Karch had had to pull off in Barstow and calm her. Mostly he bribed her with French fries and a Coke. He got her to agree to stop the outburst until they got to the hotel in Las Vegas where her daddy was waiting. The one good thing was that all the crying made her tired and she slept most of the rest of the way.

'Remember our deal. No crying and no outbursts until we get to the hotel room and you see your daddy. Okay?'

'I don't care. I want my daddy.'

'We're almost there,' he said. 'You're going to be with your daddy real soon.'

He smiled, though he knew she would never comprehend the joke.

'Are we in France now?'

'What?'

He checked the mirror and saw her staring out the window to her right, the reflection of neon light playing on her young face. He looked out the windshield to the right and saw what she was looking at. They were passing a half-size Eiffel Tower fronting a casino.

'Could be, kid. Could be.'

After a few more minutes he turned the car into the Cleopatra's entrance and followed the signs that said SELF PARKING to the rear of the property. He drove into the west parking garage as he had told Grimaldi he would. He found a parking slot on the fourth level and then he and the girl took the stairs down to the ground floor. Karch walked quickly, holding the girl by the hand and tugging her along.

An emergency exit door that Karch knew led from the elevator lobby of the Euphrates Tower directly to the parking garage had been left propped open for them with a towel tied around the inside push bar and then looped around the edge of the door and tied to the outside handle. By entering here he would be able to bypass all of the cameras in the casino. He could not allow there to be any video documentation of himself with the girl. Once they were through the door Karch yanked the towel free so that the door closed and locked. He left the towel on the floor.

In the elevator lobby Jodie Shaw stopped and tried to jerk her hand out of Karch's grip. It reminded him of the slightest tug of a throw-back fish on a fishing line. He looked down at her.

'Where's my daddy?'

'We're going up to see him right now. You want to push the button?'

He pointed to the elevator call buttons.

'No, I'm almost six years old. Not three.'

'Oh, okay then.'

Karch pulled her to the panel and pushed the button. He then glanced around and made sure no one was paying attention. He dipped his fingers into the sand jar below the buttons and eventually pulled out the card key Grimaldi had had planted there for him. An elevator opened and Karch pulled the girl into it. He used the card key to engage the penthouse button. Once the door was closed he let go of her hand. He looked up at the camera in the corner. There was no light or other means of determining if it was on or had been shut down per his instructions.

He looked down at the girl and he could tell she was confused and about to start crying again. He squatted down to her level and smiled.

'It's all right, kid. This will all be over in a few hours.'

'I want my mommy and daddy now.'

'You will all be together real soon. I promise. Hey, tell you what, did I show you this?'

He took the pack of cigarettes out of his pocket and shook one out. He then performed the in-the-ear-and-out-the-mouth transfer flawlessly. The girl's eyebrows arched in wonder. He lit the cigarette with a lighter and blew the smoke up over her head.

'That's magic,' he said. 'My daddy taught me that.'

He stood up.

'Or at least the guy who thought he was my daddy.'

The doors opened and he led the girl out into the alcove. They stepped into the hallway and went to the first door to the right. He used the card key to open the door and the girl charged in ahead of him.

'Daddy!'

He watched her look around expectantly and then go through the open double doors leading to the bedroom. Karch closed and locked the door, dropped the card on a little table beneath a mirror in the entranceway and followed her into the bedroom. She was leaning against the bed, her face down on the spread.

'Where's my daddy?'

'I guess we have to wait for him.'

She turned and looked up at him with accusing eyes. 'You told me he was here.'

'Don't worry. He's around somewhere. We just have to wait for him to come back. I'll make some calls to see if I can't find him, okay? In the meantime, this here is the room where you are going to wait. You can get on the bed and go back to sleep or you can watch TV, whatever you want. They have a channel just for cartoons, right? Why don't you check it out?'

He looked at the girl nodding and smiling but she wasn't with the program. She hardly seemed mollified and Karch was just about out of patience. The next move would be to tie the kid up and put her in the shower with a gag in her mouth. He decided to try once more before going to that extreme.

'Tell you what, you hungry? I'll order us up some room service. I'm fucking starved. How about a nice, juicy steak?'

'Gross. And you talk dirty.'

'That I do, that I do. All right, no steak. What would you like instead?'

'Spaghettios.'

'Spaghettios? You sure about that? They got some great cooks down there. You sure you want Spaghettios?'

'Spa-*ghettios*.'

'All right, all right, Spaghettios. Tell you what, you watch the TV in here and I'll go call room service.'

He took the remote off the top of the TV and turned it on. He handed her the remote and walked out of the room. He then remembered something and came back in and disconnected the phone. She watched silently as he left the room with the phone. Just as he closed the double doors she called out from within.

'And a Coke, too.'

He wondered for a moment whether a child that age was allowed to have Coke. He then dismissed the thought because it didn't matter.

'Okay, one Coke coming up.'

Karch took the phone cord and wrapped it around the necks of the two doorknobs. He doubted she would try to make a break but it didn't hurt to be thorough. He then walked over to the little desk and picked up the phone. He dialed Grimaldi's direct line again and the casino director answered immediately.

'You're in.'

'You turned the elevator cams off, right?'

'And the garage. Just like you asked. Routine maintenance. If you stayed clear of the casino then there's no record of you coming in.'

'Okay. What about the stairs?'

'I've got people in every stairwell. And we know she doesn't have a card because Martin got his back. So she can't use the elevators. Just the stairs. You want somebody up there in the penthouse, like in the hallway?'

'No.'

'You sure she's going to come back with the money? Just for the kid?'

'She's coming, Vincent. I guarantee it.'

'With your life, Jack. You understand that?'

Karch didn't answer. Grimaldi was trying to reassert himself but it was too late for that. Karch still had control.

'She says she didn't put Hidalgo down on the bed like that.'

'Who says this?'

'Cassie Black. She says she didn't pop him.'

'Bullshit. What's she going to say? "Things went

wrong up there and I did it?" No, they never cop to anything, Jack, you know that.'

Karch thought about this.

'All right,' he finally said. 'I guess you're right.'

'I know I am. So you're all set up there?'

'Yeah – oh wait, one last thing. I need you to call room service and have them send up a steak. Make it bloody rare. And . . .'

He looked toward the doors to the bedroom. The low sound of cartoon gunfire was coming from the room.

'What?'

'And do they have any Spaghettios down there?'

'That canned shit?'

'Kids like it.'

'No, Jack, no fucking Spaghettios. This is a four-star kitchen.'

'Well, then something close to it. And two Cokes, no ice. Tell them to knock on the door and leave it outside. Tell them I don't have to sign for it. Nobody can see me up here, Vincent. You understand?'

'Perfectly. Anything else?'

'That's it. This will all be over by midnight, Vincent. You'll have the money, everything. Miami will get the Cleo, you'll run the show, and Chicago gets fucked.'

'I'll be very grateful, Jack.'

'You bet your ass you will be.'

He hung up. He then took the cell phone out of his pocket and used it to check his messages. There were a couple of new missing persons referrals but nothing else. Karch knew that one way or another his missing persons days were going to end soon.

When he put the phone back into his inside suit pocket he felt something in there and remembered he had taken Leo Renfro's date book. He took it out and opened it. He had only glanced through it before, at the time hoping there would be a clue to the whereabouts of the money or Cassie Black. Instead, he found the calendar pages filled with penciled notes about astrological conditions. It fascinated him that there were people who made life decisions based upon configurations of the stars and the sun and moon. He felt that it was stupid and what happened to Leo sure proved it.

He now paged through the calendar to see what Leo had written about the future he didn't live to see. He started to smile when he got to a particularly large notation penciled into the block denoting the current date.

'Hey, we got a void moon rising tonight,' he said out loud. 'Ten-ten till midnight.'

He thought maybe there was something valid to all of this. After all, he knew the night was going to be bad luck for somebody. He put the date book down and stood up. He stepped to the corner and opened the curtains, revealing the floor-to-ceiling window. He stood back and appraised the view and the glass. He pinpointed the spot where Max Freeling had hit the glass and crashed through.

He looked over at the bedroom doors. He heard the signature *Beep Beep* of a Road Runner cartoon and he knew the coyote was on the case.

42

Cassie analyzed and reanalyzed everything Karch had said during the cell phone-to-cell phone conversation. She was in Vegas now, parked in the Flamingo garage again. She sat with her hands on the wheel even though the car was stopped in a parking slot. She stared at the wall in front of her and analyzed the conversation once more. At one point Karch had mentioned the scene of the crime. He also said that when she called after arriving he would have someone bring her 'up' to him. This meant to Cassie that he was waiting for her in the penthouse of the Cleo. In room 2014 to be exact. The scene of the crime.

But then she overanalyzed things and began to wonder if the clues he had dropped into the phone call had been dropped intentionally. Perhaps Karch knew she had been lying and was on the road just behind him. Perhaps he knew that she would make a move to rescue her daughter. Finally, though, she dismissed this latter possibility. Looking at it from the standpoint of Karch's believing he held all the cards this time, she decided that he had something else in mind when he chose 2014 for their meeting and supposed exchange of money for the girl.

One thing that needed no analyzing was the exchange. Cassie knew as an absolute given that there would be no trade. Whatever Karch had in mind did not include

Cassie's leaving Las Vegas with her daughter. She knew that if she went through with this Karch's way that she would be going to her death. Karch was a no-witnesses man. And to him an ex-con hot prowler wasn't worth a second thought. While she was pretty sure that she could and would trade her life for Jodie's, she was also absolutely sure that Karch's no-witnesses ethic would even apply to a five-and-a-half-year-old innocently caught in the crosswinds of her mother's fatal mistakes.

So after all the furious thinking there was no choice. It came down to a given. She had to get back into the Cleopatra and up to the top floor. She then had to get into room 2014 again. Using that resolve as a foundation, she finally hatched a plan from which she hoped at least one person – a child – would come out alive.

Thirty minutes later she was moving through the casino at the Cleopatra with a new wide-brimmed hat on and a determined step in her walk. She carried a matching black gym bag she had also bought at one of the shops at the Flamingo. It contained more cash than was on the entire casino floor at the moment. It also contained the fanny pack with the tools of her trade but no gun. If things worked out as she planned a weapon would not be necessary. If a weapon became necessary she knew she'd already be lost.

She had to assume the stairwells were being watched. It was the only way up without a key. So she ignored them and headed directly to the Euphrates Tower elevator alcove. She pushed the up button.

Before an elevator arrived two couples walked into the alcove, the male half of each pushing the already lit call button. Cassie needed an elevator to herself. When one arrived she stepped back and let the others have it, then pushed the button again. This happened two more times until she started to think she would never get her own elevator. Finally, she decided to take her chances and got on an elevator with a woman carrying a plastic change cup. She waited until the other passenger chose her floor – luckily it was the sixth floor – and then punched the button for the nineteenth floor.

While they rode up Cassie checked her watch. It was ten o'clock. As soon as her fellow passenger stepped off the elevator, Cassie pushed the buttons for the seventeenth and eighteenth floors as well. She then removed her hat and hooked it over the camera in the upper corner. She did it in such a way that the hat was held between her face and the camera until the camera was blocked. Her hope was that when the tampered camera was discovered and investigated it would be written off as a prank.

Cassie slipped her lock picks out of her back pocket and put them in her mouth. She hooked one arm through both straps of the gym bag, then put one foot up on the railing that ran along the side wall of the elevator. She hoisted herself up with her back to the corner and put her other foot on the railing on the rear wall. Braced against the corner she went to work with the picks on the lock on the elevator's overhead door.

The elevator stopped on seventeen and the doors opened. Cassie glanced down and out into the empty alcove and then went back to work on the lock. She was having trouble because of her uncomfortable posture and having to work on tumblers in vertical alignment. The door closed and the elevator made a quick jump to the next floor.

Just as the doors slid open Cassie heard the click of the final tumbler and turned the lock. She pushed the door upward and open, then looked down as she pulled the gym bag off her arm. She saw a man standing in the elevator looking up at her. He was wearing a Hawaiian shirt tucked into beltless pants. Cassie didn't know how much he had seen but she knew there was no valid explanation for what she was doing. His eyes moved from Cassie to the black hat hooked over the camera. The doors started closing behind him but he suddenly shot his arm out and hit the bumper with his hand. The doors opened again.

'I think I'll catch the next one,' he said.

'Thank you,' Cassie said, one of her picks still in her mouth.

She didn't know what else to say. The man stepped out and the doors closed behind him. Cassie shoved the gym bag up through the hatch, which was about two feet square. She then reached her arms up through the opening and braced them on the top of the elevator roof. She pulled herself up and through.

The elevator started moving upward again. Cassie quickly closed the hatch and heard its lock click into place. Dim light came down from the top of the elevator shaft where a single bulb hung from a roofing beam.

Cassie stood up with the gym bag and maintained her balance while waiting for the elevator to stop at the nineteenth floor. When it did, she stepped off the elevator onto an iron crossbeam that separated the elevator shaft from the one next to it. After a few moments, the elevator she had ridden up in began descending, leaving her on a six-inch-wide piece of metal nineteen stories from the ground.

The doors to the penthouse alcove were just across the chasm and up another six feet. She slowly moved along the ironwork until she reached the front wall of the shaft. There was latticework of steel cross struts creating a support cage for the elevator. She began climbing these, finding the going slippery and treacherous because the struts were caked with dust.

When she had reached a point where she was level with the penthouse doors, she gripped one of the struts with one hand and reached across the open chasm to the doors. Once she had a grip on the inside lip of one of the doors, she reached a foot across to the five-inch ledge below the doors. She swung her body across to the ledge. In doing so the gym bag slipped down her arm and was going to drop when she caught one of the straps in her hand. The bag, heavy with bricks of currency and her tools, banged sharply on the thin metal of the elevator doors. The sound echoed loudly down the shaft below her. Cassie froze. She thought the noise must have been just as loud in the alcove and the penthouse hallway.

Karch looked up from Leo Renfro's date book. He had heard a loud banging from somewhere out in the hall. He stood up and pulled the Sig from its holster while his other hand went into his pocket for the silencer. Then he thought better of it. He holstered the weapon and his hand went under his jacket to his rear beltline. He pulled the .25 out and went to the door.

Through the peephole the hallway was empty. He debated whether to investigate the noise or to call Grimaldi. He decided it was better not to wait for someone to be dispatched. He stepped back and grabbed the card key off the entranceway table and opened the door.

In the hallway Karch saw no one. He stood with the .25 palmed in the same hand in which he held the card key. He paused and listened. He heard nothing but the buffered sounds of the elevators from the nearby alcove. He walked that way and stepped into the alcove. Again he stood still and listened.

Cassie gripped the door with taut muscles, her ear

pressed to the crack between the panels. She had thought she had heard a door open and close but then there was no other sound. After a minute she decided it was time to move. She released one hand's grip and removed a penlight from her back pocket. She flicked it on and put it in her mouth. She then directed the beam over the door's framework until she saw a spring-activated release lever on the upper left side. She inched her way over to that side of the door. Just as she reached up and put a hand on the lever she felt a strong rush of air from below. She hesitated and looked down, just as the elevator directly below her loomed up out of the darkness and came up to crush her against the door. In a split second she had to decide whether to pull the lever and try to push through the doors or to catch the elevator by stepping back onto its roof as it came up.

The light over one of the elevators went on and there was a soft chiming sound. Karch quickly stepped backward out of the alcove. He looked both ways down the hall and saw the double-push doors leading to the housekeeping station. He quickly stepped over and pushed through the doors.

He held one of the doors open an inch and looked back out into the hallway. He heard the elevator doors open and close. Then a man and woman stepped into the hallway and headed the opposite way from Karch's position. The man looked like he was in his fifties, the woman her twenties. Karch watched as the man reached behind the woman and stuck his hand up the short black dress she was wearing. She giggled and playfully slapped his hand away.

'Wait till we get to your room, sugar,' she said. 'Then you can grab whatever you want.'

He watched until they went into a room down the hall.

He then looked around the housekeeping station. On one end there were linen and bathroom supplies locked in a fenced closet. On the other side was a service elevator. Also in the small space was a room service table piled with dirty dishes. It smelled rancid and Karch thought it had been forgotten about all day.

He stepped back into the hallway and went back toward 2001, pausing at the entrance to the elevator alcove but again not hearing or seeing anything that raised his suspicion. He moved on to the door of 2001 and used the card key to go back in.

After thirty seconds the elevator was called to another floor and dropped down the shaft. Cassie stepped off the roof onto the crossbeam and once again worked her way to the door. This time she secured the gym bag when she made the final move to the door ledge. She made it without a sound, then reached up and pulled the spring-release lever. She heard a metallic click and the two panels of the door separated a half inch. She worked her fingers into the crack and then pulled the door panels apart.

She stepped out into the elevator alcove, then turned around and slid the door panels closed until there was a click as they locked back into place.

She quickly moved into the hallway and headed toward 2014, unsure what she was going to do when she got there. But as she passed the door to 2001 she suddenly stopped as she realized something. *Synchronicity.* Karch had said the word when she had called and he thought it was someone named Vincent on the phone. She had immediately jumped to the conclusion that the Vincent he had referred to was Vincent Grimaldi, director of casino operations. The same Vincent Grimaldi that Hidalgo had referred to. The same Vincent

Grimaldi who was chief of security six years earlier. But now who Cassie thought Karch was speaking to seemed less important than what he had actually said. *Synchronicity*. Cassie knew what it meant. It had been in the *Las Vegas Sun*'s crossword puzzle at least a dozen times during the five years she religiously worked it. The aspect of seemingly separate events occurring in conjunction over time: *synchronicity*.

She knew Karch's plan. From suite 2001 a man had fallen to his death almost seven years before. Tonight that man's lover – and their child – would do the same. Karch would take the money. All other things could be laid to blame on Cassie, the distraught mother who shot her co-workers and her parole agent, abducted her daughter and then returned to Las Vegas to end it all as her lover had.

The plan was smart. She knew it would work. But knowing it wrested an advantage to Cassie's side of the board. She leaned forward, her head close to the door. She heard the faint sounds of cartoon mayhem coming from a television inside the suite.

Cassie gently placed a hand against the door and whispered, 'I'm coming, baby. I'm coming.'

43

Karch unwound the telephone wire from around the two doorknobs and looked in on the girl. She was lying on her stomach at the end of the bed, her hands propping up her head as she fought to stay awake and watch cartoons.

'Everything okay in here, kid?'

'Where's my daddy?'

Karch looked at his watch.

'Soon . . . real soon.'

He closed the door and wound the wire back around the knobs.

'More like where's the goddamn food,' he said to himself.

He walked over to the phone and called Grimaldi's number. Again the call was answered immediately.

'Anything?' Karch asked.

'Not on this end.'

'Did you call in that room service order?'

'As soon as we hung up.'

'Vincent, your four-star kitchen isn't worth a shit. I'm fucking starving up here.'

'It's busy down there. But I'll make another call.'

'All right. And let me know the minute somebody has her.'

'Will do.'

'Oh, and Vincent?'

'What, Jack?'

'You better close a few craps tables down there. You don't want anybody getting hit.'

'Jesus! Are you sure it has to be this way? Can't we just—'

'Vincent! Vincent! You don't want questions, right?'

'No, Jack.'

'Then there is no other way. Synchronicity, Vincent. Call the pit chief. Close the tables.'

He hung up and walked over to the window. He banged a fist on it, hoping to get a feel for the tension in the glass. He wondered if he shot the glass out first, to make it easier, if the Metro investigators would be able to tell that. Would they actually gather the glass and examine it? Probably not, he decided. Too much trouble, especially for what looked like an obvious murder-suicide.

He decided the plan would be to shoot the glass out and then immediately drop the bodies. The girl first and then the mother. A classic murder-suicide: distraught mother tosses her daughter, then jumps herself.

In the housekeeping station Cassie moved the room service table into a position directly below one of the panels of the drop ceiling. She then cleared the dirty dishes to one side of the table and climbed onto the other. The table was constructed with large wheels so that it would roll smoothly across the deep carpets in the penthouse suites. This made it unsteady as a platform. Cassie slowly stood up on it and reached to the ceiling. She pushed the panel up and to the side. She then gripped the tracks of the frame that held the panel and tested them against her weight. She was 110 pounds in her clothes, the gym bag another 20 or so. The tracks held secure. She tossed the gym bag up first, then grabbed the frame again and swung her legs up. She climbed into the utility crawl space between the false ceiling and the real one.

The crawl space was no more than four feet top to bottom. It was crowded with electrical conduits, water lines and the fire sprinkler pipes. But what took up the most room was the network of air-handling ducts for the heating and air-conditioning system. Twin return and delivery ducts ran the length of the hallway and branched off in smaller tributary lines that went to vents in each suite on the floor. The main ducts were three feet square and large enough to crawl through easily. The tributary lines were smaller but Cassie knew from experience that the air-return ducts were large enough for her to move through, provided she pushed her equipment bags in front of her. She also knew that if she could make it through, Jodie could as well.

Her plan had serious faults and difficulties. Noise would be a major factor. Any sound in the ventilation tunnels was magnified by the time it got to the room vents. She wasn't as much worried about her entry as she was her exit with Jodie. Keeping a five-and-a-half-year-old quiet in what was going to be a frightening situation would be difficult. She hoped the cartoons were still on the television and could be used as sound cover when they made their escape.

Another problem that Cassie knew for sure was ahead would be the removal of the vent cover once she got to the room where Jodie was being held. The cover would be screwed on from inside the room. The difficulty would be in accessing the screws. Her plan was to use a small pry bar from the gym bag to bend the vent slats. She would then reach out with a screwdriver and remove the screws that held the vent in place. This, she knew, would be laborious and time consuming. If she dropped the screwdriver or even one of the screws the resulting noise could bring Karch right to her.

Its success was predicated on her belief that Karch most likely had Jodie in the bedroom of the suite, while he was in the sitting room. But if she was wrong and Karch was keeping the girl close to him, then Cassie knew her chances of getting a shot at a rescue were infinitesimal.

Despite all of this she pressed on. She carefully moved into the crawl space and slid the panel back into place. Once again she put her penlight into her mouth and directed it along the main air-handling ducts until she found the bolted seam of two conjoining segments. She crawled that way, careful to keep her weight at all times on the framework of the drop ceiling.

Cassie started removing the bolts from the bracket that held the two segments of duct together. The work was difficult. Each of the eight bolts had been spot welded as an apparent security measure. It had been almost seven years since Cassie had been in this same crawl space – when she had set up the job Max then wouldn't let her do – but she still remembered and she knew the spot welds were new. It took all of her strength to break the weld on the first bolt and a half minute to remove it. The process instilled a feeling of panic in her. It was taking too long.

Cassie had just started working on the last bolt when she heard the chime from the service elevator in the housekeeping alcove. She put her wrench down and quickly crawled back to the panel she had climbed up through. She lifted it a crack and looked down just as the elevator opened and a room service waiter pushed a table out onto the landing.

As the elevator closed behind him the waiter slipped a

leather check folder out of the inside pocket of his red uniform jacket. He opened it to double-check on his destination. Cassie was three feet above him and could easily read the notations on the check inside the folder.

#2001
Leave in hallway.
– V. Grimaldi

Seeing the note was one more confirmation of Vincent Grimaldi's involvement. It also gave Cassie an idea for a new plan.

The knock on the door startled Karch from his reverie at the window.

'Room service,' a voice called from the hallway.

He turned and stared at the door and waited but there was no second knock or sound. He picked the .25 up off the desk and cautiously approached the door. Before putting his eye to the peephole he put his ear to the jamb and listened. He heard nothing.

He looked out through the convex view of the peephole. He saw a room service table sitting in the hallway. It was covered with a white tablecloth and was set for two. A small vase of cut flowers was placed at the center. He saw no one else in the hallway. He continued to watch and wait, just in case the room service waiter was waiting by the elevator alcove. Karch had no idea what Grimaldi would have instructed and if his instructions would have made the waiter curious.

After thirty seconds he opened the door, looked both ways in the empty hallway, and then down at the table. He realized there were no plates on the table. He lifted the tablecloth and looked underneath. There was a warming oven built in below the table. Satisfied, Karch pulled the table into the suite. The table was difficult to move and he made a mental note to tell Grimaldi the carpets were too thick in the rooms. He kicked the door closed and pushed the cart toward the bedroom doors, putting the .25 down on the entrance table as he went by.

After opening the doors he pushed the cart into the room and beside the bed.

'Come and get it,' he said to the girl.

'I'm not hungry,' she said.

Karch gave her a look and said, 'Suit yourself. I'm starved.'

He flipped up the end of the tablecloth and opened the plate warmer. A blast of warm air greeted him. There were two dishes with aluminum covers sitting on a shelf. He pulled the first plate out and was holding it with both hands when he realized it was burning him. He quickly brought it up and put it down on the table.

'*FFFFFUUUUCCKKKK*, that's hot!'

He shook his hands out and bent down to look under the shelf. There were three cans of Sterno flaming directly below the aluminum shelf where the plate had been.

'Fuckers!'

He looked at the girl to make sure she wasn't finding humor in what had happened. She was just staring at him, a note of fear on her face.

'I know, I talk dirty. I gotta put some water on this.'

As soon as Cassie heard the water running in the bathroom she crawled out from beneath the other end of the room service table. Kneeling on the floor next to the table, she took a quick look around to see if Karch had left a weapon nearby. He hadn't.

'Hey!'

She turned to Jodie and quickly leaned over the bed. She had her ears trained on the sound of the water. The bathroom door was open and she could see Karch's back in a mirror reflection. She knew as soon as the water went off she had to be out of sight.

'Jodie, I'm here to take you away from that man,' she whispered quickly.

'Good, I want—'

Cassie put her finger across the girl's lips.

'Whisper, whisper, so he won't hear. Do you want to go with me?'

The girl was a fast learner. She nodded.

'Okay, then you have to do what I tell you, okay?'

Jodie nodded again.

Karch pulled his hands out of the cold water and looked at them. Both his thumbs and index fingers had red marks. He cursed again. He felt like going down to the hotel kitchen and grabbing whoever was responsible and holding his head down on a hot stove. He went into a short reverie in which he envisioned doing it, then realized the person whose head he was holding over the stove was Vincent Grimaldi. Karch looked at himself in the mirror and smiled. He was sure there was something a shrink could do with that.

He turned the water off and went back out to the bedroom. The girl was now standing at the other end of the table and looking under the tablecloth. Karch came over quickly and, realizing the .25 was in the other room, brought his hand inside his jacket to his Sig. He didn't want to draw it in front of the girl if he could help it.

'What are you looking at?'

'Nothing.'

He pulled her aside and then whipped up the tablecloth, ready with his other hand to pull the Sig. There was nothing underneath on this side.

'Looking for a place to hide, huh?'

'No, just looking.'

Karch grabbed one of the napkins off the top and went back around to the plate warmer. He used the napkin to take the second plate out.

'So let's see what we've got,' he said.

Still using the napkin he removed the cover from the first plate. It contained a New York strip steak in a pool of still sizzling butter next to a pile of mashed potatoes. The steak was rare and bloody juices were mixing with the hot butter.

'Gross,' Jodie said.

'What are you talking about? This is a goddamn thing of beauty. Now let's see what you got.'

He removed the other cover revealing a large bowl of rigatoni with meat sauce.

'That's not Spaghettios.'

'You're right. But what do you care? You're not hungry, remember?'

He walked over to the bed and took the pillowcase off one of the pillows. He folded it to quarter-size and then put it in his open palm. He used the napkin to push the hot steak plate onto the pillowcase and then put a set of utensils into his shirt pocket.

'Tell you what, I'm going to eat out there and leave you with your cartoons in here. Eat, don't eat, I don't care, kid. Doesn't bother me one way or the other.'

'Fine, I won't, then.'

'Good. Just don't burn yourself on that plate.'

He carried his food out to the desk, then went back to the bedroom for his Coke and the salt shaker. After he left he tied the doorknobs again with the phone wire. He then went over to the entrance table and brought the .25 back to the desk. He started sawing through the steak and putting large hot chunks of it into his mouth.

'This is fucking good,' he said with his mouth full.

44

Cassie rolled out from under the bed, put her finger to her lips to remind Jodie to be quiet, and picked up the television remote. She slowly raised the volume so that it would better cover their whispering and any other noises that were made. She then walked around the side of the bed to where Jodie was sitting. Cassie pulled her daughter into a heartfelt embrace but noticed the girl's arms were held down at her waist. Jodie had no idea who this woman was who was hugging her. Cassie pulled back and put her arms on the girl's shoulders and leaned down close to her to whisper.

'Jodie, are you all right?'

'I want my mommy. I want my daddy.'

Cassie had thought about this moment for a long time. Not these circumstances but the moment when she would be close to her daughter and what it was she would say and try to explain.

'Jodie, I'm . . . ,' she started but didn't finish. In that moment she decided this was not the right time. The child was already confused and scared. 'Jodie, my name is Cassie and I'm going to take you out of here. Did that man hurt you?'

'He made me—'

Cassie quickly put her finger across Jodie's lips to remind her to whisper. The girl then started over.

'He made me go in the car with him. He said he was a

magician and that my daddy was having a party here for my mom.'

'Well, he's a liar, Jodie. I am going to get you away from him and out of here. But we have to be very—'

Cassie stopped when she heard a sound from the doors.

Karch unwrapped the telephone line from the knobs and opened the bedroom doors. He stepped in and looked at the girl lying on the bed, her face propped in her hands. He stepped further in and surveyed the room and saw nothing amiss.

'Loud enough for you?' he asked.

'What?'

'I said, "Loud—"'

He stopped when he saw her smile, realizing the joke. He pointed a warning finger at her and stepped over to the curtains. He opened them, revealing another floor-to-ceiling wall of glass. He stepped close enough that he could see his breath on the glass and looked down. He could see through the atrium below to the crowded gaming tables.

'They're all suckers,' he said. 'Nobody beats the house.'

'What?' Jodie said from behind him.

He turned and looked at her. Then his eyes moved to the room service cart and her untouched plate of pasta.

'I said you better eat your dinner, kid. You won't be getting another.'

'I'll eat when my daddy comes.'

'Have it your way.'

He stepped through the door, closed it and this time decided the telephone wire wasn't necessary.

'Where's she gonna go?' he said to himself as he returned to his steak.

*

After she heard the bedroom doors close Cassie closed her Swiss Army knife and got down off the toilet, where she had been poised to jump and attack if Karch had come in to search the bathroom. She went out to the bedroom and whispered into Jodie's ear that she had done a fantastic job in handling his visit to the room.

'Now, I have to go back into the bathroom, close the door and make a phone call. This time I want you to come with me. This way if he comes back you can say you're going to the bathroom and that he can't come in.'

'I don't have to go to the bathroom.'

'I know, sweetie, but you can tell him that.'

'Okay.'

'Good girl.'

Cassie kissed the top of her head and realized that the last time she had done that had been in the hospital ward at High Desert. A nurse was standing impatiently next to her bed, waiting for the baby with her arms outstretched.

Jodie's hair smelled like Johnson's baby shampoo and for some reason Cassie's identification of it served to remind her of all she had missed. She faltered for a moment while leaning over her child and the bed.

'Are you okay?' Jodie whispered.

Cassie smiled and nodded that she was. She then led the girl to the bathroom and quietly closed and locked the door. She took one of the bath towels off a shelf over the bathtub, put it on the floor and pressed it against the bottom crack of the door.

'My daddy does that when he smokes in the bathroom,' Jodie whispered.

Cassie looked up at her and nodded.

'Mommy doesn't like him to do it because it smells funny.'

Cassie got up and picked Jodie up and sat her on the

closed toilet. The black gym bag was on the tank behind her.

'Now if he tries the door or knocks, you tell him he can't come in because you're going to the bathroom. Then flush the toilet and go on out, okay? But remember, before you go out take that towel from the door and throw it into the bathtub so he doesn't see it, all right?'

'Okay.'

'Good girl. You stay here. I'm going to go into the shower stall to make the phone call.'

'Are you calling my daddy?'

Cassie smiled sadly.

'No, baby, not yet.'

'I'm not a baby.'

'I know. I'm sorry.'

'He called me that.'

'Who did?'

'The magician. He said I was a baby.'

'He was wrong. You're a big girl.'

She left her there, grabbed the gym bag and another towel and went into the shower stall. She carefully and quietly closed the door and then got her cell phone out of her pocket and unfolded it. She had a page of blank note paper she had torn from a hotel pad in the bedroom. The toll-free number for the Cleopatra was printed on the bottom. She pulled the towel over her head to further deaden the transmission of sound out to Karch and punched in the number. In a low voice she asked the operator for Vincent Grimaldi. The call was transferred and picked up by someone who was not Grimaldi. He told Cassie that Mr Grimaldi was too busy to take a call at the moment and that he would be happy to take a message.

'He'll want to talk to me.'

'How so, ma'am?'

'Just tell him there are two and a half million reasons to talk to me.'

'Hold, please.'

She waited a nervous minute, wondering how long it would be before Karch checked on Jodie again, saw the bed empty and came to the bathroom door. Finally, another voice came on the line. It was calm and smooth and deep.

'Who is this?'

'Mr Grimaldi? Vincent Grimaldi?'

'Yes, who is this?'

'I just wanted to thank you.'

'For what, I don't know what you're talking about. Two and a half million reasons? What two and a half million reasons?'

'Then I guess Jack hasn't gotten it to you yet.'

This was met with a long silence. Cassie lifted the towel and looked out through the glass door of the shower stall. Jodie was where she had left her. She was rolling the toilet paper into a pile on the tile floor.

'You say Jack Karch has this money?'

Cassie dropped the towel back down. She noted Grimaldi's use of the word *money* for the first time in the conversation. Also the name *Karch*. He was getting hooked in.

'Well, yeah, I gave it to him like we agreed. I was calling just to thank you. He told me it was you who okayed the trade.'

Grimaldi's voice took on an urgent tone now. Cassie was getting juiced because she thought it was working.

'I'm not clear on what you are – could you speak up? I can hardly hear you.'

'I'm sorry. I'm in the car on the cell phone and my

daughter's sleeping. I don't want to wake her. Plus out here in the desert, I think I'm losing reception.'

'What exactly did Karch say I okayed? What trade?'

'You know, the trade. My daughter and me for the money. I told him, we didn't know about the payoff or Miami or any of that. We didn't want to be greedy. As soon as we opened the case and saw all that money we knew we'd made a mistake. We wanted to give back the money. I'm just glad we were able to—'

'You're saying Karch has the money now?'

Cassie closed her eyes. She had him.

'Well, I think he was going to bring it down to you. But he had some arrangements to make first, he said. He was on the phone when we left. He was—'

The line went dead. Grimaldi had hung up.

Cassie closed the phone and slid it into her pocket. She dropped the towel and came out of the shower. She went right to Jodie and knelt down in front of her. She started untying the girl's sneakers.

'We're going to go now, Jodie. We have to take these off so we don't make any noise.'

'How come?'

'Because we're going to climb up into the wall and crawl through a tunnel that will take us out to the elevator.'

'I'm afraid of tunnels.'

'You don't have to be afraid, Jodie. I'll be right behind you the whole time. I promise.'

'No, I don't want to do it.'

The girl looked down at her hands, which were in her lap. She looked as if she might be about to start to cry. Cassie reached a finger under her chin and tilted it up.

'Jodie, it's all right. There won't be anything to be afraid of.'

'No . . .'

She shook her head. Cassie didn't know how to budge her. If she threatened her she would only scare her. And she didn't want to lie to her, either.

She leaned forward, her forehead against her daughter's.

'Jodie, I can't stay here. If that man comes back in and finds me he'll take me away. So I have to go. I wish you would go with me because I want you to be with me. But I have to go now.'

She kissed Jodie on the forehead and stood up.

'No, don't leave me,' the girl protested.

'I'm sorry, Jodie, I have to go.'

Cassie picked up the gym bag and went to the bathroom door. She kicked the towel aside and put her hand on the knob. Jodie whispered behind her.

'If I go with you, will I have to see that man again?'

Cassie turned and looked back at her.

'Never again.'

45

The steak was a bloody mess, just the way Karch loved it. He had been so hungry and the piece of meat was so good that he was on the verge of having a religious experience as he worked his way toward the last bite, dipping each chunk that he cut into the mashed potatoes before delivering it to his mouth. Being totally consumed in this process, he was taken by surprise when the door to the suite opened. He looked up, a forkful of meat and potato poised in front of his mouth, and saw a man he remotely recognized entering the sitting room followed by Vincent Grimaldi and then Grimaldi's top thug, Romero. The new man and Romero held guns at their sides.

Karch put the fork down on his plate.

'How's it taste, Jack?' Grimaldi said.

'It's excellent, Vincent. You know, you're a little early.'

'I don't think so. More like a little late.'

Karch frowned and stood up from the desk. He instinctively knew something was wrong and that he was in trouble. He picked up the napkin from the desk and wiped his mouth. He then held his hands down at his sides, the napkin still in his right hand. Very casual. Michelangelo's David.

'She's going to call any minute now,' he said. 'But you don't want to be up here when it all goes—'

'Really?' Grimaldi interrupted. 'A little bird told me

she's already been here. Come and gone, as a matter of fact.'

Grimaldi nodded to the man who had led the procession into the suite.

'Check him.'

The man came over to Karch, who raised his arms outstretched. He held the napkin hanging loosely from his right hand. The man held his gun in his left hand and pointed at Karch's gut while his right hand went inside Karch's jacket and pulled the Sig out of its holster. He then patted down the rest of Karch's body, finding the silencer barrel in a coat pocket. His hands went up under his crotch without hesitation and he finished by flipping up the cuffs of his pants looking for an ankle holster. It was a professionally thorough job but not thorough enough. The whole time Karch watched him and tried to place where he had seen him before. When the search was finished the man shoved Karch's Sig under his belt and silently stepped back to the side of Grimaldi.

'What's going on, Vincent?' Karch asked.

'What's going on is you fucked up, Jack. Letting her go like that, it puts a big kink in my plan. I'm going to have to chase her down now.'

'What plan is that?'

After removing the first three, Cassie loosened the last screw of the air-intake vent and carefully pulled the vent forward and pivoted it on the remaining screw. The duct was now open and the vent hung below it. She then looked down from the room service table on which she was standing and signaled Jodie up. The girl climbed onto a chair and stepped up onto the table. Cassie lifted her up, careful not to lose her balance, and pushed her toward the opening into the duct system. Jodie struggled and put one hand out and against the wall, stopping Cassie from pushing her in.

'It will be all right, Jodie,' Cassie whispered. 'Just go in and I'll come in behind you.'

'Noooo,' the girl replied in a small voice.

Cassie pulled her down into a hug and whispered in her ear.

'Remember you told me you weren't a baby, that you were a big girl? Well, this is something a big girl would do. You have to go, Jodie, or I have to leave you here.'

Cassie closed her eyes, the last threat making her feel awful.

The girl didn't say anything. Cassie raised her toward the duct again and this time she climbed in. As she moved into the opening her knees banged on the aluminum siding and Cassie froze. But the stern tones of the voices in the other room continued without interruption. Once Jodie had crawled completely into the vent, Cassie handed her the penlight and told her in a whisper to go farther in. Cassie then hoisted herself up and climbed into the duct, catching her belt pack on the edge of the duct at first. Once in the duct, she unbuckled the tool bag and pushed it through the vent in front of her.

The space was so tightly confining that she could not reach back to pull the vent cover back into its place on the bedroom wall. She urged Jodie forward to the main air-return duct, thinking she would have room to turn around there and then crawl back to pull the vent cover back into place.

But after they were only twelve feet or so into the duct there was a junction where another similar-sized duct joined it. Cassie looked down this branch and could see light and hear voices. She realized it was Karch asking, 'What's going on, Vincent?'

Silently she went past this duct, then backed into it.

She then turned and slid herself back in the direction of the bedroom. When she got there she reached down to the vent cover and slid it up the wall and back into its place. She then started backing herself up in the duct.

Karch was rapidly trying to assimilate the situation and figure out what was happening. He then hit upon the only possible explanation.

'She called you, didn't she, Vincent?'

Grimaldi didn't answer, just as he hadn't when Karch had asked him about his so-called plan. Grimaldi just stared with eyes that seemed dark with anger and hatred.

'Look, Vincent, I don't know what she told you, but it's bullshit, okay? She hasn't been here yet and I don't have the money. I'm waiting, Vincent. She's gonna call and I'll get her up here. I'll take the money and she and the kid go out the window. Like I said, synchronicity.'

As he said the last word Karch felt an internal falter. He remembered he had let the word slip when Cassidy Black had called. He wondered if that had been enough. Had he given her enough with that simple slip to read his plan and come up with a counter?

'Look, Vincent, please. Tell me what's happening here.'

Grimaldi's eyes were scanning the suite.

'What's in the bedroom, Jack?'

'Not what. Who. The kid's in the bedroom.'

Grimaldi nodded to the man who had searched Karch and the man went to the bedroom doors. He disappeared inside the room and Karch and Grimaldi just stared at each other while they waited. Romero took two steps to his left. Karch guessed he thought this put him in a better position in case he had to make a move in the room.

'I'm telling you, she's playing you, Vincent,' Karch said. 'She's play—'

He stopped when he saw the man emerge from the bedroom carrying a black gym bag. Its zipper was open and Karch could see into the bag. He saw the face of Benjamin Franklin. Several times. The bag was filled with bricks of hundred-dollar bills. Karch's mouth dropped open. Cassidy Black, he thought. She had somehow made the switch. He started toward the bedroom door but the man with the gym bag and Romero both raised their weapons and told him to hold where he was.

'There was a girl,' he said.

'Sure,' said the man with the bag. 'There ain't now.'

He walked over to Grimaldi and pulled the two handle straps wide, opening the bag and completely exposing several of the plastic-wrapped bricks of cash.

'Vincent, that's not . . .'

He didn't finish. He didn't know what to say and he could see Grimaldi was intent on the money, not him. Grimaldi put his hand into the bag and laid it flat on one of the bricks as if touching the shoulder of a long-lost friend. He then nodded to the man holding the bag.

'Okay, Martin, close it.'

Karch watched the bag being closed and then he looked at the face of the man who held it. Martin? He remembered the videotape. Hidalgo riding the elevator up with his security escort. Martin. Who was supposed to be dead. Martin, whom Grimaldi had asked Karch to bury in the desert.

'Martin?' he said.

He looked from Martin to Grimaldi as it all came to him. It was all a bluff, all part of a more elaborate plan.

'You,' he said to Grimaldi. 'You staged this whole thing. It was all a setup.'

He then looked at Martin, who held the gym bag in his right hand and his weapon in his left. He remembered Hidalgo's body on the bed. The bullet in the right eye, delivered by a gun held in the left.

'And you,' he said to Martin. 'You're the one who hit Hidalgo.'

One side of Martin's mouth turned upward in an approximation of a proud smile.

'It wasn't the girl,' Karch said, looking back at Grimaldi. 'All she did was take the money you wanted her to take.'

When Cassie turned around in the junction she heard intense voices from the sitting room. She didn't wait to listen. She headed toward the main air duct and covered the ground in about ten seconds. She saw the penlight that Jodie was holding and realized the girl was still in the smaller tributary vent and had not moved into the main conduit.

As she got closer she realized why. Jodie had reached a dead end. Metal bars criss-crossed the opening to the main duct. Cassie reached around the girl and out into the larger duct. She felt the end of each bar to determine how they were attached to the wall of duct. She felt the smooth metal weld joints. They could go no further.

'What –' Jodie started to say before Cassie got her hand over her mouth. She gave the silence signal and the girl continued in a whisper. 'What do we do?'

Cassie gripped one of the bars. She shook it and then braced her back against the upper wall of the duct and pushed on the bar with all of her strength. The bar didn't move or show any weakness in its weld points. Cassie shook her head. The operators of the hotel had put bars in the air ducts but hadn't bothered to replace the half gears in the deadbolts. It made no sense to spend money in one area and not the other. That was why hitting this dead end was so surprising and distressing.

'What do we do?' Jodie whispered again.

Cassie looked at her innocent and beautiful face in the shine of the small light. She then looked at the bars and realized something.

'Jodie, you can fit through.'

'What about you?'

'Don't worry about me. You go through. I'll go out and come around and get you.'

'No, I want to go with you.'

'No, you can't. This is the only way. You squeeze through and wait for me to come get you.'

She pushed the girl toward the bars. Jodie reluctantly stuck her head between the bars and into the larger duct, then worked her upper body through. She then pulled her legs into the new space and looked back at Cassie.

'Good girl,' Cassie whispered. 'Now you wait there. I'll come around as soon as I can but I have to wait for those men to leave the room, okay?'

'How long will that be?'

'I don't know, darling. You'll have to wait. Do you know how to tell time?'

'Of course, I'm almost six.'

Cassie took off her watch and handed it through the bars. She showed her the button to press to light the face. She then gave the girl her cell phone and showed her how to open it. Jodie said her daddy had one but never let her play with it.

'If I don't come for you by twelve o'clock you open that phone and call nine-one-one. Do you know how to do that?'

The girl did not immediately answer. Cassie took the cell phone back and showed her what to do.

'You press nine-one-one and then this button – the

send button. You tell whoever answers that you are stuck on the top floor of the Cleopatra. Can you remember that?'

'Of course.'

'Where are we?'

'The Cleo-pah-tra. Top floor.'

'Good girl. I'm going to go now and listen for the men to leave. Then I will come around and get you. Come here.'

The girl leaned forward and Cassie leaned her face through the bars and kissed her forehead. She could smell her hair again. She hesitated and then started backing toward the junction, where she would be able to monitor what was happening in the suite.

Cassie saw Jodie wave to her through the bars and had a premonition that she was seeing her daughter for the last time. She waved back and then blew her a kiss.

Grimaldi was beaming as he watched Karch come to an understanding of his scheme.

'I was just like Leo and the girl, a piece you used,' Karch said.

'A piece I used beautifully and that performed beautifully,' Grimaldi responded.

'And Chicago, did they have anything to do with this?'

'That was the beauty of it. I used Chicago and they didn't even know it. But I knew just the mention of the Outfit would get your blood boiling and you'd go off like a loaded gun. Leo Renfro had markers with some people I know. I bought his paper and sent Romero and Longo over to L.A. to let him know there was a new sheriff in town. They told him they were from Chicago, that they worked for Tony Turcello. He bought it and started shitting his pants. Then they gave him a way out: hit

Hidalgo on the hot prowl and his debt is clear. He went for it. Just like you went for it, Jack.'

Karch nodded.

'Yeah, I went for it. My job was to follow the trail, wipe out all parties and collect the money.'

'And you did a fine job – all except for letting the girl go. Now she's a loose end but we'll take care of it. This is the important thing.'

He raised the gym bag full of money. Karch tried to keep any physical showing of his anger in check.

'You're making a big fucking mistake, Vincent. I didn't –'

'I don't think so, Jack. I don't think so at all.'

They stared at each other for a long moment, their hatred enough to warm the room.

'So what happens now?' Karch finally asked.

'What happens now is that we still need someone to disappear with the money. Someone Miami can send their people after.'

'And that would be me.'

'You were always a smart man, Jack.'

Karch shook his head. The shortsightedness of Grimaldi's plan was staggering.

'And you always thought small, Vincent. Short range. You should have just gone along with the plan. That bag of money would have been just a drop in the bucket once Miami got the license and got into this place. You sold off the long run for the short end; one bag of money. That was stupid.'

Instead of getting angry, as Karch expected he would, Grimaldi laughed loudly and shook his head as if amused by a child's naïveté.

'You still don't get it, do you, Jack?'

'Get what? Why don't you tell me, Vin-*CENT*?'

'Miami will *never* get the license. Don't you see?

There never was going to be a payoff. This is the new Las Vegas, Jack. Miami will never get in here. I set this up from day one. Me, Jack! I called Miami and said they had a problem and it would cost them five million to get it fixed and to get in here. Half up front and half after the license app was approved. They're greedy and they went for it. Just like you.'

Now Karch saw it. A perfect plan. Grimaldi would get away with two and a half million and Miami would forever search for Karch – only he'd never be found because he was about to be escorted out to the desert on a one-way trip. Karch dropped his eyes to the floor. He no longer wanted to look at Grimaldi.

'You know what *your* problem was, Jack?' Grimaldi asked. He was so full of himself and his success that he couldn't help but turn the knife further. 'Your problem was that you thought too *long* range. I know all about you. The looks, the comments behind my back, the bullshit. You wanted to get to me and you thought this was the way. I knew that and I used it, man. I played you like a fucking piano and now the song's over. So fuck you, Jack. Tonight you sleep in the sand. We're gonna take the service elevator down and then we'll use your car – it probably knows its fucking way. You already have the shovel in the trunk, right, Jack of Spades?'

Grimaldi waited for Karch to respond but there was only silence in the room. Grimaldi then delivered his last turn on the knife.

'We'll pick a nice spot for you near your mother.'

Now Karch brought his eyes back to Grimaldi's. The older man nodded.

'Yeah, I know all about it. You and your old man – the favorite spot out there. But here's something I bet you didn't know. I was the one, Jack. I took her away from him. Ten years I was with her behind his back. But she

381

wouldn't leave him because of you. I loved her and then he . . . Tell me, what kind of kid helps his old man bury his mother? You sick fuck. I'm going to enjoy this. Let's go.'

Martin and Romero took two steps back and maintained a safe distance as they escorted Karch out of the suite. As Karch walked his mind grew dark with pain and rage. He concentrated his vision on the man walking in front of him. Vincent Grimaldi. Now Karch knew every last secret.

The four men moved down the hallway until Grimaldi directed them through the push doors into the housekeeping station. Martin hit the button and they waited for the elevator. Karch had his head down and still carried the cloth napkin in his right hand like a flag of surrender. Grimaldi saw it and smiled.

'How was your last supper, Jack?'

Karch looked at him but didn't answer. When the elevator arrived Romero stepped on first to hit the door-open button. He kept the black hole of his gun's muzzle focused on Karch's body the whole time. Grimaldi then stepped on, passing for an instant between Karch and Romero. It was the instant Karch had been waiting for. He raised his right hand toward Martin, who stood to his side. Martin watched the hand holding the napkin come up toward his face.

There was a pop as the .25 hidden in the napkin and Karch's hand was discharged. Martin's head snapped back in the same instant, the bullet catching him in the left eye and entering his brain. At the same moment he was falling lifelessly to the floor of the housekeeping station, Karch was swinging his arm over Grimaldi's shoulder. He fired the first shot at Romero too early.

The slug hit the wall of the elevator, a foot to the right of Romero's face.

Romero straightened his shooting arm but hesitated. Grimaldi was in his shot. The delay in his action was all the time Karch needed to correct his own mistake. His second shot hit Romero on the left cheek. The third hit his forehead, snapping his head back. The fourth shot hit the soft underside of Romero's chin and went up into the brain. He dropped to the floor of the elevator without ever getting a shot off.

Karch grabbed Grimaldi by the tie and yanked him to the door of the elevator. Karch had his foot firmly planted against the bumper so the door would not close. He drove the .25 up under Grimaldi's chin so that his face was angled upward while his eyes looked downward and back at Karch.

An evil smile slowly spread across Karch's face.

'So, Vincent, how's the short range looking now?'

'Jack . . . please . . .'

'Be sure to say hello to Mom for me.'

Karch waited for the comeback but there was none.

'You don't know, do you?'

'Know what, Jack?'

'Let me tell you a quick story. About ten years ago the old man got sick. Cancer. It was shot through him and the only way he was going to make it was if he got a bone marrow transplant. I wanted to do it and they took my blood for the match test.'

Karch shook his head.

'No match, Vincent. I told them to do a few other tests and they did. I didn't match because he wasn't my father.'

Karch just stared into Grimaldi's eyes.

'Thanks, Vincent. Back in there you filled in the last part of the story for me.'

'You mean—'

Karch squeezed off two quick shots and watched Grimaldi drop on top of Romero's body. He then looked down at his hand and saw the napkin as well as his fingers and the gun bathed in blood. He felt a tremendous rush move through him. Three against one and he had beaten the odds. He looked around as if hoping someone had seen the magic act he had just performed and would applaud.

And what was more stimulating than the adrenaline blitz of surviving was the release and relief of knowing he was leaving one of life's rooms and going through the door to the next.

He dropped the napkin and reached down and wiped his bloody hand and gun back and forth on Grimaldi's white shirt until they were reasonably clean. He then tucked the gun back into its pocket in his pants and jerked the gym bag out of the dead grip of Grimaldi's right hand.

Karch backed up, grabbed one of Romero's legs and pulled his body out into the elevator's threshold so that the bumper would hit it and the door wouldn't close. He then moved from body to body checking pulses and pulling his Sig Sauer out of the waistband of Martin's pants. He checked the weapon to make sure there was no blood on it and then holstered it. He patted Martin's body until he found and removed the silencer from a front pants pocket.

Finally, he looked around the housekeeping station and saw in the fenced enclosure there was a large laundry basket on wheels. He checked the door but it was locked. He stepped back and shot his leg out, his heel striking the fencing just above the key lock. The door snapped open and inward and he went in for the basket, turning it over first and dumping several stacks of fresh towels onto the floor.

It took almost all of his strength to load all three bodies into the laundry cart. He then used some of the towels to mop up the blood. When he was done he grabbed a blanket off one of the shelves and used it to cover the cart. He pushed it into the fenced enclosure and closed the door.

46

Cassie heard the series of pops that she knew to be gunfire. It sent an electric chill down the muscles of her back.

'Cassie?'

It was Jodie's urgent whisper. Cassie looked toward the reflected glow from the penlight in the duct ahead. Jodie was scared. It was impossible to tell where the shots had come from. She crawled toward the light.

Jodie was huddled by the bars. She put the light on Cassie as she got closer.

'Cassie, I heard loud noises.'

'It's all right, Jodie. It's all right. I'm going to go around now and come get you. You wait right there, okay? You wait for me.'

'No! Don't—'

Cassie had to put her hand over her mouth. When she did it she felt tears on the girl's cheeks.

'It's okay, Jodie. We're almost done. You have to wait here. It's the only way. I will be coming around for you in five minutes. I promise. Look at that watch and see how short five minutes is, okay?'

'Okay,' she said in a small voice. 'I'll be here.'

This time Cassie just reached a hand through the bars that separated them and touched Jodie's cheek. She then started pushing herself backward through the duct toward suite 2001.

When she got to the vent she tapped it with her foot to push it out of its frame. It swung down the wall on the one screw still in place. She climbed out feet first and dropped down to the room service table, carrying her belt bag of tools with her. She took the fact that the table was still in place as a good sign. She went to the television console and was about to turn it off so she could hear better when a voice from behind stopped her.

'Nice move getting in here.'

She turned and Karch was standing in the alcove leading to the bathroom, which was blocked off by the room service table beneath the overhead vent. He held the gym bag down at his side with one hand and a gun pointed at her with the other. She saw the gun had the silencer attached. He pushed the room service table out of his way with a foot and stepped into the room. Cassie backed up against the television, which was showing another Road Runner cartoon.

Karch smiled but there was no warmth or humor in it.

'The Trojan horse,' he said. 'The enemy was inside and they rolled it right in. One of the best magic tricks ever.'

Cassie still didn't say anything. She stood perfectly still and just hoped the television noise was loud enough that Jodie didn't hear this.

'You know those bars you ran into up there in the duct?' Karch asked. 'They were put in after your little spree with Max seven years ago. All the hotels did it. I guess you could say you did your little part to help make Las Vegas what it is today. A safe place for the gambler and his family.'

He smiled again.

'Where's the girl?'

Cassie pointed to the bag in his hand.

'You have the money, Karch. You have me. Let her go.'

Karch frowned as if he was actually considering the suggestion. Then he shook his head.

'Can't do it. I hate loose ends.'

'She's not a loose end. She's not even six years old. What possible danger is she to you?'

Karch ignored the question and wagged the gun at her.

'Let's go into the other room. I like that window better. There's a symmetry to it. That was Max's window.'

Cassie turned and started to move slowly toward the door as she tried to consider options. She decided her only chance was at the door. She had to make a move there, even though he would be expecting it. She gripped the strap of the tool bag tighter and was a few steps from the door when again a voice stopped her. But this one wasn't Karch's.

'Don't you hurt her!'

As Cassie turned she saw that the voice had also caught Karch by surprise. He was instinctively turning, swinging his gun hand up toward the air vent behind him. Cassie's eyes followed the movement and saw Jodie crouched in the air duct, looking down on them.

Cassie acted instinctively, too. She moved toward Karch and swung the tool bag in a wide overhead arc at the same time she yelled to Jodie.

'Jodie, go back!'

The tool bag came down on the back of Karch's head, the steel tools impacting heavily and propelling Karch forward and downward. He fired a shot – which was still quite loud despite the silencer – but the aim was way low and the slug spiderwebbed a mirror in the bathroom alcove.

Cassie moved quickly into him while he was bent over and jerked his suit jacket up and over his head. She then brought her knee up into the tangle of the jacket and felt it connect solidly with Karch's face.

Karch desperately started turning and swinging his arms. A forearm caught Cassie across the side of the face and knocked her away. Karch turned in the direction of the impact and started firing the gun blindly. Stunned by the blow to the face, Cassie was still able to leap onto the bed and roll across it, coming down into a crouch on the floor behind Karch.

Karch continued to fire as he swung his arm right to left. The shots peppered the walls and hit the floor-to-ceiling window twice, causing twin spiderwebs to craze across the glass. He finally was able to straighten up and jerk his jacket back down over his head. He dropped the money bag to do so.

As the jacket came down off his head and his vision cleared, Karch was confused by his location. He was looking out at the Las Vegas night through a wall of shattered glass. There was no sign of Cassidy Black. He realized how vulnerable he was and started to turn just as something solid and hard crashed into the back of his thighs and he was propelled into the glass wall.

The weakened glass gave easily and he crashed through. As he went he let go of the gun and grabbed desperately with both hands for any purchase. His left hand found the curtain and he grabbed on as his upper body went through the glass into the chill night air.

As the glass fell away into the night Karch was momentarily poised on the precipice like a rappeller on a sheer cliff facing. Clinging now with both hands to the golden curtain, his body hung out into the night and was bolstered by his feet on the edge of the window sill.

His weight swung him gently to his left and the curtain started to close. He quickly spread his feet to stabilize himself and the curtain stopped at the halfway mark. He looked back into the room and saw Cassidy Black staring at him, both her hands flat on the room service cart she had hit him with. His eyes dropped to the floor and he saw the money bag and the gun. He reached one hand further up the curtain and started pulling himself back into the room.

With his first pull he heard a popping sound and the curtain gave way a few inches. He froze and waited. Nothing else happened. He looked in at the woman who had put him in this position and their eyes locked. Karch smiled and reached further up the curtain again.

This time the shifting of pressure and weight on the curtain brought a long ripping series of pops as one by one the curtain hooks gave way. The curtain started coming off its attachments and Karch started dropping. He kept his smile, looking at Cassidy Black until the curtain ripped completely free and he was falling through the night.

Karch did not yell. He did not close his eyes. To him his plummet seemed to be in slow motion. Above him he saw the golden curtain waving like a flag. The windows went by, some lighted and some not. Above the building he saw the moon in the blue-black sky.

The void moon, he realized.

His last thought was of the trick. The mail sack and the crate. The secret zipper and the false bottom. How he had to reach up and place the playing card – the Jack of Spades – in the right spot. He remembered how proud his father was. And the applause from the audience.

The clapping was loud and ringing in his ears when he hit the atrium glass. His body crashed through and landed in the empty crow's nest. His eyes were open and there was still a smile on his face.

Glass shattered down on the casino and cries of panic followed. But as the players looked up they saw the gaping hole in the glass and nothing else. Karch's body could not be seen from below. Then the golden curtain dropped through the shattered atrium like a failed parachute. It seemed to open at the last moment as it glided down into the crow's nest. It draped over Karch's body like a shroud.

A hush settled over the casino and all eyes remained fixed on the gaping, unexplained hole above them. Then out of the blackness of the night sky money came floating down and into the casino. Thousands and thousands of bills came floating in. Hundred-dollar bills. Soon the shouting started again and people began rushing to the money, hands outstretched, jumping and snatching hundred-dollar bills out of the air. A blackjack table was overturned. Men in blue blazers ran into the melee but were overrun by the crowd. Some of them joined in the fight for the money.

Cassie broke open another brick of hundreds and threw the loosened currency out into the night air. The five hundred bills spread apart and started languidly floating down. She heard screams from far below. She looked down and saw that some of the bills were being carried on air currents out to the fountains at the entrance and even over to the Strip. Cars were stopping, horns blasting. People were running into the traffic and the wading pools. People were fighting over the money. She had needed a diversion for an escape. She had one now.

She turned and pushed the room service cart back beneath the open air vent. She climbed up and peered into the darkness.

'Jodie! It's all right. It's me, Cassie. We can go now.'

She waited and then the girl crawled from the shadows of her hiding spot and into the light. Cassie reached her hands in to her and hooked them under her arms. She pulled the girl out and lowered her to the table. She then got down and brought Jodie down. She hugged her for a long moment.

'We have to go now, Jodie.'

'Where's that man?'

'He's gone. He can't hurt us.'

As she turned to lead the girl from the room she saw on the floor two green passports. She picked them up and realized they must have fallen from Karch's jacket when she had pulled it over his head. She opened one and saw her own photo staring back at her. Jane Davis. Clipped to the page was an Illinois driver's license with the same name.

'What's that?' Jodie asked.

'Just some things I dropped.'

She opened the other passport and looked at the photo of Jodie for a long moment. She then closed it and shoved both passports into the back pocket of her jeans. She took Jodie's hand and started leading her out. As she went she bent down and grabbed the gym bag with her other hand. She hadn't kept count but she was pretty sure there were still more than twenty bricks in the bag. More than a million dollars.

She looked at the gun lying on the floor near the open window. She thought about it for a moment but decided to leave it. No guns.

'Let's go,' she said to herself more than Jodie.

As they went through the bedroom Cassie glanced back into the room. In the bullet-fractured mirror she caught a disjointed image from the television. It was

Porky Pig doffing his hat. He said, 'Th-th-th-that's all, folks.'

The disorder in the casino was still in full thrust when they came out of the elevator alcove and started making their way toward the exit doors. Cassie picked up Jodie and carried her. They skirted around two men who had wrestled each other to the ground as they fought over a sheaf of bills that had apparently fallen without coming apart.

'What are they doing?' Jodie asked.

'Showing their true hearts,' Cassie answered.

They made it to the exit doors without Cassie seeing a single blue blazer. Cassie turned to push the glass door open with her back because her hands were full with Jodie and the gym bag. She glanced back across the casino, her eyes rising above the melee to the crow's nest. She saw one corner of the gold curtain hanging over the edge. Otherwise it looked empty.

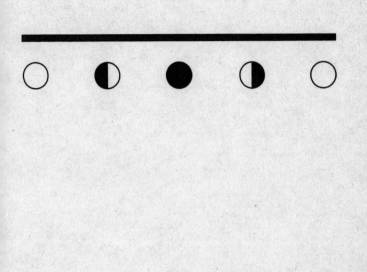

47

Cassie's full focus was on getting to the car and then getting out of Las Vegas. So she and Jodie did not speak until the Boxster was on the freeway heading toward Los Angeles. It was as if Cassie could not take a breath until she was far from the neon glow of the Strip. When she had pushed the Boxster into fifth and set the cruise control at seventy-five, she finally looked over at the little girl belted into the seat next to her.

'Are you okay, Jodie?'

'Yes. Are you?'

'I'm fine.'

'You have a bruise on your cheek where that man hit you. I saw him. That's when I hid in the tunnel.'

'Bruises go away. Are you tired?'

'Nope.'

But Cassie knew she was. She reached across and reclined Jodie's seat to the maximum so that she could sleep. She put the Lucinda Williams CD into the player and put it on low. She was listening to the lyrics and thinking about the choice she had to make at some point on the drive to L.A. when Jodie spoke again.

'I knew you would come for me.'

Cassie looked over at her. The glow from the dashboard revealed her daughter's face looking back at her.

'How did you know?'

'My mommy told me I have a guarding angel watching me. I think it is you.'

Cassie looked back at the road ahead. She felt tears welling in her eyes.

'Guardian angel, baby. *Guardian.*'

'I'm not a baby.'

'I know. I'm sorry.'

They drove in silence for a half minute. Cassie thought about her choice.

'I know,' she repeated.

'How come you're crying?' Jodie asked.

Cassie wiped the tears aside with the heels of her palms. She then tightly gripped the steering wheel and willed herself not to shed another tear in front of the girl.

'Because I'm happy,' she answered.

'About what?'

Cassie looked over at Jodie and smiled.

'Because I'm with you. And because we got away.'

A confused look crossed Jodie's face in the dim light.

'Are you taking me home?'

Cassie nodded slowly.

'Jodie, I'm . . . From now on you're going to be with your mother.'

Jodie fell asleep soon after and dreamed all the way to Los Angeles. Cassie took long looks at her as she slept and thought she saw both Max and herself. She definitely had Max's high forehead. It made her love her all the more.

'I love you, Jane,' she said, using the name she would have given her.

By five the dark tunnel of the desert had turned to a predawn gray and the desolate landscape was overtaken by the gradual buildup of the Los Angeles sprawl. Cassie gulped the last of the cold coffee she had gotten at the window of a twenty-four-hour McDonald's in Barstow. She was on the 10 Freeway heading toward the interchange with the Golden State Freeway, the north-south route which could take her south to Mexico in three hours.

She turned the radio on low and tuned in KFWB, the all-news station that repeated the top stories every twenty minutes. She caught the tail end of a feature report on champagne hoarding for the millennium and then the news anchor broke to a traffic report before starting at the top of the news.

Hers was the first story. She looked over at Jodie to make sure she was still asleep and leaned forward toward the dashboard speaker to hear it better. The anchor had a deep and smooth voice.

'This morning authorities were searching for a female ex-convict believed responsible for a one-day crime spree that included two separate shootings and a kidnapping. LAPD spokesmen said Cassidy Black, a thirty-three-year-old woman who served five years in a Nevada prison for a manslaughter conviction, was being sought as the chief suspect in the double murder of two co-workers yesterday morning. The shootings at Hollywood Porsche, where Black had worked as a saleswoman for less than a year, were followed by the shooting in Black's Hollywood home of her parole agent, identified as Thelma Kibble, a forty-two-year-old resident of Hawthorne. Kibble, according to authorities, had gone to Black's home on a routine parolee check and was apparently unaware of the shootings at the dealership earlier. Investigators believe there was a confrontation and Kibble was overpowered and shot once in the chest with her own weapon. Kibble was in critical but stable condition last night at Cedars-Sinai Medical Center. She is expected to recover.'

Cassie leaned forward, closed her eyes and made an audible sigh of relief. Thelma Kibble had made it. She opened her eyes and checked Jodie once more. The girl was still asleep. Cassie focused on the rest of the radio report.

'Authorities said Kibble had not yet been interviewed because of her condition. Late Friday investigators confirmed that Black had also been linked to the abduction of a five-and-a-half-year-old girl from the front yard of her Laurel Canyon home. Authorities said Black is Jodie Shaw's natural mother but gave the girl up for adoption shortly after she was born at High Desert Correctional Institution in Nevada. It was believed that Black abducted the girl in a late-model Lincoln or Chrysler that was black in color with dark-tinted windows. LAPD detectives initially were handling the abduction investigation separately until they learned the missing girl had been adopted and her natural mother was Black. More on this developing story will be available today as the investigation progresses.'

Cassie turned off the radio. She could now see the spires of downtown ahead. She thought about the radio report. The police were following Karch's plan to the letter. She realized that even in death he might succeed.

'Thelma,' she said out loud.

She knew Thelma Kibble was the key. If she made it through she would tell them and the real story would be revealed.

Still, it did not absolve her, she knew. She was guilty. So many deaths. All because of her desires.

She tried to push the thoughts and the guilt away. She knew they would always be near and one day would have to be answered. But for now she had to put them aside.

She reached to her back pocket for the passports. She hit the light over the rearview and opened them side by side on the steering wheel so that her photo was right next to Jodie's. Her eyes fell to the line marked employment. It said Homemaker and she had to smile. Leo's last joke.

She folded the passports closed, one inside the other, and held them against her heart. A sign that announced the Golden State Freeway interchange in two miles went by. Two miles, she thought. Two minutes to decide the future of two lives.

She looked at the gym bag on the floor between Jodie's shoeless feet – her sneakers had been left in the bathroom in the room at the Cleo. The bag contained more money than she had ever conceived of. More than a new start. She knew she could dump the Boxster in South L.A., where it would be picked to a clean skeleton in a day. Take a cab to an auto mall in Orange County and pay cash as Jane Davis. There'd be no connection, no trace. Cross the border and take a flight from Ensenada to Mexico City. From there she could pick the destination.

'The place where the desert is ocean,' she said out loud.

She put the passports back into her pocket and turned off the light. In doing so her hand hit the I-Ching coins she had hung from the mirror. Leo's good luck coins. They swung back and forth and hooked her eyes like a hypnotist's gold watch.

Finally, she pulled her eyes away and looked at her

sleeping daughter. Jodie's lips were slightly parted and revealed her small white teeth. Cassie wanted to touch them. She wanted to know every part of her daughter.

She reached over and moved a strand of hair from the girl's face and hooked it behind her ear. It didn't wake her.

Cassie looked back up at the road just as the Porsche approached an overhead sign with arrows pointing out the proper lanes for all traffic heading south.

48

Jodie slowly came awake under Cassie's gentle hand. Her eyes opened and at first seemed concerned as they moved about the car. When they came to Cassie's face the concern was replaced by a look of trust. It was almost imperceptible but it was there and Cassie read it.

'You're home now, Jodie.'

The girl sat up straight and looked out the window. They were driving up Lookout Mountain Road, about to pass Wonderland Elementary.

'Are my mommy and daddy there?'

'They'll be inside waiting for you. I'm sure.'

Cassie reached up and unwound the string of I-Ching coins from the mirror. She handed them to the girl.

'Take these. For good luck.'

The girl took the coins but the concerned look crept back into her eyes.

'Are you coming in to meet my mommy and daddy?'

'I don't think so, sweetheart.'

'Well, where are you going?'

'Away. Someplace far away.'

She waited. All the girl had to say was *Take me with you* and she would change her mind, turn the car around. But those words didn't come and she hadn't expected them.

'But I want you to remember something, Jodie. Even if you can't see me, I'm there. I'll always be watching over you. I promise.'

'Okay.'

'I love you.'

The girl didn't say anything.

'And can you keep a secret?'

'Of course. What is it?'

They were a few blocks from the house now.

'The secret is I have somebody else to help me watch over you. All the time, even though you can't see him.'

'Who is it?'

'His name is Max but you can't see him. He loves you very much, too.'

She looked over and smiled at the girl, remembering her promise to herself not to cry – at least not in front of her.

'So now you have two guarding angels. That's pretty lucky for one girl to have, don't you think?'

'*Guardian* angels. That's what you said.'

'Right. Guardian angels.'

Cassie looked up and saw that they were there. Even though it was not yet five in the morning, the lights were on inside and outside the home. There were no police vehicles at the house. Only the white Volvo was in the driveway. Cassie guessed that the cops figured the last place she would turn up was at Jodie's house. She pulled to a stop next to the curb and kept it running. She immediately reached across and opened the passenger door. She knew she had to do this quickly – not because the cops might be hiding in the house. But because her decision was that close and was that fragile that in another five seconds she knew she might change her mind.

'Give me a hug, Jodie.'

The girl did as instructed and for ten seconds Cassie held her so tight she thought she might be close to hurting her. She then pulled back and held her daughter's face in both hands and kissed both of her cheeks.

'You be a good girl, okay?'

Jodie started to try to pull away.

'I want to see my mommy.'

Cassie nodded and let go. She watched as Jodie climbed down and ran around the picket fence and across the lawn to the well-lighted front door.

'I love you,' she whispered as she watched the girl go.

The front door was unlocked. The girl opened it and went inside. Before the door was closed Cassie heard Jodie's name called out in a piercing scream of relief and joy. Cassie reached across and pulled the passenger door closed. When she straightened back up she looked over at the house and saw Jodie in the arms of the woman the girl thought was her mother. The woman was fully dressed and Cassie knew she had not slept a minute during the night. She cradled Jodie's head in the hollow of her neck, holding her as tightly as Cassie had a few moments before. In the porch light Cassie could see tears streaming down the woman's face. She also saw the woman mouth the words *Thank you* as she looked out at the Porsche.

Cassie nodded, though she knew that in the darkness of the car the gesture probably could not be seen. She put the car into gear, lowered the hand brake and drove away from the curb.

49

She cut up Laurel Canyon to Mulholland and then drove the snaking road east. At a pull-over point overlooking the Valley she watched the sun creep over the mountains to the east and flood the flats below. She put the top down on the Boxster before taking off again. The dawn's air was bone cold but it kept her awake and somehow made her feel good. Where Mulholland dipped down to the Hollywood Freeway she crossed over to the freeway entrance and started heading north.

In her mind she conjured a vision of Max in his Hawaiian shirt on the night in Tahiti when they had made life promises and, in her heart, Cassie knew that their daughter had been conceived. She remembered how they slow-danced barefoot on the beach to music crossing the inlet from the distant lights of a fancy resort. She knew what they had together was inside. All inside. It had always been that way. The place where the desert turned to ocean was the heart. And she would always have that.

By the time she hit the Ventura County line she needed to put on her sunglasses. The air was warming up and whipping her hair around her ears. She knew she had to dump the car and get another. But she couldn't stop. She believed that if she took her foot off the pedal and even slowed down for a moment everything that was behind her would catch up and overtake her. All the death and guilt would come roaring down on her in the road. All she knew was that she had to stay ahead of it.

She just drove.

ACKNOWLEDGMENTS

The author gratefully acknowledges the help and efforts of several people during the writing of this book.

Special thanks to Jerry Hooten for his expertise in surveillance equipment and systems and their surreptitious installation. All surveillance technology described in the book actually exists and is available to the public. Any mistakes made herein belong exclusively to the author.

Also thanks for excellent creative input to Bill Gerber and Eric Newman, as well as Bryan Burk, Mark Ross, Courtenay Valenti, Steve Crystal, Linda Connelly and Mary Lavelle.

Thank you to Joel Gotler for his guidance and the title of the book. Also, thanks to Philip Spitzer, Betty Power, Dennis McMillan and Gene Griepentrog, formerly of the California Department of Corrections, Parole and Community Services Division.

The book titled *The New Modern Coin Magic* by J. B. Bobo, published by Magic, Inc., was also a valuable resource to the author.

Thank you to Jane Davis, of See Jane Run, designer and manager of www.michaelconnelly.com, for keeping the web site up to date and interesting.

Lastly, thank you to Michael Pietsch, editor-in-chief at Little, Brown and Company, for another excellent edit.

If you have enjoyed

VOID MOON

don't miss Michael Connelly's
thrilling bestseller

THE BRASS VERDICT

Out now in Orion paperback

ISBN: 978-1-4091-0203-8

Price: £7.99

PART ONE

Rope a Dope
1992

ONE

Everybody lies.

Cops lie. Lawyers lie. Witnesses lie. The victims lie.

A trial is a contest of lies. And everybody in the courtroom knows this. The judge knows this. Even the jury knows this. They come into the building knowing they will be lied to. They take their seats in the box and agree to be lied to.

The trick if you are sitting at the defense table is to be patient. To wait. Not for just any lie. But for the one you can grab on to and forge like hot iron into a sharpened blade. You then use that blade to rip the case open and spill its guts out on the floor.

That's my job, to forge the blade. To sharpen it. To use it without mercy or conscience. To be the truth in a place where everybody lies.

TWO

I was in the fourth day of trial in Department 109 in the downtown Criminal Courts Building when I got the lie that became the blade that ripped the case open. My client, Barnett Woodson, was riding two murder charges all the way to the steel-gray room in San Quentin where they serve you Jesus juice direct through the arm.

Woodson, a twenty-seven-year-old drug dealer from Compton, was accused of robbing and killing two college students from Westwood. They had wanted to buy cocaine from him. He decided instead to take their money and kill them both with a sawed-off shotgun. Or so the prosecution said. It was a black-on-white crime and that made things bad enough for Woodson — especially coming just four months after the riots that had torn the city apart. But what made his situation even worse was that the killer had attempted to hide the crime by weighing down the two bodies and dropping them into the Hollywood Reservoir. They stayed down for four days before popping to the surface like apples in a barrel. Rotten apples. The idea of dead bodies moldering in the reservoir that was a primary source of the city's drinking water caused a collective twist in the community's guts. When Woodson was linked by phone records to the dead men and arrested, the public outrage directed toward him was almost palpable. The District Attorney's Office promptly announced it would seek the death penalty.

The case against Woodson, however, wasn't all that palpable. It was constructed largely of circumstantial evidence — the phone records — and the testimony of witnesses who were criminals themselves. And state's witness Ronald Torrance sat front and center in this group. He claimed that Woodson confessed the killings to him.

Torrance had been housed on the same floor of the Men's Central Jail as Woodson. Both men were kept in a high-power module that contained sixteen single-prisoner cells on two tiers that opened onto a dayroom. At the time, all sixteen prisoners in the module were black, following the routine but questionable jail procedure of "segregating for safety," which entailed dividing prisoners according to race and gang affiliation to avoid confrontations and violence. Torrance was awaiting trial on robbery and aggravated assault charges stemming from his involvement in looting during the riots. High-power detainees had six a.m. to six p.m. access to the dayroom, where they ate and played cards at tables and otherwise interacted under the watchful eyes of guards in an overhead glass booth. According to Torrance, it was at one of these tables that my client had confessed to killing the two Westside boys.

The prosecution went out of its way to make Torrance presentable and believable to the jury, which had only three black members. He was given a shave, his hair was taken out of cornrows and trimmed short and he was dressed in a pale blue suit with no tie when he arrived in court on the fourth day of Woodson's trial. In direct testimony elicited by Jerry Vincent, the prosecutor, Torrance described the conversation he allegedly had with Woodson one morning at one of the picnic tables. Woodson not only confessed to the killings, he said, but furnished Torrance with many of the telling details of the murders. The point made clear to the jury was that these were details that only the true killer would know.

During the testimony, Vincent kept Torrance on a tight leash with long questions designed to elicit short answers. The questions were overloaded to the point of being leading but I didn't bother objecting, even when Judge Companioni looked at me with raised eyebrows, practically begging me to jump in. But I didn't object, because I wanted the counterpoint. I wanted the jury to see what the prosecution was doing. When it was my turn, I was going to let Torrance run with his answers while I hung back and waited for the blade.

Vincent finished his direct at eleven a.m. and the judge asked me if I wanted to take an early lunch before I began my cross. I told him no, I didn't need or want a break. I said it like I was disgusted and couldn't wait another hour to get at the man on the stand. I stood up and took a big, thick file and a legal pad with me to the lectern.

"Mr. Torrance, my name is Michael Haller. I work for the Public Defender's Office and represent Barnett Woodson. Have we met before?"

"No, sir."

"I didn't think so. But you and the defendant, Mr. Woodson, you two go back a long way, correct?"

Torrance gave an "aw, shucks" smile. But I had done the due diligence on him and I knew exactly who I was dealing with. He was thirty-two years old and had spent a third of his life in jails and prisons. His schooling had ended in the fourth grade when he stopped going to school and no parent seemed to notice or care. Under the state's three-strike law, he was facing the lifetime achievement award if convicted of charges he robbed and pistol-whipped the female manager of a coin laundry. The crime had been committed during three days of rioting and looting that ripped through the city after the not-guilty verdicts were announced in the trial of four police officers accused of the excessive beating of Rodney King, a black motorist pulled over for driving erratically. In short, Torrance had good reason to help the state take down Barnett Woodson.

"Well, we go back a few months is all," Torrance said. "To high-power."

7

"Did you say 'higher power'?" I asked, playing dumb. "Are you talking about a church or some sort of religious connection?"

"No, high-power module. In county."

"So you're talking about jail, correct?"

"That's right."

"So you're telling me that you didn't know Barnett Woodson before that?"

I asked the question with surprise in my voice.

"No, sir. We met for the first time in the jail."

I made a note on the legal pad as if this were an important concession.

"So then, let's do the math, Mr. Torrance. Barnett Woodson was transferred into the high-power module where you were already residing on the fifth of September earlier this year. Do you remember that?"

"Yeah, I remember him coming in, yeah."

"And why were you there in high-power?"

Vincent stood and objected, saying I was covering ground he had already trod in direct testimony. I argued that I was looking for a fuller explanation of Torrance's incarceration, and Judge Companioni allowed me the leeway. He told Torrance to answer the question.

"Like I said, I got a count of assault and one of robbery."

"And these alleged crimes took place during the riots, is that correct?"

With the anti-police climate permeating the city's

minority communities since even before the riots, I had fought during jury selection to get as many blacks and browns on the panel as I could. But here was a chance to work on the five white jurors the prosecution had been able to get by me. I wanted them to know that the man the prosecution was hanging so much of its case on was one of those responsible for the images they saw on their television sets back in May.

"Yeah, I was out there like everybody else," Torrance answered. "Cops get away with too much in this town, you ask me."

I nodded like I agreed.

"And your response to the injustice of the verdicts in the Rodney King beating case was to go out and rob a sixty-two-year-old woman and knock her unconscious with a steel trash can? Is that correct, sir?"

Torrance looked over at the prosecution table and then past Vincent to his own lawyer, sitting in the first row of the gallery. Whether or not they had earlier rehearsed a response to this question, his legal team couldn't help Torrance now. He was on his own.

"I didn't do that," he finally said.

"You're innocent of the crime you are charged with?"

"That's right."

"What about looting? You committed no crimes during the riots?"

After a pause and another glance at his attorney, Torrance said, "I take the fifth on that."

As expected. I then took Torrance through a series of questions designed so that he had no choice but to incriminate himself or refuse to answer under the protection of the Fifth Amendment. Finally, after he took the nickel six times, the judge grew weary of the point being made over and over and prodded me back to the case at hand. I reluctantly complied.

"All right, enough about you, Mr. Torrance," I said. "Let's get back to you and Mr. Woodson. You knew the details of this double-murder case before you even met Mr. Woodson in lockup?"

"No, sir."

"Are you sure? It got a lot of attention."

"I been in jail, man."

"They don't have television or newspapers in jail?"

"I don't read no papers and the module's TV been broke since I got there. We made a fuss and they said they'd fix it but they ain't fixed shit."

The judge admonished Torrance to check his language and the witness apologized. I moved on.

"According to the jail's records, Mr. Woodson arrived in the high-power module on the fifth of September and, according to the state's discovery material, you contacted the prosecution on October second to report his alleged confession. Does that sound right to you?"

"Yeah, that sounds right."

"Well, not to me, Mr. Torrance. You are telling this jury that a man accused of a double murder and facing the possible death penalty confessed to a man he had known for less than four weeks?"

Torrance shrugged before answering.

"That's what happened."

"So you say. What will you get from the prosecution if Mr. Woodson is convicted of these crimes?"

"I don't know. Nobody has promised me nothing."

"With your prior record and the charges you currently face, you are looking at more than fifteen years in prison if you're convicted, correct?"

"I don't know about any of that."

"You don't?"

"No, sir. I let my lawyer handle all that."

"He hasn't told you that if you don't do something about this, you might go to prison for a long, long time?"

"He hasn't told me none of that."

"I see. What have you asked the prosecutor for in exchange for your testimony?"

"Nothing. I don't want nothing."

"So then, you are testifying here because you believe it is your duty as a citizen, is that correct?"

The sarcasm in my voice was unmistakable.

"That's right," Torrance responded indignantly.

I held the thick file up over the lectern so he could see it.

"Do you recognize this file, Mr. Torrance?"

"No. Not that I recall, I don't."

"You sure you don't remember seeing it in Mr. Woodson's cell?"

"Never been in his cell."

"Are you sure that you didn't sneak in there and look through his discovery file while Mr. Woodson was in the dayroom or in the shower or maybe in court sometime?"

"No, I did not."

"My client had many of the investigative documents relating to his prosecution in his cell. These contained several of the details you testified to this morning. You don't think that is suspicious?"

Torrance shook his head.

"No. All I know is that he sat there at the table and told me what he'd done. He was feeling poorly about it and opened up to me. It ain't my fault people open up to me."

I nodded as if sympathetic to the burden Torrance carried as a man others confided in — especially when it came to double murders.

"Of course not, Mr. Torrance. Now, can you tell the jury exactly what he said to you? And don't use the shorthand you used when Mr. Vincent was asking the questions. I want to hear exactly what my client told you. Give us his words, please."

Torrance paused as if to probe his memory and compose his thoughts.

"Well," he finally said, "we were sittin' there, the both

of us by ourselves, and he just started talkin' about feelin' bad about what he'd done. I asked him, 'What'd you do?' and he told me about that night he killed the two fellas and how he felt pretty rough about it."

The truth is short. Lies are long. I wanted to get Torrance talking in long form, something Vincent had successfully avoided. Jailhouse snitches have something in common with all con men and professional liars. They seek to hide the con in misdirection and banter. They wrap cotton around their lies. But in all of that fluff you often find the key to revealing the big lie.

Vincent objected again, saying the witness had already answered the questions I was asking and I was simply badgering him at this point.

"Your Honor," I responded, "this witness is putting a confession in my client's mouth. As far as the defense is concerned, this is the case right here. The court would be remiss if it did not allow me to fully explore the content and context of such damaging testimony."

Judge Companioni was nodding in agreement before I finished the last sentence. He overruled Vincent's objection and told me to proceed. I turned my attention back to the witness and spoke with impatience in my voice.

"Mr. Torrance, you are still summarizing. You claim Mr. Woodson confessed to the murders. So then, tell the jury what he said to you. What were the *exact* words he said to you when he confessed to this crime?"

Torrance nodded as if he were just then realizing what I was asking for.

"The first thing he said to me was 'Man, I feel bad.' And I said, 'For what, my brother?' He said he kept thinking about those two guys. I didn't know what he was talking about 'cause, like I said, I hadn't heard nothin' about the case, you know? So I said, 'What two guys?' and he said, 'The two niggers I dumped in the reservoir.' I asked what it was all about and he told me about blasting them both with a shorty and wrappin' them up in chicken wire and such. He said, 'I made one bad mistake' and I asked him what it was. He said, 'I shoulda taken a knife and opened up their bellies so they wouldn't end up floatin' to the top the way they did.' And that was what he told me."

In my peripheral vision I had seen Vincent flinch in the middle of Torrance's long answer. And I knew why. I carefully moved in with the blade.

"Did Mr. Woodson use that word? He called the victims 'niggers'?"

"Yeah, he said that."

I hesitated as I worked on the phrasing of the next question. I knew Vincent was waiting to object if I gave him the opening. I could not ask Torrance to interpret. I couldn't use the word "why" when it came to Woodson's meaning or motivation. That was objectionable.

"Mr. Torrance, in the black community the word 'nigger' could mean different things, could it not?"

"'Spose."

"Is that a yes?"

"Yes."

"The defendant is African-American, correct?"

Torrance laughed.

"Looks like it to me."

"As are you, correct, sir?"

Torrance started to laugh again.

"Since I was born," he said.

The judge tapped his gavel once and looked at me.

"Mr. Haller, is this really necessary?"

"I apologize, Your Honor."

"Please move on."

"Mr. Torrance, when Mr. Woodson used that word, as you say he did, did it shock you?"

Torrance rubbed his chin as he thought about the question. Then he shook his head.

"Not really."

"Why weren't you shocked, Mr. Torrance?"

"I guess it's 'cause I hear it all a' time, man."

"From other black men?"

"That's right. I heard it from white folks, too."

"Well, when fellow black men use that word, like you say Mr. Woodson did, who are they talking about?"

Vincent objected, saying that Torrance could not speak for what other men were talking about. Companioni sustained the objection and I took a moment to rework the path to the answer I wanted.

"Okay, Mr. Torrance," I finally said. "Let's talk

only about you, then, okay? Do you use that word on occasion?"

"I think I have."

"All right, and when you have used it, who were you referring to?"

Torrance shrugged.

"Other fellas."

"Other black men?"

"That's right."

"Have you ever on occasion referred to white men as niggers?"

Torrance shook his head.

"No."

"Okay, so then, what did you take the meaning to be when Barnett Woodson described the two men who were dumped in the reservoir as niggers?"

Vincent moved in his seat, going through the body language of making an objection but not verbally following through with it. He must have known it would be useless. I had led Torrance down the path and he was mine.

Torrance answered the question.

"I took it that they were black and he killed 'em both."

Now Vincent's body language changed again. He sank a little bit in his seat because he knew his gamble in putting a jailhouse snitch on the witness stand had just come up snake eyes.

I looked up at Judge Companioni. He knew what was coming as well.

"Your Honor, may I approach the witness?"

"You may," the judge said.

I walked to the witness stand and put the file down in front of Torrance. It was legal size, well worn and faded orange—a color used by county jailers to denote private legal documents that an inmate is authorized to possess.

"Okay, Mr. Torrance, I have placed before you a file in which Mr. Woodson keeps discovery documents provided to him in jail by his attorneys. I ask you once again if you recognize it."

"I seen a lotta orange files in high-power. It don't mean I seen that one."

"You are saying you never saw Mr. Woodson with his file?"

"I don't rightly remember."

"Mr. Torrance, you were with Mr. Woodson in the same module for thirty-two days. You testified he confided in you and confessed to you. Are you saying you never saw him with that file?"

He didn't answer at first. I had backed him into a no-win corner. I waited. If he continued to claim he had never seen the file, then his claim of a confession from Woodson would be suspect in the eyes of the jury. If he finally conceded that he was familiar with the file, then he opened a big door for me.

"What'm saying is that I seen him with his file but I never looked at what was in it."

Bang. I had him.

"Then, I'll ask you to open the file and inspect it."

The witness followed the instruction and looked from side to side at the open file. I went back to the lectern, checking on Vincent on my way. His eyes were downcast and his face was pale.

"What do you see when you open the file, Mr. Torrance?"

"One side's got photos of two bodies on the ground. They're stapled in there—the photos, I mean. And the other side is a bunch of documents and reports and such."

"Could you read from the first document there on the right side? Just read the first line of the summary."

"No, I can't read."

"You can't read at all?"

"Not really. I didn't get the schooling."

"Can you read any of the words that are next to the boxes that are checked at the top of the summary?"

Torrance looked down at the file and his eyebrows came together in concentration. I knew that his reading skills had been tested during his last stint in prison and were determined to be at the lowest measurable level—below second-grade skills.

"Not really," he said. "I can't read."

I quickly walked over to the defense table and grabbed

another file and a Sharpie pen out of my briefcase. I went back to the lectern and quickly printed the word CAUCASIAN on the outside of the file in large block letters. I held the file up so that Torrance, as well as the jury, could see it.

"Mr. Torrance, this is one of the words checked on the summary. Can you read this word?"

Vincent immediately stood but Torrance was already shaking his head and looking thoroughly humiliated. Vincent objected to the demonstration without proper foundation and Companioni sustained. I expected him to. I was just laying the groundwork for my next move with the jury and I was sure most of them had seen the witness shake his head.

"Okay, Mr. Torrance," I said. "Let's move to the other side of the file. Could you describe the bodies in the photos?"

"Um, two men. It looks like they opened up some chicken wire and some tarps and they're laying there. A bunch a police is there investigatin' and takin' pictures."

"What race are the men on the tarps?"

"They're black."

"Have you ever seen those photographs before, Mr. Torrance?"

Vincent stood to object to my question as having previously been asked and answered. But it was like holding up a hand to stop a bullet. The judge sternly told him he could take his seat. It was his way of telling the prosecutor he was going to have to just sit back and take what was coming. You put the liar on the stand, you take the fall with him.

"You may answer the question, Mr. Torrance," I said after Vincent sat down. "Have you ever seen those photographs before?"

"No, sir, not before right now."

"Would you agree that the pictures portray what you described to us earlier? That being the bodies of two slain black men?"

"That's what it looks like. But I ain't seen the picture before, just what he tell me."

"Are you sure?"

"Something like these I wouldn't forget."

"You've told us Mr. Woodson confessed to killing two black men, but he is on trial for killing two white men. Wouldn't you agree that it appears that he didn't confess to you at all?"

"No, he confessed. He told me he killed those two."

I looked up at the judge.

"Your Honor, the defense asks that the file in front of Mr. Torrance be admitted into evidence as defense exhibit one."

Vincent made a lack-of-foundation objection but Companioni overruled.

"It will be admitted and we'll let the jury decide whether Mr. Torrance has or hasn't seen the photographs and contents of the file."

I was on a roll and decided to go all in.

"Thank you," I said. "Your Honor, now might also be a good time for the prosecutor to reacquaint his witness with the penalties for perjury."

It was a dramatic move made for the benefit of the jury. I was expecting I would have to continue with Torrance and eviscerate him with the blade of his own lie. But Vincent stood and asked the judge to recess the trial while he conferred with opposing counsel.

This told me I had just saved Barnett Woodson's life.

"The defense has no objection," I told the judge.